TRUE SOLDIER GENTLEMEN

Adrian Goldsworthy

PHOENIX

A PHOENIX PAPERBACK

First published in Great Britain in 2011
by Weidenfeld & Nicolson
This paperback edition published in 2011
by Phoenix,
an imprint of Orion Books Ltd,
Orion House, 5 Upper St Martin's Lane,
London WC2H 9EA

An Hachette UK company

1 3 5 7 9 10 8 6 4 2

A CIP catalogue record for this book
is available from the British Library.

ISBN 978-0-7538-2836-6

Printed and bound in Great Britain by
Clays Ltd, St Ives plc

The Orion Publishing Group's policy is to use papers that
are natural, renewable and recyclable products and
made from wood grown in sustainable forests. The logging
and manufacturing processes are expected to conform to
the environmental regulations of the country of origin.

www.orionbooks.co.uk

To Georgina, Kate, and Rosie, Andrew, Julian,
and Kevin, with thanks

Hark, now the drums beat up again,
For all true soldier gentlemen,
Then let us 'list and march, I say,
Over the hills and far away.

Over the hills and o'er the main,
To Flanders, Portugal and Spain,
King George commands and we'll obey,
Over the hills and far away.

Over rivers, bogs and springs,
We shall live as great as kings,
And plunder get both night and day
When over the hills and far away.

Over the hills and o'er the main,
To Flanders, Portugal and Spain,
King George commands and we'll obey,
Over the hills and far away.

We then shall lead more happy lives,
By getting rid of brats and wives,
That scold on, both night and day,
When o'er the hills and far away.

• • •

First included in a 1706 play as a satire on soldiers;
by the end of the eighteenth century the song had
become a favourite march of the British Army.

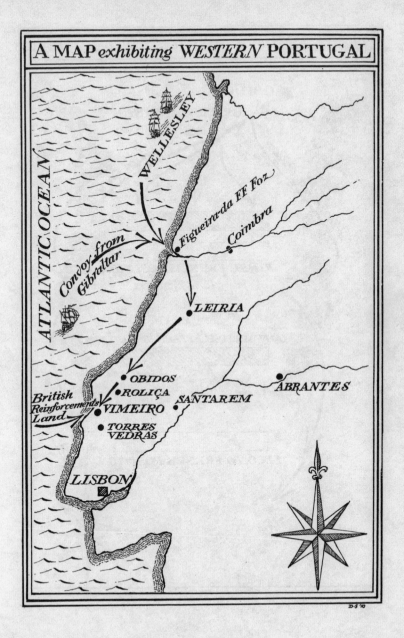

A MAP *exhibiting* WESTERN PORTUGAL

ATLANTIC OCEAN

WELLESLEY

Convoy from Gibraltar

Figueira-da FF Foz

Coimbra

LEIRIA

OBIDOS

ROLIÇA

VIMEIRO

SANTAREM

ABRANTES

British Reinforcements Land

TORRES VEDRAS

LISBON

D·S '10

The BATTLE of ROLIÇA 17th August 1808

OBIDOS

BRITISH ADVANCE

Flanking Column

Flanking Columns

FIRST FRENCH POSITION

Roliça

MAIN BRITISH ATTACK UP RAVINES

106th

SECOND FRENCH POSITION

The BATTLE of VIMEIRO 21st August 1808

2nd Flight

To the Beach

1st Fight

BRENIER

VENTOSA
FARM

SOLIGNAC

FRENCH Flanking Columns

Initial British position
including 106th

TOLEDO
FARM

20th LD

VIMEIRO

MAIN FRENCH ATTACK

Maceira Stream

D·S '70.

PART ONE
Madrid, 2nd May 1808

PROLOGUE

William Hanley watched the pride of imperial France ride up the Alcala. It was a magnificent sight, and the Englishman could not resist stopping to watch the soldiers pass. He had seen them before, had watched the parades since the French had first arrived in Madrid several weeks ago, and had even chatted to some of the officers. They had come then as allies, but now things were different, and the horsemen clattering along the paved road were moving with grim purpose. Hanley had taken care to crouch down behind a small cart left at the mouth of an alleyway. This was not a day to be too visible.

First came the Mamelukes, a strange legacy of Napoleon's Egyptian adventure. They did not wear strict uniform, although most had red fezzes surrounded by great white turbans and immensely baggy scarlet trousers. They carried curved scimitars, had pistols at their belts and wide-mouthed blunderbusses hanging from their saddles. From the beginning the people of Madrid had hated and feared them. Women had fled to the opposite side of the street when they passed. Men spat at their shadows and crossed themselves. The Mamelukes looked like an oriental fantasy, but to Spaniards they had stepped straight out of old nightmares from the time when the Moors had ruled most of Spain and trampled the Church beneath them.

Next came the Chasseurs. Once known as the Guides, they had guarded General Bonaparte since his Italian campaigns, and still remained his favourites. Napoleon was far away in France, but that did not make these tough old soldiers any less determined. Veterans to a man, they were immaculately turned out in their

3

green jackets and overall trousers. The jackets were heavily braided, with brass buttons like the ones running along the seams of their overalls. They were light cavalry, so were mounted on modestly sized horses and carried curved sabres. Hungarian Hussars had set the fashion for European light horsemen more than a generation ago, and so each Chasseur had a second jacket, known as a pelisse, which they wore draped over their left shoulder. The pelisses were red, again heavily braided and also trimmed with black fur which matched the round fur caps each man wore on his head. Tall green and red plumes nodded with the motion of the horses.

The last men were larger and rode bigger and darker horses. These were the Empress Josephine's Dragoons, dressed in dark green jackets with white waistcoats and breeches. Their boots came up to the knees and were polished like black mirrors. Each dragoon wore a high brass helmet bound with a mock leopard-skin turban. They had dark horse-tail crests and high white plumes. A long straight sword rested on each shoulder.

These men were La Garde Impériale – not ornamental toy soldiers, but hard-fighting regiments recruited from veterans. They had left behind some infantrymen who could not keep up. The men who had ridden over the enemy at Austerlitz and Eylau did not need the help of mere conscripts. The Guardsmen were perfectly turned out. Only the strictest NCO could (and no doubt would) have found fault with them if they had been at this moment on the Field of Mars in Paris. They made a spectacle of colour, all set off by the backdrop of the pale brown stone of the grand houses along the Alcala. Yet combined with the beauty of the scene was a sense of menace and brutal self-confidence.

It was that savage intent combined with swagger which Hanley knew he could never capture on canvas. For years he had dreamed of being an artist, had studied and practised. He knew he was not good enough, was doomed to be able to recognise great art, but never to create it himself. He could imagine mixing the colours, reproducing both the detail of the background and the soldiers, their horses and equipment with great accuracy and precision. Yet his picture would still be utterly lifeless.

Anyway, that dream was gone – had died at the same time as his father. He had never met his father, had seen him only twice and then from a distance. It was not that different with his mother. She was an image of beauty, but he could remember just a handful of occasions when they had been together. Mary Hanley had only been beginning to make a name for herself on the stage when she fell pregnant. It was an interruption to her career, and meant a rapid severance of relations with her lover. Hanley's father never openly acknowledged his bastard, but granted him an allowance. A year later Mary became mistress to another man, who made it clear that she would never be allowed to have the child with her. The boy was left with her own mother, who did the best she could. Hanley received an education, and when he grew older was allowed to travel and study art and antiquities. His allowance was moderate, but now it had come to an end. His father was dead, and his half-brothers had no intention of subsidising the product of an indiscretion.

A shot was fired, echoing off the houses. Hanley could not see where it had come from, did not see horse or man fall, but it jerked him from his reverie. Orders were shouted, and the French horsemen broke into a trot. It was also time for him to go. Madrid was tense today. The French had systematically removed Spain's Royal Family, spiriting them away into captivity, but the attempt to take one of the young princes this morning had led to a riot. Hanley had already come a long way through the city and could sense the growing anger. People he had passed had called out 'Today is the day!' and 'We strike soon!', or simply muttered 'Death to the French'.

The Englishman was leaving Madrid, but first he must say one last goodbye. Maria Pilar was a dancer with the ballet, a small, sad and very pretty girl who had been his model and then lover. 'Mapi' – her stage nickname which all her friends used – had enjoyed cooking and cleaning for him, creating a home she had never had before. It had taken him a while to realise how important he was to the Spanish girl. Now he must tell her that he was going away and that she could not come. Mapi would not argue, and in many ways he feared even more her mute acceptance of the parting, the quiet sorrow that he would see in her clear brown eyes. It was true that her prospects in Britain would be poor, but he knew that really he longed to be free of her cloying affection. Hanley did not especially like himself for this, and it was harder now to hide behind ideas about a creative soul needing to be free of all attachments.

His money had almost gone – buying a horse to take him north to the coast had taken much of it – and he could not stay in Madrid. The way things were going it would anyway not be healthy to stay there as an Englishman. So far his pretence of being an Irish exile had satisfied the Frenchmen he had met, but that was unlikely to last. Ironically enough Hanley's only income now came from his half-pay as a junior officer in the British Army. His father had secured his commission when he was just ten, back in the days before such abuses were banned. Hanley had never seen his regiment, had never served a day with the army, and even now had no desire to do so. Hopefully he could find something better than this last resort when he returned to England. Still, in the unlikely event that his status was discovered, it would scarcely help to persuade the French that he was merely an artist, with scant interest in politics and in fact a strong sympathy towards France and her empire.

As Hanley threaded this way through the narrow alleys of Madrid he heard sporadic shots. Within half an hour he had passed half a dozen corpses. Four were French soldiers, very young and thin. One had tried to grow a pathetic moustache, but now lay stripped of all his uniform apart from a dirty white shirt which was covered in a mass of dark, almost black, blood from his cut throat. The fourth Frenchman was older, grey haired and fat. He still wore his officer's uniform as he hung with his arms and legs nailed to the large timber gates at the back of a nobleman's house. His jacket had been ripped open and his chest was a mass of congealed blood over which the flies buzzed thickly. Hanley could not tell whether the man had been dead before whoever had done this had fastened him to the gates. He was not sure he wanted to know and so hurried on, rushing away from the sight as well as the stench, which made him gag. A little farther on were two Spaniards, one with a hole neatly in the centre of his forehead and the other with stab wounds in the belly. From now on the few live people he met said nothing, but hurried on their way.

Maria Pilar was not at her lodgings, nor at the house where one of her friends lived. Hanley spoke to the girl, a desperately thin, hollow-eyed creature whose racking coughs betrayed the sickness that would kill her before she was twenty. She seemed to look accusingly at him as she told him that Mapi had gone with a group to the Puerta del Sol to 'show the French'. The sick girl said that she would have gone too, but that it had not been a good night. Surprising himself, Hanley gave her some of the few coins he had left. She hesitated for a long moment before taking them.

Hanley headed towards the grand square at the heart of Madrid. The streets were strangely empty, but the noise grew. A crowd was chanting and there were more gunshots. Then for a moment everything became silent.

In the Puerta del Sol Marshal Murat, Grand Duke of Berg and brother-in-law to the Emperor, confronted the angry crowd. As always his uniform was a riot of colour, for he took care to set off his good looks with a uniform outshining that of the gaudiest hussar. Years before Murat had led the horsemen who had followed up Napoleon's whiff of grapeshot with a vicious charge against the Paris mob and so saved the Directory. Now he repeated the exercise in another capital city.

Cannon fired, the metal canisters bursting open at their muzzles and spraying dozens of musket balls into the packed crowd. Infantrymen added their volleys, filling the square with echoing noise, black smoke and blood. Then the Guard Cavalry charged, swords and sabres thrusting and hacking as the crowd panicked and people started to run.

When Hanley turned into one of the larger side streets he collided with a fleeing man. He was short, thickset and wild eyed, and his flailing elbow struck the Englishman hard and winded him. Hanley struggled both to breathe and to stay upright. The

Spaniard's red headscarf fell off and fluttered down beside him, but the man kept running, looking neither right nor left. Many more people came after him, their faces pale and blank. Some were women, but none were Mapi. Hanley leaned against a wall and let the fugitives flow past him. Behind them were others, coming a little more slowly. A few carried knives or ancient muskets, and one had a sword. This man was old, and his coat of yellow silk was rich in lace and had last been fashionable thirty years ago. There was blood on his right leg and he was limping along, supported by a plump friar. Two younger men walked behind the nobleman and his priest, both with fowling pieces, and they turned now and again to watch behind them. Suddenly one of the pair shouted and an instant later fired, flame and black smoke gouting from the muzzle of his firelock.

The French cavalry were silent as they galloped into the street. Their formation had long gone, but the Chasseurs came in a dense group led by a tall officer with a blond moustache. There was blood splattered on the chests of the horses and on the men's legs. Their curved sabres chopped and thrust down with the precision of long practice. The officer beheaded the first of the nobleman's attendants, riding a little past the retreating man before slicing back with massive force. A fountain of blood pumped up from the severed neck as the body pitched forward. His sergeant killed the other attendant with far less effort by a thrust of his sabre's razor-sharp point into the man's neck. He let the momentum of his horse free the blade from the clinging flesh, and it was just a few seconds before he dealt with the priest in the same way.

The nobleman managed to parry the officer's first wild cut, but he screamed in pain as he had to put his weight on to his wounded leg. The Frenchman cut down again, severing the old man's thin arm a few inches from the wrist. The nobleman's sword dropped to the ground with his hand still grasping the hilt. Reining back, his horse's hoofs skidding for a moment on the flagstones, the officer stood up in his stirrups and cut down again, almost chopping the old man's head in two.

The Chasseurs flooded along the street, blood spraying as the sabres rose and fell. There were no orders, and no words spoken, the horsemen merely grunting with effort as they drove steel into flesh and through bone. Even the screaming had stopped, and to Hanley that only made the scene more horrific. He stared for a moment, fascinated, as he saw the green-uniformed horsemen slowing down to give themselves time to kill.

Then Hanley turned and ran. He no longer knew what he was doing and just fled, his bag banging against his back with the motion. There were hoof-beats behind, closing with him as he ducked around a corner. He had enough control to turn again, sprinting for an alleyway. A man appeared there, wearing a dark waistcoat over a light brown shirt and raising a wide-mouthed blunderbuss. The muzzle looked massive and Hanley saw the man open his toothless mouth in a tight smile and threw himself forward, knowing the scream he heard now was his own. Then there was a massive detonation, the noise magnified in the narrow alleyway, and the sense of a force punching the air above him. He rolled as he fell, losing his bag, but turning over to look behind him. A horse was rearing in pain, one of its eyes destroyed, and its rider's face was a mass of shattered bone and blood where he taken the full force of the scrap iron and nails fired from just a few feet away. The man could not scream, but made an unearthly moaning sound as his hands went up to clutch at his appalling wound. His sabre still hung from his wrist strap.

Hanley tried to dodge the feet that surged past him as a group of Spaniards ran from the alleyway to drag the man down. A few more had muskets or pistols and fired these at the Frenchmen now coming to help their comrade. At least some of the citizens of Madrid were fighting, and they would make these enemies know it. Hanley paused only to scoop up his valise, and then ran away.

He never found Mapi. There were bodies everywhere, and once he saw a thin black-haired girl lying on her face in the porch of a house, her skirts bunched up above her waist. He was shuddering, tears in his eyes, as he turned the young woman's body over. She had clearly been raped, then a knife thrust between her bare breasts.

It was not Mapi, but Hanley wept for a woman he did not

know. Lifting her body, he carried it to a shrine to the Holy Mother set into a high wall. He covered the corpse with his coat, and made the sign of the cross, although he was neither a Catholic nor even a believer in God. Then there were more shots and shouting from near by.

Hanley fled, overwhelmed by fear and disgust at the horrors he had seen. The sound of gunfire followed him until he reached the very edge of the city. Some was regular, as the French firing squads methodically dispensed punishment. A few shots were fired by Spaniards, but the retribution was always terrible. Hanley was never to know, but the house where he had rented a room was stormed by a party of the Empress Dragoons. They cut down the lame doorman and ransacked the place, smashing whatever they did not steal. In Hanley's room one of the soldiers found a sketch of Mapi, reclining in the nude on a couch. The Dragoon grinned appreciatively and stuffed the paper into his jacket before looking round for anything else worth taking.

No one tried to stop Hanley as he left the city, and he saw no more soldiers, for Madrid was a big place and the French still few in number. He drove his horse hard, till the beast's flanks were white with sweat. It was breathing hard, and would not stay in a canter no matter what he did. He realised it was close to exhaustion and that he needed to give it some rest if it was to last out the journey. Fast as he had gone, the shock and horror of what he had seen stayed with him. A new hatred of the French fought with resentment of his own fate. His life had changed, his dreams collapsed, and he did not know whether the lover he had not loved was alive or dead. The failed artist was going home. He was escaping a war and going to join an army.

I

The battalion was in trouble, and Williams did not know how to extricate it. Everything had started so well, the ten companies deployed side by side in line. That was the fighting formation for attack or defence, with the thousand soldiers of the 106th Foot in two ranks so that all could fire their muskets. His grenadiers were in the place of honour on the right of the line, as befitted the biggest and, he was sure, the best soldiers in the regiment. On the far left were the light bobs, not yet sent forward as skirmishers. They were supposedly the best shots and the most agile men, although personally he was unconvinced about their claims to greater intelligence and initiative, most of all where their officers were concerned. Still, the Light Company was in its place and he could rely on them to do their duty.

The order came to advance and, since no enemy was close, or even likely to be close, Williams put the battalion into open column. They formed on the centre company – or actually Captain Mosley's Number Four Company, which stood just to the right of the colours in the middle of the line – because that would take minutes off the manoeuvre. The grenadiers marched forward, wheeled twice and took up position at the head of the column. They were still in two ranks each of fifty men covering just over ninety feet of frontage. Behind them at half that distance was the identical line formed by Number One Company, then Number Two, and so on. The lights and Numbers Eight to Five had to turn about to take up station behind Four Company. The colour party with the battalion's two flags stood in the centre between Four and Five Company. On his order the battalion marched forward at a steady seventy-five paces a minute.

They came to a defile, so Williams put each of the individual companies into a narrow column of route to pass through it. Back in the open once more, they reverted to a battalion column with the companies at half-distance, then went into line again. Side by side the ten companies covered some three hundred yards of frontage. Ordered to resume the advance, he put them back into column again.

Williams thought the serried ranks of redcoats looked magnificent, and was pleased with his handling of the regiment. Then the enemy appeared.

'French cavalry!' yelled Lieutenant Truscott. 'Over on the right front!'

Williams followed the pointed finger. Infantry in a column at half-distance like this were desperately vulnerable to horsemen. He heard the drumming of hoofs, knew he needed to form square, but could not remember how. It was easy from a denser column at quarter-distance – he could remember those diagrams as clearly as anything.

'A whole regiment. Cuirassiers. Big blackguards in armour on massive horses!' Truscott sounded almost enthusiastic as the regiment's doom approached. 'Come on, sir, make up your mind.'

'We're dished,' chipped in young Derryck. 'Bloody grenadiers,' he added as an afterthought.

Truscott smiled as he drummed his fingers even more loudly on the oak table. 'They are getting closer. You have one minute left.'

Hamish Williams hesitated, then he reached down and moved the blocks representing the Grenadier and Number One Company together to form a dense line four deep. The two ranks of grenadiers would be kneeling, bayonets fixed and the butts of their muskets braced against the ground so that the weapons pointed upwards. No horse would willingly commit suicide by charging a hedge of bayonet points. So as long as the redcoats remained steady – and Williams was utterly confident that they would – then they were safe against a charge from the front. The problem was the flanks, which were still wide open.

'Thirty seconds. They are spurring into a gallop now. Their swords are about three feet long and they are all aiming at us, arm straight and wrist bent in the charge.'

'Bloody grenadiers.'

Each company was represented by a wooden block some three inches long. They were white, but painted on each side were seven miniature redcoats standing at the present, staring blankly forward as if they did not have a care in the world. They wore the old-fashioned cocked hats long since replaced by the shako, and there were plenty of chips on the paintwork as testimony to heavy usage. Someone had drawn in a pair of glasses on the centre grenadier to make him look like Lieutenant Pringle. The latter was stretched out on his bed, using Williams' heavy brass telescope to peer out of the window. It was an immensely heavy piece, designed to be held on a stand, so Pringle was resting it on the headboard of the bed.

Pringle looked up for a moment. 'Am I about to be called upon to lay down my life for King and Country once again?' he said wearily.

Truscott ignored him. 'Come on, man, what do you do?' he demanded of Williams once again.

'Only it will be the eighth time this afternoon,' continued Pringle, who was now looking back through the telescope. His glasses were on the top of his head and he adjusted the brass eyepiece to sharpen the focus. 'I only ask because if I'd known I would have got Jenkins to do a better job of polishing my boots. Seems a shame to die looking shabby.'

'Why change the habit of a lifetime?' chipped in Anstey, one of four officers playing cards at the other end of the long table from the wooden blocks representing the battalion. There were appreciative guffaws from his companions. The game was progressing slowly, but they were already well into the second bottle of claret so it was clear that their time had not been entirely wasted. Thin clouds of cigar smoke also attested to their comfortable leisure.

Williams had a sudden revelation. He could do it if he broke each company into two platoons. Quarter-distance meant that

13

there was room for the platoons to wheel outwards and form the sides of the square. They would be only two deep, which was very thin, but if they timed their volleys just right then they could stop a squadron in its tracks. Williams started to move the blocks, but each was a solid company piece so he was going to have to explain what he meant.

'Time's up,' said Truscott. Derryck helpfully jabbed at the blocks with a toasting fork, scattering the painted battalion. Truscott leaned against the back of his chair and complacently crossed his legs. His lean, intelligent face showed little trace of amusement and considerable disappointment. 'It seems that once again we all have an opportunity to find out the answer to the great question, courtesy of our young gentlemen. Well, I suppose some of the battalion might survive. Be hard for the French to kill everyone.' He paused, frowning. 'Their arms would get tired for a start. Anyway, they are usually pretty decent about taking prisoners.'

'Bloody grenadiers.' Williams glared at the young ensign, who grinned back cheerfully. Derryck's own attempts at manoeuvring the blocks had produced an even more rapid and spectacular disaster. Neither of the other ensigns had managed much better.

'Nobody survived when you were in charge.'

'I do like to be thorough,' said Derryck. He was just sixteen, but was no more than five foot two inches tall and thin as a rake in spite of the vast quantities of food he devoured whenever he got the chance. He looked about twelve, and managed to give off an air of innocence utterly out of keeping with his character. Williams liked him. Most people did.

'I fear doing just a little better than Mr Derryck is not quite sufficient,' put in Truscott. 'This regiment expects somewhat more than the survival of one hundred men out of a thousand. Especially before any of them have had a chance to fire a shot. His Majesty's government has invested considerable money in raising, feeding and training this battalion. Think of all those poor rich people having to pay their taxes.'

The lieutenant could see that the young gentlemen were

unmoved by the plight of the wealthy. He could not blame them. None of the officers of the regiment was titled, and only the new colonel had any real claim to wealth. The 106th Foot was the most junior regiment of the line and was not fashionable. Truscott's own family's moderate income was stretched very thin to support seven children. He reached for a battered copy of the drill manual approved for the entire army by the Duke of York. It was written by General Dundas and detailed the manoeuvres to be performed by a battalion on parade and in the field. He flung the book at Williams, who instinctively swayed back and only just caught it.

'Both of you study "Old Pivot". You know, study – something Billy never had to do at his pitiful place of education.'

'Too true,' said Pringle, without taking his eye from the telescope. 'It wasted valuable time when a fellow could be dining and drinking.'

'And whoring, no doubt,' said Anstey.

'An Oxford gentleman does not speak of such things in polite conversation.'

Anstey scoffed at this statement so out of keeping with Billy Pringle's normal talk. Most of the others laughed, although Williams just looked solemn. Truscott shook his head.

'What the Church lost in you, Billy! Still, sending you to Magdalen was probably a bad idea.'

Pringle looked back at him for a moment. 'A scriptural joke. Is that the best Clare College can come up with?' He resumed his intent observation through the window. 'Now if they had let me study Molly Hackett at Oxford I would have been the most avid of students.'

'Who is Molly Hackett?' asked young Derryck rather nervously.

Truscott had no wish to discuss Mrs Wickham's maid with the pink-cheeked ensign. 'She is not Sir David Dundas, and he alone should consume your attention at present,' he said sharply.

'She is an indiscreet young lady,' Pringle replied, ignoring his fellow lieutenant. 'Very, very indiscreet, who has not closed the shutters on the window of her chamber.' He clearly had the attention of Derryck, and several of the other officers were listening more intently. Williams blushed, realised that he had done so, and the consciousness of this only made things worse. He thought Truscott had noticed.

'I strongly suspect that Mr Williams' good mother did not present him with such a fine telescope in order to allow you to spy upon innocent young girls,' said the lieutenant.

'Nonsense, I have no doubt she would thank me for keeping temptation away from her son. It is an excellent glass and no doubt will aid her boy in smiting the King's enemies. We do not want him distracted from that task, so I will look after the thing until those enemies appear.'

'Damnation to them all!' cried Derryck, his voice cracking midway through and rather ruining the effect of this statement of patriotic zeal. The others ignored him anyway.

Williams found himself staring at the scattered blocks. He tried to imagine the wreckage of a battalion caught unformed by enemy cavalry. The war with France had been going on for more than half of his lifetime. Tens, probably even hundreds, of thousands had died in those years, but he was still new to the army and had never been in a battle. Nor had any of the other subalterns, even confident men like Truscott and Pringle. There were no battle honours on the colours of the 106th.

It was so hard to picture the carnage, to think of these men he knew sprawled on the ground, their bodies slashed and stabbed by the enemy's blades. In the pictures of famous battles the dead were always decorously draped over the landscape, their wounds tiny or even invisible. Yet the limbless and scarred beggars who prowled the streets still wearing ragged red coats or sailors' pigtails hinted at the true horrors of battle. How many would die quickly and with only brief pain, and how many would lie screaming in dreadful agony? Williams wondered whether the others had similar thoughts, but could see no sign of it.

Somehow it was difficult to believe that similar violence could possibly touch Truscott in his immaculate uniform or the ever cheerful Derryck. They were soldiers, but their world was one of neatness and precision and there seemed almost no place for bloodshed and chaos. Williams frowned as he realised that even now he assumed that he would himself come through unscathed. Why should he be special and invulnerable? His foot brushed against something and he looked down, noticing that the block marked Gren. Coy had fallen on the floor. Williams picked it up. For a moment he stared at the little figure with the inked-in glasses.

'Sorry, Billy,' he muttered, and then put it back on the table. He began reassembling the shattered battalion. The little painted soldiers looked unmoved by their recent ordeal.

Truscott noticed the gesture. 'Don't worry, my dear fellow. Grenadiers are too stupid to die.'

Williams felt a rush of anger, wondering whether Truscott had thought he was concerned about his own life. The idea that anyone would consider him so selfish or indeed so lacking in courage horrified him. Yet to deny such a thought openly would surely reinforce the impression. Truscott's face betrayed no particular emotion, and he was already saying something to Derryck. Williams hesitated, and then was saved from the decision by a knock on the door.

Lieutenant Brotherton came in accompanied by an unknown officer. The man was tall, his face dark from the sun, and he had short black hair. That was odd because all the other officers in the room wore their hair long, tied with a black ribbon and coloured white with powder. The newcomer's jacket was creased and looked a little too small for him, his dark red sash was untidily wrapped around his waist, and his top boots and breeches were splashed with mud. Behind him two soldiers carried a trunk, although for all their emphasised effort it appeared to be fairly light.

'Gentlemen, I would like to present the newest addition to our happy family.' Brotherton gave a sweeping gesture towards his companion. 'This is Mr Hanley, of the Grenadier Company. Put that in the corner there.' He spoke to the two redcoats. 'Thank you.' The men left. 'Now, if you will forgive me, I will leave you to introduce yourselves. I must resume my work – the life of an acting adjutant is one of unending toil and sorrow.' Brotherton departed amid jeers.

Hanley stood for a moment, unsure of what to do. The coach journey down from London to Dorset had been long and uncomfortable, and followed weeks of travel as he had gone to Spain's north coast to catch a ship back to Britain. Some letters, then a meeting with the representatives of his late father's family, had been necessary to equip him for service with the 106th. It was under the sworn understanding that this would permanently terminate their contact. There was no question of giving him an allowance, and the sum of £200 was the last money he would ever get from them. It was already mostly gone – the cost of uniforms and other essentials had surprised him. Now he was fully a soldier, and one who would have to live off his pay. Neither were things he had ever especially desired. The soldiers he had met in the past had all been either dull or pompous. Still, he was here, had nowhere else to go, and he would inevitably be spending a good deal of time with these fellows. In spite of all that had happened so recently, Hanley was nervous. He looked down the long attic room at the top of the small coaching inn. Just under half of the 106th's officers currently stationed in the village were billeted here. They were in various states of dress, several just in shirtsleeves, but their powdered hair gave them a strange uniformity. For what seemed an age they simply stared at him. As usual it was Truscott who made an effort to be friendly.

'Welcome to the Senior Common Room – it is where the more distinguished of we subalterns are billeted. The others live like swine in some hovel or other. I'm Truscott of Four Company. The red-faced rogue over there playing cards is Anstey of Two Company, and next to him is Hopwood of Three – they are from the hovel!' The two men nodded affably. 'They are both visitors to this establishment trying to fleece these young griffins of their money.'

'What else are ensigns good for?' said Hopwood cheerfully. 'These are Quincy and Clarke, by the way.' The flow of new names was already washing past Hanley. There seemed nothing remarkable about most of their owners.

Truscott resumed, although his fastidious nature was slightly offended by this interruption to seniority. He would have preferred introducing the only other lieutenant before moving on to their juniors. 'That elegant wastrel lying on the bed is Billy Pringle. He is a grenadier like you so we must make allowances for lack of manners and wit.' Pringle raised an arm, but his eye remained fixed to the eyepiece and he showed no great urge to welcome the newcomer any more enthusiastically. 'Oh yes, and this is Williams, also of the Grenadier Company. Ensign Redman is on duty so you will have to meet him at some other point. And finally, in so many ways, we have Mr Derryck here, our drill master and junior ensign – at least until now.'

'No, Hanley here is senior,' cut in Pringle, finally setting down the immense telescope, rolling over on to his side and getting up. 'In fact, I think he may be at the top of the list for the whole battalion. He has certainly been on the company's books since before I joined.' He flicked his glasses down, adjusting them slightly on his nose.

'You know, it is always a shock when you actually demonstrate knowledge.' Truscott smiled. 'What is the matter, has the girl closed the shutters?'

'Just ignore him, he seems obsessed with the female gender.' Pringle shook hands with the new arrival. 'So you are our errant knight, the secret strength of the 106th Foot. A pleasure to meet you at last. Come on, Williams, and make the man feel at home. Now we have another grenadier it will raise the whole tone of this place. This is our volunteer, Mr Williams. Although you might not expect such a thing, his Christian name is Hamish. Well, I suppose it had to happen to somebody.'

Hanley and Williams made appropriate noises as they shook hands.

In a stage whisper Pringle added, 'Williams is our moral conscience, a man of virtue and faith. He is a Quaker or Hindoo or Druid or something.'

'I am a sinner saved by Grace,' said Williams with a fair degree of militancy. Hanley could not think of anything in particular to say to that, so endeavoured to keep his expression neutral. Religious fervour always made him uncomfortable. If feigned, then he despised the hypocrisy, and if genuine it seemed unlikely to produce stimulating or imaginative company. He was six foot tall, but Williams must have had an inch or so on him, and somehow seemed too big for the low attic room. He was also much broader, something emphasised by the thick stripes of lace running in horizontal pairs up the front of his jacket and the tall wings, ending in a woollen fringe on his shoulders. Pringle was a little shorter, and a good deal plumper, but had a ready smile, and a brightness to the eyes behind the lenses of his glasses. In fact he had a throbbing headache from the previous night's heavy drinking, and it took a conscious effort to appear as affable as a gentleman should on such occasions.

'Are you also a lieutenant, Mr Williams?' asked Hanley, assuming that the extra decoration implied superior rank.

Hamish blushed. 'No, Mr Hanley, I am a volunteer with the regiment. I do not yet have a commission.'

'That means he is waiting around for one of us to die so that he can step into the vacancy,' Pringle explained. He followed with another stage whisper. 'If I were you, I should think twice if Bills here ever offers you some soup!'

'Bills?'

'He is called Williams so we assume there must be more than one of him.'

'It also means the intellects of our grenadiers are not overtaxed in remembering more than one name,' put in Truscott. 'By the way, what did the vicar call you after you were sprinkled?'

'William, actually,' replied Hanley.

Truscott and the others laughed. 'Damme another one. Will you take a drink with us, Hanley?' The lieutenant gestured at the remaining claret. 'There should be enough. Williams barely touches the stuff, and anyway he and Pringle will be leaving us before too long to stretch their legs. Can't have them marching in less than a fully sober condition.'

Pringle had wanted a drink, and guessed that his friend realised this and was determined to make this difficult. He was not sure whether to curse him or grin, so instead spoke to Hanley. 'Captain MacAndrews is leading the Grenadier Company on a ten-mile march. Have you reported to him yet?' Hanley nodded. 'Well, he must have thought you needed to rest or he would no doubt have requested that you join us.'

'May I?' asked Hanley, rather surprising himself. Anyway, it seemed a better alternative than making conversation here. Pringle seemed companionable enough, and even if Williams did not then at least he could remember his name. Hanley was stiff after the journey and had always enjoyed walking. More than that he wanted to be tired. When there was time to think he was plagued by memories of Madrid, and gnawed by self-pity at his own fate. It was hard to sleep unless he was so exhausted that thought ceased.

'Really. Well, up to you, old boy. Still, we can't have you going like that. They won't have allocated a soldier servant to you yet. Bills, will you give Hanley here some assistance – for a start sort that damned sash out. I'll get Jenkins to take a look at those boots.'

Hanley was puzzled. 'Is there much point? I dare say I will get dirty again pretty soon.'

The plump lieutenant raised an eyebrow. 'You did not see MacAndrews for long, did you?'

2

The Grenadier Company paraded at five o'clock on the green opposite the duck pond and overlooked by the spire of St Mary's church. A few villagers watched them, one group of small boys doing so with great seriousness, mimicking the parade movements with shuddering intensity. There were also a number of young ladies from the area – since the half-battalion of the 106th had arrived in the village their visits had become more frequent in their coincidence. Matching that coincidence was the presence of several officers from the other companies, who were thus able to bid these charming acquaintances good afternoon, and express their pleasure at this happy chance. Inevitably, conversation soon turned with eager anticipation to the ball that was to be held in two days' time.

Captain Alastair MacAndrews was above concern for such trivialities, and ignored the hubbub as he carried out a quick inspection. He gave the slightest of winces at an especially loud burst of giggling, which could have only one source. At forty-seven he was comfortably old enough to be the father of most of the officers in the regiment, let alone the local pink-bonnets. Still, he would be happier once the company set out and lost its audience, but it was important not to rush the preliminaries. Sergeant Darrowfield's barked command brought the company into open order.

'Pre-sent . . . arms!' Even after thirty years in the army the sheer power of most NCOs' voices still amazed MacAndrews. It was a mystery how such confident, capable men kept on emerging from the handless raw recruits who took the King's shilling.

The elderly Scottish captain was content with the drill of his men, and they went through the three movements neatly. MacAndrews only just restrained a nod of approval, helped by the fact that there was some frenzied clapping from one of the observers and a cry of 'Oh, Jane, you are such an enthusiast!' in soprano, followed by bass and baritone voices laughing and calling bravo. For a moment there was a pang, for his daughter's name was Jane, and MacAndrews had not seen her or his wife for two years. It was the briefest of thoughts, and he was already beginning his inspection as he felt the thrill of knowing that they would soon be with him.

He hoped that he was not smiling, although in fact duty was by now so much a part of him – had always been – that none of the company would have guessed that his attention had strayed even a fraction beyond the details of their turnout. The cost of that duty had been terrible, the little graves dotted in garrison cemeteries around the world, and he wondered whether he would have chosen as he had chosen if he had known the price. Yet it was hard to imagine ever having been anything other than a soldier.

MacAndrews missed nothing as he passed steadily along the front rank. Things were as they should be, for the sergeants had done their job well. Yes, he was content. When he was young he might have been tempted to imagine some minor flaw and reprimand the man just to show the company that they could not take his approval for granted. He had learned sense quickly, for the Highlanders he had led in America readily smoked out a fraud and as readily showed their opinion of an officer, stopping just short of punishable insubordination.

A man never forgot his first company – the faces, names, some of the jokes which had been repeated so often at the time. Since then there had been other men, other companies, and the faces changed even if the basic work of leading them did not. These were nearly all new men, and quite a few were shorter than was ideal for grenadiers. Normal practice tucked such men away in the centre of the second rank, so that from the front the impression was of a line of big men. MacAndrews knew that some of the recruits were barely over five foot six and in normal times would not have been accepted. Perhaps they would grow, given regular meals in the army. At the moment the shoulder wings on their jacket made these youngsters look small and squat.

MacAndrews reached the end of the front rank and passed the reassuringly battered face of Dobson, one of the few old hands and every inch a grenadier. When the 106th had been posted to the West Indies the Grenadier Company had listed three sergeants, two corporals and eighty-three privates on its books. That had been 1804. When they came back from Jamaica three years later MacAndrews had led just nine men off the ship. The regiment had never once seen an enemy during the entire posting, had not suffered from fire or shipwreck. The men had simply died, and the battalion been consumed as so many other British regiments had been consumed in postings to the Fever Islands. Even without battles the army lost more than twenty thousand men every year.

On the return to England it had been almost like raising a regiment from scratch, and it was impressive how much had been accomplished in the year or so since then. MacAndrews was pleased with his sergeants, satisfied with his men, and so far judged his officers to be adequate. It was too early to decide about Hanley. His willingness to join the company on a march when he did not have to was in his favour, but might simply be sycophancy or, even worse, a desire to be popular. He was clearly not yet up to a parade, so MacAndrews had sent him with a message to the acting adjutant so that he could join them as they marched through the village.

The Scotsman was content – with this parade and with the company in general. He was not yet proud of them, but that should come in time and if they got the opportunity. Rumours continued to circulate that their new colonel was using his influence to have the regiment sent abroad. MacAndrews hoped they were true, but had heard too many rumours in the last thirty years to rely on them now. What mattered was being ready, and so he would drive his company hard, for he was proud of his prowess as a soldier. Fortune and the lack of money and interest had denied him a glittering career, not want of effort or skill. No one could ever say that his company was not the best he could possibly make it. So now he would take them on a march when the rest of the half-battalion was resting. Major Hawker had not minded, and indeed was content to give his captains considerable licence when it came to training. Still, it was hard to tell his mood these days and good to be away, if only for a few hours.

The Grenadier Company would have preferred an easier night, but as they marched to the beat of the drum through the village they did so with great pride, especially whenever they passed strollers from the other companies. The choice was not theirs. The captain had decided. That did not mean there was not a pleasing sense of superiority, even a little joy in demonstrating that they were tougher men and better soldiers than their comrades. The biggest men in the battalion, they straightened up and threw their chests out even more, standing even taller and prouder. Williams had seen it before – did not know that he was doing the same – but it still puzzled him, how much the mood changed the appearance of men.

Ensign William Hanley walked along the main street of the village in search of the acting adjutant. Brotherton had seemed a pleasant enough fellow when they met earlier, but was now proving elusive. Lieutenant Anstey had sent him to the Red Lion, assuring him that the adjutant should be in the side room used as a temporary headquarters. There had been a few officers outside the inn however, who had sent him back to the Senior Common Room. This time Anstey had explained that this was only a welcoming jape at the expense of a raw ensign like himself, and that Brotherton really was there. The fellows playing cards had all thought this was hilarious.

Hanley had been pleasantly surprised by his first glimpse of the regiment's officers, for his view of soldiers in general was not high. Now, his worst expectations of them as a set of childish boors seemed to be confirmed. He wondered for the hundredth time whether he had made a mistake, although he could not think of any alternative. His skills were few, his pocket almost empty, and there was no real alternative to a soldier's life. The logic was impeccable, which did nothing to make it any more comfortable.

By the time he returned to the Red Lion the officers who had been sitting outside were gone. As he was about to go in, Hanley caught his own reflection in the windows, and had to admit that he cut quite a figure in uniform, and the artist in him was pleased with the image. His red jacket with its brass buttons and gold lace fitted snugly, and the two long tails were edged with white from where the material was turned back. The other fellows had helped him tidy up his breeches and boots before he left, but the stroll through the village had undone most of their efforts. Even so, with his cocked hat and its tall white plume on his head, his sword – something he had never worn or thought to wear before in his life – trailing behind him in its scabbard, he admitted that he looked heroic.

He struck a pose, one hand on the hilt of his sword and the other pressed to his chest, and tried to adopt an expression of valour and fortitude. In spite of himself he was impressed, and smiled to think how appearances could be so deceptive. Then he frowned because it set him to wondering who he really was. His hand moved from his chest to finger the gorget at his throat. The horseshoe-shaped piece of metal was purely decorative, but apparently an essential part of the uniform. His outfitters had told him that it was a reminder of the time when officers had worn armour like medieval knights. He wondered about that, and at least it interrupted the bleaker thoughts and questions he could not answer. Better to keep busy and deliver the papers to the adjutant.

As Hanley turned he noticed that he had been watched. A young woman – indeed, scarcely more than a girl if it were not for the knowing gleam in her eye – stood a few yards away. She wore a simple white blouse and a dark blue skirt, the hem of which was dirty. Her hair was dark brown, the thick curls falling on to her shoulders. There was amusement in her expression as she stared directly at him for a moment.

'Most handsome,' she said with a half-smile, and then walked away at a slow pace, swaying her hips with the motion.

'Who is this Johnny Newcombe?' said a high-pitched masculine voice from the inn doorway.

'Damn him, I say. Who's the dollymop?' The second voice was even more affected. Hanley saw two of the officers who had misdirected him earlier. The first was very fat and red faced and the second much taller and thinner with a long hooked nose. The pair seemed to have stepped straight out of a cartoon, and Hanley could almost see their words printed in bubbles beside them.

'Oh, just some slut from one of the soldier's families. A grenadier, I believe.'

'Yes, her upper regions are well developed.' The taller officer laughed uproariously at his own wit.

'Tow row row,' said his companion. 'Scrub her up and I'd join the grenadiers myself.' They both found this hysterical. The girl must have overheard their comments, but only walked more slowly and sinuously. Hanley found it all revolting, and gave them only a curt nod as he walked past them and went to find Brotherton. His spirits sank further as he thought of living with such oafs as his companions.

At least Brotherton was jovial.

'Less than an hour with the regiment and already carrying important dispatches. This augurs a great future for our newest officer.' The acting adjutant was no older than twenty-five, but already had little creases round the edges of his eyes and mouth. He had also lost his hair very early in life, and wore a luxurious but ill-fitting wig. Papers were strewn across the table in front of him, but he immediately laid down his pen, winced as he left a blot on the page he had been writing, and reached up to snatch the message. 'I am most favourably impressed. Perhaps the fate of this regiment and our nation depends upon this small piece of paper. Are these orders to depart for war and glory?'

Brotherton unfolded MacAndrews' note and read it intently, then whistled softly through his teeth. Hanley was not sure what he was supposed to do, so simply waited, standing loosely, with his arms hanging down at his sides. The urge to look heroic had vanished. There were two clerks in the inn's side room, which was serving as the office. The redcoats scribbled away and paid him no attention. A cracked voice broke into song from behind the side door of the room. Hanley looked puzzled, but the others ignored it. They were used to Major Hawker's ways, and anyway had seen the steady procession of bottles being taken in to him by one of the maids.

'I was right! It is war!' yelled Brotherton. The clerks, used to their officer's moods, barely paused for a moment in their work.

'War?' Hanley asked automatically. The singing had become louder, but still the others appeared not to hear it.

'Yes, you know, lots of bangs and crashes and shouting. It is what soldiers are for. Occasionally it makes the newspapers.'

'Haven't we been at war with France for some time?'

'It has become traditional, it is true. Never felt right to me back in '03 when we had the peace. Seemed especially ironic as I had only just joined the army. Still, old Boney soon got over that fright and started the ball rolling once again. Decent of him, really. At least as decent as a monster can be.'

Hanley confessed that he had never thought of Napoleon's proclaiming himself as emperor in quite these terms.

'Well now you know. "Truth will out", as the headmaster of my school used to say before he flogged us. Now it is our task to flog the Corsican Ogre and his lackeys until they see sense and start behaving like Englishmen. Well, as far as is possible for so many garlic-eating Frogs.'

'I rather like garlic,' said Hanley, enjoying Brotherton's nonsense.

'The mood will pass.'

'So, are we to go and fight the French in Spain?'

'Bloodthirsty sort of fellow, aren't you? Make a note of that, Fuller.'

'Yes, sir, certainly, sir,' answered Private Fuller without looking up or interrupting his work. 'It is noted for ever, sir.'

'Splendid. It is important to keep records. "Truth will out", as my nanny used to say before she flogged me.' Brotherton had picked up his pen, but succeeded only in sprinkling ink across the table and was now dabbing at the blots with a piece of grubby cloth which may once have been a handkerchief. 'So you wish to chastise the Spanish as well as the French?'

'I thought we might help the Spanish against the French.'

'Can't think why. The Dons have rarely been any friends of ours. Used to be very chummy with Napoleon, though. Invited him to visit, and now look at the mess they're in.'

'The French have taken over the country, deposed the king and killed anyone who opposed them.'

'Yes, they do that sort of thing,' commented Brotherton mildly. 'Damned silly to have them as guests in the first place. Should at least have asked them to leave their cannon in the hatstand and wipe their feet before messing the carpet up. Wasn't too friendly of the Dons to let Boney's legions stroll through Spain on their way to Portugal. Spain shouldn't have lifted her skirts up in the first place,' concluded Brotherton. 'Who but a fool would trust Boney to be a gentleman?'

'The Spanish are fighting. It is their country, after all.'

'Not any longer, by the sound of things.'

Hanley tried to get back to the point. 'But are we going to Spain?'

'You should be going about your own duties, and leaving a poor adjutant to toil into the midnight hours, unthanked and aided only by his stalwart companions, Corporal Lane and the admirable Private Fuller.'

'And the war?'

'Is far more serious than the mere infants' struggle against Napoleon to see who will be first at the jam pot. Captain MacAndrews once again denies knowledge of a dozen haversacks which battalion records maintain were issued to the Grenadier Company in '05. This is serious, costs His Majesty's government many shillings and perhaps conceals a conspiracy of wider import. For all we know one of the grenadiers is selling this vital military equipment to the French to be used in anger against us. That is the real war. Any one of us may be a spy purloining haversacks for the Emperor. Oh well, truth will out in the end.'

Hanley grinned. 'Who gets flogged this time?'

'If there was justice in this world it would be the people who waste my precious time. Now get about your business.'

Hanley left.

'And if you ever see a haversack guard it with your life!' called Brotherton after him. Hanley shook his head. Brotherton seemed amiable enough, but he was rapidly coming to the conclusion that his fellow officers were all buffoons.

The Grenadier Company had already passed the Red Lion as Hanley came out. He jogged after them, nearly tripping when the scabbard of his sword got caught between his legs. Billy Pringle waved his arm in greeting and gestured to show the new ensign that his position was at the right, just behind the last rank of the formation. Hanley lifted his sword's hilt to keep the scabbard out of mischief and tried to match the redcoats' steady pace. Unable to keep step with them, he found himself alternately hurrying to keep up and then almost treading on the heels of the redcoat ahead of him. Once they left the village they dropped into a more comfortable stride, and it was a while before he realised that he was moving in time with the rest. It was an odd feeling for a man who had always thought of himself as an individual. Hanley marched with the company away from the village and longed for weariness and untroubled rest.

3

It was a warm sunny evening on the last day of May, ideal weather for walking through the green fields and rolling hills of Dorset. Half an hour after they started clouds came and soon hid the sun. There was the sweet, almost too sweet, smell of blossom in the air, warning of the rain that began within an hour. It grew steadily heavier. Williams heard Private Tout wonder aloud whether the captain had expected the weather to turn.

'Do you think he knew?' asked Private Tout. The company had paused, taken greatcoats off the tops of their packs and put them on. Now they trudged up a long and gentle slope, sweating under the weight of the thick woollen coats over their uniform jackets.

No one replied. Their heads were bowed, at least as far as their leather neck stocks allowed. It meant that they gained some small shelter from the peaks of their shakos.

'I said, do you think the cap'n knew it would rain?' They were marching at ease, naturally rather than consciously in step, and allowed to talk. Even so Tout had waited until MacAndrews had gone back to the rear of the column, before insisting on this point to the other men in the front.

''Course he did,' Dobson replied. 'Went specially to the sergeant major to order it.' He marched on the left, with Williams between him and Tout. Private Hanks completed the front rank to Tout's right.

'Wouldn't put it past the old bugger,' muttered Tout.

'Could be worse. Could be much worse,' said Dobson. Forty if he was a day, Dobson was the oldest of the handful of veterans in the Grenadier Company, indeed in the entire 106th. In

31

spite of that he was loping along, looking almost comfortable.

'Yes, he could have asked for snow,' said Williams. Dobson snorted, and Tout laughed. Hanks remained impassive, but then he usually did.

A moment later Williams wondered whether even this mild joke at the expense of his commander was inappropriate. A gentleman volunteer served in the ranks, wore an ordinary private's uniform, did the same duties as the soldiers, but lived with the officers. Such men hoped to be commissioned, but nothing was certain, and it could take years. All the time they were neither fish nor fowl. The men were wary of the volunteers, suspicious that they would not pull their weight and so make more work for them. There was also inevitably a degree of nervousness around a man who might one day have them flogged, and who already was close to the officers. Some men saw them as little more than spies. It was only a little easier with the officers, for the good ones realised that they could not be seen to show any favouritism. The bad ones, and those nervous of their own standing, were apt to show disdain.

Williams had joined the regiment at the start of the year. He was twenty-four, so would be old if he did gain an ensign's commission, especially compared to infants like Derryck. Yet for as long as he could remember he had wanted to be a soldier. As a boy he had read every story of adventure he could find and every history of war. In his pack, carefully wrapped in oilskin along with his Bible, was a battered translation of Caesar's *Gallic War*, its spine cracked and with more than a few loose pages. There was something about the great campaigns of the Ancients which still fascinated him, and he read anything he could afford on such subjects. As a child, he had often managed to convince his younger sisters to play at being Alexander and Darius, or Scipio and Hannibal – the girls had especially liked being elephants.

His mother had not been keen. Married at sixteen, she had been left widowed and with four children before she was Hamish's age now. His father was an engineer, a good one in an age when machines were changing the world and how everything was made. Then one day there had been an accident at the factory, and the promising young engineer was killed. Hamish could still remember the faces of the men who had come to tell his mother, and that she showed no emotion. Never in his life had he seen her weep.

The factory's owner gave the widow a pension. It was extremely modest, for he assumed, if he cared at all, that the young woman would marry again and find another man to provide for herself and her offspring. That was not unreasonable, for the golden-haired Frances was undoubtedly pretty, if more than a little stern. There were suitors, as soon as it was decent, and several were handsome and even modestly well off. Mrs Williams was always courteous, but adamant. A few of them persisted for some time, until finally they gave up. Interest faded, and eventually so too did gossip from those jealous of the attention she received. Gradually a grudging acceptance grew that the young widow had no wish to change her status – still less for any liaison of a less formal kind. Any suggestion of the latter prompted a fierce, icy look, and indeed most people came to consider her as an extremely cold woman.

They had lived in Cardiff for a while, where his mother rent-ed a small house and let two spare rooms to respectable guests. There was little new in the furnishings, but the food was ample, if basic, and the entire house was kept spotlessly clean. Laundry was done, clothes mended and other little tasks performed with ruthless efficiency. A few years later the family moved to Bristol, where she began to run a larger establishment of the same sort. In both places many of the guests were mates and sometimes even the masters of merchant vessels. Mrs Williams encouraged no familiarity, but she enjoyed listening to the men talk of distant shores and storm-swept seas. For quite a few the house became their only real home – a somewhat austere home, but a home none the less. There was no question of deep affection between the landlady and her staff or guests, but all knew where they were with Mrs Williams.

Hamish had to admit his own feelings were similar. His mother's approval was never lightly given and he cherished those rare occasions when he had been granted it. Sometimes he was proud of her, especially when she put on her bonnet, best dress and gloves and took the children to church, singing Mr Wesley's hymns in her beautiful voice. Those were the only times he felt she showed passion. To him she was beautiful, but distant – a queen to be feared and obeyed, but loved only in the way a country was loved.

She had hoped to raise him for a doctor. His grandfather had been a physician – a very good one according to his mother. Dr Campbell had also been a poor one, because she said he would treat anyone whether or not they could pay. Yet the schooling needed for that was expensive – far too expensive for a widow to afford – and so Mrs Williams had set her ambitions lower. Her son and three daughters had all been taught to read and write. In time the girls also learned to sew and to cut material, and along with their mother they brought money into the house by doing work for people apart from the guests. Hamish had been kept in school until he was sixteen, and then, scorning mere apprenticeships, his mother's persistence had secured him a post as junior clerk in the office of a shipping corporation.

It was dull work, with lists of cargoes and delivery dates, of ships and their provisioning, of harbour fees and pilots' fees, of sailors and their pay and allowances paid to families during a voyage, and always of timber, ropes, sailcloth and the myriad of supplies needed to keep vessels at sea. Hamish had felt his youth was slowly drowning under the weight of lists. Every day was the same, with the same petty rivalries and little jokes among the half-dozen leathery old men who worked in the office. Yet he was good at his job, temporary employment became permanent, and slowly, painfully slowly, his wages rose. The money helped the family, for as his sisters grew older his mother was intent that they should be dressed properly, and be able to attend decent functions in the hope of finding good, respectable husbands.

Until he was twenty-one Hamish stayed in the office and dreamed of adventure and glory. Then one day he told his mother than he was resolved to be a soldier, and would enlist as soon as he could. He was not sure what he had expected. Not rage certainly, for his mother never showed so much emotion. There was disappointment, but no surprise, and he had readily agreed to the condition that he must wait until a suitable place could be found for him.

Frances Williams had set about the task of securing an officer's commission for her son with all of her usual determination and perseverance. In his youth Dr Campbell had been an assistant surgeon with a regiment, so she wrote letters to its present colonel, and to a pair of officers who had served at the same time and were now elderly and obscure generals. There was no response. In any case her choice would have been a Highland regiment, so she wrote to the colonels of these. Hamish's father may have been a garrulous Welshman, but as far as his mother was concerned he was a Scot, and better than that, a Campbell. The commander of the 91st Foot replied with a polite letter explaining that there were no vacancies for ensigns at present, and unlikely to be for some time. The 93rd did not respond at all.

Undaunted, she dispatched more letters to general after general, any whose address she could find, humbly (and that was something which did not come naturally to Mrs Williams) requesting a place for her son, a young gentleman of good education and sober character. It took years until finally a letter had arrived from Major General Sir Augustus Lepper, colonel of the 106th Foot, 'The Glamorganshire Regiment', informing Mrs Williams that although he could not offer her son a commission at this time, he would be glad to accept him in the regiment as a volunteer. It was less than she had hoped for, but that was something so familiar from her life. Mrs Williams showed no emotion when her son 'went for a soldier'. She had agreed and that was that. He promised to write and to send them what money he could and she simply nodded, and let him kiss her on the cheek. His sisters provided tears and embraces enough to add drama to the scene, but when he thought back it was only his mother, standing straight and stern, that he remembered.

Williams joined the 106th at the beginning of 1808. A few

weeks later another gentleman volunteer arrived and was sent to a different company, and Hamish did not come to know Mr Forde at all well, but the latter seemed to adapt more readily to the new life. For the army was not quite what Williams' dreams had made it. The routine was dull, with day after day of drill. Unlike the officers who had their servants, he was expected to care for his own uniform, equipment and musket. He learned to polish his boots, the pair identical with no left and right. Veterans like Dobson changed them to the opposite foot at the end of each week to spread the wear. He learned the mysteries of pipe-clay, which whitened his cross-belts, and how to polish the brass buttons on his tunic and gaiters without dirtying the material around them.

Now, after five months, his uniform felt comfortable − or at least as comfortable as the rough wool and the stiff leather neck stock allowed. His first parade, when nothing seemed to fit and it all felt so awkward and ungainly, had left him wondering how the sergeants could be so impossibly smart. Even now these men seemed to possess some magic he lacked, but Williams felt that he was a master of the chief mysteries of soldiering. He could pick out his musket from all the other India Pattern firelocks by the tiny notch on the butt plate and the stain on the wood just behind the trigger, which no amount of oiling and scrubbing could remove. It was 'his' musket, unique among all the hundreds of thousands owned by the army. Williams felt himself to be fully a soldier, but he remained an outsider wherever he was.

MacAndrews gave the company five minutes' rest after march-ing for an hour, and then a longer break after the second hour. By then they had gone a good six miles, and the weather had improved, so the order was given to remove their greatcoats and tie them back on top of their wooden-framed packs. That done, Williams was unsure what to do as the grenadiers took their ease. Should he go and join the officers as they leaned against a nearby wall, or stay and converse affably with the grenadiers, showing that he was not too proud to acknowledge them? Would either welcome him or would he be seen as sycophantic to the officers and patronising to the men? Pringle was always friendly, and when the lieutenant was present the supercilious Redman was at least formally polite. As Williams glanced towards the officer, he noticed Hanley looking back at him. After a moment, the new ensign nodded and smiled, but it was hard to know whether that was meant as an invitation, and Pringle had his back to him so was no guide. Williams nodded in reply, but did not move.

'Mr Williams, sir, did you bring your tinder box?' asked Dobson from behind him. The 'sir' was a courtesy. Tout and another private named Murphy also came up holding their clay pipes. After that Dobson stopped any of the other soldiers from asking for the same service. Murphy was one of a dozen or so Irishmen in the grenadiers, and there were similar numbers in the other companies. In spite of its name, the 106th had few soldiers from Wales, and fewer still from the county itself. Like other regiments they took recruits wherever they could find them. 'We don't want to wear out Mr Williams' flint,' added the veteran.

'No, he's not married yet,' quipped Murphy. Williams allowed himself a smile in spite of the coarseness.

'That's why he's still happy,' put in Dobson automatically, although he had buried one wife and been with his Sally now for sixteen years. They rowed sometimes, especially when he drank, but even then he had never laid a hand to her and was proud of that. Their eldest girl was now nearly sixteen – there had been some urgency about their wedding – and was a constant source of worry to him. 'Would turn me to drink, if I had not long since spun that way,' he often said. Jenny Dobson was too full of herself, and he feared that she was making eyes at the officers. That way lay ruin, for 'gentlemen' all too easily used and discarded maids like her. She had a brother, aged fourteen and now on the strength as a drummer, and a sister just ten.

Dobson had been raised to sergeant several times over the years, but then been broken for drunkenness. Like so many soldiers, Dobson all too easily threw off all restraint, drowning himself in alcohol, which tended to make the big man violent. Williams did not think the officers much better – had been astounded by the sheer quantities they could drink in an evening. Personally he drank little, mainly because the taste nauseated him, and had never been drunk in his life, although that was on principle.

'How's that lock?' asked Dobson. Some weeks ago he had shown Williams how to wrap a rag around the lock on a musket in wet weather, stopping water from getting into the pan, where it would soak the powder and so stop the weapon from firing. They were not marching with loaded muskets today, but the old soldier was keen for the volunteer to learn to do things properly. In the company's formation Dobson stood directly in front of Williams, and front and rear rank men depended upon each other utterly in battle. The veteran wanted his to be up to standard.

'Not bad,' he said as Williams showed him the tightly wound rag. 'That would keep it out if anything will.' Dobson grinned and patted the volunteer on the shoulder. 'Well done, Pug.'

Only Dobson used the nickname to Williams' face, but it had generally supplanted his earlier one of Quaker – the inevitable slang for any man who neither swore nor drank. The Hastings Pug was a prizefighter, not the best, but he had won several bouts in the county during the last year. The grenadiers had not known what to make of their volunteer for a long time, for he said so little. Then in March he had been sent with a party of fifteen men to help a supply wagon which had become bogged down on its way to the battalion. It had been hard work in foul weather, digging around the wheels to free them. Dobson had stared aghast at Williams' energetic, almost frenzied plying of his spade.

'Good God, sir, don't you even know how to dig. Look, watch me, and do it this way.'

They had got the job done in two hours of exhausting labour, had let it drive on to the battalion, but Sergeant Probert – one of the few genuine Welshmen in the regiment – had taken them into an inn to shelter and refresh themselves before they returned. On that day even Williams enjoyed some warm punch. Reluctant to venture out into the weather, they stayed drinking for some time. Then Hope, not an especially big man, but very broad in the chest, had suddenly grabbed one of the maids as she passed.

The girl struggled and squealed as the man yelled out that he must have a kiss for every mug he had drunk. Some of the soldiers laughed for the man was obviously drunk, indeed known for the readiness with which the drink took hold of him. Others told him to let her free, but Hope ignored them all, and gave the maid a long slobbering kiss. One of his hands began to grab at her skirt and lift it.

The girl screamed loudly now, and reaching around on the table beside them, flung a bowl of stew at him. It was still hot enough to make Hope let her go, and she fell to the ground, cap falling from her head and legs waving in the air amid a flurry of skirts and petticoats. The grenadier stood up, fingers rubbing at his eyes, and howled in rage. Probert should have done something, but was more amused than worried and ignored Dobson's warning looks.

Then Williams got up, strode over to Hope and punched him just once squarely on the jaw. It surprised everyone, including the volunteer, but he had taken more drink than usual and the adventures he read so avidly were about strong men who protected the weak – most of all who behaved with chivalry. Williams just found himself there confronting the drunken private. Much of it was fluke, for although he leaned into the blow and was a big man, still it was chance that he struck in just the right place. Hope went back, skimmed over the tabletop scattering tankards and plates in all directions and landed unconscious on the other side.

For a moment two of his friends seemed inclined to continue the fight. Yet Williams was big, and still looked belligerent, although in truth he was as much amazed at himself as anything else. Then the huge figure of Dobson came to stand beside him and Probert finally acted.

'Now, lads, it's all over. A fair fight and he deserved it,' he said, looking round the room to see that they all accepted this. 'King and Rafferty, you wake him up.' His friends promptly did this with a jug of water. Hope came back to life spluttering, but surprisingly passive. He was not normally such an aggressive drunk. He stood, rubbing his jaw.

'Come, then, you two boys just shake hands like men and end it,' continued Probert. There was no warmth when they did so. There was more enthusiasm when the maid stood on tiptoe and pecked Williams on the cheek. The grenadiers cheered that, even Hope, who did not seem to remember what had provoked all this in the first place. Hamish blushed, which made them laugh and cheer all the more.

'Listen, all of you,' this was Dobson, 'nothing happened, see. We all just had a quiet drink. Right?' They nodded. 'Old Hope just had too much and fell on his arse like always.'

It had taken a while for Williams to understand. Although he served as an ordinary soldier he was supposed to be a gentleman. For a gentleman to strike a soldier – indeed, to strike anyone other than a King's enemy – was unthinkable. Had it become officially known then he would have had no choice but to resign or be dismissed. It was chilling to think that a moment's anger could have ended his career before it had even begun.

What surprised him was the reaction of the company, for the brief confrontation made the grenadiers accept him as they had not done before. They were soldiers, and the one thing above all else they respected was pluck. He had shown that and more, and now they gave him some respect, even trust. They were a little more free when they talked to him. Dobson in particular began taking an almost paternal interest in him. He had become 'Good Old Mr Williams' or simply the 'Pug'. Even Hope seemed to carry no ill will, although he had always been an easygoing man when sober.

The rest was soon over, and Sergeant Darrowfield barked out the order to fall in. Pringle and Ensign Redman lingered for a moment, struggling to restore some order to Hanley's uniform. They could do nothing about the mud spattered across his white breeches – somehow Hanley had seemed to attract more than either of them – but straightened his belts and once again tried to wind his dark red silk sash back into place.

'There, as good as new,' lied Pringle. 'Damp, of course, but a drop of water won't harm you, and I should know, coming from a long line of sailors.'

'Yet here you are in the army?'

Pringle smiled. 'I seem not to have inherited my ancestors' sea-legs. A naval officer is not supposed to spend every voyage draped over the side or lying moaning in his cot.'

'Was not Nelson prone to seasickness?' asked Redman, who was a tall but desperately thin eighteen-year-old. He had been disappointed to learn that Hanley was his regimental senior, but still did his best to be friendly.

'Yes, I am sure I read that somewhere,' said Hanley.

'Ah, the difference was that with him it would wear off in time. It just didn't seem to with me. I rather doubt England's hero would be quite so celebrated if he had spent the Nile or Trafalgar puking his guts out over the side.'

'Apart from that these were a problem.' Pringle had taken off his wire-rimmed glasses and was polishing their lenses with his own sash. 'His Majesty's Navy isn't keen on officers with bad eyesight. At least Nelson had one good eye.'

'Are French soldiers easier to see than their warships?' asked a grinning Hanley.

'Apparently. Perhaps the Horse Guards have arranged that we will only fight against particularly tall and fat Frenchmen.'

Their musings were interrupted by Sergeant Darrowfield. 'Mr Pringle, sir, would you and the other gentlemen care to join us.'

The three officers strolled over to take their places in the formation.

'Amazing how they can make "sir" sound like a question,' said Pringle quietly.

The company marched on as the sun began to set, the clouds shading into rich pinks and reds. Hanley was now content and weary enough to take pleasure in the scene. In the last weeks even the most magnificent landscapes had left him unmoved. For a moment he wanted to stop and sketch, or better yet use the box of watercolours he carried in his trunk. Then he thought of Mapi. He had often dreamed of the dead girl from Madrid, and sometimes it was his lover's face he saw when he turned the corpse over. Despair flooded back and all desire to make or create

41

vanished. His mind came back to where he was and he laughed grimly as he thought that he had come to an army to seek peace.

Pringle raised a quizzical eyebrow, but Hanley did not notice. The lieutenant had worries enough of his own. His memories of the previous night were still hazy, but after the hours of drinking in the inn, he remembered a vigorous coupling by the wall of the stable yard. He had hoped that it was with Molly Hackett, but when he had encountered her that morning she had not returned his smile and certainly gave no hint of intimacy. Anyway, she was a blonde, and he was now sure the girl in question had had dark hair. When the company had left the village, he had noticed young Jenny Dobson watching them. She had winked at Hanley – and that was a surprise – and then treated him to a broad smile. Had this been more than her habitual flirtation?

Anyone but her, thought Pringle, please God, anyone but her. Jenny was pretty, but a good officer should not be rolling one of his soldier's daughters. Dobson was a good man, one whose respect Pringle wanted to earn. Apart from that, the veteran could be frightening, and was certainly not a man to make angry. Billy Pringle made a familiar pledge to restrain his fondness for liquor, this time with more fervour than usual.

The Grenadier Company trudged on in an easy rhythm.

4

'It could be Spain,' said Sir Richard Langley, and was not surprised when his companion merely grunted. Sir Richard was a man who noticed details, and that was one of the things that made him important. He held no formal office, but seemed to know everyone in Lord Portland's government, at the same time as maintaining the friendliest relations with the leaders of the Whig opposition. Now he noted the slight movements, the gentlest squeeze of the knees, followed by slight pressure on the reins, as Lieutenant Colonel Moss slowed his borrowed mount.

'Indeed, I begin to think it very likely. London seems to have fallen in love with the Spanish.' Sir Richard was happy to provide both sides of a conversation. 'Of course, they have rarely been friends of ours.'

'Bugger friendship.' Moss sniffed, finally breaking his silence of the last ten minutes.

'Quite so,' said Sir Richard, and as so often wondered whether his younger friend was consciously acting, for he had seen him behave in different manners in various company. At times he was garrulous, often charming, whereas today he was the gruff, even crude soldier. 'Yet for all that, life without friends is difficult, for a country as much as an individual. England has few friends, with the Austrians and Prussians battered into submission. They say Russia's Tsar is apparently now positively affectionate to Bonaparte.' Moss knew that Sir Richard's information would be as reliable as any available in the country.

'Affection need not be lasting in statecraft,' said Moss, his voice now softer and manner more intent.

'Interests can indeed change, but at present there is very little reason for any of the Great Powers to side with Britain. The Spanish have less choice, unless they want to fight Boney on their own. For our part, a weak ally is better than none. You remember the fervour in town when the news came of the rising in Madrid.'

'Which the French crushed.'

'Yes, but that has not prevented a wave of enthusiasm for all things Spanish. I understand that one of my clerks has been enjoying the favours of several ladies by pretending to be a Spaniard. He wears a broad red sash and speaks to them in a mixture of Latin and a speech of his own invention. I would scarcely have credited him with the initiative, but for a small, ill-favoured lad, it appears that he is doing remarkably well.

'More importantly, you saw the crowds welcoming the delegation from the Spanish junta. England, or at least fashionable opinion, wants us to help their noble struggle.' Sir Richard spoke dispassionately, but without amusement. Not part of the crowd, he did not despise it, for it was an element – even if only one element and rarely the most important – of what made politics work, and that was Sir Richard's world. Moss was the son of an old friend and business associate, a banker who helped Langley to become wealthier with every passing year. Finance was as inseparable from politics as it was essential for a comfortable life. 'There are sound reasons for action as well as enthusiasm.'

Sir Richard broke off to greet an elderly couple walking arm in arm. Hyde Park was busy, and they had barely been able to trot for more than a few minutes. He could sense Moss's frustration, as he stopped the hot-blooded mare he was riding, curbing her urge to run. It was typical of the man to choose the tallest and fastest horse on offer. Sir Richard could sense his frustration in not being able to give the bay her head, and deliberately prolonged the conversation, and even when they bade the couple farewell he kept his own gelding at the gentlest of walks.

The young lieutenant colonel of the 106th Foot was inclined to obsession. Old General Lepper was the regiment's colonel, guiding from a distance, and approving important decisions and promotions, but Moss commanded the battalion on a day-to-day basis and would lead it into battle, if only Horse Guards had the sense to send them on campaign. The young lieutenant colonel did not care where, as long as there were the King's enemies to fight.

A short man, George Moss whenever possible moved at high speed. Even when inspecting a parade he paced so rapidly along the ranks that officers not used to it struggled to keep up. For all that he had an eye for detail, and seemed at a glance to be able to spot the tiniest flaw in turnout. His speech was fast, although socially he was also prone to these long bouts of silence. At his infrequent rest he looked gloomy, almost mournful. When talking he could soon become aggressively enthusiastic, sweeping people along before they had a chance to think.

Moss had purchased command of the 106th at the end of the previous year, but had as yet spent little time with the battalion. His agents had arranged the purchase while he was serving on a staff appointment in Dublin, and some time elapsed before a successor was found and he felt free to leave. In the following months there had been brief whirlwind visits. Orders came in flurries, with changes to routine and details of drill. Patience was not one of Moss's virtues and he expected the changes to be instant. Then he would depart, usually to London, where he would plunge himself head first into the politics of the army and the country itself where the two overlapped. At twenty-nine he was young to command a battalion, although not as young as some, especially in the years before the Duke of York had taken over the army and imposed tighter regulation on careers. Moss had not been badly affected by this, but any delay enraged him, wasting time when he could be winning glory.

Eight years before he had been the first up the beach in Egypt, a young captain charging ahead of his company, which was itself at the head of the entire army. He had made a name for himself, but it had been brief. Twenty minutes later he was shot through the cheek by a spent musket ball. The wound looked dreadful, although it scarcely slowed the small man as he led his men up the dunes. They told him later that no one could understand what he was saying as his cheek flapped whenever he spoke, but his redcoats followed him anyway. He staggered and fell when another ball buried itself in his side. Then he was up again, still roaring and waving his sword, until a third shot broke his left leg and knocked him down for good.

For Moss, Egypt had been a short war, and his glory was soon submerged in the greater glory of Abercromby's victory at Alexandria a few weeks later. The captain had still been with the surgeons at the time, damning their eyes and threatening to shoot anyone who tried to take his leg. The doctors had shaken their heads, but eventually given up on the irascible captain and let him take his chance. By then they had too much other trade from the Battle of Alexandria to worry overmuch about one fool. The fever had come and gone, and if anyone had had the time to think they might have been amazed at Moss's recovery. He kept his leg, and was walking on it long before anyone else thought this wise. Years later there was not even the slightest trace of a limp. The side wound had also healed. So did the injury to his face, but that gave him a permanent scar. Most people – and especially the ladies – felt this was a marked improvement. Before then he had looked immensely boyish. With a dark red slash on his cheek he looked piratical, and his smile changed from innocence to roguish charm.

Alexandria had been the army's last great victory. Back in '06 a small force had shattered an equally small French army at Maida in Italy, but that had been little more than a skirmish. Since then there had been little glory, and more than a few humiliations. South America was the worst, but even in Egypt things had turned sour. Moss despised failure. He knew he was a good soldier, a bold man who would not hold back until victory was won. Yet he had had no chance to smell powder since Egypt. Britain's navy ruled the waves and covered itself with the laurels of triumph time after time. The army did not get its chance, and Moss chafed at years of inaction. It seemed so absurd when the world was in the middle of the greatest war in history.

When Moss gained his own battalion he was adamant that he would take them to war. Enough time had already been wasted and there was a good deal of lost ground to recover. His cousin was an MP, and he had connections at high levels in Horse Guards, the headquarters of the army, but Sir Richard was a family friend and by far the best guide to the mechanisms of power and influence in London. Following his advice, Moss flung himself head first at any opportunity to influence those who determined the postings given to regiments. The 106th was not a famous corps and had few obvious patrons. It was now the junior regiment of infantry in the entire British Army. There had once been regiments with higher numbers, even a 135th Foot, but most had existed only on paper and these ghost units had been abolished by the Duke of York, along with all the opportunities for corruption they had brought. The 106th had survived, but there was a danger that it would only ever get the worst assignments. Moss had no intention of taking his men back to the Caribbean or to any other unwholesome backwater.

He lobbied hard, spending his own money to entertain generals, ministers and senior clerks alike. He paid court to the men themselves and anyone who might persuade them. Over the months he seduced the wife of an elderly general, at the same time lavishing gifts and favours on the mistress of another. He gambled with men in government, letting them win enough to enjoy his company, but never making it too obvious. Finally, it had worked. The outbreak of smallpox among a battalion stationed in Ireland and allocated to a force bound for South America had provided the opportunity. A replacement was needed, and Moss could boast that his regiment was the bravest and best trained in the army, and that it would be a criminal waste to leave them guarding Dorset against imaginary enemies when there were battles to be fought. Adding the 106th to the expedition would be the simplest solution. Sir Richard called in favours and gave advice.

Moss was almost there. Sir Richard assured him that his regiment would join the force soon to embark at Cork, and his assurances were as certain as anything could be in politics, even if Horse

Guards had not yet written the order. What he did not know is where the expedition would be sent, and that was because as far as he could tell no one had actually made up their minds. There was no more mention of South America, which made him suspect that plan had been abandoned, at least for the moment.

Sir Richard liked the thrusting, impatient Moss, as well as being obliged to his father. As importantly he guessed that the young officer would go far in the army, at least if he stayed alive. Furthermore, Moss had no brothers or sisters, and so was sole heir to a great fortune. Langley had long since considered the many advantages of a union with his own daughter.

They rode slowly for ten minutes, the silence broken only to acknowledge acquaintances as they passed. At the end of this time, Moss turned to his companion – in spite of a smaller horse their faces were level. 'Spain, eh,' he said, nodding to himself with a look of fixed intent. 'Good.' There seemed to be no more for a while, but Sir Richard waited, knowing that Moss was not listening and anyway never one for needless talk. 'Any idea of who will be in charge?'

Sir Richard Langley smiled, the tight skin of his long face fracturing into a web of wrinkles. 'Ah, now that I do know.' There was open ground ahead of them and he kicked his horse straight into a canter. Moss instinctively followed and found himself laughing as the strong mare pounded across the firm grass.

'Damn you, sirs! Damn you all to hell! Is this the pledged word of England?' The little man's English was excellent, until his fury grew too incandescent and he could express it only in Spanish far too rapid and heavily accented for Sir Arthur Wellesley and his companions to follow. General Francisco Miranda had come to London from Venezuela to persuade the British to help him raise rebellion in Spain's American possessions. That aid had been promised, and Wellesley appointed to lead a strong British expeditionary force. They had met several times to plan the enterprise. Now, at the last minute, Britain's government had changed its mind.

'You betray us!' Miranda reverted to English, his voice lower, but more precise as he controlled his rage. 'You betray freedom itself! God will judge you for this treachery. You will be lost!' The last words were bellowed as once again the anger overcame him and he stalked off down the street.

The British had deliberately arranged to meet the general and his followers in the street, hoping that this would prevent too unpleasant a scene. It had not gone entirely to plan, and more than a few passers-by had paused to watch the gaudily uniformed man's explosion of anger. Wellesley did not blame the would-be revolutionary.

'He is angry enough to lead a revolt on his own,' said one of his companions, both civilians sent by the government.

'If they do, then well and good,' said Wellesley. The government men looked at him, but already knew him sufficiently to understand that he was unlikely to expand on this comment. In truth he had been uncomfortable with the plan from the very start. To raise a people to revolution seemed too great a responsibility, for so many things could go wrong and there was no knowing where such impulses would stop. Yet the command was still a command, and any chance of active service was better than the drudgery of administration in Ireland. Apart from that, he was *nimmukwallah* – even in thought he liked using the Indian word. He was the government's man, had eaten their salt and was duty bound to go where they sent him.

The night after that uncomfortable episode, he sat in contented silence in his house in Harley Street. There was great relief that the South American adventure had been cancelled, and far greater satisfaction that he and his army were to be put to better use in Europe itself. Whether in Spain or Portugal was yet to be decided, but the former seemed more likely, and it would no doubt enrage General Miranda even more to know that the troops once promised to him were now likely to find themselves fighting alongside the Spanish.

His command of the force waiting at Cork had been formally confirmed, whatever its final destination, and many of his

London friends had gathered to dine the previous night in celebration. Their host, Sir Jonah Barrington, plump and red faced, his speech slurred before the evening was half over, had done a good job and enjoyed himself immensely. There was a brief moment of discomfort when he talked of the previous year's attack on Copenhagen as 'robbery and murder'. Wellesley had led a brigade in that expedition, something which Sir Jonah had only then remembered. His cheeks grew even more ruddy, and an apology formed. Wellesley had smiled at his old friend, and asked aloud whether the latter also suspected him of purloining some of his spoons. The host shamefacedly joined in the guffaws of laughter and the awkwardness quickly passed.

It was hard to be proud of the whole Danish affair. Britain had demanded that the Danes hand over their powerful fleet of well-built warships to prevent them from falling into Napoleon's hands. Neutral Denmark had not unreasonably refused, and so Britain had used force, bombarding Copenhagen until the Danes surrendered and the ships were destroyed or taken. 'Robbery and murder' just about summed it up, but Wellesley saw that if it was a crime, then it was a necessary one. Bonaparte would in time no doubt have ridden just as roughshod over Danish neutrality, and grabbing the Danish fleet might just have allowed him to challenge the Royal Navy's dominance. The government had been right to act. Even so, he was *nimmukwallah*. At least the short and one-sided campaign had been well run, and offered a break from the drudgery of administration in Dublin.

Tonight's supper had been a quieter affair, with just a single guest joining Sir Arthur and Lady Wellesley. John Wilson Croker was a friend and ally from Ireland, and after Kitty had retired the two men plunged into business, running through the details of improvements to Dublin's water supply. That settled, Sir Arthur fell silent, staring into the fire, which was a comfort on an unusually cold spring evening. The shadows added to the sharpness of his face, and most of all his great beaked nose. Croker had similar pale grey eyes, a nose almost as hooked, but there the resemblance ended, for his lips and chin were weak.

Few people trusted him until they knew him well – and some not even then. Wellesley commanded confidence and respect of a different sort, and even at rest his friend saw an intent concentration in him which he had never seen in anyone else. For a good twenty minutes Croker said nothing, savouring the taste of an excellent brandy and allowing his companion to pursue his own thoughts. Only then did he break the silence.

'Sir Arthur, as a lawyer I always endeavour to know that I shall win a case before it reaches court. I should imagine that a soldier's struggle is similar. You must be giving great thought to confronting Bonaparte's men.'

Wellesley looked up sharply, fixing his gaze on his friend, and then gave the faintest of smiles. In fact his mind had been wandering more over the past few years, the disappointment of returning from victories in India to dull years of monotonous work. Indian reputations were ten a penny, almost a disadvantage in the army, especially since most of the men making decisions could not match them with achievements of their own. Marriage had proved a disappointment. Whether or not Kitty had changed in the years he had been away, he had certainly changed too much. Honour commanded that he marry, but they were now utterly unsuited. *Nimmukwallah*, once again, although this time duty bound to a wife he no longer loved or even respected. The last few months offered hope at last of serious work and great opportunities. He had been promoted to lieutenant general, at thirty-nine the youngest in the British Army. Then came the command and the chance of leading an army to war. So in truth the thought of how to beat the French had concerned him especially closely of late, if not that particular evening up until this point.

'I have not fought the French for fourteen years. They were good then, and from all I have heard have since grown better.' Sir Arthur shook his head when Croker gestured towards the decanter. The young lawyer helped himself to another glass and then settled back into his chair.

'From what I understand, we made a lot of mistakes in Flanders,' he asserted in his best barrister's voice.

'That is most certainly true. It would have been difficult to make a greater hash of things. I suspect that the main thing I learnt from that campaign was how not to wage a war.'

'Well, I suppose that is something.'

'Rather an expensive way to learn a lesson.' As always, waste appalled him, and there was bitterness in his voice. 'Since then Bonaparte has devised a new system of strategy which has outmanoeuvred and overwhelmed all the armies of Europe.' Sir Arthur gave another faint smile. ''Tis enough to make one thoughtful; still, no matter.'

'I would guess that consideration has produced an answer – a remedy to this new strategy?'

Again the smile. 'Well, let us hope so. In any case my die is cast. The French may overwhelm me, but I don't think they will out-manoeuvre me. First, because I am not afraid of them, as every-body else seems to be; and secondly because if what I hear of their system of manoeuvre is true, I think it a false one as against steady troops. I suspect all the continental armies were more than half beaten before the battle was begun.' Suddenly he burst into something that sounded like a cross between a sneeze and a horse neighing. Croker knew his friend well enough to recognise his unique laugh, although as with most people its volume and abruptness still took him by surprise. It stopped just as unexpect-edly, but Sir Arthur's smile was broad as he continued. 'I at least, will not be frightened beforehand.' The smile faded and his face was once again a mask of confident purpose. 'I think I shall beat them.' He opened his hands in a gesture. 'But I can't help think-ing about them.'

Comforts were fewer in the cabin of a small merchantman, beat-ing as close as it could into a south-westerly wind in the Bay of Biscay. They had not seen the sun for days, and late spring or not, the atmosphere below decks was cold and damp. The ship's captain had left them, and the three men sat around his table. One was slumped over, arms resting on the wooden sur-face and cradling his head as he snored loudly. The younger of the other two men watched with mild interest as a spilled pool of wine flowed against the sleeping man's sleeve every time the deck rolled beneath them, and then trickled away back to the raised rim of the wooden table whenever it pitched back the other way. He was half surprised the sleeper did not wake up, lick the puddle dry and then resume his slumbers, for the man had spent almost all the voyage either drinking or asleep. Would he be any more active once they arrived and he took charge of one of his Imperial Majesty Tsar Alexander's warships? Would he have drunk himself to death before they arrived?

The racking cough interrupted his thoughts, but Major the Count Denilov barely registered it, for the sound had been so very frequent in the last weeks. Surprise had long since gone, and even the disgust had faded. The third man in the cabin had skin that hung loose around his neck, the sign of severe loss of weight. His complexion had already been as grey as death and his eyes bloodshot before they got on board. He coughed again, his whole body in spasm, and when he brought his grubby handkerchief away from his mouth there was blood on the cloth.

The general knew he was dying, and that was why it was so important for him to talk to his younger colleague. Their mission mattered more than the agony of sitting upright, more than the squalor of the voyage in this tired old wine ship, which leaked water through every joint and yet still seemed covered in filth. Only Denilov looked clean, his dark green uniform somehow neat and pressed, his black leather belt shining. The count always looked immaculate, just as he always looked bored, observing other people as if they were insects. The general watched as Denilov poured some of his own wine to add to the pool running up and down the table.

'The English . . .' Another vicious spasm of coughing interrupted the general. Again he pressed his handkerchief to his lips. He no longer even bothered to look at the contents. There was no surgeon on board, and anyway even the best doctor could do nothing for him. It might have been better to have sent someone else, but there was no one that all the senior generals and also the Tsar himself trusted so fully. The price of talent, he thought to himself, then his smile dissolved into another cough that sent pain through all his body. He recovered, swore wearily and continued. 'In the end it all comes down to the English. We need to know what they will do. Bonaparte plans to strangle their commerce. He will close off all the ports of Europe to English ships and starve them of trade.'

'It seems a very practical response,' conceded Denilov, but his voice suggested no more than casual interest. 'He cannot hope to beat the English navy at sea. He does not have either the ships or the men and it will take years to build them. If he does not control the sea then he cannot send his legions to march into London. So why not hit *les rosbifs* in the pockets.' Both Russian officers conversed comfortably in flawless French, for they were educated men and this was still the language of culture. Still, the general found the use of such slang more than a little jarring. He wondered whether his subordinate had intended this.

The general nodded, began to cough again, but then for once the spasm quickly subsided into nothing. For a short moment, he knew relief from the pain. 'It is reasonable, and now he has overrun both Portugal and Spain and so is able to extend his ban on English trade. All Europe is now closed to them. Again, the question is what will they do about it.'

'We are France's ally.'

The general nodded again. He had been with the Tsar the previous year when he had met the French Emperor on a specially prepared barge floating on the River Niemen. The only two doors to the wide cabin faced towards the opposite banks and the idea had been for both to enter at the same time. Napoleon had of course hurried across, and was there waiting for the Tsar. Napoleon always got there first.

The general had been close behind his ruler, and remembered that his first words had been 'I hate the English as much as you do' and how gladly Bonaparte had lapped that up. Maybe it was true. Russia, encouraged by English money and enthusiasm, had fought Napoleon in Europe and had paid the price in three years of defeat and tens of thousands of dead.

'The Tsar and Bonaparte are friends,' noted Denilov, although as ever his voice was detached. There was no judgement in the tone, no indication of whether he thought this good or bad, or indeed whether it touched him at all. Still, the general had almost forgotten that the count had been present in the series of banquets following the negotiations. No doubt he remembered the warmth between the young and handsome Tsar and the short, stocky French Emperor. Prussia's king had been publicly humiliated, but Napoleon carefully cultivated the Russian monarch.

More coughing, and this time the attack was worse and the general struggled to control it, his whole body sheathed in agony. Finally he recovered enough to speak.

'The Tsar must act like any good ruler and cope with defeat.' The general did not add that his monarch was also still young, and not always wise. 'At present we cannot fight the French. Our armies need time to recover. Our generals need to learn how to win. God willing, one day we will find another Suvarov.'

'Better to stay their friend if Napoleon's plan works.' As far as the general could see Denilov felt little shame in Russia's defeat, showed no regret for all those dead men. The count had made a name for himself in the campaigns, showing courage at times when there were influential witnesses. Had it not been for his reckless gambling, shameless affairs with married women, and the frequency and ruthless effectiveness with which he duelled, his career would have prospered far more. Denilov did not appear to care.

'If it works?' the general continued. 'The French face risings in Portugal and throughout Spain. Napoleon's soldiers are good, but they are stretched thinly from Poland to the Atlantic. If the English send an army to aid the rebels . . .' He broke off for another spasm of coughing.

'The English spend money, not their own blood,' said Denilov dismissively.

The general breathed deeply, and waved one arm in the air. For some reason it seemed to help. 'Even lavish use of money would aid the rebels greatly. Yet this time they may also fight. They have done it before, and perhaps now have reached a point where they have nothing left to lose. If Bonaparte's plan works, then England will be lost, sooner or later. Do we want a world run by Bonaparte?'

Denilov shrugged. 'Paris is still a long way from St Petersburg.'

'For the moment. What of the future? Is Bonaparte always to dictate to us, and Russia must come to heel like a whipped cur?'

Another shrug, but there was just the hint of more interest in the count's gaze. The idea of Britain making a last desperate gamble appealed to him for it mirrored his own life. He also knew from experience that the cards did not always favour either the desperate or the bold. It was a truth which made the wager all the more intoxicating. For himself there were still more hands to play. The British were finished. Whether they fought or not, they would lose in the end and Napoleon's empire would dominate the world. That was the reality, and a sensible man would accept it, and make himself as comfortable as possible in the new order.

The general was pleased to see the spark of real attention, accepting it as a sign that whatever Denilov's failings of character, he remained a true Russian and loved his country. It calmed him, and with little more than a clearing of the throat, the automatic raising of his handkerchief to brush his lips, and a slight wave of his hand, he was ready to continue.

'That is our task. To go to Lisbon, and judge what will happen next. Siniavin will help us, but he is not an imaginative man and he must not know our purpose for his opinion will be worth little. All sailors respect the English fleet too much to understand the weakness of their army.' When Russia had made peace with France the previous year, the Tsar and his ministers had made many concessions to the French. One was giving up all of their Mediterranean bases. That left the squadron of warships stationed there with a long journey home, unsure whether or not the Royal Navy would treat them as enemies. Admiral Siniavin was their commander, and he was a cautious man who had put in to the broad mouth of the Tagus and anchored off Lisbon on the pretext of repairing storm damage. He maintained friendly relations with the French there, but kept his distance even though he was an ally. He also ensured his crews were prepared for anything. Denmark had shown how little the British regarded neutrality when there were warships at stake. The three men would join this fleet – their sleeping companion was to replace the captain of one of the ships who had died in an accident.

'Siniavin is instructed to introduce us to the French leaders, and as many of the Portuguese as possible. The English we will simply have to watch.'

The general coughed again, and, when he had recovered a little, he silently prayed that he would live long enough to see and to write his report. Denilov would have to carry it back, for he knew that he would not survive to do so. He wished there had been someone else, but the elegant count still had some powerful friends and they had arranged for him to be sent – the rumour was that he was fleeing the creditors who would bankrupt him – and at least now he had shown some trace of love for Mother Russia. The general allowed himself hope. The great hope that cracks were at last about to appear in the upstart empire of Bonaparte, and the smaller hope that Denilov would belie his reputation and serve the Tsar well. Then the coughing began again, and all he knew was the terrible pain.

Denilov looked at the old general as if the man were already dead.

George Moss stayed in London until the middle of June when he received official confirmation that the regiment was to join the expedition. He and Sir Richard watched from the gallery when Parliament decided to support Spain. It now looked as if it would definitely be Spain, and Moss decided that it was time to join the regiment and hurry its preparations. He had got what he wanted, and when he left there was a general sense that London had become a more restful place. The politicians won less often at cards. The general's wife wept for a day and a half. The mistress had already grown bored with him so was not greatly concerned and simply returned her main interest to her old protector.

5

A lot had happened in the regiment by the time Moss arrived, and the biggest change had come on the day after MacAndrews had taken the Grenadier Company on its march. At eight o'clock sharp on that bright morning, they and the other companies were ordered to parade and witness punishment at a spot half a mile or so outside the village. The muscles in Hanley's legs ached from unaccustomed use, but at least he had slept well and dreamlessly for the first time in over a week. Williams was by now well used to marching, and as usual had slept like a log. MacAndrews had arranged for hot stew and an issue of rum to be waiting on their arrival and let the men enjoy this before giving them the bad news. It meant several hours cleaning equipment to be fit for parade. All of the men's boots and gaiters were covered in mud and most also had grime on their white trousers. The order was to parade without packs, so there was less urgency about cleaning greatcoats. Still, the shakos needed attention, as did their belts, which once again needed to be whitened with pipe-clay. There was a good deal of cursing and complaining – about their captain, the army in general, the Regent and the King themselves. Tout even seemed to blame the Archbishop of Canterbury.

Most of the men had had less sleep than they would have liked, but the grenadiers were every bit as smart as the other four companies. Together they formed the right wing of the 106th – in battle, when the entire battalion was present, their station was the right of the line. The left wing, with the remaining four centre companies and the Light Company, was somewhere near

Taunton, and had been for the last two months. At the same time the right wing had gone to Dorchester. Both detachments were supposed to be aiding the civil powers against rumours of organised sedition among millworkers. There were very few mills in the area, and as far as anyone could tell no more than usual discontent among the folk who worked in them, so instead the 106th had paraded and trained, carrying out field exercises with some militia stationed near by and with the local yeomanry. After a few weeks they moved away from the towns and were billeted in villages which offered better scope for training.

Now the grenadiers and the men of Companies One to Four paraded to watch a flogging. They formed up as three sides of a rectangle. The fourth side was composed of the high brick wall that enclosed the garden of Hanscombe Hall – the Hall itself was almost a mile away and not in sight. The field had been chosen because this was a private matter, to be dealt with within the regiment and not under the gaze of outsiders. Against the wall a tripod made from sergeants' half-pikes tied together had been erected. The Grenadier Company stood in line at a right angle to the wall, with Number Four Company facing them. The other three companies formed the long side of the box.

Major Hawker spoke for half an hour about honour, glory and damnation to the King's enemies. MacAndrews let Hawker's words flow past him. The stocky, red-faced major had always had a sudden and vicious temper. More recently his behaviour had become highly erratic. Mostly he kept to himself, drinking alone in his room – his speech sounded a little slurred even at this time of the morning. Hawker had no family, had never much sought the company of the other officers. It had been the same in the West Indies, where his consumption of wine and spirits had amazed even the hard-drinking planter society. Then the old colonel had taken a very active role in running the day-to-day affairs of the battalion. He was a man who liked the small details of soldiering. The 106th's second major had not been with them, having secured a comfortable staff appointment in Ireland which kept him well away from such a dangerous posting. Hawker had been required to do very little, for often the companies were detached individually.

Inactivity seemed to have suited him. Oddly enough, so had the climate, in spite of his hard drinking. Disease had cut as big a swathe through the officers as through the men of the battalion. Almost all the ensigns had died or become so sick that they would not be fit for service for some years, and perhaps never. The lieutenants were nearly as badly affected. Half the captains had died or been forced to sell out and leave the army. Yet Hawker had remained robustly healthy.

It would be wrong to say that MacAndrews actively regretted this. Yet he was the senior captain in the 106th, and had been even before the battalion went to the Indies. When a vacancy for major occurred, whether through death, transfer or promotion, he was the rightful successor to the rank. That was assuming no one purchased over his head. That was the way of the army, and no one could let it become personal. He did not especially like Hawker, and thought he was a bad officer, but the only thing that really mattered was that the major was still there, and most unlikely to be promoted or leave the service.

'. . . so damnation to the French! Let us slay our enemies again and again!' Hawker's voice was always rather high pitched, and in this climax of his speech he became positively shrill. MacAndrews happened to know that the major had never once fought the enemy in all his eighteen years of service. Still, at least he had finally ended his oration. The Regimental Sergeant Major brought the right wing to the present, and then allowed them to rest arms.

The prisoner, Private Scammell, was brought in, wearing loose white fatigue trousers and bare from the waist up. Mr Hughes, the assistant surgeon, certified that he was fit to receive the punishment of four dozen lashes. Then the two guards and a sergeant took him up to the tripod and tied his hands together at its top. The charges were read, and two drummers came forward to inflict the punishment. There were a number of boy drummers in the battalion, but most, like these, were grown men, for army drums were heavy. Anyway, an experienced sergeant stood beside them to ensure that they performed their task properly this morning.

It was the second flogging in a week, the third since the half-battalion had been detached under Hawker's command, and that was more than had been inflicted in the 106th in the entire year before that. They were not a flogging battalion, preferring other lesser punishments and appeals to a man's honour. Yet recently the mood had changed, and the major had become far more savage in his punishments. In the previous week he had broken to the ranks Sergeant Reade, also from Number Three Company, and then awarded the man three hundred lashes. His crime was to have been found asleep when supposed to be mounting guard. This was widely believed to have been an honest mistake, for Lieutenant Wickham had not passed on the order, but that officer had failed to speak clearly before Major Hawker. There was still much bitterness over this, kept fresh because Reade had received only one hundred lashes, and was now in the room serving as a hospital, waiting until he had recovered sufficiently to receive the balance of his punishment. A soldier of previously unblemished record, most felt that the shock of losing his rank had shattered him physically before the flogging had begun. The remaining two hundred lashes might easily kill him. The redcoats felt a good man had been unfairly and unnecessarily broken.

There was little sympathy for Scammell. He was known to be a thief, and worse, a thief who would steal from his own comrades, and was a sullen, unpopular man. Even so there was a feeling that the sentence was too harsh, and Mr Wickham had regained a little of his lost reputation by speaking up for the man and asking for leniency. Another man, Thompson, widely held to be even more of a rogue than Scammell and patently guilty, had actually been let off identical charges. The new harshness of Major Hawker's punishments made the men of the Right Wing nervous. That his decisions seemed so arbitrary and unpredictable was far worse. There was a sense that Scammell had not been treated fairly, which was as close as anyone could come to feeling sorry for such an unpleasant man. They watched in silence, faces wooden, as the two drummers alternately lashed the man's back, till the blood ran down and soaked his white trousers. Scammell made not a sound, and that was admired, for strength was respected in anyone.

All but Hanley had seen a flogging before. Not long ago he might have been troubled by the sight, but Madrid had changed that. He had the same odd sense that what he was seeing was not real – the blood and lacerated flesh on the man's pale back no more than oils cleverly painted on to canvas. Indeed, some paintings had seemed more real to him. Perhaps it was because he did not know the man? Or was it just that he had now seen worse things? It began to bother him that he felt no pity – indeed did not feel anything at all. Williams tried to empty his mind, just like the old soldiers on parade. Simply stand there, not thinking and responding only to the next order. It did not quite work. He accepted that flogging was necessary – was indeed surprised at how readily men like Dobson accepted it – but wished that a better way could be found. Pringle was at the rear of the company, and glad that his view was poor.

'Forty-eight, and all done, sir!' bellowed Sergeant Forster, who had been in charge of the punishment detail.

For what seemed like a long time Major Hawker said nothing. His face looked taut, his eyes staring into the distance at nothing. During the punishment he had stood with the acting adjutant and the Regimental Sergeant Major in the centre of the box formed by the half-battalion. He had not watched the flogging, but had instead continually scanned the ranks of the companies, looking at each man in turn. He seemed to be in discomfort and more than once had rubbed his left arm.

'Punishment complete, sir,' said Sergeant Major Fletcher to prompt his commander. Hawker nodded, but said nothing.

'Remove the prisoner,' bellowed Fletcher in a voice that must have echoed as far as the village. Mr Hughes rushed forward to staunch Scammell's wounds while the drummers undid the ropes tying him to the triangle.

"Talion will order arms,' Fletcher continued, his voice seeming to do the impossible and grow in volume. 'Order . . . Arms!' The companies went crisply through the three movements. The sound seemed to stir Major Hawker into life.

'Behold the price of treason!' he yelled, gesturing wildly at Scammell, who had refused help and was walking stiffly off parade beside Hughes. Hawker did not look at him, but glared at the paraded redcoats, his expression one of intense malevolence. 'Traitors to their King and revolutionaries must suffer!' Once again his voice had become shrill. The adjutant was trying to catch the eye of any of the other officers. Even the RSM's face betrayed traces of surprise.

'They will suffer the consequences of their evil crimes. This man plotted against his King and has been flogged! Only His Majesty's clemency prevented the supreme punishment of death.'

The men of the 106th were stunned. A few in the more distant parts of the line even turned their heads to stare at the irate major. There was some muttering. Such was the shock created by his words that it took a long moment before the sergeants standing behind the companies barked out an order to face front and be silent. Major Hawker's outburst seemed to have come from nowhere, but the noise from the ranks stopped him in mid-flow. His face, already bright red, seemed to glow.

'Is this mutiny?' he screamed, his voice so unnaturally high pitched that there was more murmuring.

'Silence in the ranks!' boomed Sergeant Major Fletcher.

Hawker turned unsteadily towards the RSM, but his eyes did not seem to focus. His cocked hat dropped from his head into the grass. He turned again so that he faced the Grenadier Company.

'Traitors everywhere,' he croaked. 'You!' He pointed towards Hanley and Dobson in the front rank of the formation. His arm was waving wildly. The old soldier managed to remain stiffly at attention, but the ensign found himself vaguely gesturing with his right hand and mouthing the word 'me?'

'Not you. The rogue lurking at the back. Come out, you scoundrel, you revolutionary. I can see you.'

Williams pushed his way between Hanley and Dobson. He straightened up, then marched as formally as possible five paces forward and came to attention. (He did not quite know why he did it. Later he assumed it must just be the habit of obedience. Billy Pringle suggested that it was the sign of a guilty conscience.)

Hawker was swaying as he stood. His face was now more purple than red. His voice revived to uncanny strength and he delivered his words in almost a screech.

'Ah, Robinson. I know you, you blackguard. Thought you could escape me, you rogue, you dastard! I'll have the skin off your back. Captain Smythe, give this man a thousand lashes!'

Smythe lay buried in Jamaica. No one knew any Robinson. Williams stood so rigidly to attention that he found himself quivering. His right leg felt as if it was about to give way. He was trying to stare above the major's head, but Hawker suddenly lurched towards him. The adjutant was coming up behind him. Williams did not see it, but MacAndrews had left his station on the right and a pace ahead of the company's line and was now marching straight at the major.

Spittle flew from Hawker's mouth. He almost collapsed when Brotherton the adjutant put his hand on the gold epaulette on his left shoulder.

'Sir, Mr Williams is a gentleman,' whispered the acting adjutant. Gentleman volunteers, like the officers they hoped to become, were not subject to corporal punishment.

Hawker had dropped to one knee, shrugging off Brotherton's grasp, but now he sprang upwards towards the trembling Williams. 'Goddam it. I'll kill the son of a bitch myself,' he yelled, reaching for his sword. Brotherton tried to grab him again, and MacAndrews was almost up to them, also stretching out his arms towards Hawker.

For Williams, time seem to have slowed to a snail's pace. He saw the major's eyes roll upwards till all that was visible was the whites, then Hawker simply dropped forward, falling like a sack of flour, even as Brotherton and MacAndrews reached towards him.

Hawker's face struck Williams' boots. The world had gone

silent. The 106th were stunned, frozen in shock. Even the oldest soldier had never witnessed anything quite like that. MacAndrews was the first to break the spell.

'Mr Hughes!' he shouted for the assistant surgeon, who after a moment's hesitation came running. The RSM followed at a steady, more dignified pace. 'Captains to me,' added MacAndrews.

Brotherton was kneeling, turning Hawker over and trying to support him. MacAndrews also crouched, but already knew the signs.

'Good Lord,' said Brotherton, his voice wavering. 'I think he's dead.'

MacAndrews just nodded. In a few moments Hughes examined the major and confirmed the matter.

'Stone dead. I'd never have believed it,' he said. Feeling that more was required from the only medical man present, he added, 'Apoplexy perhaps? Or some kind of fit?' His career had not prepared him for anything like this. Army surgeons were rarely the best qualified of their profession. Still, his voice carried to the grenadiers.

'Well, I'm buggered,' whispered Dobson, loud enough for Hanley to hear. 'The daft old sod's dead.' The wording may have varied, but that seemed to be the sentiment throughout the half-battalion.

The other four captains had joined MacAndrews by this time. They all knew that he was senior in the regiment, and therefore it was natural and proper that he took charge. The army oper- ated under the assumption that men would die and be replaced. Hawker had gone in bizarre circumstances, but the routines applied.

'Mr Fletcher. We will give the men an hour's drill as a wing. After that, break up into companies for another hour and a half. Drive them hard.' The captains nodded. It was better not to give anyone time to brood. 'Mr Hughes, assemble a party and take Major Hawker back to his lodgings for the moment. Perhaps, Tom, you will be so kind as to see the vicar and make the neces- sary arrangements.' Tom Mosley acknowledged the order. He was a good, sensible man, with sufficient tact to deal with the matter with the minimum of fuss. MacAndrews took out his watch, feeling the old dent in its case.

'Mr Brotherton and myself will return to the village. The first thing is to write to Lieutenant Colonel Moss. It's now nine thirty. If the captains and Mr Fletcher will join me at the inn at eleven, the companies can march back and stand down at noon. We will have a short officers' conference at half past. Thank you.'

MacAndrews, Brotherton and Mosley rode back to the village. Major Hawker's body went more slowly, wrapped in blankets and carried on a stretcher. Private Scammell accompanied the party, marching with surprising reverence and stiff backed in spite of his wounds. Behind them, the Right Wing of the 106th drilled.

6

MacBooby was in charge. Even Redman of the grenadiers used the nickname when he gossiped with the subalterns from other companies, especially his crony Hatch. The Scotsman was an ancient relic who had fought in America before they had been born, and that had been in a war Britain lost. It did not seem much of a recommendation. 'Ought to be off taking the cure in Bath,' said Redman to anyone he thought would find it amusing. 'Twenty years of gathering dust in garrisons in the middle of nowhere. How can a man like that know anything of modern warfare? At least old Hawker didn't bother us with all this drill.'

'You grenadiers always did a lot,' said Hatch, finally deciding to interrupt the monologue.

'And only now do you understand what we went through.' MacAndrews had given orders filling every day of the week with duty. There would be drill and more drill, and long marches, and especially musketry training. Worse still, they were to leave their billets in a couple of days and sleep under canvas as they marched away from the village.

'I know,' suggested Hatch. 'Why don't you pay his coach fare to Bath and take charge yourself? Each company could get drunk and chase dollies according to a strict rota.' There was laughter from the small group of discontented subalterns, and as so often Redman wondered whether his friend was laughing with him or at him.

MacAndrews would not have been surprised at such talk, or have cared in the slightest. It was not his principal task to be liked.

There was also far too much to do to concern himself with such things, and that was why later in the day he sent all four gentlemen of the Grenadier Company to meet his family. Redman did not dare to express his disdain for the acting commander as he waited with Pringle, Hanley and Williams outside the Red Lion.

'With the benefit of my university education, I am able to inform you that the coach is late,' announced Pringle.

'It usually is,' commented Williams. Then he sighed as he noticed that Hanley had leaned against the courtyard wall and come away with his back covered in powder from the drying whitewash. By the time they had brushed him down, his sash had unwound itself and somehow got caught in the buckles of his sword belt. Pringle began to wonder just how long their new officer's clumsiness would be amusing rather than irritating.

'In future try to remain immobile. It is probably safest,' he suggested to Hanley.

'Perhaps you could get turned into a pillar of salt, like Noah's wife,' said Redman, his smile broad until Williams corrected him.

'I believe you mean Lot's wife.' Privately the ensign seethed at being corrected by a jumped-up nobody without the connections or money to become an officer. In truth Redman's family had barely managed to arrange for his own commission, as his father somehow kept the debtors at bay and yet maintained his household in a style appropriate for a gentleman. Education had largely passed him by, and he fell into silence when Hanley spoke of Medusa, and that took them on to all things Hellenic. Hanley was pleasantly surprised at Williams' knowledge, still more by his and Pringle's enthusiasm for such a serious subject. He was almost disappointed when the coach finally pulled into the inn's yard.

The driver called to the servants from the Red Lion to take down the two large trunks and the three valises. He then climbed down, lowering the steps and opening the door. The four gentlemen of the Grenadier Company stiffened into respectful poses which stopped just short of being at attention. The three officers had doffed their cocked hats, and Williams held his shako in his left hand. Hanley was almost tidy.

An exceptionally tall lady appeared in the doorway. She wore a dark green travelling habit with matching jacket. On her head was a broad-brimmed hat of light straw, tied beneath her chin by a green silk sash. A few raven-black curls peeped in an ordered way from beneath it. Her eyes were vividly blue, her skin lightly touched by the sun, and a few wrinkles suggested that she was at least of middle age. Even so the young officers were struck by her looks, and even more by her commanding manner.

She looked at them with a wry smile.

'Do not tell me. My husband sends his apologies, but duty prevents his attending on his wife and only child?'

For once even Pringle was momentarily lost for words at such directness. He coughed nervously. Mrs MacAndrews brushed aside the hand of the driver and skipped down the carriage steps, her skirt lightly lifted in one hand. She was wearing somewhat old-fashioned and rather worn boots with heels a little higher than was now the taste. On the ground she was only a few inches shorter than Pringle and Hanley.

'I suspect the captain's orders did grant you the liberty of addressing me.' Her accent was unusual. Pringle had grown up in Liverpool and recognised it as from one of America's Southern states.

He coughed again. 'My profound apologies, Mrs MacAndrews.' The other three chorused similar regrets. 'It is just that I did not expect someone so young.' Again there was an echoing chorus.

Esther MacAndrews looked offended at such forwardness. Immediately the young gentlemen fell silent. Williams and Redman were blushing, and even Pringle and Hanley were worried. She had known many subalterns over the years and understood just how to work them. For a few seconds she let them squirm, then unleashed a smile, showing her still very white teeth.

'Flattery, however insincere, is always welcome. It is good to know that my husband has under his command such fluent and generous liars.' This provoked the expected confusion, the half-smiles as they tried to work out whether they were being complimented or insulted. Redman's mouth was hanging open until Pringle noticed and gave him a nudge with his boot.

The lieutenant finally rallied, at least to a level of coherence if not his usual ease in the company of women. 'May I present Ensigns Hanley and Redman, and Mr Williams. I am Lieutenant Pringle, ma'am, and we are all at your service.' He bowed, and the gesture was quickly followed by a general bobbing of heads.

'That is delightful, I am sure that I do not know how I have managed without it,' drawled Esther MacAndrews. She stepped to one side and looked back over her shoulder. 'Now may I in turn present my daughter.'

In the last minutes it had been hard for the grenadiers to notice anything other than their captain's lady. Williams gasped aloud as they all looked up at the doorway of the carriage. A young woman stood there. She was dazzling.

Miss Jane MacAndrews looked nothing like her mother. She was small, little more than five foot high, and slightly built. Her dress was a dark blue, with a lighter jacket with black lace ribbons and braid that fitted snugly. Her bonnet was also blue, again with a black ribbon, but from beneath its edge unruly wisps of red hair were trying to escape. Apparently lacking her mother's supreme self-confidence, she cast her blue-grey eyes downwards, although this was also to help her negotiate the carriage steps. One hand held tightly on to the carriage door, and the other grasped her dress and raised the hem so that it did not get in the way. On her dainty feet were black shoes fastened with little buckles. Her ankles – even a few inches above them were visible – were sheathed in white silk stockings.

The young gentlemen were staring wide eyed at the sudden vision. Only when the coachman proffered Miss MacAndrews a hand to help her down did they start to recover. All four surged forward. Pringle and Redman stopped short immediately to save themselves from walking into Mrs MacAndrews, and before the other two could arrive, Jane had taken the coachman's hand and lightly jumped down the last long step to the ground. She straightened her dress, looked up and nodded thanks to the coachman, and treated Hanley and Williams to the briefest of smiles, before once again looking demurely down.

Again there was a round of introductions. Jane offered the merest touch of three fingers to the proffered hands. Each time one of the gentlemen was presented to her, she curtsied and they bobbed down. The girl's eyes flicked briefly past their face before looking high above them. After the introductions she resumed a close inspection of the ground around their feet. She could be no more than eighteen or nineteen, with smooth and flawlessly white skin.

There was no doubt that Miss MacAndrews was beautiful. Williams was already in love. His gaze soon began to mirror the young lady's, focusing either high or low and avoiding looking directly at her. Hanley was intrigued and attracted, although he had never in the past found innocence especially fascinating. Pringle wondered how she would look stripped, realised he might be inspecting her too closely, and turned with a light smile to the mother instead. Redman was simply staring, although part of him was scornful that the captain's wife and daughter were unaccompanied by even a single maid. His mother had always maintained that a true lady never had less than one attendant, an obligation his father had struggled to provide for her and Redman's two sisters.

'Well, this is most pleasant,' said Mrs MacAndrews. She was enjoying their confusion, and had a mother's complacent satisfaction at the obvious power of her daughter's charms.

'I am so sorry,' stammered Pringle. 'Let us take you and your things to Captain MacAndrews' lodgings.'

'That would be nice.'

The trunks were heavy — exceedingly heavy. Pringle and Williams took one, each grasping one of the brass handles, and Hanley and Redman managed the other. They then draped the valises over their shoulders. There were also some hatboxes, which they piled on to the trunks as best they could. It seemed to work for the first few yards, before arm muscles began to scream in protest. There was strain in Pringle's voice when he spoke.

'It is not far, Mrs MacAndrews. The captain has taken one of the nicest cottages in the village.'

Esther smiled. 'Are you managing, Mr Pringle? I fear our few things have grown into a great burden.'

'Not at all. It is a mere nothing. An honour to be of service.' Behind him Redman lost his grip on the trunk, which swung hard against Hanley's shins. There was muffled cursing.

'Perhaps we should summon additional help?' suggested Mrs MacAndrews.

'Yes, Mama, it is too much for these poor young gentlemen,' said Jane, speaking for the first time since the introductions. She may just possibly have been older than Redman, but confidently assumed an air of superiority. Still, for the first time she looked straight at them.

'I do assure both you ladies that we can manage. Anyway, I suspect that the gallant officers of our regiment will rush to aid us as soon as they see the beauty of the captain's family.' The other three managed a chorus of agreement, broken only when Redman once again let the trunk slip.

Mrs MacAndrews' accent became thicker. 'Why, Mr Pringle, I do declare you are far too generous to two weary and weather-stained travellers.'

'Not a bit of it, ma'am,' said Williams. For a moment they waited for more, but he seemed frozen by his own boldness. He was also worried that his voice had sounded gruff, even vulgar.

'Well, if you are sure. You are all such fine, big men. Are they not, Jane?'

'Yes, Mama,' replied Jane, and once more resumed her downward gaze.

In the event the first officer of the 106th they encountered was Lieutenant Wickham, promenading with his wife. He raised an elegantly gloved hand to his cocked hat, then plucked it off his head to welcome the ladies more fittingly. Presentations were made, and the grenadiers took the opportunity to lower the trunks to the ground.

Wickham was widely acknowledged as the handsomest man in the battalion. He was tall – tall enough to be a grenadier, in fact – with an elegant figure and natural grace. Both were always shown off by a finely tailored uniform. His smile was open and welcoming.

His wife was of medium height, and pretty enough in a round-faced way, with thick brown curls beneath her pink ribboned bonnet. Her expression was completely untroubled by any hint of intelligence, but her smile was broad and even more full of welcome.

She was delighted to see them – had heard so much about them – for they were expected for more than a week now – she had been dying to meet both Mrs and Miss MacAndrews – was not their husband and father respectively the finest of men? So like her own dear father, who was so kind and noble to a silly child like herself – were they tired from their journey? They must be – she dearly liked to travel – had been to many parts of the country, but would dearly love to see more – but travel was always such a wearying business, so of course they must be tired – and to have come from America, just think of that – well, they were welcome to the regiment and now part of our happy family. The 106th were the most gallant gentlemen in the world – but then, they had already met our heroic grenadiers – the finest and handsomest of men – next only to her champion Wickham, of course – and the nice Mr Truscott – oh, and Anstey and Mosley . . .

The flow seemed endless, and was regularly punctuated with a laugh surprising in both its volume and harshness. It did not seem to matter what anyone else said. Wickham took Mrs MacAndrews' hand, staring into her eyes as he expressed his honour in meeting so fine a lady. He did the same with Jane, who surprisingly met his gaze. While this went on Mrs Wickham happily showered the grenadiers with compliments, flirting with each in turn. When her husband had stepped back she returned her focus to the ladies – was sure they would be the best of friends – especially Miss MacAndrews – and did they know there was to be a ball . . .

Wickham drew Pringle aside.

'How are you enjoying commanding the company, Billy?'

'Haven't had to do much yet,' replied Pringle. 'Although I

rather suspect that is going to change. I only have to do a little this evening and Hanley is helping prepare the targets for tomorrow.'

'I am sure you are doing a fine job.'

'I am just keeping the place warm for MacAndrews. It is a good company.'

'Are you sure he will come back? There were rumours a year ago that he might get his majority, until Toye purchased the vacancy.' Major Toye commanded the left wing of the 106th, having come in from the Royal Fusiliers.

'There are always rumours,' said Pringle. He rather liked Wickham, although they were not close friends. The latter was married, for one thing, and when he did spend time with the other subalterns he had more enthusiasm for gaming than suited either Pringle's taste or funds.

'That's true, but there were good ones that General Lepper wants to promote him if he can. So there may be a vacancy.'

'Isn't Brotherton senior?' It was odd to think of the diminutive Brotherton taking command of the tall grenadiers.

'It doesn't have to go with seniority,' suggested Wickham quietly.

'Oh, I see. Have you got the gilt?' Everyone knew that Wickham was associated with a rich and powerful man. The connection was old, and had been reinforced more recently when this same man married his wife's elder sister. Still, in certain company the lieutenant would launch mournful attacks on the selfish and wicked conduct of this same man and his wife, of how they had ignored the spirit of their inheritance, and provided him with only niggardly support. Yet now it seemed they were obliging him with the money needed to purchase the captaincy of the Grenadier Company.

Wickham smiled.

7

Williams thought of Miss MacAndrews, picturing her gentle blue-grey eyes, which had looked into his for just one brief moment. He thought of her fair skin, her wide mouth and the smile which revealed her neat white teeth, and her flowing red hair – deciding that he would think of this as burnished copper, although he knew it did not do the magnificent colour justice. Then he pulled the trigger.

The flint sparked, igniting the powder in the pan, then setting off the main charge. The musket slammed back into his shoulder as a cloud of dirty white smoke obscured the target. There was the now familiar smell of bad eggs.

They were firing at circles of canvas three foot in diameter and placed a hundred yards away. At fifty yards Williams had hit the same target nine times out of ten, with more than half of the shots in the bull's-eye itself. At this range all the flaws of the army's smooth-bore muskets made accuracy much more chancy. Still, he was pleased with his shooting, especially since he had never once fired any weapon before joining the 106th. He knew that he must at the very least have been close to the target.

Mechanically, he went into the motions of loading the last of the ten rounds he would fire at this range. He let go of the grip with his right hand, allowing the butt to fall to the ground. His fingers felt for the next cartridge from his open pouch, raised it to his lips and bit off the top of the paper that contained the ball. The taste was salty on his lips. Pringle had told him this was the saltpetre in it. Taking a pinch of the black powder, he poured it into the pan of his musket, flicking its cover open to do so, and then closing it again. Then he straightened the musket, empty-ing the rest of the cartridge into the muzzle. He leaned forward and spat the lead ball down on top, drew his ramrod, reversed it so that the wider head pointed downwards, and thrust down just once. He plucked the ramrod out, spun it in his hand and slid it back into place in its holder beneath the muzzle. As he raised his Brown Bess he pulled the lock back to full cock, reassured by its definite click.

All the while he thought of Miss MacAndrews. Williams did not yet feel confident enough to think of her as Jane. He won-dered whether he would have the courage to ask her for a dance at tonight's ball. What were the proper words? 'Would you do me the honour' . . . or perhaps 'May I beg the privilege?' Hamish was not sure, and had little experience of social occasions of this type. He had been to only a few since joining the regiment and had found each one desperately awkward, spending most of his time on the fringes of conversations. Once or twice Mrs Kidwell, the rotund and elderly wife of the quartermaster, had taken pity on him and either danced with him herself or led him to one of the free young ladies and made most of the arrangements.

He doubted that he would ever feel comfortable in the social world. He dreamed of holding Miss MacAndrews, of whirl-ing with her around the dance floor, seeing her looking up at him with warmth and affection. At the same time he knew that he was afraid even to speak to her. On the day when Captain MacAndrews' family had arrived she had spoken only once to him. As they had talked with the Wickhams, more and more of the 106th's officers had arrived to join them. When finally they moved off, most of the subalterns accompanied the mother and daughter, all struggling to be most of service and warmest of welcome. The hatboxes piled on top of the trunk he carried with Pringle had wobbled, threatening to fall, and Williams had somehow managed to keep hold of the handle and scoop the boxes up with his other hand. Miss MacAndrews had just for a moment looked at him, given him a brief but lavish smile and thanked him. Williams had managed no more than an incoherent grunt, immediately cursing himself for such absurd shyness.

By the end of that day, Jane MacAndrews' beauty and charm had become the chief talking point of the 106th. Most of the younger officers quickly decided that they were her devoted admirers. By the next day a measure of reflection had set in. Her father was an elderly and virtually penniless captain. For the moment he was acting commander of the half-battalion, but no one knew whether this would become permanent. Even then, if MacAndrews was gazetted major, the salary of that rank was scarcely a fortune.

On the following day there was a note of renewed optimism. Mrs MacAndrews was an American, and obviously a great lady. Rumours spread of family plantations vast in extent and generous in profits. Later this enthusiasm dampened. The captain had evidently not been able to advance his career through access to such a fortune, and its existence was quickly dismissed by all but the most optimistic and romantically inclined. Miss MacAndrews could well be a most delightful companion, but only those of substantial personal means could afford to condescend to seek her hand in marriage. Since she was the daughter of their current commander, any less formal arrangement would clearly need to be pursued with extreme caution. The young gentlemen still called at the MacAndrews' cottage, but their ambitions were more limited, and a few returned to their pursuit of the daughters of the local gentry, however less favoured by looks.

Williams scorned such thoughts. He loved Miss MacAndrews, and intended only ever to marry for love. He had no doubt that so perfectly beautiful a lady must be perfect in every other respect. For a moment he was resolved. He was to be a soldier, and intended to be an excellent and brave one. Surely he must have the courage to ask a young lady to dance. The confidence lasted for several minutes.

Hanley blew a whistle to signal that the shooting was over and that each man should go and inspect their targets. Whistles were formally used only by the light infantry as a means of conveying orders. MacAndrews had given one to each of his grenadier officers and insisted that they learn to use them as well. The sharp tone could carry better over the noise of battle than shouted words.

Williams walked forward to his target and was pleased to find six hits, including two bulls. Dobson nodded approvingly. The old soldier had managed only three hits, half as many as at fifty yards.

'Eyes going,' he said.

The section formed up and then marched over to join the rest of the company. In another part of the field there were large canvas screens forty foot wide and six feet high supported by wooden frames. Hanley and a party of men had worked on these for long hours on the instructions of MacAndrews. His idea was to make a target the size of a company of enemy infantrymen. The other companies had already torn four of the screens to shreds, firing in concentrated volleys rather than shooting individually. The Grenadier Company directed its fire at the last remaining target. Pringle gave the orders and MacAndrews observed. They began at one hundred and fifty yards – long range for a smooth-bore musket – and then gradually closed the distance. MacAndrews had tried to drum into them the care needed when levelling a piece at each range. Over longer distances the heavy lead musket balls dropped, and so the men needed to point their firelocks higher than the target.

The grenadiers were in two ranks. Then, at the order, the men of the second rank like Williams stepped to their right and forward a pace, closing the distance and allowing their muskets to project through the gaps between their front rank men. Volleys shattered the summer air. The noise was like the tearing of very heavy cloth, as a great cloud of smoke covered the front of the company. Hanley recorded the hits, marking them as accurately as he could on a quick sketch. The last volleys were fired at just fifty yards.

Afterwards, MacAndrews took the officers and Williams to inspect the results. Hanley had totted up the total of hits for each volley. Pringle needed only a quick glance to provide average scores for the various ranges. The results were encouraging. Everyone knew that the Brown Bess was built to be sturdy rather than accurate. Even so almost two-fifths of the shots fired at the maximum range had hit the screen. At one hundred yards it had been nearly three-fifths, and at fifty yards the result was devastating. Between eight and nine out of ten shots had punched through the canvas, leaving it as ragged as the screens savaged by the other companies earlier in the day. At that range, it seemed difficult to miss. MacAndrews nodded his approval. They had done marginally better than the other companies.

Hanley was impressed, and more than a little horrified at the thought of such devastation. He was also puzzled. 'Assuming a hundred men in a French company, wouldn't we kill them all before we got to fire the closer volleys?'

'Your screens are very fine, William, but real Frenchmen are not square, and there will be gaps,' commented Pringle.

'Do not the French also get to fire back?' asked Williams.

'Aye, they are allowed to,' responded the captain, prompting smiles from the others.

To Hanley that suggested only mutual annihilation. Williams was trying to imagine the chaos as men fell all around him. Redman looked pale, but obviously felt a demonstration of confidence was in order. 'But we are better trained. I have heard the French never practise with real powder and ball.'

'So they say,' confirmed MacAndrews. 'But plenty of them have seen a lot of real fighting.' He waited for a while, wondering whether they would see the implication.

'I would guess a target that fires back is a little distracting,' said Pringle.

Good, thought MacAndrews, they were getting there. 'In America,' he began, 'the Yankees used to say that we always fired high. It was true as well, I have seen the treetops peppered with hundreds of balls, the leaves sheared off and branches shattered. The strange thing was that if you looked behind our positions it was exactly the same. Both sides seemed to have taken a profound dislike to the enemy's woodland.

'Men do strange things in battle. It's like,' he struggled for a moment for words, 'nothing you can quite imagine until you have seen it. The noise, the smoke . . .' He wondered about speaking of the blood, the screams and the stench, but decided that was too much. Mere words could not prepare anyone for such things.

'Soldiers are just men, not machines. We train them to make them keep doing their job even with all that is going on and with their comrades falling beside them. They are still men. They are nervous, and the line between courage and panic is thinner than paper. I have known men not notice that their musket has misfired, and keep on loading it with round after round even though the whole thing is so jammed up that it is never going to fire.'

The captain paused. He had always been inclined to make his officers think, but in the last days his talks had been more frequent and extended to the other companies.

'So what do we do, sir?' asked Hanley with genuine curiosity. A clever man, he liked to feel that anything could be understood, and any problem solved. At the same time he found the calmness with which they discussed the destruction of other human beings disturbing. He thought with a chill that he was now trapped in a profession whose purpose was death. Would he become as callous as those French horsemen who slaughtered the crowd in Madrid? Yet here in England everything seemed unreal. Each morning he was still surprised to wake up and find himself to be a soldier, a man who destroyed instead of creating. He barely heard MacAndrews continue.

'First thing to do is to stay calm. Or at least look calm. The men look to each other. It's their fellows who reassure them, but before even that they look to us. As officers you need to show no fear, and to look as if you have no doubt of victory. That is why you are there. What else?'

'Try to gain an advantage,' suggested Pringle.

'If you can. You are there to think, not to fight, although you may have to do that as well. Still, sometimes there are just two lines of men facing each other in an open field and no one has an edge.'

'Get close,' put in Williams, surprising himself with how confident he sounded. 'So close we can't miss.'

'You'd be surprised how easy it is to miss – but yes, Mr Williams, you are right. Never fire at more than fifty yards unless you have no choice. Better yet, close to half that. If the enemy are already firing at you long before you get there then let 'em. The odds are they'll be missing. Firing too much and too soon is a sign of bad soldiers.'

'Can we not get the men to aim more carefully?' said Redman, feeling rather left out and slightly annoyed that the volunteer had beaten him to a suggestion and, still worse, been praised.

'It's hard when the others are firing all around you,' said Williams, feeling that for once he knew more about a matter than the officers. It had astounded him just how loud the company volleys had been, and it must have been worse for the front rank with the second rank's muskets just inches from their heads. No wonder Dobson was a little deaf.

'True, but Mr Redman has a point. Get close and tell the men to aim low. Aim at the knees and you will probably hit the chest.'

'Or we can always give the French trees a good pasting,' said Pringle. 'Destroy French horticulture to defend the forests of Old England.'

MacAndrews did not mind the flippancy. Quiet by nature and made more reserved by years of disappointment, he disliked making speeches, but wanted these men to learn. The sergeants had already dismissed the company for their meal. There would be more drill later this afternoon, but he had decided to let everyone finish early. The officers would then have time to preen themselves for this evening's ball. For a moment he almost regretted his family's arrival, for that would mean that he must attend. He wanted to spend time with them, with Esther especially, but would have preferred a more private occasion. There was also so much work to do. Deep in thought, he strode ahead at a rapid pace on the path back to the village. Very soon he left the others behind.

'It is going to be glorious,' said Redman. Eager anticipation for once revealed the boy he still was. 'The Hansons shall be there I am sure.' He was convinced Miss Emily favoured him.

'I am sure it will be a most pleasant distraction,' was as far as Pringle was willing to go, and neither he nor Hanley showed any desire to discuss the subject further. Redman hurried away to find Hatch, leaving the other three strolling along in silence. Williams trailed a little, for he had decided now that he dared not request a dance from Miss MacAndrews and was busy despising himself.

8

Pringle, Hanley and Williams stuck together after arriving at Mr Fotheringham's house. Most of the seventy or so guests were already there, but their arrival was not so late as to cause either offence or excessive attention. They slid into the crowd, and were soon joined by Truscott. Together they watched their younger colleagues as they flirted, made too much noise, and generally made asses of themselves. At times their enthusiasm almost drowned the orchestra, which it was said their host had brought down from London.

Mr Fotheringham had retired to the county after a career in government, buying the Old Hall on the edge of the village. He had only a single daughter, a quite startlingly severe woman who seemed far older than her twenty-three years. No doubt in time she would nevertheless find a husband, drawn by the family fortune if nothing else. She was already much in demand this evening, something which came as a relief to Pringle and the others, who felt absolved from the courtesy of asking the host's daughter for a dance.

The four drifted over to a table and began to take some food, where they were joined by a Yeomanry officer named Thompson, who seemed sensible enough by the low standards of Britain's volunteer cavalry. His splendidly braided blue jacket was tight fitting, and rather outshone their own red tunics. Truscott had met him before, and swiftly made the introductions. Servants quickly found them and refilled their glasses, although Williams had in fact taken little of his wine. For courtesy's sake, he would sip at the glass every few moments, trying to take as little as possible.

'Fourteenth-century?' Hanley had almost to shout to be heard over the music and general hubbub. The main hall was certainly a grand and high-roofed structure, with the musicians seated way above in a minstrel's gallery.

Pringle nodded to a rotund matron trailing two daughters behind her. 'No, sixteenth.' He winked at Hanley. 'She looks Tudor to me.' Whether or not she heard, the mother passed the group by, looking for more likely dance partners for her offspring. Still, their presence had been noted, and no doubt she would return if spaces remained in the girls' commitments.

Billy Pringle was hoping not to dance or drink too much this evening. He liked both things exceedingly, and even more he liked and thought of women for most of his waking hours. By now the fear that he had made love to Jenny Dobson had receded. She paid him no particular attention when they had passed each other earlier that day and her father's demeanour towards him had not changed in any way. He was almost certain that his partner had been someone else. In spite of this, the fear made him cautious. Too young and indeed not really sufficiently wealthy or well placed to contemplate a serious courtship, and anyway not especially intrigued by any of the local belles, he felt that there was not one of them with whom he *had* to dance. There was pleasure in simply looking at the young ladies, most of whom appeared at their finest on such an occasion. Dancing permitted an intimacy and contact which might raise his ardour too far. If he then drank too much, he might leave in such a mood that another encounter with a more available woman was likely. Pringle wanted to remain in enough control to make certain that this time it would not be with any girl who was inappropriate. Moderation in both drink and passion was now his goal. Then he noticed a tall dark-haired girl with elegant carriage and an excellent figure and felt his restraint weaken. He gestured to a servant to fill his glass.

Truscott liked observing, even more than he enjoyed dancing. He had tried to point things out to Williams, but the latter was too nervous to converse freely, and after a while the lieutenant turned his attention to Hanley. The artist in the latter had already appreciated the scene, and the flickering shadows cast by the chandeliers. Truscott drew his attention to the patterns formed by the people, the wider dance already started before the partners took to the floor.

'We are just in the middle,' he said, indicating the older officers who had retired to the even darker corners in the hope of remaining inconspicuous.

Hanley smiled, and part of him pictured the scene as a cartoon. He had never attempted such a thing, concentrating on the pursuit of the highest art, but one of his friends in Madrid had been a devotee of Hogarth, and had always been asking him to explain some of the more English references and objects in his collection of prints. Military life might well offer fruitful subjects. That took his mind back to the musketry drills, and from there it was but a small leap to the shots and death that haunted his memory. He changed the subject.

'Our friend appears to be the perfect audience.' He gestured at Williams, juggling a nearly full glass and an overburdened plate and with an expression of solemn interest as Thompson spoke to him of horses. The subject was clearly his great passion and he needed no more encouragement to continue at considerable length. Truscott suspected that Williams could hear little and understood even less, for his background had clearly not permitted the keeping of a stable. Thompson took his nods for agreement, and became more and more convinced that the volunteer was an excellent judge of horseflesh.

It was nearly time for the dancing to begin, and since there were decidedly more ladies than men at the gathering, efforts to remain inconspicuous were doomed to failure. One by one the recalcitrant groups were hunted down, usually by a mama intent upon finding suitable partners for her daughters. The arrival of the MacAndrews saved them for the moment, as they hurried to greet their commander and his family.

Miss MacAndrews looked magnificent. She wore a white gown, its fashionable high waist gathered with a turquoise sash. A silk ribbon of the same colour bound her piled hair. Around her neck hung a silver chain, ending in a pendant which lay on the bare skin just above the fringed line of her dress. This rose to short puffed sleeves, leaving her arms bare down to her long white gloves. She walked on her father's left arm, while her mother was on his right. Mrs MacAndrews was once again in green, although this time a much paler shade, apart from the very dark turban around her black hair. The captain looked somewhat embarrassed as rather a hush fell across the room, although it was clear that his wife enjoyed making an entrance.

Mr Fotheringham, his florid wife and icy daughter welcomed them formally and without any warmth. Pringle and the others were then the next to greet the family. Bows were exchanged, and the young gentlemen showered the ladies with compliments. After that there was an awkward pause, which Mrs MacAndrews decisively ended.

'Mr MacAndrews, I wish to dance. Is it necessary for me to order one of these young gentlemen to ask Jane?'

'Of course not, ma'am,' said Hanley, feeling that there could be worse ways to spend the time. 'Miss MacAndrews, if you would do me the honour.'

'Seniority, old boy,' interrupted Pringle.

'Indeed yes,' added Truscott, placing a hand on his shoulder. 'Regimental seniority.' He bowed low to Jane.

'That is settled, then. Well, Jane, we have your first four dances. I must say they all look more handsome without that dreadful white paint on their hair.' For the ball the officers of the 106th had followed the normal practice of washing their hair and simply tying it back with black ribbon. 'Look at Mr Williams, with his blond hair. You are quite the Viking, sir. Be careful, Jane, or he might carry you off to his ship!'

Mrs MacAndrews ignored Williams' blustering and confused denial of any such evil intention. 'Come, husband, we shall dance. And watch where you are placing your great clumsy feet!' The pair disappeared happily, closely followed by Truscott and Jane, and went to take their places among the line of couples on the dance floor.

'She is a terrifying woman, in the nicest possible way,' said Billy Pringle. Before they could escape to the fringes of the crowd they were trapped and caught. Mrs Wickham bore down on them with the fixed gaze of a determined matchmaker. In tow were two Miss Stocktons, Miss Crabbe and a Miss Dawlish. There was the usual flood of words.

They had been deliberately hiding – she was sure they had – for none of them had yet asked for the dance they must know she was saving for them – it was most ungallant (the last remark emphasised by striking each of the three men lightly with her fan) – and why were they neglecting such fair companions as these ladies – did they not know them – then introductions must be made.

Williams was trying to watch Truscott and Jane and did his best to ignore the flow of chatter. He saw the couple now and again, marked how gracefully Miss MacAndrews moved and felt excitement that her mother seemed to have arranged a dance for him.

Out on the floor, Lieutenant Truscott complimented his partner on her dancing.

'You are too kind, sir,' said Jane. Her eyes looked for a moment into his, and then flicked down and instead focused on the golden epaulette on his right shoulder. Truscott saw her blink.

'Are you disturbed, Miss MacAndrews?' he asked with real concern, as they once again passed close, her right hand held high in his left as she turned.

'It is merely a bad memory. My first ball was two and half years ago, when the regiment was in Port Royal. All the uniforms brings it back so very vividly.' He noticed that her eyes were glassy as she looked up at him once more, the move complete and they again followed the other dancers down the length of the ballroom.

'But surely that was a happy event?'

'It was, but nearly all the men I danced with that night were dead by the end of the year. The fever, you know.'

Truscott, like Pringle and most of the other officers, had joined the regiment after it had returned or had been at the depot during its service in the Caribbean. Still, everyone knew of the losses.

'It is a soldier's fate, ma'am. Sad, but we all must take the risks. At least . . .' He struggled for a moment. '. . . at least those men first enjoyed a dance with a most beautiful and kind young lady.' He knew it was a peculiar compliment, but his always generous nature warmed to the girl's sympathetic spirit and he yearned to lift her sorrow.

'You are too kind.' Jane gave him a brittle smile. They spoke no more, but Truscott could not remember having ever enjoyed a dance more than this. It was with real warmth that he thanked her at its end, bowing once again, and then leading her back to the others.

Their arrival was a welcome relief to Williams even more than the other two. He had been jerked from his reverie by the sharp demand of Miss Elvira Stockton for him to explain his rank. He was so young, and yet the splendour of his jacket must mean that he was senior to the others. Hamish had borrowed white breeches, stockings and shoes from Pringle, but otherwise wore his regimental jacket. Like all those of the ordinary soldiers it had broad white lace in pairs running up the front, unlike the rather plainer officer's jacket. The shoulder wings were also higher and fringed with white wool. In the candlelight it was not obvious that it was a much duller red and of coarser weave than their uniforms.

Mrs Wickham had laughed her inimitable laugh, pointing out very loudly that she should not embarrass poor Mr Williams so. He had then been forced to explain the status of a volunteer. It was always awkward proclaiming oneself to be a gentleman – surely that should be self-evident. There was the usual reaction, as the various misses realised that he would make a most unsuitable husband. The Stockton sisters remembered that they had promised their mother to ask after Mrs Fotheringham's health, and promptly left. Miss Crabbe had evidently taken a strong liking to the bespectacled Pringle, and at Mrs Wickham's urging he seemed to have no choice but to beg humbly for the next dance. Miss Dawlish began to look expectantly at Hanley. She was a brown-haired, plump girl, not yet eighteen. Her face might almost have been pretty, were it not for its childlike petulance.

Miss MacAndrews saved him. She arrived and boldly interrupted, reminding Mr Hanley that he was already promised to her, since Mr Pringle had so selfishly vanished. She was sure that Mr Williams would be delighted to partner Miss Dawlish.

Moments later Hanley found himself holding Miss MacAndrews, who stared directly up at him.

'All this is a little tiresome, do you not think?' Jane asked softly.

'I would have agreed, until now.' He smiled. For all the whirl of the wider dance, this was the most intimate moment he had enjoyed with a woman since Madrid.

'You are kind,' she said, returning his smile and seeming to press a little closer. 'But I remember the balls in Charleston last year – the colours and the light. It is not London or Paris . . .'

'Or Madrid or Rome,' he said.

'Oh, have you been to those places?' There was a thrill in the girl's voice. 'I so dearly want to travel more.'

Williams passed them, clutching Miss Dawlish in his arms. The look of concentration on his face was almost savage in its intensity, and most of the time he looked downwards, checking that his feet were obeying him precisely.

Hanley could not help smiling. Jane also grinned. 'Poor Williams,' she said, 'I was most unkind to him just now. Well, I shall make it up to him, and dance with him later on.'

'Are you sure you want to take the risk?' Williams had made a mistake and his feet were thrashing wildly as he tried to recover. 'He is not the best of dancers.'

'He will be when he dances with me,' the girl said with an assurance that was surprising, and all too reminiscent of Mapi. The memories pressed in on his mind once more, and so he looked straight into Miss MacAndrews' eyes, and tried not to think, but to enjoy her beauty and the movements of the dance itself.

Hanley and Miss MacAndrews certainly danced well. The tall, dark officer seemed to sweep the diminutive girl effortlessly round, her white dress billowing with the motion. Everyone could see that they made a grand couple. Ensign Redman could sense that this did not encourage great affection for them from either of the Miss Stocktons.

'Who is that officer?' asked the older sister. 'Is he new?'

'That is our Mr Hanley. Like me he belongs to the grenadiers, but has only joined the regiment after a prolonged leave of absence.'

'Ah, then is he a man of means?' Her interest was pricked. Handsome was all very well, but to little end if not accompanied by a decent income. 'I must say he looks quite dashing, although that MacAndrews girl is too abandoned to be fully decent.'

'He is something of a mystery, but I fear not well connected,' replied Redman, and then decided that no one could blame him if he repeated, but did not confirm, a rumour that was doing the rounds. 'He is a grand fellow, although very dark. They do say his mother is a Hindoo ...'

By this time Williams and Miss Dawlish were several steps behind everyone else. They barged into one couple, and so he lifted his partner inches from the ground as he took long strides to catch up. Miss Dawlish gasped in surprise, then stumbled as he put her down in a patch of clearer floor. Williams at this point realised what he had done and stared back at her, his mouth agape. He grabbed at her to break her fall, nearly lost balance himself and only just kept her upright. The girl pulled away from him and then there was a sound of tearing, audible even over the music and the chatter of the now fascinated crowd. Miss Dawlish's pale pink dress had ripped a good six inches up from the hem, showing a white petticoat beneath.

Both of them froze in horror. There were cries from the crowd, quickly drowned out by gales of laughter. Williams sprang backwards, as if stepping away could somehow repair the damage. Miss Dawlish looked at him, then down at her torn dress. Then she screamed – the loudest noise Williams felt he had ever heard in his entire life. The girl fled, still shrieking, and was soon whisked away by Miss Crabbe and Miss Fotheringham herself. Williams' apologies were drowned in the noise, and now he wanted only to be away from here. He too hurried out of the ballroom.

'Poor Williams,' whispered Miss MacAndrews to Hanley, as if speaking of a small child.

The incident was one of the most talked about of the entire evening. For the men – and especially the officers of the 106th – it was a grand joke. Such things happened and no harm had been done. The ladies expressed huge sympathy for the unfortunate Miss Dawlish. Some of them were even genuine, although she was not an especially well-liked individual. Most felt repeated description of the incident made her embarrassment all the more delicious.

The ball continued. Miss MacAndrews danced more dances with other officers from the 106th, and once with Thompson of the Yeomanry, even though she knew her father would be less than enthusiastic about this, given his distaste for cavalrymen. She declined the invitations of any civilians, save for an elderly and rather stiff clergyman named Hawkins, whose parish lay next to this one. She found Pringle, and insisted he fulfil his promise to her, which he did with considerable delight. For a big man, inclined to plumpness, he had a remarkably delicate step. At the first opportunity, he complimented the girl on her elegance and grace.

Jane frowned. 'Such a tribute is rather diminished by the lack of competition.' They separated, drew back, and could not speak again until the dance brought them closer again.

'Then may I say that your beauty would shine out in any company,' ventured Pringle, still struggling to deal with her directness.

'Better, although a pretty compliment should never have to live alone.'

'Should I speak then of your perfection of figure,' Pringle whispered as they leaned close for a brief moment, then immediately realised that this crossed the boundary of propriety.

'Yes, I had observed your admiration.' His eyes followed as Jane's gaze flicked for just an instant down to the front of her dress. The pace of the dance quickened, producing an impressive motion. They stepped apart again, before Pringle could think of any response. Each spun around, and Pringle moved behind the line of men, while Jane's path took her behind the ladies. At the end they turned in, and once again faced each other. Pringle was greatly relieved to see the girl smiling. She glanced beside her to Miss Crabbe.

When the couples closed, there was amusement in her voice. 'Once again, it may be a question of comparison.' Miss Crabbe was tall and spindly, as well as notably flatchested.

Pringle waited until there was more distance between each couple, then spoke in a voice not intended to reach more than his partner. 'If you listen carefully, you can hear her knees knocking together.'

'Aren't we terribly cruel,' said Jane, but there was mischief in her words. 'I spoke with Miss Crabbe earlier, and her high estimation of people seemed to depend entirely on the size of their fortune.'

'I believe that when a wealthy gentleman shows interest, then there is no concern about her knees being together.' Pringle was amazed to have made such a comment, normal enough in chat between subalterns, but scarcely appropriate here.

The frown returned to Jane's brow. 'I am quite sure I do not know what you mean, sir.' Pringle hoped that this was true, and that his coarseness would be missed, but he was not quite sure. Her eyes were bright and the sparkle of reflected light gave them a knowing gleam. 'In case you suffer from a false impression, that was not an invitation for you to show me,' Jane added. Pringle could not help laughing out loud, startling the nearest couples, and provoking several stern glances. Miss MacAndrews shook her head in mock disapproval.

Hanley also danced a good deal, and several of the ladies, especially the younger Miss Stockton, showed him particular favour. She was rather thrilled at the idea of dancing with a man so mysterious that he might be part Indian.

Pringle drank heavily in spite of his earlier resolution, and as the evening progressed slipped away from the main room. The dance with Miss MacAndrews had been a delight, but was scarcely calculated to calm him down. A too-eager attempt to win over a pretty little maid ended with her kicking him in the shins, at which point he decided discretion was the better part of valour. A little lost, he stumbled around until he found the library and Williams sitting reading.

'What have you got there, Bills?' he asked cheerfully. 'Not a dancing manual, I trust.'

Williams looked angry for a moment, and then sagged.

'I suppose they have sent you to find me.'

'No, I'm just lost.' He reached over and lifted the book to see that it was the first volume of Gibbon's *Decline and Fall*. 'You'll be a while if you are going to read all of that.' The distant sound of music came through the open door. It was nearly midnight.

'We ought to go back, you know. Duty and all that,' Pringle added after a moment.

'I made a fool of myself.'

'Haven't we all.' Pringle rubbed his shin. 'Look, it was nothing. Accidents happen and it could have been a lot worse. My oldest sister once lost half her dress dancing with a sailor. Well, they're all clumsy as mules when they're on land. And she married the fellow, so it can't have been that bad.' He paused. 'You obviously don't have to marry Miss Dawlish, though. Well, I doubt she'd have you.'

'Should I apologise?'

'Only if you should meet her. Best not to make a fuss. I dare say she'll be trying to forget it. Come on, we had better go.'

There was a sense of things drawing to an end by the time they returned. Nevertheless, Miss MacAndrews appeared and insisted on dancing with Williams. 'Come, sir, you shall not escape my clutches so easily.'

'I thought . . . I mean that I feared . . .' he stammered, 'that you would . . .' He did not know how to finish. 'I am not a very good dancer.' He spoke as if he expected the girl to change her mind even at the last minute.

'Then it is high time you became proficient,' said Jane firmly. 'Come. You do know that you are supposed to lead me?' Her smile was warm, the mockery gentle. Williams stood tall as he took her arm and led her out on to the floor.

There was little conversation as they danced, although Jane did her best to engage him.

'Do you not think it has been a delightful evening?'

'Oh yes,' agreed Williams fervently, but said no more as he concentrated on keeping in step, all the while intoxicated to be so close to the centre of his adoration.

'The orchestra has been quite good.'

'Oh yes.'

'I believe Mother has quite worn Father out.' This time there was no response, as Williams was unsure whether or not to comment on the condition of his commanding officer.

'Do you find the yellow of Miss Fotheringham's sash a pleasing shade?'

'Oh yes.'

'Although perhaps red would suit her complexion better?'

'Oh yes.'

'Or mud-brown?'

'Oh yes.'

'Are you aware that she is the Empress of China?'

'Oh yes.' Williams looked puzzled. 'I beg your pardon. I fear the desire to prevent my dancing from disgracing you has made me inattentive.'

That at least was courteous, and Jane decided that it would be difficult to achieve any more than this for the moment. 'I am quite positive you will not,' she said, and decided to abandon attempts at further conversation. She smiled at him, and Williams' heart soared.

Miss MacAndrews did not quite manage to make Mr Williams look competent, but she emerged with both her feet and her gown unscathed, and that was probably the best that could have been hoped for.

It was now almost one o'clock, and this proved to be the last dance of the evening. Carriages had been waiting for some time. If the regiment's officers had been the hosts then they would no doubt have taken the fairest of their guests 'hostage' and insisted on several more dances as ransom for their release. Such behaviour would have been inappropriate when they were guests of the very respectable Mr Fotheringham. They too left, unsteadily in many cases. Williams, Hanley, Truscott and Pringle walked together to their billet. It was a beautiful night, and Pringle looked up at the stars until his head swam and he began to feel giddy. Truscott needed to support him the rest of the way. The other two trailed behind them.

'Did you enjoy yourself tonight, Bills?' asked Hanley, using the nickname for the first time.

'Oh yes. Indeed yes,' replied the volunteer earnestly, knowing the world to be a truly wonderful place.

9

There were plenty of sore heads among the officers when the half-battalion marched out an hour after dawn the next morning. As it was June, the dawn came early and a good number of them had not slept at all. Billy Pringle, who had drunk heavily and dozed for just a couple of hours, looked no worse than usual – he rarely showed great enthusiasm for the early morning anyway. Redman looked unnaturally pale and red eyed, and Hanley only a little better. Williams had drunk only two glasses of wine – the most he felt that he cope with for he loathed the taste, but he suffered in order to be polite. He had not slept a wink, too full of the thrill of dancing with Miss MacAndrews. Then his doubts had returned, and he cringed as he remembered how little he had said, knowing that she must have thought him dull and uninteresting, and that she had condescended to be his partner only out of pity.

His spirits revived a little as they marched, and his fatigue vanished as the familiar rhythm of the march took over. The men were in good spirits, and once they were a discreet distance from the village they took a delight in singing cheerfully, beginning with an ironic rendering of 'The Girl I Left Behind Me'. Williams joined in – he was Welsh enough to relish singing – and even sang lustily when the redcoats began to bawl out one of their favourites called 'Confound our Officers', sung to a pretty Scots tune. The 106th's officers were rather fond of this song, and some smiled or even joined in. They were all still walking. After their horses had warmed up, the captains could ride if they chose, although as it turned out most did not. There seemed to be a feeling that they should share the hardships of their juniors, at least this time.

The 106th camped after six miles, laying out tent lines in a field on an estate owned by one of Lieutenant Colonel Moss's acquaintances. A letter had arrived that morning from the colonel, informing them that at the end of the week they were to meet up with the left wing and that the whole battalion would then train together for a few more days before marching to Portsmouth. When MacAndrews informed the officers of this they all felt that it confirmed the rumours of a posting overseas. The question was where, and speculation about this filled the next few hours as they rested and had lunch. Somehow – the mechanism of such things was never clear, but was no less real for that – the word had already spread among the redcoats. Williams heard Tout adamantly maintaining that they were off to South Africa or perhaps Egypt, which he seemed to believe was near by. 'Elephants and blackamoors, I tell ye.'

Opinion among the officers varied. Pringle and Truscott both thought Sweden the most likely, although they argued over whether they would be fighting alongside the Swedes against the Russians, or with the Russians against the Swedes. They were confident, though. Williams remained quiet, but from what he had read in the papers there seemed a similar confusion on the part of His Majesty's government. Ministers had decided that an expedition to the Baltic offered distinct advantages, and were sure that given time they would be able to think of something for the expedition to do.

'Moore has been sent with an army. No doubt we are reinforcements,' asserted Truscott.

'He's a good man. One of our best,' agreed Pringle. Sir John Moore was one of the most respected young generals in the army.

'My cousin Bunbury speaks most highly of him,' said Derryck. 'He is in the Ninety-fifth and trained at Shorncliffe.' The new style of training introduced by Moore when he commanded at Shorncliffe camp was the subject of much speculation. All agreed that the brigade he had trained was among the finest in the

British Army. It consisted of two light infantry battalions and the new Rifle Regiment.

'The sweeps, what do they know?' said Redman, using the nickname of the 95th Rifles, earned by their dark green, almost black uniforms.

'No, it must be Spain.' This was from Mosley, who was trying with scant success to light a cigar. 'We'll go and help the dons throw out the French.'

Hanley pricked up his ears at this. The dreams had come again during his brief sleep; no doubt the thoughts of Mapi were brought on by the dance, for this time the dead girl who haunted his slumbers had had red hair. 'I should like that. What the French have done to the Spanish deserves punishment.' Perhaps to fight in Spain would drive away the memory and the nagging sense of guilt.

'Just being French deserves punishment,' said Anstey cheerfully. 'It is our solemn duty to cut them to ribbons. Still, you are all wrong, the wise money is on South America.'

That surprised most of them. The previous year a British exped-ition had attempted to acquire some of Spain's territories on that continent. It had started well, but ended in utter humiliation when the army surrendered at Buenos Aires.

'That is where we are going. To avenge Whitelocke,' Anstey maintained.

'They should have shot that coward,' said Redman.

'You can borrow my musket if you like,' offered Williams. Even Redman joined in the smiles. General Whitelocke was a coward and an incompetent who had been condemned by court martial, but simply cashiered. It was not all that long ago that the Navy had shot poor Admiral Byng for much lesser crimes.

Hanley scarcely listened. Since Madrid his hatred of the French Emperor had grown less passionate, but remained strong. He wanted to fight against France, and could think of no better place to do this than in Spain. It beggared belief that his col-leagues could talk so lightly of aiding the Spanish at one moment, and then invading Spanish colonies the next. None of it seemed to matter to them. They seemed perfectly willing to slaughter whichever foreigners their government chose, utterly unconcerned about the reason.

After their rest, the regiment trained hard for the remainder of the afternoon. There were close-order drills by company, and much physical exercise. Hanley found it all so frustratingly dull. As they went once again through the same exercises the prospect of going to war faded back into the distance. Soldiering seemed to consist only of dull and pointless routine. He failed to see how an obsession for neatness and polishing metal and leather till it shone would help to fight the French or any other enemy. The uniformity and the mechanical drills were an attack on all that made men individuals.

Later on, Pringle took the Grenadier Company off to practise skirmishing. This was something MacAndrews had introduced with great enthusiasm. Technically the Light Company were the battalion's skirmishers, the men who would fight in open order ahead of the main line. Yet in America the lights had often been detached from their regiments. So had the grenadiers, and all troops including the centre companies had been called upon to skirmish. MacAndrews was determined that his men should be trained to do this, for untrained men fought badly in open order.

Pringle kept half the company formed in two ranks as a reserve. The rest spread out in pairs, a few yards apart. Williams kneeled, with loaded musket – he had mimed the action – as Dobson ran to the side and forward, keeping out of his line of fire. Then Dobson was kneeling, loading, and once he brought his musket up to the shoulder he yelled 'Go!' and Williams pulled the trigger. It was soft, with no resistance, because he had no intention of wearing out the spring by firing the action for no reason and so had not cocked it. He mouthed the word 'Bang!' and sprang to his feet, and this time made it to a low stone wall. That was their objective, and Williams stood behind it while he once again mimed the loading process. He rested his piece between two of the upright stones on the wall when he was finished and shouted for Dobson to join him.

The attack came from the left with one discharge of Lieutenant Truscott's pistol and a chorus of shouts from his men. These were the sharpshooters, six men picked from each of the other companies as the best shots. The men grinned as they bobbed up from behind the side wall and ambushed the grenadiers.

MacAndrews had not warned Pringle that he had arranged this little surprise. He and Brotherton also appeared to observe the results, and the acting adjutant ran through the open gate and began tapping some of the grenadiers on the shoulder to mark them as casualties.

'That's it, you bite the ground, old boy,' he said cheerfully to Hanley.

'What?' replied the puzzled ensign as Brotherton kept on running.

'Lie down, you're supposed to be bloody dead!' called the adjutant over his shoulder.

Altogether five more men of the company were declared casualties. Dobson and Williams were at the end of the line, but the ambush had come from behind and they escaped, but were left exposed.

'Come on, back we go, Pug!' Dobson set off at a surprisingly fast run for an old man. Williams hesitated for a moment before following him back towards the new line that Pringle was forming facing the sharpshooters. Brotherton came towards him waving his hand of death. Williams swerved, stumbled, but managed to recover and swung sharp left as he kept running. Brotherton was laughing as he pursued, caught up and at the last minute changed his aim to knock off Williams' shako.

'Bills, you rogue, you have cheated death! The pox will just have to take you!' he yelled as Williams kept running. Truscott fired again, and half his men mimed firing a shot. Brotherton decided to be vindictive and declared Redman to be a victim.

'Right between the eyes. Don't worry, in your case that won't hurt!'

Redman complained as he sat down in the grass, prompting another shout. 'Lie down, sir. Trust a grenadier not to know when he's dead!' The acting adjutant was clearly relishing his role.

Pringle had committed half of his supports to join the skirmish line. 'Mr Williams,' he called, 'help Sergeant Darrowfield control the skirmishers. You take the left.'

Williams was surprised, but responded immediately. 'Yes, sir. Thank you, sir.'

'Get on with it, then!' shouted Pringle. 'Oh, and Mr Williams.'

'Yes, sir!'

'You're out of uniform!' Williams looked up at where the peak of his shako should have been. Pringle smiled.

'Yes, sir. Sorry, sir.' He jogged to the left of the line, looked at Darrowfield and saw him nod.

'Line will advance. Number One!' The front rank man of each pair jogged forward five paces, kneeled and mimed firing. 'Number Two!' The rear rank men advanced in their turn.

It did not take long. The sharpshooters were heavily outnumbered and Truscott ordered the withdrawal before the grenadiers had time to work around the flanks of their shorter line. Brotherton allocated them just a single casualty. Williams was standing near the prostrate Hanley when it was declared over. The ensign was lying on his back, staring up at the blue sky and idly chewing a straw.

'Are you feeling better?' Williams asked.

'I am quite comfortable. I may decide to stay dead for a few days.' The two men exchanged grins. Pringle appeared, and lightly kicked Hanley with his boot, declaring that the dead do not feel anything. 'Ah, resurrection,' he added, as Hanley sprang up.

'Perhaps you mistake me for the gardener,' he said, rubbing his side. Williams stiffened, his smile instantly gone, but made no comment. Hanley regretted the joke, but had not meant any harm. He almost wished the Welshman would have been more angry, but then there was no time to think as MacAndrews called them all over to him. There was praise for their conduct, interwoven with detailed criticism of mistakes and ending with encouragement. This was typical of the Scotsman's approach during the next few days. The training was hard, but it was also imaginative, and simple drills turned into mock battles. On some of the days they marched long distances. For these it was invariably either blazingly hot or pouring with rain. Tout's conviction that the Regimental Sergeant Major could control the weather grew stronger.

Most of the officers took to gathering in the evenings in a large tent set aside for the purpose. It was known that Lieutenant Colonel Moss had decided that the 106th should form a communal mess, of the type now common in many regiments. The officers and the two volunteers would contribute for their food and other provisions and regularly dine together. It was sociable, but Hanley for one was worried that this would devour almost all of his pay before any other expenses. Williams was even more nervous.

MacAndrews enjoyed the week and the command. Another letter arrived from Lieutenant Colonel Moss, and one from General Lepper, and both stated clearly that they hoped to confirm him as major. It was encouraging, yet long service and countless disappointments made him reluctant to take anything for granted. His wife showed no such reticence.

Mrs MacAndrews and her daughter arrived on the afternoon of the sixth day, riding into camp along with Mrs Mosley and Mrs Kidwell. Williams was standing guard when they arrived and felt Miss MacAndrews looked especially fetching in a russet riding habit. Her mother was spectacular in red, and the pair easily outshone the other ladies, and especially the poor quartermaster's wife, who did not ride well. Williams presented arms, and directed them to Captain MacAndrews' tent on the main road of the camp.

'Thank you so much, Mr Williams.' The captain's wife dazzled him with her warm smile. 'It is a pleasure to see you again. Please give my compliments to the other gentlemen.' Jane nodded to him, before she tapped her mare with the long whip to catch up with her mother, who had gone straight into a canter.

★

'I am getting old,' said Alastair MacAndrews.

'You were born old,' replied his wife with scant sympathy. The last half-hour had not supported his statement, but she had never been one for unnecessary flattery with anyone who mattered.

It was late in the evening, and they were lying on the floor of his small tent. MacAndrews had a travelling cot, but it was too narrow for the two of them, so he had done the best he could by spreading some straw-filled sacks on the ground. From outside came the sound of someone singing. Jane had been given a tent near by and a crowd of the 106th's officers had gathered to serenade her. The voice was a pleasing tenor, which suggested young Derryck.

The proximity of so many of his officers had meant that their lovemaking had had to be unnaturally silent.

'Reminds me of another time,' said Esther, fondly stroking her husband's cheek.

He knew what she meant. They had met a long time ago, when he was a prisoner of the American rebels. His battalion of the 71st Highlanders had been led to disaster by that damn fool Banastre Tarleton at Cowpens in January '81. The Americans knew him as 'Bloody Ban', but that was nothing to what MacAndrews or anyone else from the 71st called him.

The captivity was comfortable enough, billeted as they were for much of the time in a small town whose inhabitants were friendly. A fair few had Scottish connections, which did no harm, but it was wearisome. MacAndrews was a fifteen-year-old ensign when he had landed with General Howe on Long Island in '76. Battle followed battle, and by the time of Cowpens he was a lieutenant and acting company commander. Tarleton's recklessness left him a wounded and penniless prisoner – the poverty had always been there, but at least when fighting there was a chance of distinction and advancement. He chafed at captivity for eighteen long months.

Then came the escape. He and another officer planned carefully, but then this fellow changed everything by bringing along his American mistress, a girl eloping with him from a good family. They moved more slowly and ate more of their scanty rations. In the end they had to take chances, going to smaller settlements and hoping to find Tory aid. Betrayed, they were hunted by the militia and the other officer had cut and run, leaving MacAndrews with the girl.

Esther had been just seventeen then, and had only just realised that she was pregnant. The revelation may well have encouraged her lover's flight. Somehow MacAndrews and the girl had evaded capture and finally reached the British Army at New York. They had also fallen in love, and were married the day after they reached safety. The first time they had lain together had been in a dense thicket, militiamen hunting for them not more than twenty yards away.

Outside their tent a new voice began singing in a language neither of them knew. It was Williams, singing a love song in Welsh – indeed, the only words he knew in that language. He had a deep melodic voice, but like so much Celtic music it sounded like a dirge.

'Our Jane has plenty of admirers,' said Esther with a mother's satisfaction.

'At least they will get in each other's way,' said her husband gruffly.

'Yes, she will be safe.'

'Yes, but will they?' MacAndrews ran his fingers along his wife's arm as if to confirm that she was really there. 'She has grown so much.'

'Charleston agreed with her. For a while at least. Then she became bored. I was the same at her age.' He refrained from pointing out that before she had reached her daughter's present age, Esther had conducted a torrid affair, followed two prisoners of war in a desperate flight, taken and married a second lover before giving birth to the child of the first. MacAndrews hoped that Jane was taking things rather more gently. Not that it had ever bothered him that he had not been Esther's first choice. Although he had admired her looks, he had come to love her only as they travelled secretly together in the last stages of their escape. That love had only grown stronger with the passing years. It still amazed him that such a spectacular woman should choose to be with such an ordinary man. He had tried to tell her this so many times, but had always been brushed aside, and had long since given up saying it. Instead he returned to the subject of Jane.

'Was she tempted to stay?' he asked. Esther had gone home because her father had died and her mother had written wanting to make peace. There had been offers of a good position for her husband and herself if he settled in Carolina, talk of finding a wealthy match for Jane.

'No more than I was. It is a petty, small society, however rich. And the climate. I had forgotten just how oppressive the heat can be. It turns men to drink and women to religion.' He smiled. 'Anyway,' Esther continued. 'She is a soldier's daughter and she'll be a soldier's wife one day. It's in her soul.'

'I had hoped she might have better,' said MacAndrews wistfully.

'We have been happy,' she said firmly.

'In spite of everything?'

'Because of everything.' Esther shook her head. 'I still think you don't believe me. Alastair, together we have lived, and our companionship has been closer than anything experienced by most people. If there has been pain and sorrow there has been so much joy. You know there has been sorrow. Three great sorrows. I carried those babies which we had to bury, and not a day goes past when I do not see their tiny faces or hear their voices.' The first had been a boy, the child of her fugitive lover and with the same soulful brown eyes that had won her heart. He had been five when a fever took him.

'That was the hardest. All three times.' MacAndrews emphasised the number.

'I know, all three. You did care for them all and that is one reason why I love you. So we have known sorrow. Few have not. But we have a daughter to be proud of and I have revelled in the love of the finest man alive. Happiness is much rarer than you think and we have known our full share.'

When young, MacAndrews would probably have demanded

to know who this rival was, but now he just looked fondly into her blue eyes. They had had this conversation so many times, but still he felt he had somehow let her down.

'Fine, but poor – it sounds like a poem. Couldn't we find Jane a man that was fine, but rich?'

'She will choose for herself. Like I did, and I did not do so badly.' MacAndrews resisted the urge to remind her of the lover who had abandoned her. His wife continued, 'Don't worry, she won't rush. She is just practising. Maybe he will be rich or poor. I was rich once and it did not make me happy.'

MacAndrews had never had the chance to test this from personal experience. There was no point arguing. He would never win with Esther – would never want to win. She would get her way. It was no coincidence that she had brought along the two other wives when she came to the camp. If just she and Jane had come Esther knew that her dutiful husband would have felt obliged to send her away, so that he alone did not enjoy a privilege. It was best simply to be glad that she had not dragged Mrs Wickham along as well. The lieutenant was certainly pleased, and had been an eager participant in the frequent evening card games played in the mess. Apparently his wife could not ride and had no access to a carriage.

'I fear Jane may be a sore distraction to my officers,' he said with a shake of his head.

Esther laughed. 'You even sound like a major now.'

10

Lieutenant Colonel Moss arrived the day after the two wings of the 106th had reunited. He ordered an immediate parade and inspected the men. Then he led them in two hours of battalion drill, driving them hard, wanting every formation change performed at his own rapid speed. After that he gathered the officers together in the main room of the inn where he had set up his headquarters. The regiment's two volunteers were included – Forde had nodded amicably to Williams – and altogether thirty-seven men sat on the high-backed wooden chairs and benches around the dark oak tables. Moss looked down on them from the open first-floor corridor which ran along one of the narrow sides of the tavern. There was a solid wooden banister, but George Moss was never one to lean. Occasionally he gripped the bar hard with both hands, to stop himself from pacing up and down. The faces were watching him expectantly. It took an effort to wait a few more moments just to be sure that he had their attention.

'Gentlemen,' he announced. 'I intend the 106th to be the finest regiment in the British Army.' They liked that, pounding the tables with their right hands. Moss waited for the din to die down.

'We shall be the best because I expect you all to be the best. The 106th is the youngest regiment of the line. As yet, it has not seen action. I know some of us have with other corps. I know Mr Anstey was with us in Egypt.' That was true, but Anstey was surprised the colonel was aware of it. 'Captain Mosley is an old India hand. If the enemy come at us with elephants he's the man who will know what to do!' Moss let them laugh, pleased that

108

Mosley joined in. 'Mr Kidwell has seen more service than I have enjoyed hot dinners.' It was good to include the former ranker and now quartermaster in his praise.

'Finally we have our two majors, and they were fighting before we were born. However, for the benefit of our younger gentlemen I am able to quash the rumour that Major MacAndrews was at Agincourt.' They liked that, although one or two needed a whispered explanation before they got the joke. Moss had brought confirmation that MacAndrews was to be gazetted as major. Lieutenant Wickham had also purchased his captaincy and would now command the Grenadier Company. He certainly looked the part of a dashing flank company officer.

'Now comes the answer to the question you have all been asking. In a week's time we will march for Portsmouth, there to join with the Twentieth Light Dragoons and some gunners and embark on board transports.' There was hush now, the faces eager and craning up to find out which of the rumours was true. 'From Portsmouth we shall sail to the Irish Sea and join a much stronger force of some eleven thousand men off Cork. It is commanded by Lieutenant General Sir Arthur Wellesley.'

There was a burst of conversation and Moss let them talk. Wellesley's victories in India were well known, and he was young and aggressive. Moss had seen a little of him in Ireland and liked what he saw, sensing a man after his own heart. In a few years, it should be General Moss leading one of England's armies on a great expedition.

Moss raised his voice. 'From Ireland we shall sail again to land in Europe and confront the legions of Bonaparte.' The hubbub increased in volume. He raised his hand and brought silence. 'Our destination – Spain! We are to help the Spanish chase out the French invaders.

'Gentlemen, we are going to war!' Cheers now as well as hands pounding on the table. Moss raised his own hand. 'At last we have the chance to show what the 106th can do. I know that none of you will disappoint me. On and off the field you shall conduct yourselves as English gentlemen. Do that, and we shall drive the

King's enemies before us like the dogs they are!' That had them cheering again. Moss let them go on longer this time. A servant arrived bearing a tray. The colonel held up his hand until there was silence.

'As officers you will lead your men. You must always go first.' He paused for a moment. 'And I shall always lead you.' Moss raised a glass. 'Gentlemen, the King.'

They rose to their feet for the toast. Standing straight, they raised their glasses. 'The King' came from thirty-seven throats.

A moment later, Moss gave them another. 'The 106th and glory!' This time the emptied glasses were followed by three cheers for the colonel.

Moss gave the regiment a light day by his standards. There were company drills for an hour, and then a thorough inspection of the regiment's tent lines. Everywhere there was activity and excitement. News that they were to go on campaign had spread rapidly and lent a new urgency to everything.

One of the colonel's new regulations was greeted with enormous enthusiasm. He had announced it at the end of this morning's parade. The army had decided to abolish queues and the practice of putting powder on hair. The new code had not yet been formally announced, but Moss had decided that the 106th would lead the way. Sufficient clippers had been found – somehow the RSM had known how to procure such things at short notice – and as the afternoon wore on each company took delight in removing the hated queues. In barrels of water the men washed out the equally loathed white powder, which mice were apt to nibble at while they lay asleep. Barbers were appointed for each company and one by one the long pigtails were chopped off. Hair was now to end just above the collar. Every company had built a fire and burned the hair in a strange ritual. Each left behind a pool of lead, for the end of each queue was weighted down by a musket ball.

'Well, that should stop witchcraft,' said Hanley as he watched the grenadiers go through the process. There was something very pagan about the scene, but Hanley was the only man in the company who already had short hair and so did not need to be shorn.

Williams looked a little disconcerted, while Pringle was curious. 'How so?'

'Parts of the body have power. You are supposed to be able to control the person if you have part of them.'

'Well, you have travelled and know about these things. Anyway, I don't think the French employ magicians so you needn't worry,' said Pringle.

'Heathen nonsense, anyway,' asserted Williams. He was waiting for the barber, his long fair hair hanging down past his shoulders.

Hanley and Pringle exchanged looks. 'You know, Bills,' said the lieutenant, 'I sometimes think you might have been happier serving with Cromwell's Ironsides.'

'Oh, I don't know. I haven't taken part in a witch-burning for ages.'

Pringle laughed, but decided to change the subject. It always seemed wiser to avoid discussion of organised religion with the earnest Williams.

'So, Hanley,' he said, 'do you welcome the prospect of going back to Spain?' Hanley had told them a little of his travels in the last few years. He thought for a moment before replying.

'Yes, I believe I do. When I left Madrid I was full of hate for the French. The things I saw them do there . . .'

There did not seem to be any more. 'Well, you must tell us everything important about the place. You know, what are the women like?'

'Very pretty. Brown eyes and trim figures. And unpredictable. Curse you one minute and then kiss you the next.'

'Doesn't sound that different from here.'

'Well, it's hotter, and the curses are stronger. Their nails are sharper too.'

'You must teach me some useful expressions. "Is your husband away for long?" – that sort of thing.'

'Isn't it enough to have the French to fight without outraged husbands?' asked Williams, being as flippant as he could on what

III

he felt was a serious subject. In his case, he was utterly sure that no Spanish lady could possibly compare to the exquisite Miss MacAndrews.

'I shall be discreet.'

'You never have been before, Billy,' said Wickham as he strode up behind them, trying to keep pace with Lieutenant Colonel Moss. The new captain of the grenadiers looked immaculate. He had long ago cultivated thick sideburns, which had always looked a little odd when his hair was powdered. Now they set off the thick and curly brown hair, which seemed just a little neater than anyone else's. He had had his hair cut privately, like the colonel and a few other officers. Most had cheerfully joined in with their men. There was something of a holiday atmosphere that day in the 106th's camp. The officers' wives were all discreetly absent, but many of the men's wives watched and cheered on the haircutting. Hanley noticed Dobson's pretty daughter, and was shocked when the girl winked at him again. No wonder her father was worried.

Moss waved the men down as the nearest sprang to attention. This was not a formal visit. 'Discretion is to be expected of all my officers,' declared Moss. 'Any lady must always be treated with utmost respect. So always take your boots off.' The laughter was genuine and even Williams joined in. Moss was already popular.

'Mr Hanley was telling us about Spain, sir,' volunteered Pringle.

'Yes, I heard. I shall make sure I am careful not to get scratched too heavily.' More laughter. 'How long did you spend in Spain, Mr Hanley?'

'Nearly two years, sir.'

'And you speak the language – beyond enquiring about the whereabouts of husbands?'

Hanley grinned. 'Yes, sir.'

'Excellent, that may prove very useful. I know that I can rely on all of my grenadiers.' Moss had raised his voice to carry as far as possible. His quick stride had already taken him past the chair where Dobson was having his queue cut off.

'Bet this must feel odd for an old soldier like you,' said the colonel cheerfully.

'Glad to see the back of it, sir.'

Moss smiled warmly. 'Well, there is one thing I do know, and that is that the French will never see the backs of us!' They cheered that. Moss was already halfway towards the lines of Number Three Company, and simply waved vaguely back in acknowledgement. He was pleased, and decided to try the same joke again. George Moss was going to war again at last.

Lisbon gleamed white in the bright sunlight as the pilot boat came alongside the Russian merchant ship. Its captain yelled at the group of soldiers to get out of the way as his men prepared to take the ship into the Tagus, and tried to ignore the deliberate hesitation before the surly, one-eyed sergeant in charge gestured to the men and took them below.

No one disturbed Count Denilov, who leaned on the rail and stared hungrily at the city. Three days earlier they had let the general's wasted body slide down a board and into the sea, the soldiers firing a salute with their muskets. His orders – vaguely worded, but commanding full co-operation with the bearer and his deputy in the pursuit of their mission – were now in Denilov's pocket. He had also taken the purse of gold coins intended to finance their mission.

It was more money than he had carried for some time, but would have been only a drop in the ocean of his debts. He had left Russia because all that remained for him there was suicide or a debtor's prison. Voluntary exile had been one way out, but had little to commend it. This mission was an opportunity, another game of chance, and already the hand was going his way. Denilov had the general's orders and now his authority. Admiral Siniavin would have no choice but to assist him in spite of his modest rank, for he was a representative of the Tsar himself. It would give him access to the French high command, and to the remaining aristocracy of Portugal, including those who resented the invader.

There was a war on, and he knew that wars meant chaos, and also opportunity for a bold man. It was a question of sniffing around to catch the scent of profit. The French were looting widely and no one was likely to be able to trace the source of anything he was able to grab for himself. If fortune smiled, then he might go back home rich again and with the fresh prestige of performing a service for Tsar Alexander. If not, then a good man with a sword should have no trouble finding employment in Napoleon's armies, especially since he would bring with him the names of disloyal Portuguese nobles, and knowledge of the concerns of the Russian court.

To Denilov, Lisbon looked ripe for the plucking.

11

Williams tried to concentrate on his letter in spite of the noise. The colonel had instituted an officers' mess on the day of his arrival, hiring the main room of the inn exclusively for the purpose. The money came out of his own pocket. There were mess bills to be paid by each member, but the adjutant had taken Forde and Williams quietly aside and informed them that they would not be required to contribute anything for the first three months. Moss covered this expense, making clear that this was a gift and not a loan. He was also matching every penny paid by the other officers from his own funds. These 'secret' arrangements were common knowledge and only added to the high esteem that Williams and the others felt for their commander. The story was that Moss planned to eat and drink only what was available to his officers. Since he had no desire to live like a Johnny Raw Ensign then he would ensure that everyone else could live at his standard.

The colonel also expected every officer to spend as much of their off-duty time in the mess as possible, although some leeway was given to the married men. Williams would have preferred to write his weekly letter home in the privacy of the tent he shared with Pringle, Redman and Hanley. Although past ten it was a bright night and the light would have been adequate even without lighting a candle. Inside the inn it was gloomy, filled with smoke. Williams rubbed his hair. It was still a pleasant sensation to be free of powder. Less pleasant was the lack of any real privacy. If his duties permitted he would try to take a long walk tomorrow evening, getting away from everyone for at least an hour or two.

The volunteer was struggling to think of things to say. One paragraph had described his admiration for Colonel Moss. Then he had detailed the duties they had performed, and been as charitable as he could about his fellow officers, while noting, 'sadly all too many are given over much to drinking and are prone to cursing'. Personally he disliked the smell of tobacco, but knew his mother liked the scent and so did not add that as a criticism. He reported the promotion of Major MacAndrews and mentioned the delight of his family. That was as far as he came to mentioning Miss MacAndrews. It was hard not to spend pages telling of her wonderful qualities. He did not have the right to do that. Instead Williams described the appointment of Wickham to command the company, describing him as a true and handsome gentleman.

He glanced across at the new captain, who was playing cards with Hanley and a couple of officers from the Light Company. They had been at it for hours. Wickham was one of the most frequent gamers in the 106th, and often seemed to show no enthusiasm to return to his billet and his wife. He was generally lucky, seeming to win far more than he lost, but this evening the cards were going against him. Pringle was watching, joining in the conversation, but not the game. The lieutenant often declared that gambling was the one of the few vices that held no appeal for him. He had reversed a chair and sat with his legs either side of its back, his hands resting on the top.

Williams decided against mentioning the card school to his mother. Another omission was the raucous laughter and often crude jokes of the younger – and in most cases well-liquored – officers. Forde was one of a group who now began an enthusiastic, if scarcely musical, rendering of 'Spanish Ladies'. Since they had heard of their destination it had become one of the most popular songs in the regiment. Williams could remember some of his mother's lodgers singing the same song when he was a boy, and decided that he could at least make that part of the evening sound picturesque. Still the words did not come easily and he found himself rubbing his chin. He was also thirsty, having long since finished the second glass of wine which was all that he would allow himself in an evening – indeed, was all he could stomach. Perhaps some water would help. Williams got up, leaving his papers and the stubby pencil on the table.

At the far end the colonel, Major Toye and some of the more sober captains were deep in conversation. MacAndrews was not there, having already taken his leave and gone to see his wife and daughter. Howard of Number Eight Company was reading aloud from a newspaper. Moss noticed Williams passing and beckoned him over to join them.

'This will interest you, Mr Williams. It is from the debate in Parliament which committed our expedition to help the Spanish. I was there,' the colonel threw in a matter-of-fact way, 'but it will be good for all our officers to know.' Moss gestured to Major Toye, who raised his voice.

'Quiet now,' he yelled. 'This is important.' Several voices were still bidding farewell and adieu to the ladies of Spain, and it took more shouting before they were hushed into silence.

Spanish ambassadors had come to London on 8th June, prompting a debate in the Commons a week later to discuss their appeal. For once the Whig opposition agreed with the Tory government. So did the newspapers and even old Cobbett, the former Dragoon and radical champion of the ordinary soldier's rights. Howard read extracts from the speeches. Mr Sheridan of the opposition had argued cogently and in great detail for supporting the Spanish with both financial and military aid.

Moss let them in on a secret. 'Of course, that's not what he actually said. It was all going so slowly that morning that old Dick Sheridan wandered off upstairs and joined some friends. By the time he came back he was as drunk as a lord. Poor fellow could hardly stand.'

They laughed as Moss had known they would. Williams joined in, since although he rather disapproved of the country's leaders misbehaving, there was something so essentially comic about the image.

'So what happened next? Did Canning embrace him and swear

undying friendship?' suggested Pringle, who had come over to join them.

The laugh was smaller, as befitted a joke made by a junior officer, but Moss hesitated only for a moment before joining in, and that encouraged the rest.

'No, Billy' – using the familiar name was a careful touch – 'Canning was as sober as a judge. His speech is fairly accurate.'

'So he did really say there was "The strongest disposition on behalf of the British government to afford every practical aid to the Spanish People"?' Howard was reading carefully from *The Times*. 'So is the practical aid bit about us?'

'Well, everyone above the rank of ensign anyway,' suggested Major Toye, producing more laughter. That seemed to end things and the group dispersed. Williams heard Derryck saying to another ensign that he was strongly disposed to ask on behalf of himself for the loan of five guineas. He grinned, and then realised he was still standing beside the colonel. Moss noticed his confusion, but was still in a generous mood. 'Mr Williams, will you take a glass with us?'

It was obviously impossible to refuse, but Williams felt awkward as he sat. Moss asked him a number of questions, chatting affably although in his usual rapid manner. The port came and Williams dutifully consumed the glass, and tried not to grimace each time he took a sip. He realised that this was expensive stuff, from the colonel's own cellar, and that he ought to be privileged. That did not stop it tasting foul to him, or reduce the sense that his throat was burning.

Perhaps it loosened his tongue a little, for at one point he found himself talking with great enthusiasm about Caesar, Hannibal and Marius. Major Toye had merely asked politely whether he had studied any military history. Williams' voice had risen sharply in volume as he warmed to such a favourite theme.

'I confess I know little of the ancients, especially of Marius,' said Moss briskly.

'He said one thing worthy of note. One day an enemy general wanted to fight a battle, but Marius would not bring his Romans down from a high hill. "If you are such a great general, Marius, come down and fight!" his enemy said. Marius just replied, "If you are a great general, then make me."' Williams looked immensely pleased with the story.

'We shall keep that advice in mind,' said Howard. 'Now, Mr Williams, would you mind returning his paper to Mr Anstey? Thank you.' He held *The Times* out.

'Oh yes, of course.' Williams rose and left, still looking pleased at having been included in the conversation.

'A keen young man, though rather sober,' said Toye, once the volunteer had moved off.

Moss nodded, but looked a little doubtful. 'Rather a cautious moral to his story. Still, he may learn. Another glass, gentlemen?'

Williams' admiration for the colonel had increased still further. He felt proud to be in the 106th, confident that with such a true gentleman at their head they would win fame. With luck he might get his commission sooner rather than later. He pictured himself as a wise and noble colonel, condescending to his juniors as easily as Moss. He was clearly the model he should endeavour to match.

Having returned the newspaper, Williams headed back to the table where he had left his unfinished letter. He tried to think of a modest way of describing his conversation with the colonel. When he reached the spot his papers were missing. Behind him he heard a voice.

'Dearest Mother, I do hope the pox has cleared up.' Williams turned to meet a gale of laughter. Redman had his head back and his mouth wide open, showing his bad teeth as he guffawed. Ensign Hatch had hold of the letter and was pretending to read aloud.

'How is sweet sister Emily and her latest bastard? Can she remember whether it was the parson or the sweep who is the father this time? Tell her she must take payment immediately next time and not rely on their good faith.'

Williams was furious. He strode towards them and grabbed the letter from Hatch. It tore slightly as he pulled it away, but the man was too drunk to resist properly or make a game of it. For a moment he kept staring at where the pages had been, not noticing that they had gone.

'Do not judge my family by the standards of your own,' said Williams as coldly and calmly as he could. He felt rage within him, was flexing the fingers of his free hand, itching to ball them into a fist and slam it into the man's face. With an effort, he spun on his heels and walked off, knowing that acting quickly was the main thing.

'That told you,' said Redman to Hatch.

'I left a bit out. All about having to share a tent with an ugly bugger called Redman,' replied his friend. 'How he kept making unwelcome advances on poor Williams.' Some of the nearby gentlemen howled with laughter. Redman looked confused and then glared at his friend. Hatch froze for a moment. 'You know, I do believe I am going to be a little ill.' He staggered up and left.

In the corner Williams was still fuming. He flinched, turning angrily when Pringle patted him on the shoulder.

'Well done, Bills.'

'I should have knocked them down.'

'They are drunk, and will fall down well enough on their own. That would not have proved anything.'

'I would have enjoyed it, though.'

'Would you also enjoy being expelled from the regiment? If officers fight it must be an affair of honour properly conducted. You can count on me as a second if you need me.'

Williams began to understand. 'That is most kind of you.'

'Think nothing of it. What little honour William Pringle still has is always at your disposal.' He smiled. 'But not over nonsense like this. Best to show you can take a joke. Anyway, Redman is a damned fool, but he is our goddamned fool and we have to live with him. What was it you were saying earlier – only fight when your enemy makes you? If it's good enough for Marius I am sure it's good enough for you.'

'You heard that?'

'Half the room did,' said Hanley, appearing from nowhere.

'Your speech was a little loud and forceful,' confirmed Pringle. 'I wish I had a voice as strong!'

'Oh dear, should I apologise, do you think?'

'Of course not. You were perfectly polite if a little deafening,' said Hanley.

'Given up the game?' asked Pringle.

'Too rich for my liking. I have lost fifteen shillings and that is enough. Anyway, I thought I would seek some intelligent company for a change. But . . .'

Pringle finished the sentence. 'You couldn't find any so decided to make do with us. Bills, we are desperately undervalued. Tell him something about Caesar and prove him wrong.'

'Well, he's dead for a start,' said Williams, grateful for their company.

'Oh, I am so sorry. Had I known, I would have sent flowers.'

'He is supposed to have killed a million Gauls,' said Hanley.

'Obviously not enough, as there are still plenty of Frenchmen out there,' replied Pringle. 'Apparently you cannot rely on an Italian to finish a job.'

'He fought in Spain a few times. In fact he fought nearly everywhere,' added Williams.

'Had affairs with women everywhere too,' said Hanley.

Pringle's smile broadened. 'Ah, now you interest me strangely. I had almost forgotten why I enjoy history so much! Tell us more.'

12

Lieutenant Colonel Moss was impatient and was never a man to suffer in silence.

'Damn it, Toye, where the hell are they? Thomas has been gone for nearly an hour.'

Mr Thomas the adjutant had ridden off to look for the two missing companies less than twenty minutes earlier, but Toye did not think it prudent to point this out. 'I am sure they will be back soon, sir,' said the major guardedly. They were not too far from the men, and he was uncomfortable with appearing to criticise any other officer in front of them. Anyway, Thomas was reliable and would no doubt be back as soon as he could. The adjutant had joined as a private soldier and risen through sheer merit. If he was not the most elegant horseman among the officers, he was more than competent, and his little chestnut cob had plenty of stamina. Thomas would be back as soon as was possible. It was not as if they faced a real enemy.

Today Moss had divided the battalion. MacAndrews had been given the grenadiers and Companies One and Eight and sent off before dawn. They were to build a small redoubt on a prominent hill some three miles away. At ten the rest of the 106th would advance to take the position, forcing their way across a river en route. Moss himself led the main force of five companies to the bridge. The Light Company along with Number Five Company had been sent downstream to cross by the cattle ford and then move round to outflank anyone MacAndrews had posted to defend the bridge.

Yet when Moss and his men had arrived at the bridge there was no sign of anyone. The 'enemy' were not waiting for them, nor were the Light Company's Captain Headley and his men. Moss had waited for five minutes and then the main force advanced over the humpbacked bridge to a low rise beyond it. They waited, and after a while he let the men sit down to rest. It was a warm day, and some were soon lying stretched out in the long grass. Quite a few of the older men dozed off, taking advantage of any chance to rest. Others were smoking their pipes. Most of the officers clustered in the centre of the line formed by the five companies. They remained standing, and a few had lit cheroots.

Hanley was the senior ensign in the battalion and so today was detached from the Grenadier Company and carrying the King's Colour of the 106th. At the moment the large silk Union flag – it was more than six feet high and a little longer – remained covered by its protective leather case. He had been given a white shoulder belt fitted with a metal holder in which to rest the butt of the pole when he raised it high, but for the moment he let the heavy standard stand on the ground.

'I suppose we ought to think of you as a spy, Hanley,' said young Derryck cheerfully. He had only a week's seniority over Ensign Trent, and so the latter was given the task of carrying the regimental colour. This had a small Union flag in the top left-hand corner. Normally the main field matched the colour of the collar and cuffs of a regiment – its facings. The 106th, however, had red facings identical in shade to the rest of the jacket. (As Pringle said, it rather suggested that their first colonel was not a man of great imagination.) As was usual in such cases, the 106th's standard had a white field with a large red cross on it. In the centre of this, like the King's Colour, was a green wreath containing the regimental number CVI in gold lettering. This colour also remained in its case, however. It was clear the weight was already tiring the diminutive Trent, but he stubbornly refused to let Derryck or anyone else hold it for a while to ease his burden.

Moss and Toye stood about fifteen yards ahead of the group of officers. At least Toye stood. Moss paced up and down restlessly. Now and again his angry tirades against the delay carried back to where the others waited. Their horses were held by two soldiers who knew enough to keep their expressions utterly blank.

'Where is the bloody man?' asked Moss for the tenth time. 'The goddamned ford is only half a mile away, what in the name of all that's holy is damned well keeping him?'

'I am sure Mr Thomas will be back very soon. Either with the companies or at least with news of them. Perhaps they got lost?' suggested Toye, more for something to say than out of any conviction. He instantly realised it was the wrong thing.

'For God's sake they can't have got lost. Even Thomas can read a map. So can that arse Headley. Bloody hell, it is a simple lane, and then they can follow the river to us.' Moss was red in the face, his anger boiling over. Someone would pay for this. Still, he was a soldier and in war things went wrong. There was nothing to be done but carry on.

'That's it. I am not wasting any more time. They can catch up with us if they are able.' Moss was already striding back towards the companies. 'Mr Fletcher, fall them in if you please.' The RSM's voice echoed through the wide field.

'Are you sure, sir?' asked Toye.

Moss barely managed to bite back a cutting remark. 'We must always be sure, Major Toye.' With a struggle he managed to pause for a long moment. 'If we wait any longer they may not arrive, and all the time we wait MacAndrews' boys can be strengthening their position. So we go.' Moss grinned. 'If in doubt, go straight for the enemy's throat!' he declared cheerfully. Toye was unconvinced, but he smiled back, the habit of obedience strong. MacAndrews' men had very few tools and were unlikely to construct anything too formidable. When Moss waved away the private leading his horse, the major felt obliged to do the same. They would both walk the last mile with the men.

Moss put the five companies into open column. They were not one of the wings of the battalion. Whether through design or chance the colonel had broken up the usual subdivisions of the 106th and scattered the companies. The change from line into column was a little slower and less tidy than usual. Moss

124

was displeased, and once they were on the move beckoned to the RSM and had a few words with him. Speed was what mattered, and he was not unduly concerned whether this offended the sergeant major's fondness for precision in drill. 'Being fast is the key, Mr Fletcher. That way you can respond to anything the enemy throws at you before they have time to think.' He liked that, and made a mental note to tell his officers the same thing at some point.

Finally – it was now long past noon – the main force arrived at the foot of a gentle ridge. On a modestly projecting spur the dark red earth of a rampart stood out. It stretched for little more than thirty yards and was scarcely three foot high. There was a flurry of activity when Moss's men appeared, and soon the earthwork was lined with two ranks of redcoats, the men in front kneeling.

'Can't see any sign of side walls,' said Toye, as he and Moss studied the position through their telescopes. The colonel grunted in agreement, but was more concerned with the deployment of his men. He turned to see the RSM bellowing at the companies. To make the change into line more speedy, Moss had instructed him to form with the first company in the column as the centre of the new line. Arnold's Number Three Company was at the head of the column, Davenport's Number Seven behind them, then Mosley's Number Four, Hamilton's Number Six, and finally Kitchener's Number Two Company at the rear.

With the men unused to their positions in this ad hoc formation, things had quickly gone wrong. Davenport's men had wheeled to the left rather than the right and that left both them and Hamilton's company trying to occupy the same position to the immediate left of Arnold. Both had to halt. The sergeant major marched stiffly over, yelling orders as he did so. Davenport's men were already in place, so it was easier to turn Hamilton's company about, wheel them round ninety degrees and then march them to form at the very far left of the line next to Kitchener's Number Two Company. That left Mosley's company on the far right, with a company-sized gap between them and Arnold's Number Three. Fletcher had them turn to their left and then march until they were in contact with the rest of the line. A good deal of more minor shuffling was required before the five-company line was ready, somewhat to the left of where it was originally intended to be.

'A bloody shambles, Mr Fletcher!' yelled Moss, unable any longer to hide his displeasure with his subordinates. The RSM stiffened slightly, but remained otherwise unmoved. Inwardly he was cursing his commander, who criticised him for his own haphazard instructions.

'Sir, sir!' A voice was crying out, and Moss heard someone run up beside him. He turned to see Mr Thomas on foot.

'Where the hell have you been?' Moss spat the words at his adjutant.

Thomas was breathing hard as he came to attention in front of the colonel. 'I beg to report that the flanking force has been captured, sir.'

'What? What the devil are you blathering about, man? And where's your screw of a horse?' demanded Moss.

'Ambushed, sir. Both companies were defiling through a sunken lane, and found MacAndrews had his men waiting for them. They rolled wagons behind and in front to block the lane, and then two of his companies popped up from the hedges. Had Headley and his men cold.' For once Moss was speechless. 'A neat piece of work. They had just sprung the trap when I arrived. It seemed only fair to declare the flanking force dead or captured.'

'You did what?' Moss was beginning to marshal himself.

'Told them to pile weapons and sit down. They said that I was a prisoner and I told them that I damned well was not. So MacAndrews took my horse and said if that was the case I should walk back.' Service in the ranks had long since taught Thomas to let a superior officer's anger flow past him. He also took care not to reveal any trace of his own amusement.

Moss rallied, realising an opportunity. He turned to Toye, who was still studying the makeshift earthwork with his telescope. 'Who can you see up there, John?' he asked, deliberately using the major's Christian name.

'Captain Wickham. He is standing on the rampart. Couldn't be anyone else.'

'No other officers?' enquired Moss eagerly.

'No, sir. Not that I can see.'

'Excellent,' said Moss. 'We have them, gentlemen. MacAndrews must still be away with the two companies and has just left the grenadiers to hold the redoubt.' The term was rather grand for what Toye could see, but that was just the colonel's way. Still, he had his doubts.

'Maybe we just can't see them?' he suggested cautiously.

'Nonsense. Use your head, man. Thomas here was on his own and has only just got back. Marching men move more slowly than an individual. MacAndrews is still away being clever and we outnumber the grenadiers by five to one.' Thomas thought it unnecessary to mention that MacAndrews had made him pledge to wait half an hour before he started back.

'Mr Fletcher,' Moss called. 'The 106th will prepare to advance. Uncase the colours.' He would have liked to give the order to fix bayonets, but that could easily result in accidents and it was prudent to keep the sharp spikes in their scabbards. Still, the unveiling of the two flags gave the moment some drama. Moss felt the excitement rising, feeling the thrill of leading his own battalion – if today only part of it and not against a real enemy. That moment could not come too soon for him.

Moss waved away the soldier with his horse, and so of course Major Toye immediately did the same. The young colonel drew his sword, an expensive curved blade with an oriental-style hilt. He turned back to face the five-company line.

'Boys, we're going to take that hill! No shooting, we'll just go straight at them.' He nodded to the RSM. 'Mr Fletcher, if you please. The battalion will advance.'

''Tallion will advance. Forward march!' Moss was moving before Fletcher had finished calling the order. Toye was left behind and had to jog to keep up. Yet as the five companies moved forward the colonel slowed to the steady pace of the drill book. This was not a heady charge up the beach in Egypt, but a formal attack on a strong position, and Moss wanted it done properly.

The 106th marched in silence. Even Hanley at the centre of the line found this stillness a little eerie. There was only the rattle of pouches and equipment, the swish of feet tramping through the long grass, the steady beat of the drums and now and again the sharp call of a sergeant rebuking any man who strayed even slightly from his position in the formation. The sergeants carried a six-foot pike known as a spontoon rather than the muskets of the ordinary soldiers. In each company they were stationed behind the second rank, ready to steady the men, and in extreme cases use the shaft of their pike to straighten the dressing or even force soldiers back into their position. A sergeant stood between Hanley and Trent. Another was to the young ensign's left and four more stood in the second rank behind them. These men had as their sole duty the protection of the colours. As Hanley understood it, the protection of the ensigns carrying the flags was at best a secondary concern.

The line went up the gentle slope. The men still had their muskets shouldered. This made them easier to carry, but also its very nonchalance suggested a confidence that could unnerve a real enemy. There was no wind, and the silk colours hung lazily down. Hanley was glad of the belt to help him support the weight. He tried to look as rigid as the men around him, but still found something unreal about his life as a soldier and kept wondering when he would wake up from this dream. The playacting element of today – 'fighting' against their fellow soldiers and his own friends – made the whole thing more than a little absurd. The thought made him giggle, and it was difficult to suppress this and impossible not to smile in spite of the stern look from the sergeant next to him.

At one hundred and fifty yards, Moss saw the redcoats behind the low rampart level their muskets. Wickham had stepped down and the tall white plume of his cocked hat was just visible behind the shakos of his men. Then the whole line vanished in an explosion of dirty smoke. The sound of the volley came a little later.

Moss wondered for a moment whether to launch the charge

now, but knew it was too soon. He turned and walked backwards for a few paces, smiling cheerfully at his men. The second volley came thirty seconds later. The noise was louder now, although not as loud as when using a full charge and a ball. Moss had turned back to face forwards. He raised his sword high. It was time. Rush the enemy so that even if some had reloaded by the time they arrived they would be flustered and not fire in an ordered way. Boldness always paid.

'Come on, boys,' he screamed, his voice becoming high pitched in the excitement. 'Charge!' The colonel ran on, waving his sword in circles over his head. The redcoats behind him cheered and surged, each individually dropping his musket from his shoulder and grabbing it in both hands. There had been no order to bring the firelocks down into the charge position.

The colonel was the first to reach the small fortification, with the closest of his men five yards behind. The neat line was now very ragged, broken into small clumps and individual running redcoats. Hanley was lagging with the weight of the colour and little Trent was behind him, in spite of the best efforts of the sergeants to keep them together. The men of the attack force were still cheering as Moss jumped lightly down into the ditch in front of the rampart. Muskets went off above him, but he had managed to deny the defenders their organised volley. The ditch was as deep as the wall was high, so that Moss could not reach the top. He tried to scramble up, but the earth was soft and gave under him, causing him to tumble back down. As he scrambled to his feet, cursing, the first men landed down beside him. A hand reached down from the rampart as he tried again. He looked up to see a toothless smile from one of the older soldiers. The man beckoned to him, and Moss took the proffered aid and let himself be pulled up. He knocked down the turf lying on top of the rampart as he came, staggered and grabbed at the man's shoulder, yanking hard on the woollen tuft at the fringe of his epaulette. There was something odd about that, but it escaped him at the moment.

Moss barged through the men, looking for Captain Wickham.

He was planning to be complimentary about the defenders in his declaration of the attack's success. Then the air was shattered by the thunder of a large volley. It came from beyond the redoubt, but men were in the way and Moss could not see what was happening, did not see Major MacAndrews leading his two companies against the attackers' left flank.

MacAndrews had been waiting with the grenadiers and Number One Company below the crest to the rear of the ridge. Wickham had been left at the redoubt to look conspicuous, but was not in command. His role was to signal as soon as the first man came within ten yards of the ditch. A wave of his cocked hat and MacAndrews began to march his men up and around the attackers' flank. Thomas, who had hung back in the attack, had watched the neat line of almost two hundred men breast the crest and swing round, wheeling till they were at ninety degrees to the ragged line in and around the ditch. MacAndrews halted them when they were just twenty yards away and fired. In a real action he would then have charged, but a little tact seemed necessary when fighting against your commander. He let the men load and began platoon volleys, a quarter of each company firing in turn, then the section to its right and so on, so that fire rippled along the front.

Moss declared the attack a victory, although a costly one. He paraded the battalion after they had marched back to camp and told them how pleased he was, but his speech was shorter than usual. He told them to be bold, to follow his lead and never give the enemy a moment's relief. His dented enthusiasm rallied at this, and there was a big cheer when he declared that after fighting against other heroes from the 106th, just facing mere Frenchmen would be child's play. Inwardly he fumed.

13

Williams whistled as he strolled along the well-shaded lane. The late afternoon sun was strong and hot, and even without pack and belts his woollen jacket was heavy. It was pleasantly cool under the trees that grew on either side of the muddy track and closed over it like a tunnel. He was now a good two miles from the regiment's camp and as usual there was a thrill in the sense of freedom this brought. There was no need to worry about how to behave, balancing the need to be sociable, but not over familiar, and respectful and enthusiastic in his duties, without appearing sycophantic. Worse still, there was never any privacy. Solitary by nature, and used over the years to spending so much time alone happily reading or dreaming, it was this he found most difficult. That made these occasional walks in his off-duty moments all the more precious. It was simply a relief to be away from pipe-clay and shouted orders, from tobacco smoke and constant talk.

As usual Williams found himself thinking of Miss MacAndrews. He knew that she was beautiful, and yet still found it hard to picture her face clearly in his mind. If only he had a likeness, and perhaps a lock of her red hair to keep with it and wear around his neck. The married officers had taken quarters in the small town near the camp, and Williams had seen the girl only twice in the last week. Admittedly the colonel had kept them all busy and his enthusiasm for them all spending as much time as possible in the mess had prevented most evening strolls and with them the hope of a chance meeting. This evening, however, Moss was attending a dinner at a house some miles away and so attendance in the mess was less important. The mood among the officers was also a little strange and there was a general sense that it would not be an especially convivial evening. Several others planned to be absent.

Williams had enjoyed this morning's mock battle. It had been exciting doing more than simply manoeuvring for the sake of practice. The ambush of the flanking force had gone perfectly, and it was especially satisfying for the grenadiers to surprise and overwhelm the light bobs who were always so apt to swagger. Then came the rapid march back to the defences, MacAndrews driving the men hard. Number One Company was determined not to be outdone by the grenadiers and so both moved quickly. He could feel a sense of excitement as the men took to the idea of proving themselves better than the rest of the battalion. The waiting had been harder, once they were in position behind the ridge. MacAndrews had let them sit, but it was difficult not knowing what was happening. Then they heard the defenders of the redoubt fire their first volley and knew that the attack had started. Ordered to their feet, they had still not begun their own advance for what seemed like an age, until Wickham waved his hat as a signal.

The defenders knew that they had won, and Williams suspected that they would make this clear to the men from the other companies at the first opportunity, whatever the colonel's judgement. The mock battle had anyway become just a little more real around the redoubt, resulting in a good few bruises and the odd black eye. Williams admired the way MacAndrews had out-thought the enemy, even if it was a little disconcerting since that enemy was their own commanding officer. It had also been reassuring for the company to be led by Pringle. Captain Wickham was a fine gentleman, and yet there was a vagueness about his manner that was just a little unsettling in a commander. MacAndrews always had been – and still was – so definite and precise in his instructions.

Sadly, it seemed as if the last days of training would be spent in more familiar drills. Williams knew that most of the officers in the attacking force wished for another opportunity and were convinced that they would do far better next time. The lights in particular wanted a chance to outwit the clodhopping grenadiers. Moss had announced, however, that there would be no more mock fights. There were whispers that he was angry with the officers of the attacking force for letting him down, and the defenders for doing too well. Williams hoped that was just malicious gossip, and still admired the colonel, although a small part of him wondered whether he might be a little too rash. Of the two, MacAndrews seemed to possess a surer hand, even if he lacked the colonel's flamboyance and charisma.

Williams left the track and climbed over a stile. A path led over a low hill and then down through a little patch of woodland to the river. Ten minutes later he was swimming lazily in the gentle current, enjoying the coolness of the water around him. His uniform was carefully folded and piled on a fallen tree trunk. This was luxury and relaxation, and even a huge sense of freedom. Worries about tensions within the battalion faded as he enjoyed the moment. He ducked his head under the chilly water and swam beneath the surface.

'The tone of this place has really fallen of late,' said a voice as Williams burst back up. The sneering tone was familiar, but for a moment he could not see who it was.

'Yes, full of bloody peasants,' agreed another voice. That was Hatch, which meant that the other was Redman. The spot was well known and often used by the 106th's officers, but even so Williams had hoped for some peace.

'Go to the devil, both of you,' yelled Williams, slightly surprised at his own vehemence.

'Oh, doesn't he know some bad words, Redman,' said Hatch.

'Well, he mixes with common soldiers, Hatch.'

'Look, can't you leave me in peace. It was so agreeable until you turned up,' tried Williams in a softer tone.

'So, he doesn't want our company. Not good enough for him, I suppose,' said Hatch. 'Not agreeable indeed. He's been reading books. Well, we will leave His Grace to his ablutions.'

'Anyway, we had better move upstream where the water is clearer,' said Redman. There was female laughter at this. Williams

133

had now cleared the water from his eyes and turned towards the bank. Redman stood by the tree trunk, his arm around the waist of young Jenny Dobson. His other hand prodded Williams' clothes with a stick. Hatch was behind them, holding the reins of a pair of horses.

'Jenny, does your father know you are here?' asked Williams, realising as he spoke how fatuous it must sound.

She looked a bit sheepish, but then rallied. 'I'm a woman now, Mr Williams, and go where I choose.' She lifted her chin defiantly. Her face was a little thin, but had a gentle prettiness about it, perhaps even beauty, and this was well set off by her thick brown curls.

'That's true enough for anyone to see.' Redman dropped the stick and reached round to undo the lace at the front of the girl's blouse. He struggled for a moment. Jenny looked a little shocked, but then used her own hand to help him. The tie undone, the young ensign pulled the top down and began to fondle the girl's left breast. 'And she knows how well gentlemen will treat her. A lady, is our Jenny.'

Williams was shocked, a little ashamed, but did not manage to look away. He was a quite glad that he was shoulder deep in water. It was only when Jenny Dobson moved to push Redman's hand away and refasten her blouse that Williams himself managed to shift his gaze down.

'You should go home, Jenny,' he said as gently as he could. 'You parents will be worried. Best to stop now before you make a mistake.'

'There's no mistake.' Redman was now stroking the girl's cheek. 'We'll look after her and all have a pleasant time.'

'Go home, Jenny,' repeated Williams. He started to swim towards the bank. Hatch had already mounted.

'Mind your own business and don't pretend to understand the ways of gentlemen.' Redman's voice was dripping with contempt. He put his hands round Jenny's waist and lifted her up. Hatch took her arms and pulled the girl on to the horse behind him. She did not resist, but Williams noticed that she would no longer look at him. Redman then mounted.

'Let me take you home, Jenny,' implored Williams.

'Goddam it, stop interfering, you Welsh prick!' screamed Redman. Hatch rode away with the girl. Redman walked his horse over to the trunk, and reached down to grab the pile of clothes. Williams' shirt fell away, but the ensign galloped off hal-looing and waving his jacket and trousers in his hand. They were fifty yards away by the time Williams scrambled up on to the bank. Their scorn for him did not matter, but to be leading Dobson's daughter astray brought on a cold rage. He could not catch them now, but he could at least follow them, and maybe bring the girl away before she was disgraced. The two young officers were more than a little drunk and so there just might be time.

Williams pulled the shirt on to his wet skin. It was long and fell to the middle of his thighs and would almost be decent if it were not that the dampness made it more than a little transpar-ent. The same was true of his drawers, which he had worn while swimming. He pulled on his boots, and was glad that he had not worn the long black gaiters when he went walking in his fatigue trousers. He lifted his shako up from the ground and put it on his head. It was easier than carrying the thing. Then, in shirt-tails, boots and hat, the gentleman volunteer went off on a quest to preserve a maiden's honour, in spite of herself.

On reflection it was probably a bad choice to cut through the woodland in the hope of getting ahead of the riders following the towpath. Tactically it made sense. The river curved in a great loop before it came to the next spot where the bank was gentle and a little beach favoured bathing or indeed other activities. Practically, the route was overgrown, and at times he had to force his way through. Williams reflected that at least knights errant had their armour to protect against brambles and nettles instead of just bare legs. He was not sure just what he was going to do if he caught up, and hoped that an idea would come to him. If Jenny refused to leave then he could not force her, and he doubt-ed that he could shame the two ensigns into letting her go.

After a few minutes, Williams started to wonder whether he was losing his way. He pressed on, knowing that the woods were not large and that he should strike the path at some point if he kept going. A little later he saw the ground rise slightly, and realised that he must have gone too far to the left. He veered the other way and finally came to where the trees were thinner. The path was near and suddenly he heard hoof-beats. There was a rocky outcrop crowned by a long-rooted elm just where the path turned away from the riverbank. Williams had just enough time to get into its shelter. There was excitement that he had beaten them and would have surprise on his side. He waited, readying himself to leap, and when the sound of a trotting horse came so close that it must be at the bend itself, Williams sprang out. He was shouting, with his shako in one hand as he waved his arms and placed himself in the middle of the path.

Jane MacAndrews screamed. Her horse reared and she struggled to keep her balance and rein the mare in. Williams gaped in astonishment, then just managed to jump backwards and avoid the animal's front hoofs as they thrashed against the air. Jane lost her hat, and her red hair came unpinned and flew around her face. A good rider, she had ridden this grey only once before and knew her to be skittish. She felt herself slipping, her weight shifting backwards and to the left and her knee coming off the support of the side saddle. The mare was now turning in close circles. Dimly she recognised that it was Mr Williams who now seemed to be running round and flapping his arms in half-hearted preparation to catch her or give support. The idiot plainly knew little about horses and was only making the beast more nervous.

The mare reared again, and Jane lost her balance altogether and felt herself falling backwards. The horse cantered away back down the path. For a moment the girl fell, then she struck Williams, knocking him down and landing on top of him. Jane was a little dazed, and Hamish winded and at first unable to speak. There was silence for a while.

'Well, I trust your intentions are honourable,' said the girl. She was staring up at the blue sky, her back resting on the body of the volunteer. One hand reached down and touched bare skin, but she did not feel real alarm and certainly kept any trace of this out of her voice.

Her hair was in Williams' mouth and brushing over his face. It felt quite wonderfully soft, and he had to cough before he could speak, although what came out was still barely coherent.

'I . . . of course, of course. Must apologise . . . Have behaved abominably . . .'

'Do you make a habit of jumping out on poor innocent girls whenever they go riding? And apparently half naked as well.'

'It's all a mistake,' Williams blurted out, sounding rather like a child caught in the midst of some prank and hoping to escape punishment. 'I thought you were Redman and Hatch.'

'Then I shall modify the question. Do you make a habit of wandering about half naked and jumping out on your fellow officers?' Williams could hear the amusement in her voice and suddenly was himself laughing. Jane joined in, and for a while they both simply laughed at the ridiculous situation. Williams laughed until he could hardly breathe.

'Mr Williams, I am quite safe and unharmed,' said Jane eventually. 'You can let go of me!'

Hamish realised that his right hand had slipped around the girl's slender waist. His left rested on her skirt and could dimly feel her thigh beneath.

'I am so very sorry,' he said nervously, through another mouthful of wispy red hair. 'I did not realise.'

The girl rolled off him and knelt up on her hands. She smiled as she looked at the discomforted Williams.

'Mama called you a Viking. I do not think that is adequate. You are clearly a satyr.' The volunteer babbled more incoherent apologies and claims that she had misunderstood. Jane stood up, taking care not to tread on the skirt of her russet riding habit. Then she very pointedly looked up at the sky.

'Is it impolite to enquire why you are not wearing breeches?' she asked.

Williams rose to a crouch and then stood up, all the while frantically tugging his shirt-tails downwards and uttering even

137

more apologies. Finally he managed a coherent account of what had happened.

'Is this Miss Dobson dark haired and wearing a deep blue skirt?'

Williams nodded. He thought Jenny's skirt was blue, although could not say that he had noticed.

'Then your quest may have been unnecessary. I passed her some while ago walking back to camp. She bid me good day by name so I guessed she was from the regiment. From what you say the girl must have come to her senses. She cannot have been with those two for very long. No harm done.' At least not today, thought Jane, but kept it to herself. She was not sure how well the evidently quixotic Williams might cope with such a cynical suggestion.

Jane MacAndrews shaded her eyes as she looked down the path. Her grey had long since vanished. The girl patted her unruly hair. 'I must look a mess,' she said, half to herself.

'You look perfectly beautiful,' said Williams, surprised at the assurance of his own voice and the boldness with which he spoke.

'A gallant satyr. You really are an unusual gentleman, Mr Williams.' He held out her hat, which had been sadly trampled by the horse and looked beyond repair. 'Oh dear,' she said, 'I was rather fond of that. Now, I would be grateful if you would assist me in recovering my horse. She was only borrowed.'

They walked side by side along the path, Miss MacAndrews carefully keeping her gaze high, either scanning the landscape for her horse or occasionally looking up at the tall man beside her. Williams could not remember being so happy. To his amazement his shyness had vanished, and they talked lightly. Jane first spoke of horses, but as it soon became clear that his knowledge was extremely limited, she asked instead about his earlier life. He spoke of bustling ports, of sailors and their stories of far-flung voyages, of his sisters, and his mother. Miss MacAndrews appeared to be entranced, and whenever he tried to turn the conversation to her own life and her time in America, she quickly asked him another question about himself.

To Williams' lasting regret, they found the grey mare before very long. It was standing under the shade of a tree, happily crop-ping the long grass. As he made to creep towards it and grab the trailing reins, the girl stopped him. She approached cautiously, talking softly and making sure that the animal was calm. The grey's ears flicked back, but it remained still and let the girl pat its neck. Only then did she take the reins and lead it round and back on to the path.

'Would you give me a leg,' she said, reaching up to grasp the horn of the saddle. Williams leaned and cupped his hands so that the girl could place her booted foot into them.

'Thank you, Mr Williams, for a quite extraordinary ride,' she said with a warm smile as she looked down at him. 'I will see you again this evening.'

'Miss MacAndrews?' he asked.

'At eight, I believe, yourself and several of the other young gentlemen are invited to dine with us at the cottage. Be prompt, mind you. Father hates unpunctuality.'

'Major MacAndrews has mentioned nothing.'

'Oh, I doubt Father knows, but Mama has arranged it and that is all there is to it.'

It was hard to argue with such assurance. 'In that case I shall look forward to it.'

'By the way, we are fairly informal at home. However, I should warn you that we do have some standards. The wearing of breeches, for instance.'

Rather foolishly Williams found himself looking down, having almost forgotten his unorthodox state of dress. When he looked up again the girl was already riding fast down the towpath, one arm raised in a leisurely wave.

14

Lieutenant Colonel George Moss savoured the taste of Sir Richard Langley's port. It was exceedingly good, as were the cigars and the conversation, but his warm glow owed even more to his satisfaction with the events of the evening. He had arrived at Longville House at 4.30 after a hard ride from his regiment's camp. The annoyance at that morning's exercise had only served to make him ride even faster and more recklessly than usual. At 5.15 he had proposed to and been accepted by Sir Richard's daughter, Emily. By six her father had given his consent to the marriage. Sir Richard's fortune was moderate – less than Moss's own family – but certainly acceptable when combined with his influence. The girl herself was pretty enough, if a little insipid, but would not disgrace Moss in any company and could no doubt run a household well enough. All in all Moss was satisfied.

After the ladies had retired the serious talk began. Sir Richard's guests included an admiral and a general. Moss already knew much of what Langley told them, and was warmed by this sense of greater confidence. Yet he still learned new things, as Sir Richard confirmed the rumour that the Duke of York had been desperate to take command of the expedition to Spain, but that the government had adamantly refused. The general was cautious about the whole business, although the admiral assured him that the navy would land the army wherever it wanted to go, and take it off again if needs be. Both were concerned about the size of the French army in Spain and Portugal. Sir Richard let them know that Sir John Moore's force, due to return from an ineffective cruise to the Baltic, would be sent to reinforce Wellesley.

This was important news to Moss. 'Will Moore take command? He is senior.' Sir John Moore had a fine reputation, only partly dented by the recent shambles, when he had briefly been arrested in Sweden.

Sir Richard shook his head. 'Moore is Whig. Apart from that he is only a little older than Wellesley. They are sending several more senior generals so the command will go to one of them.' He did not know who it would be, because again even the government had not yet managed to work that out. 'Everything is changing by the day. Indeed, George, you have been especially fortunate to be included in the enterprise at all.' Moss raised an eyebrow and hoped he did not betray the alarm he felt. 'There were several other regiments clamouring to go in place of you, claiming seniority and a higher state of preparedness. Lord Johnny was especially ardent in pushing the claims of his fusiliers.'

'There is no regiment as fit for active service as the 106th,' Moss asserted. 'Just let us at the French.' The general and the admiral thumped the table appreciatively. In truth Moss was less happy than he had been, no longer sure of some of his officers. Toye seemed a little too cautious, and he was now less convinced of the wisdom of promoting MacAndrews, although he knew that not to have done so would have caused resentment. Already he was wondering how he might dispose of both majors, as well as some of the captains.

'What really happened with Hawker?' asked Sir Richard with artificial innocence. 'Lord Johnny made a lot of that. Said a regiment that had been led by a madman could not be in much of a state.'

'There have been plenty of those before,' put in the admiral, delighted with his own wit.

Moss took care to stay calm, and was glad that the laughter gave him a moment. 'Major Hawker was simply ill and died suddenly. Nothing more. I trust that Horse Guards no longer have any doubts about the 106th.'

'Officially, no.' Sir Richard was choosing his words carefully.

'Privately, I should avoid any hint of scandal or disorder. At least until you are on board ship.'

A much less grand dinner was held at the MacAndrews' rented cottage, and the talk was initially more frivolous. Mrs Mosley and Mrs Kidwell were the only other ladies. The Wickhams had been invited, but had declined owing to an existing engagement. As well as their husbands, there were also Truscott, Pringle, Hanley, Williams, Anstey and young Derryck.

The major had not been overenthusiastic about the evening gathering when his wife informed him about it. After the morning's exercise he was uncertain of the colonel's mood and had no wish to give the impression that he was creating a faction within the battalion. Still, he had long since admitted to himself that his wife would have her way when it came to social events. It was even more impressive than usual how well and how quickly she had prepared everything, especially since Jane had been out for so much of the day on one of her rides. She had returned with a ruined hat and slightly mud-stained clothes, but as yet he had been unable to discover just what had happened.

The meal was pleasant. He had to admit that. Even Derryck, who normally ate like a man who had been starved for a month, appeared to be satisfied and refused an additional helping of beef. At first MacAndrews had managed no more than formal politeness, but as the evening passed he relaxed and genuinely began to enjoy himself. He was proud of his wife and daughter – used to how the former could get away with some outrageous comments, and impressed with the latter's ease at conversing with anyone. She even managed to draw out the quartermaster, who was notoriously uncomfortable and taciturn in most company.

At 9.30 the ladies went for a walk in the small garden behind the house. The men took their ease, sharing some brandy once the single bottle of port was exhausted. The subject quickly turned to the coming campaign.

'The French are good. Very good,' said Mosley after a burst of enthusiastic bravado from Derryck. He had fought in India with another regiment before exchanging into the 106th.

'Aye, they are brave men,' agreed Kidwell. As a young private soldier he had served in Flanders and later in another disastrous expedition, this time to the Dutch coast. 'Skilful, too.'

'We should never forget that they have hammered half of Europe. However much we despise their upstart of an emperor, he and his men know how to fight.' Mosley seemed to decide that that was enough and relapsed into silence, taking a long draw from his glass.

'Napoleon isn't in Spain, though,' said Pringle after a pause, when it was clear that Mr Kidwell was also disinclined to add anything.

'Not yet, anyway, according to the papers.' Truscott paused to refill his glass. 'He could be there before we arrived if he chose to join his forces. Depends a bit on how far he trusts the Austrians and Prussians to keep quiet.'

'A lot of his best regiments are still on the Rhine and Danube.' Williams spoke with a surprising confidence, feeling for once less awkward in formal company. He was wearing a jacket borrowed from Private Murphy, who was close to his size. His own was at this moment being repaired by Mrs Dobson, for he had managed to spot it caught on a branch that hung over the river. His trousers had vanished altogether. Fortunately he had another pair, although this evening he had donned the more formal breeches and gaiters.

'Yes, the French officers I spoke to in Madrid complained that most of their men were half-trained conscripts.' They all looked at Hanley in surprise. Although some of them knew that he had been in Spain during the invasion, he had said next to nothing about it. 'I saw some of them. They looked younger than our Mr Derryck.' For a moment he had a vision of the mutilated corpses in Madrid. 'They know how to kill, though.'

'We are not the most mature battalion ourselves.' Kidwell the quartermaster was in his late thirties, but looked older. 'I was only seventeen in my first battle. In some ways it is easier for the young. At that age death is something that can only happen to other people.'

They asked for more details of Hanley's experiences. Grudgingly at first he told them of the parades through the streets, the exhibition of the Emperor's own tents and equipment in one of the parks, and finally the savagery of 2nd May. He tried to keep his account restrained, but his face grew taut when he thought back to the sabres rising and falling amid the fleeing crowd.

There was a sober silence after he had finished.

'War is rarely a pretty business,' said MacAndrews eventually. He had spoken little earlier on, content mainly to listen and ask only occasional questions, but was aware of his duty as host. 'Especially a war when civilians fight.' His mind had gone back to the brutal struggles in America, the skirmishes and battles when no one British had been present, but Loyalists had fought Patriots, Tories had fought Whigs, and lynchings had been common. That scarcely seemed a suitable topic for the table, so instead he retold a favourite story.

'I mind the time I first fought the French. They had landed an army to help the rebels attack us in Savannah. Worst country you ever saw in your life. Swamps and streams and forests as thick as jungle. And flies, always flies.' It was rare to hear MacAndrews talk socially, and even rarer to hear him speak with such enthusiasm. Before his wife arrived it would have been unimaginable. They all craned forward to listen.

'Well, anyway, they had decided to launch a surprise attack at dawn, moving against what they thought was the weakest bit of our fortifications. My old corps – the seventy-first – were the only regulars there. The rest of the garrison was a ragbag of volunteers. Brave enough, but inexperienced.

'We knew the French and the Yankees were coming, so the seventy-first were moved to meet the attack. Our pipers greeted the dawn by playing "Hey Johnny Cope". Let them know we had smoked them and the highlanders were waiting to entertain them.' MacAndrews smiled at the memory. 'They still attacked. Hard to say by then whether it was heroism or folly. Probably just too late to call it off. Well, we simply mowed them down like wheat before the scythe. Never saw men come on better, though. It was hopeless, but the French especially just kept on coming.'

'Ah, my husband is talking of Savannah once again.' They had not noticed Esther MacAndrews enter at the head of the ladies. 'It always cheers him up, although I dare say he has failed to mention that one of my own cousins was killed that day, fighting to make a new country.'

'You never liked him much,' retorted the major cheerfully.

'That is beside the point. Charles Swanson may well have been an ugly louse of a man, but he was still my kin, and you and your Scotsmen spilt his blood.'

'Well, we were brutal tyrannical redcoats.'

'I know, I married you.' MacAndrews kissed his wife's hand. 'Enough of this martial talk,' she declared. 'I have decided that there is enough light for you to escort us ladies on a short stroll through the town. So you must all make yourselves respectable.' Williams noticed that she looked at him knowingly as she said this, and wondered whether her daughter had repeated the whole story. It was hard to say, most of Esther MacAndrews' looks were knowing. Sadly, Pringle and Derryck rushed to escort Jane, one on either side. Williams moved to accompany the Kidwells, but at an imperious gesture from Mrs MacAndrews he fell in alongside the major and his wife.

'I hear you are well read in the classics, Mr Williams,' the major's wife drawled after a while. 'Come now, you must tell us all about nymphs and satyrs.'

'I think I shall hire a new maid,' said Maria, looking at the handful of gold coins Count Denilov had put on the table. She spoke in English, for he had no Portuguese, and she now hated to use French, since Napoleon's men had invaded her country.

'You make a good maid,' he said with an easy smile. His accent was strong, but there was no hesitation in his use of the language. Maria had a number of costumes which she knew her clients enjoyed. One was a plain black dress, with the white apron and mob cap of a servant girl. The skirt of the dress was hooped in the outdated fashion, and much shorter than any normal clothes. She would pretend to clean the place, bending over so that her legs were visible as far as her knees or even higher. Sooner or later the man would pounce, and then she would pretend to be a surprised innocent, resisting in a way that pleased them, until she 'let' herself be seduced or overcome.

'But I don't get to do much cleaning,' she replied, and smiled at the handsome Russian officer, who lay in just his breeches and shirt on the bed. 'Especially with you.' Denilov had discovered her costumes and insisted that she wear each in turn, but showed a great fondness for the maid. He paid, and paid well, but there was something extra, for in the last two weeks she had taken no other clients. For the first time in months she had felt secure. He was a hard man, and she was glad of it.

Most of the other clients with money were French, and she refused to accept them at any price, but many were very persistent. She had been with an ambitious young lawyer, who had decided that it was better to win the trust of the occupying army than die fighting it. He had even been willing to sacrifice his new mistress to the whim of a fat French colonel who showed an interest when Maria had accompanied her lover to a formal reception. The lawyer had vanished, but then Denilov had appeared through the crowd and frightened the Frenchman away. Maria had willingly taken him back to her room that night. Since then he had scared away any more of the conquerors who had pestered her. Mainly she stayed in her rented room, and when he came to visit each day they rarely chose to go out.

'Look at that.' Maria was naked except for her stockings and a red ribbon in her hair, but could feel him watching as she picked up a plate of stale bread that lay on the floor and carried it over to the window. It was open, for it was a warm afternoon, and she broke the bread with her fingers and tossed the pieces out. 'There, the mice shall starve and the birds grow fat.

'This place is so squalid,' she said wearily. They were in the attic of one of the tall houses beneath Lisbon castle, overlooking the harbour. Some of her clothes were piled on chairs, for there were few cupboards. A jug with water lay beside a basin on the table, but the pump was down in the yard and she had to go herself to fetch more. 'A year ago I could have entertained you in splendour.'

'A year ago you would not have needed me. You had the duke.'

The black-haired girl stuck her tongue out at him. 'What I need and what I want are not the same. Nor is what I get.' She walked back towards the bed. 'You would have wanted me and the duke was not jealous as long as I was discreet. I can be very discreet.' Her hands were on her hips.

'So I see,' he said. Maria grabbed a pillow and hit him.

'He is a good man,' she declared after a moment. The duke had been her protector for eighteen months. Her family had once been his tenants, running a farm near the coast. Maria was not quite fifteen when her mother had taken sick and died. Her father did not cope, and drank himself into debt. They lost their home, and travelled wherever he could get work, and often he was too drunk to know when the men came for her. Then one morning he simply did not wake up.

Maria had survived. She learned to please and manipulate men and somehow keep a small part of herself locked away. She was very pretty and she was very charming. Soon she could refuse the brutes and drunks, and take her pick from clients who were rich and fairly kind. It surprised her how desperate many of them were to please her. In the better years a series of protectors paid for her apartment, her maid and a lifestyle that was close to opulent. Then the duke saw her on the arm of another man at a dinner in Coimbra. He recognised her, and there was genuine pity along with the lust. The duke took Maria as his principal mistress and she lived in comfort and the greatest security she had known since her childhood.

Then the French came, and the duke escaped to Portugal's American colonies along with the royal court. He took all of the treasure he could readily gather, and he also took his wife. She did not permit him to take his mistress. He had tried to send Maria gifts sufficient to keep her safe in the turmoil of war, but his wife had prevented his steward from passing them on.

'If I could have seen Varandas I am sure that I could have convinced him,' said Maria firmly, playfully stepping back when Denilov reached out for her. 'The old man was always drooling after me.'

The Russian leaned back. 'And Varandas is the steward.' His expression had changed subtly, and Maria realised for the first time that she might have made a mistake. She did not answer for a while.

'Of course he is, who else would he be.'

Denilov lit a cigar and took a deep, almost sensual breath. The duke had not had time to collect all of his valuables, and nor did he altogether trust the safety of banks when invaders were overrunning the country. Denilov had heard the rumours along with so many others as he mixed with the occupying army and the leading Portuguese who collaborated with them. He might have thought no more of it, and followed another trail, until someone pointed out Maria to him as the duke's former mistress.

Denilov trusted his luck and immediately knew that this was the path to follow. He had brushed aside the Frenchman bothering her, then spent the next two weeks cultivating her. Now he knew almost everything. Varandas' name was virtually the last important piece of the puzzle, for he had been the man the duke trusted to conceal and protect the rest of his fortune when the French were looting Portugal down to its bare bones. The presents to Maria were just a small part of the gold and gems hidden somewhere on the man's estate. Some was to be entrusted to the religious orders to fund charitable works, and more simply to be kept safe. He had found out this much from the girl, confirming what he already suspected.

'Of course I would have told you about Varandas. You will need to know to help me find what is mine.' Maria tried to sound confident, but there was now a coldness about the Russian officer which she had not seen before. She had so wanted to find a man who would rescue her, someone she could trust, perhaps even love for longer than just a few weeks. The handsome foreign officer had seemed so strong, and so kind when she had known little kindness for some time. Maria had wanted to trust. Now he frightened her. She crossed her hands over her chest. She had not felt nervous at being naked in front of a man for many years – not unless it was part of an act to please a lover.

Denilov noticed the gesture and smiled.

'You won't find him without me.' Maria had not been sure whether she wanted the treasure apart from the presents marked for her by the duke. Sometimes she imagined herself rich for the rest of her life. Sometimes she was a patriot, spending the duke's money to pay and arm the soldiers who would drive the French from her homeland. She would be a heroine, and perhaps that would make people forget her past, and she could be respectable. There were vague pictures in her mind of a house with some land, of a husband who was a good man, and of infants – a world as secure and truly happy as the memories of her own childhood.

The Russian said nothing, but drew deeply on his cigar.

'If you ask too many questions people will guess what you are looking for.'

'You know where he is,' he said, breaking his silence, but the words were in French.

'I can show you,' the girl said, sticking to English.

'You will tell me. Now.' He stood up and flexed his arms, but his eyes never left her for a moment.

'I could scream,' she said with a confidence she did not feel.

'They have heard it before. Who do you think would come?' The Russian threw down his cigar, and smiled again.

Denilov left half an hour later, walking out into the warm sunshine and then standing for a moment to let the heat soak into him. The girl had not told him where Varandas would be, and after a while he had no longer even bothered to ask the question. It did not matter, and it should not be too difficult to track the man down. Denilov paused by the door, feeling in his pockets for another cigar. His last was gone, so he walked out to buy some more, with the coins he had picked up from the girl's table. He had enjoyed taking her by force, seeing real emotion and fear instead of the studied performance of a whore. She ought to be terrified enough to cause him no problems, but in truth there was little that she could do.

Back in her room, Maria crouched beside the bed, clutching a sheet around her, her knuckles white with intensity as she sobbed. There was pain and shattered hope, but for the first time in years all the worst memories had come flooding back. Her whole body shook as she wept. An hour later she stopped, and began to swear. She called Denilov every insult she knew in Portuguese, then switched to English and finally even flung at his memory the filthiest names she could recall in French. Someone knocked on her door, complaining at last of the noise. Oddly it calmed her. Maria called out an apology, ignored the sullen response, and then stood up, wincing because of her bruises. She wanted what was hers, and she wanted to hurt Denilov, but despair came back when she could not think of a way to achieve either of these. Yet she did not cry any more. Using the water that was left in the jug, Maria began to clean herself.

15

For the next three mornings the adjutant drilled the battalion from eight o'clock until half past ten. Then there were company drills and musketry until one. After a break of two hours to rest and refresh, there were route marches or runs and other physical exercises. Moss pushed his battalion in the final days before they were to march to Portsmouth and embark. There was little time for further social pleasures, although life in the mess was still sometimes boisterous. The colonel had let it be known, however, that no serious misbehaviour would be permitted. Officers were reminded that above their own sense of personal honour they owed a duty to the regiment. Their conduct over the next week was to be impeccable. Moss drove the 106th hard.

Hanley was weary as he sat at the end of the third day and sketched Jenny Dobson. A week earlier he had been moved to draw for the first time since he had left Madrid. He had sat in the tent lines and sketched the grenadiers as they took their meal, sitting or standing in all states of uniform, with their wives and children around them. Jenny had seen him, had come to look over his shoulder. Normally he hated anyone watching him work, but there was a childlike enthusiasm about the girl which was winning and more than a little at odds with her normal manner. When he had finished, he gave her the picture, and she had asked him whether he would take her likeness. There had not been an opportunity until now, although on several occasions he had been moved to pick up his pencil and pad since then, and had done several hasty outlines of men on the march or drilling. Rather to his surprise, he was starting to enjoy this new life and was happy enough to want to draw. He had even wondered about obtaining some better paper, and digging his watercolours out from his trunk.

Once again he sat on a bale of straw among the company's tents. The girl sat on a folding stool borrowed from Billy Pringle with the white of a tent behind her. At first they had gathered quite a crowd, with a few of the men making faces at the girl and trying to make her laugh. She had joked and cursed back at them, until eventually most lost interest and went about their ordinary tasks.

Hanley had always liked the clarity and contrast of a pencil sketch, enjoying the way that shape and texture needed to be hinted at. He was shading the girl's face as delicately as he could. Jenny was young, her features not yet set, and Hanley tried to capture that softness. Her curly hair reminded him a little of Mapi, at least when he drew it and it became black like the Spanish girl's. No one yet seemed to know where in Spain they were going. Some said Gibraltar and others the north coast. Both were a long way from Madrid, but he wondered whether they would end up there and if he would see Mapi again, assuming she was alive. If so, then what would he say?

Jenny was trying to stay very still, even though he had told her it was not necessary. Her nose began to twitch, and after a bitter struggle she finally gave in and reached up to scratch it. The girl looked guilty.

Hanley smiled. 'Nearly done, Miss Dobson.' He kept his tone formal, wishing to show the girl's formidable father that he was employing proper respect. The family had announced only yesterday that the girl was to marry the large and quiet Private Hanks. Rumours were rife, both about her allegedly wanton behaviour and the suggestion that she might be with child. Dobson had taken the young couple before Captain Wickham and received his permission for them to marry. There would be a brief service after the church parade on the next day. Jenny was wearing the new dress bought for her by her parents, which she would also don for the ceremony. It had lace around the collar and she was very proud of it. Hanley took care to draw the detail as well as he could. The sketch would be his main present, although the company officers were making a collection to give to the young couple.

Money was a worry for Hanley. As an ensign he was supposed to receive five shillings and threepence a day. More than a shilling went before the pay came anywhere near him, lost in tax, agency and poundage. Two and a half more were deducted and paid straight to the mess, and even though Lieutenant Colonel Moss matched this fee with his own funds it was still a substantial amount. Then there was sixpence to his soldier servant, as much again to provide the necessaries for breakfast as well as a little tea for the day, and finally another fivepence to the company's wives for washing and mending his clothes. As far as he could see, service to King and country had him barely avoiding making a loss each day. It was not a life permitting of any luxuries.

He had less than a pound remaining from the money given to him by his father's family. There had been more, but thirty-five guineas was on loan to Captain Wickham. It had seemed a reasonable request at the time – a mark of friendship and trust, suggesting that he was now accepted in the battalion. Yet weeks had gone by and the loan 'till the end of the week' showed no prospect of being returned. It was also a difficult subject to broach.

Hanley looked down at the drawing. It was done. He knew that he could spend hours adjusting and modifying the sketch, but that for every improvement he made he would lose more of its essence. Smiling, he stood and walked over to the girl, handing her the pad. Jenny Dobson looked at it intently.

'That's me,' she said firmly. 'That's me.' Turning her head she called to her family. 'Come and see my picture.'

'Seen you before,' muttered her brother as he strolled towards them.

'Thank you, Mr Hanley, sir, it's lovely.' She rose, standing on tiptoe, and as he leaned over to tear the page from the pad she kissed him on the cheek. Her eyes flicked back to her approaching parents, and then she kissed him again, sliding her mouth until for just a moment her tongue flicked into his ear. The girl's thick hair stopped them from seeing anything.

Hanley straightened up, and then bowed to her, keeping his face as expressionless as he could. There was certainly not too much of the child left in this one.

'A pleasure, Miss Dobson. I have rarely drawn so agreeable a subject. May I say that Private Hanks is a lucky man.'

'Yes, he is,' said the girl.

Hanley managed to withdraw fairly quickly after only brief expressions of admiration by the rapidly gathering crowd. Dobson simply nodded his approval, thought for a moment, and then offered the ensign his hand. Even though he had expected it, Hanley was still surprised by the firmness of his grip. The man seemed to be made of iron.

After a quick visit to the tent he shared with Pringle, Redman and Williams to deposit pad and pencils and tidy himself up, Hanley reported to the adjutant for another hour's drill. This was a daily routine for all the recently joined officers and soldiers in the battalion. It was no longer something he resented. Indeed, he had discovered a strange poetry in the drill movements, an odd sense of losing himself in the group unlike anything he had ever known before. It had a dance-like, almost spiritual quality.

'Mr Hanley, sir! Keep your bloody arm straight, who do you think you're waving to!' bawled Sergeant Major Fletcher.

'Platoon, halt. Right face! Present arms!' For just a second the RSM drew breath. 'As you were, as you were.' He paced along the line, back ramrod straight, his stick tucked ferociously under his arm. 'Now I'm glad Mr Thomas can't see you. You see, he's a sick man. It'd kill him to see you! Now, we will do it again.'

If anything, there was even less of a spiritual quality to the celebrations in the mess that evening. Tomorrow was Sunday, and the battalion would rest and 'make and mend', repairing and cleaning uniforms and equipment. On the Monday morning they would begin the march to Portsmouth. The Saturday night was devoted to dinner in honour of Moss's engagement. All officers were expected to attend, but the occasion was not open to wives, which gave a good indication of the type of celebration envisaged by the colonel. Champagne specially brought down from his own stocks flowed freely for a good three hours, before other bottles appeared.

Toasts were drunk to the colonel and his lady, to the regiment, to the army, to the King, to England, and to anything else they could imagine. Songs were sung, loudly and lustily, if with scant regard for tune or rhythm. As usual 'Spanish Ladies' was one of the most popular. A pitched battle was fought between the subalterns of the left and right wings, lobbing bread rolls from the heights of the long trestle tables which ran down either side of the room. Moss and the senior officers watched from the gallery above, and periodically lobbed apples at anyone they felt deserved to become a target. After that, things became a little more lively.

The main event was the joust, with the officers paired off in teams as charger and knight. The grenadiers inevitably found themselves acting as horses. Williams carried young Derryck, who proved himself a deft hand with the pillow used as a weapon. Especially satisfying was a rapid victory over Redman as charger and Hatch as knight, aided greatly by the latter's advanced state of drunkenness. Hanley and Anstey offered more of a struggle, as surprisingly did a diminutive combination from the Light Company. In the end they faced the final challenge of Pringle and young Trent.

That battle lasted for a good five minutes, the two knights slogging away with pillows while the horses circled. Williams almost slipped on a puddle of spilled port, but managed to steady himself and grab Derryck before he tumbled down. Everything would probably have been fine had not Pringle seized the moment to shoulder-charge the volunteer. Williams and Derryck were flung back, knocking down one of the tables. Trent fell, but Pringle caught him and held him upside down by the legs, loudly proclaiming their victory. The shouted opinions on this seemed more in their favour than against, and Truscott's comments on the value of an Oxford education were all but drowned out.

All in all it was a highly successful evening, especially since the injuries were all minor. Proceedings were less formal after the joust, but continued for another couple of hours. By then, a number of officers were slumped over the tables snoring noisily and exposed to the practical pleasantries of their comrades.

Williams had managed to avoid Redman and Hatch apart from during the joust. Sharing a tent, it was impossible to have nothing to do with Redman, but the ensign curbed his now bitter hostility when the other grenadier officers were present. As far as was possible, the two men ignored each other.

It was around two when Hanley, Pringle and Williams came out into the night air. The two officers needed to relieve themselves, so the volunteer waited for them, leaning against the side wall of the inn. He had discovered that he rather liked champagne, which seemed unfortunate given the state of his finances. Although the wilder aspects of mess life had never appealed to him, there had been an air of excitement about the evening which had in itself been intoxicating. The prospect of going to war, and the knowledge that both life and honour might well depend on the quality of the men standing beside you, was a powerful bond. For all their drunkenness and ribaldry, Williams felt very close to the officers of the 106th.

The sound of violent retching came from behind him. He turned to see Hatch bent over double as he threw up on the ground. Redman was patting him on the back. Williams felt a truce was in order.

'Quite a night, eh?'

'What the devil would you know about it, you goddamned peasant!' Redman's hatred was surprising. Even Hatch looked up with a puzzled expression.

'Just making conversation.' Williams' reply was mild, but he felt his anger rising.

'Kiss my arse!' Redman was almost screaming. Hatch tried to hush him, but was ignored. 'It's a bloody disgrace, having people like you pretending to be gentlemen.'

Williams shrugged. 'You are drunk, otherwise I might take that personally.'

'I'm not drunk enough,' claimed Hatch.

Williams turned to walk away, making sure he moved slowly. Pringle and Hanley had emerged and looked confused.

'Don't you damned well dare turn your back on me,' yelled Redman. 'You hear me! You're nothing. A piece of Welsh shit!' Williams' fingers flexed, but he kept on walking.

'That wasn't the first time I've had Jenny Dobson. Same with Hatch. You liked seeing her tits, didn't you?' Hatch was straight now, nervously watching the confrontation. 'She's just a young slut. A whore like your mother!' Redman threw the taunts at Williams' back, encouraged by his refusal to be drawn.

Pringle and Hanley came up to the volunteer. They fell in on either side of him and Pringle tapped him on the shoulder. Williams started at the touch.

'Forget it, Bills. He's just a drunk. Not worth the trouble,' whispered Pringle.

'You call yourself a gentleman. Where is your honour? Damn me, you're a coward. A gutless coward.' Redman was following, enjoying his victory. Hatch tried to pull him away, but he shook his friend off. 'You think you're better than me. You and your God.'

Williams kept walking with the others, one either side of him. Redman stopped his pursuit, was about to stalk away and then added as an afterthought, 'Better than me, are you, you damned saint? What about Jane MacAndrews? We saw you. Wouldn't mind ploughing her myself. Was she good?'

Redman was laughing when Williams spun on his heels, brushed off his friends and strode right up to him.

'I will fight you any time and anywhere. With pistol or with blade.' He almost spat the words. Redman's eyes showed surprise, but no fear.

'A pleasure,' he said, seeming now a lot more sober. 'I'll enjoy killing you.'

'Mr Pringle will act for me.' Billy had forgotten his promise, never guessing that it would be taken up.

'And Hatch for me.' The nominated second was busy throwing up again.

'Then there is no more to be said. Good night to you.' Williams made a very precise about-turn and marched off five paces. Then he stopped. Slowly he turned and marched back as neatly as he had come. A few feet away from Redman he swung into a punch and his right fist struck the ensign cleanly under the chin. Redman dropped.

'I forgot the insult,' said Williams, and about-turned once again. Pringle joined him as he marched away, putting one arm around his shoulder. Hanley caught up with them.

'That's not quite the way you are supposed to do it,' Pringle said mildly. Privately he was afraid his friend had just thrown away his career.

16

If Pringle hoped that the two men would have forgotten the challenge by the time they woke up then he was disappointed. He tried reasoning with Hatch. The ensign showed little enthusiasm for the duel, but had spoken to his friend and knew that Redman was adamant. Hatch could not really understand why. Pringle took him to see the adjutant, and Thomas made it abundantly clear that the colonel would not approve. Duelling was prohibited by the *Articles of War*, the strict code of military discipline imposed on the army by Horse Guards. Anyone surviving a duel would face court martial, and anyone who killed another in a duel was to be treated as a murderer.

These were hard rules to enforce, and often all witnesses somehow forgot everything when it came to giving testimony, as the regiment accepted that honour was involved. Mr Thomas made it clear that Moss would not permit this. If the young fools did not kill each other then they would certainly be dismissed. The adjutant also promised to keep quiet about the whole affair in the hope that the pair would come to their senses.

Hatch spoke again to Redman, and Pringle spent time with him as well as trying to reason with Williams. Hanley also did his best, and after a consultation they enlisted the ever affable Truscott, letting him in on the secret. Nothing worked. Redman could not remember the cause of the argument, but knew that he loathed Williams. He simply could not permit himself to back down. Williams spoke passionately about honour and defending a lady's reputation. After a while he fell silent and simply looked stubborn and mulish.

Somehow they managed to convince them to wait. Williams in particular was a little reluctant to fight on a Sunday. They attended the church parade along with the rest of the battalion. No army chaplain was available, but Moss had pulled a few strings and secured the services of the dean of the nearest cathedral. It seemed proper to have a ceremony and ask divine blessing before the regiment went off to war. Afterwards Jenny Dobson married James Hanks in a much smaller affair conducted by the local curate, a painfully thin and lisping individual, who was very glad of his modest fee. The proper words were said and the marriage made legal, and Williams read a psalm and prayed at Dobson's request. The old soldier had wanted someone who really believed to take part in the service, hoping this would make the bond more powerful. He had chosen Hanks for the girl, although Jenny had readily agreed. A quiet, gentle man, he would most likely be dominated by her, but at least he would be kind. Her father hoped she would respond to that and be faithful in turn. A lot of girls had worse husbands. Dobson knew that Hanks was not the father of the child growing in her belly. It did not matter, he was a good man and knew the truth.

After the ceremony there was a meal with most of the company invited. Finally, the new couple were escorted to a tent laid aside for their own use for the rest of the day – the men from it were crowded into other tents or would sleep beneath the stars. It would probably be the only taste of privacy the pair would have during their army life.

Even Williams was in no mood to think of fighting for the rest of the day. It was pleasant to have a leisurely day, although he was a little piqued when Pringle and Hanley insisted on accompanying him on a walk. In the event it was pleasant. They talked of history and books, and told stories of places they had been and people they knew. There were no chance meetings, agreeable or otherwise, and the whole country seemed to be asleep.

The next day the regiment marched off at 8.30 in the morning. The band played the inevitable 'Girl I Left Behind Me' and some of the men sang, changing the verse to 'and now I'm bound for Portsmouth camp'. There was no real crowd to see them off. They had not been there long enough for there to be many girls left behind. The soldiers' families walked at the rear of the column and the officers' wives rode or travelled in carriages.

The roads were good, and though the day was hot, the regiment made good progress. Each time they came to a town the band struck up and they marched at attention, but there were never any crowds – no cheers or garlands. Soldiers were not an uncommon sight, nor an especially welcome one. The English were not fond of their army. The local belles lacked interest in regiments that did not stay long enough to flirt. Honest folk despised all redcoats as the drunks and criminals that some of them were. They took care to lock their doors and guard their livestock, both female and animal. The best the 106th could hope for in each place was the appreciation of gangs of small boys, and the sight of an old veteran standing to attention or a retired officer raising his hat. Sailors were the heroes – and usually at sea and so out of sight. Soldiers were a burden on the kingdom. Who cared that they marched off on some far-flung expedition? It would no doubt end in disaster and shame like so many others. Enthusiasm for helping the Spanish did not extend much outside London, or persuade anyone to show affection for the soldiers who would do it.

On the second day the Grenadier Company at the head of the column halted at a crossroads to permit a fine coach to pass. Moss raised his hat to the elderly occupant, who gave no more than a curt nod in response. The man's companion, an elegantly dressed lady whose mature years were artfully concealed by her make-up, was more generous and leaned towards the window and waved a greeting. Her face was striking, and enough of her visible to hint at an excellent figure. Pringle whistled softly through his teeth.

'The perks of wealth,' he whispered to Hanley. 'I wonder if I shall ever be able to afford such things?'

The ensign did not reply for a moment, and Pringle turned to see his friend staring after the swiftly departing coach.

'I do believe that was my mother,' he said at last. Pringle could think of no response beyond a hurried apology. Hanley was not inclined to speak of it any more.

The days of marching were long and left everyone weary. Pringle was able to persuade Hatch to move slowly and so no time was set for the meeting. There was no success in convincing Williams and Redman to relent. Although there were rumours of a quarrel, it remained a secret that a challenge had actually been issued. Yet suspicions were roused and the adjutant reminded Pringle of his earlier comments and expressed a wish that no meeting should occur.

Another distraction came on the third day, when the regiment encountered the 20th Light Dragoons, also on their way to embark at Portsmouth. Their dark blue jackets had yellow facings, and were richly decorated in front with rows of white lace which grew wider at the top, to make the men's shoulders look bigger. Some of the officers affected pelisses, after the style of hussars. Officers and men alike wore tall black helmets with thick crests running from front to back.

'Tarletons,' muttered Major MacAndrews sourly. The headgear had been invented by Bloody Ban back in the American War. The Scotsman could remember the British Legion cavalry wearing the same helmets and their green uniforms as they galloped from the field at Cowpens and left the infantry stranded. MacAndrews was in a sour mood for the rest of the day, not helped by the frequent and 'accidental' comments by his wife and daughter as to how handsome the dragoons looked. Yet he was forced to be polite when the officers of the two regiments took lunch together at tables laid outside an inn. Moss presided, along with Lieutenant Colonel Taylor of the 20th.

There was usually a feeling of cordial loathing between different regiments in the British Army. Hostility between infantry and cavalry was even more firmly entrenched. Cavalry officers were paid more than their infantry counterparts. Their expenses were far higher, and service in the mounted regiments was almost exclusively confined to the rich and well connected. Still, the 20th's commander was a genial man, and showed particular delight at the discovery that Pringle had gone to Oxford. Taylor had been at Christ Church and the two managed to discover a few mutual acquaintances and common haunts.

Amid the toasts and laughter the usual jokes and insults were exchanged. Pringle told Hanley the story of the cavalry officer who was so stupid that even his fellow officers noticed it. Williams chipped in to suggest that that one had first been told by Julius Caesar. The dragoons responded with jibes about yokels who had to walk everywhere, and dressed up pretending to be soldiers.

The dragoons moved on that evening. The 106th stayed where they were, but paraded to salute the cavalry as they passed. Ironic cheers went up when the third squadron of the 20th marched out on foot. Space was limited on the transport ships, and they were supposed to receive horses when they landed in Spain. Nothing delighted infantrymen more than watching cavalrymen marching in their awkward boots and tight breeches. The sergeants of the 106th gave the men a few moments before barking out the orders to be quiet.

The battalion rested for three hours, to give the cavalry time to move on. Most of the men were allowed time off, but the adjutant insisted that the recruit platoon did an hour's drill. On this occasion he watched as Redman ordered them through their paces. This he did with some competence. Afterwards, Hanley felt this was a good opportunity to talk to his fellow ensign.

'Well done, John. I felt that even I knew what was happening some of the time.' He offered Redman his hand, and the latter took it after a moment.

'Well, some of the time is at least a start.'

'Nonsensical, really, that I am senior to you, and yet they would scarcely let me give orders to a single sentry.' Hanley was doing his best to be affable. Even sober, Redman was touchy and disliked any hint that he could be inferior.

'Well, if all of us had influence.' Redman's tone was sharp.

'Had is the word. The connection which got me my commission has now been permanently severed. I have no friends outside the regiment. I even have to survive on my pay!' As soon as he said it Hanley realised that that was a mistake. As far as he knew Redman's family gave him only the tiniest allowance and this caused him shame. Fortunately they had walked out of earshot of any of the men.

'Money is not everything.' There was no conviction in Redman's voice, but pride and suspicion.

'At least you have experience and talent.' Hanley decided that flattery might work if he could appear sincere. 'In war, advancement is open to the brave. Personally, I'll be lucky not to trip over my own sword, but you could easily make a name for yourself.'

'I will do my duty,' said Redman defensively. After a while he added, 'As I am sure will you.'

Oh well, all or nothing, thought Hanley. 'Yet all that will go when you kill Williams.'

'He has a chance in a duel.'

'Oh, think, man. He's just some lump of a religious clod. I'd back you any day with sword of pistol. He might be dangerous with a cudgel, but a gentleman's weapons . . . ?'

'Williams is your friend.' The suspicion had returned.

'He is. Well, I can't help feeling sorry for the poor fool. It's a bit like having a dog.' He grinned and was pleased when Redman joined in. 'On the whole I'd prefer it if he were still alive. I'd also prefer to go to Spain with you serving with the company, not dismissed by the colonel.'

'I won't back down,' said Redman with all the pride and conviction of his eighteen years.

'There is no need. Williams is already sorry. Knows he was wrong. Well, a milksop like him can't take his liquor or he would never have done it. He's just scared you are determined to kill him, but doesn't want anyone to know it. That is why he asked me to speak to you.'

Redman looked pleased. So Hanley pressed the case. 'Damn it, man, he is just not worth it. Think of your career. He's sorry, so the two of you can just shake hands and forget about it.'

'Will he apologise?'

'He can't, can he? For the same reason you can't. Couldn't face the regiment if they knew he had backed down, but is in a blue funk because he doesn't want to be killed. Isn't that satisfaction enough? As I say, he's just not worth it. Let the French kill him.'

Half an hour later Hanley sat with Williams in their tent.

'He's scared, Bills. In a blue funk because he knows you'll cut him to ribbons.'

'It is more than possible that he is a better swordsman.' Williams' mother had been able to afford only the most rudimentary lessons in fencing and dancing as he grew up. Recent experience had very publicly demonstrated his incompetence in the second of these skills.

Hanley smiled. 'Oh, come on. You're bigger and stronger than him. And in a fight I bet you are plain nastier. They don't call you Pug for nothing.'

Williams was surprised that any officer knew his nickname. 'Not quite the same as swords. I am a good shot, though,' he conceded.

'Of course you are. Look, Redman's a buffoon at the best of times, and that night he was so drunk he didn't know what he was doing. So you'll kill him and throw away your chance of a commission. What will you do, go back to counting totals as a clerk? That's not you, Hamish. You're a good soldier. Even I can see that and I have only been here five minutes. You always seem to know what you're doing. As soon as we have our first battle you'll be an officer.'

'It is very kind of you to say so.' Williams seemed genuinely pleased. 'I can't apologise, though. Not after what he said about, about . . .' Reluctant to mention Jane MacAndrews, he finished rather lamely. 'About everything.'

Hanley was fully aware of the volunteer's adoration for the major's daughter.

'Of course not. There is no need. Anyway, a public apology would admit that there had been a grievance and then neither of you could back down even though it would cost either life or career.' Williams seemed less convinced. Damn him, thought Hanley, why does he have to take empty words like honour so seriously. 'Look, he's just not worth it. Not to throw everything away. Let the French kill him.'

'No apology?'

'None. Just shake hands and both of you can forget anything ever happened.'

Pringle, Hanley, Truscott and Hatch watched the two men shake hands. They scarcely looked at each other, but there was an air of finality and relief. Afterwards Hatch took his friend off for a drink, while the others walked away from the camp. Behind a brick-built barn a horse was tethered, and Miss MacAndrews waited for them as Pringle had arranged on Hanley's instructions.

Billy Pringle and Truscott had waited for Jane near the edge of the encampment, hoping to meet her when she took one of her regular rides. No one would think it odd that they greet and speak briefly to the daughter of one of their seniors. They were within sight of a good number of people, but far enough away to be out of earshot. Since they were to ask the girl to come to a secret assignation, it seemed to them unreasonable that they should do so at another concealed meeting, and so they conducted the interview in full view.

Miss MacAndrews' habits were regular, and they had not waited for more than a quarter of an hour before they saw her walking her horse past the tent lines. When they raised their hats in greeting, the girl nodded and gave them a courteous but not improper smile. Yet she obviously noticed the urgency in their expression, and halted her mare.

'We have come to beg a great favour,' began Truscott, after the initial pleasantries. 'In the hope that you will deign to help one whom, if not yet a friend, I am sure you nevertheless view with goodwill.'

'How intriguing,' was the only reply, and Pringle cut in before his colleague could continue in a similar vein, feeling that they needed to resolve the matter quickly if they were not to attract too much attention. 'It is Mr Williams,' he said. 'I would guess that a young lady of your wit has already realised that he utterly adores you.' Truscott gave him a look, feeling that such language was too direct.

Jane showed no sign of shock, but assumed an expression of mock disappointment. 'Only him?' Williams was a pleasantly quixotic and not ill-favoured young man, and their encounters had certainly reinforced her fondness for him, even if it was no stronger than that. There was something endearing about his odd mixture of pride and clumsiness, both of which seemed almost childlike at times. Jane loved children and the latter invariably responded. She had already made friends with most of the battalion's infants, no matter how grubby. She also liked a good few of the officers. As yet it did not go any farther than that. Marriage and children of her own would all come, but Jane was in no hurry and wished to see more of the world and of life before she made such a big decision.

Truscott smiled. 'I am sure that the entire regiment admires you, Miss MacAndrews.' He bowed, giving Pringle the opportunity to take over the conversation.

'But in the case of Williams his devotion is utter. He is a serious man, and does nothing lightly. In this case I cannot blame him,' added Billy, unable to resist the gallantry. 'Sadly, in Williams' case it could bring him ruin, should he fight the duel to which he is committed.'

That shocked Jane. For one short moment the romance of a duel being fought over her was exciting, and then it seemed both absurd and horrible. 'With whom?'

'Mr Redman, also of the grenadiers,' said Truscott.

'I do not care for Mr Redman,' said Jane, frowning. 'And yet why should either gentleman feel it appropriate to fight for my favour?'

Pringle felt that honesty was both appropriate and more likely to be persuasive. 'The quarrel is in fact over a slur to your reputation.' Quickly he explained what had happened, and the well-established dislike between the two men. 'The colonel's orders on this matter are strict. Even if neither is killed, then they will be dismissed from the regiment.'

'Then how may I help to avoid such a sad event?' The two officers told the girl what Hanley planned, and in both cases their already favourable impression of her was reinforced by the speed with which she understood and agreed. Now they stood with Hanley and watched Williams approach the girl, taking off his shako respectfully as he did so.

Miss MacAndrews offered Williams a hand as he approached. 'So now I must add champion to your list of attributes,' she said. 'I am grateful that you were so willing to sacrifice yourself to defend my reputation, but I could not have carried such a burden.'

He kneeled and kissed her hand and began to mutter assurances that he was her devoted servant and would do anything at any time for her. Jane smiled, and surprised herself because she was actually more than a little moved by his devotion – not to love, it was true, but certainly to a yet stronger affection.

The others withdrew a little, and let him play his part in this romantic scene. Of necessity it was brief, for Miss MacAndrews could not for reputation's sake spend too long away from her family now that it was evening. In the short time they had, Williams spoke with surprising fluency of his immense admiration for her. Jane deftly steered the conversation back to her gratitude, happily assured him of friendship, with the condition that he was not ever again to jeopardise his own position in this way.

'You know, I sometimes wonder if our Bills is a hell of a lot more skilled in reading women than he lets on,' said Pringle, watching the Welshman look up at Jane with an expression close to worship. He turned back to Hanley and raised a quizzical eyebrow. 'Are you sure this will work?'

'I am a fluent and convincing liar.'

'Yes, but what if Williams and Redman talk to each other?'

'They're Englishmen,' was the simple reply.

'Williams isn't. He's half Scots and half Welsh. That's asking for trouble in the first place.'

'He's English enough never to talk to a man he dislikes about an awkward subject. Trust me. If they were Spanish we'd have a knife fight in ten minutes, but he and Redman will now simply ignore each other.'

'Perhaps,' said Pringle.

'Anyway, she will convince him. He'll nobly suffer anything if he feels he is protecting Miss MacAndrews. That's why it was important to bring her.' Hanley thought for a moment. 'You know, I rather feel our Hamish is convinced he is the hero of some chivalric romance.'

Pringle smiled, thought for a moment and then frowned. 'So what does that make us?'

17

Sergeant Darrowfield held up his open haversack to the first of the Grenadier Company's wives. Mrs Howell was a plump woman with a red face and thick white arms. Although she was not yet thirty, her dark hair was already streaked with grey and made her look much older. She hesitated for a moment, and then shut her eyes and reached into the bag. For a moment she rummaged, feeling the bunched-up balls of paper, and then finally her hand seized one and pulled it out. She handed it to the bespectacled Corporal Bower. He was the company clerk and so able to read. He was also unmarried and so had no personal interest.

'Not go,' he said solemnly.

'Oh God,' gasped Mrs Howell. 'Oh my good God, no. My poor babies, and my poor Tom.' She was sobbing, but kept her eyes closed. Tom Howell took her by the shoulders and led her off. His own eyes were moist.

Mary Murphy stepped up quickly, rubbing her hands together nervously. Young and bright, she reached in and pulled out a slip.

'Not go,' said Bower once again. Mary shrieked and there were moans from the crowd because she was well liked.

No one wanted to be next. Finally Sally Dobson took her chance.

'Go,' read Bower for the first time. She let her breath out in relief. There were smiles now. Mrs Dobson had been with the company longer than anyone else and it was a relief to know that she would be one of the six wives going with the grenadiers. They and the rest of the battalion would embark in three hours. Those wives who received the slips with their fatal 'Not go' would be left on the dock.

'Why didn't we do this last night?' whispered Hanley to Pringle and Williams as they watched the next wife steadying herself to take her chance. 'At least it would have given them time for a proper farewell.' Wickham had ordered his lieutenant to oversee the ballot, ensuring that everything was fair. In truth the sergeants had done it all, but he had dutifully watched. He was dreading having to face any of the unlucky wives, not knowing how he could answer their pleas.

'Time is the last thing they need. How would it make anything better?' Billy said quietly.

'But still, this seems so callous.' Hanley had begun sketching the scene, but had stopped. It was simply too emotional.

'If we gave them time, the men whose wives lost out might well run,' Pringle replied.

'Desert?' Hanley was shocked. The regiment had not lost any men since he had joined and the idea had never really occurred to him.

'Wouldn't you?' asked Williams. Hanley was surprised at this acceptance, even approval, of a breach of discipline from a man who took duty so seriously. Pringle hushed them into silence, however, before he could say any more.

So the melancholy scene progressed. There was fear before each choice, then joy or utter horror depending on the result. Gradually the places were filled. Molly Richards was fortunate and there was little joy at her success. Ill tempered, known as a gossip and believed to be a thief, the big Irishwoman was unpopular. To make matters worse she taunted the others with her luck, especially poor Mary Howell, who once again burst into tears. Several of the other wives began to yell back and Pringle feared that a fight was only moments away. Fortunately Sergeant Probert stepped in to break them up and little Jacky Richards managed to lead his exultant wife away.

Jenny Hanks was not part of the ballot. Pringle had seen to this, persuading Wickham and the adjutant to count her still as

Dobson's daughter. There could easily have been resentment if a wife of a few days had been given the same chance as everyone else. Since Sally was going, Jenny would now go as well.

Finally, the lot was finished. Williams and Hanley stayed to support Pringle as he gave each of the unlucky wives written proof of their status. In theory this should oblige their home parish to provide them with enough to buy a roof over their heads and food. In reality few parishes welcomed a new burden. Nor did it do much to help them on the journey, often long, back to their homes. A few had families who might choose to help them. For most the prospects were uncertain and scarcely good. They did not know when their husbands would return, if indeed they ever did, and some would come back blind, limbless or crippled with just the most meagre of pensions to stave off starvation. For the wives there would be months, perhaps years, of waiting and never knowing, with the poorhouse or prostitution hovering like spectres waiting to claim them.

Officers' wives were permitted to follow them on campaign unless the commander of their regiment or the entire army expressly forbade it. No such order had been given, but as was usual there would also be no official assistance for any who chose to go. Space was at a premium on the transport ships, and none could be spared for useless mouths.

MacAndrews had been rather glad when the adjutant had informed him of this and of the colonel's resolution not to make any exceptions. The major had made a formal request for his family to accompany him, hoping to get this very response.

'I suppose you are pleased, MacAndrews,' said his wife afterwards.

'A battle is no place for a woman, let alone a wee girl like Jane.'

'We had not proposed actually to fight in any battles. And your daughter is not so "wee" as all that. Whenever you get all Scotch on me I know you're being devious. We have followed you everywhere before.'

'To garrisons, not a war.'

'And weren't those dangerous enough?' He could not deny

that. Esther noticed his eyes moisten slightly, and almost regretted reviving the old dark memories. She looked away for a moment, before she continued, trying to lighten the tone. 'So, are you tired of me already?'

Alastair put his arms around her and kissed her. They stayed holding each other for a long time before he spoke.

'You know better than to ask that.' He kissed her hair. 'These last two years were some of the hardest of my life. Since you came back it has been . . .' He struggled for words, so instead kissed her again. There was no need for more words for a while.

'I am not sanguine of success,' he said at last.

'For the regiment?' asked his wife.

'For the expedition. There are many risks and it could well end in a disaster. The regiment should do well, but that does not mean everyone else will.' He decided not to mention his doubts about Moss. There was no sense in unnecessary alarm, although their commander seemed both rash and careless. 'At the least it will be dangerous.'

'Dangers are everywhere. I might fall from my horse or sicken and die even if I stay with your dull sister in Inverness. So might Jane. The French are civilised, so it is not as if you are dealing with savages who take no prisoners. If you are captured then I will be with you. I had better after last time. Can't have you running off with some Frenchwoman!'

MacAndrews smiled. 'But if I should fall, where would you be?'

'By your side, and at least I will know that I have done whatever can be done. Better that than getting a letter and wondering if I could have made a difference. You are not usually so morbid.'

'And Jane?' he asked. 'There may be sights no young girl should have to see.'

'It will be an adventure. She will learn more than if she sits and sews in Inverness.'

'I have done my best.' His wife sniffed at that. 'There is no berth for either of you. You cannot come, my dear, and there is nothing I can do to alter that.'

'Yet if we could, would you permit it?' There was something precise in her tone which alarmed him.

'It is impossible for you to go.' Perhaps saying that firmly would make it true, but years of experience had made him cautious about underestimating Esther's ingenuity and determination.

'You are my husband, my lord and master. If you tell me I shall not do a thing then I must obey.' Their past life suggested no such thing, but she was looking him straight in the eye and very nearly appeared to be sincere. 'If you forbid it then that is that. So I must ask whether you would permit Jane and me to join you in Spain if I could devise the means of getting there.'

MacAndrews knew that there must be a catch. Yet he had been an officer for more than two decades, and one of the first and most important lessons he had learnt was never to issue an order that he knew would not be obeyed.

'In such a case, of course you may come,' he said. For the life of him he could not imagine how she would manage it, and yet his certainty wavered. He hoped that he had not just made a grave mistake.

On 29th June 1808, at three in the afternoon, the 106th went on board the ships allocated to them. The band did not play, but a pathetic group of women and children stood on the harbour-side and waved last farewells to their men. A few were mute, but Mrs Howell wailed and the two children clinging to her skirts sobbed with her. Mary Murphy held her baby tightly in her arms and hushed his cries. Her face was taut, but she somehow held back her own tears, wanting her husband to know that she was strong and would be waiting for him when he returned. Yet despair clawed at her, as an image of her Jim lying dead kept coming into her mind.

Jim Murphy clung on just as tightly to the side of the ship, his eyes fixed on his wife and tiny son. Private Howell had already gone below decks, unable to cope. So had Richards and his wife Molly, the latter no longer so keen to revel in her good fortune, for she was already nauseous with the ship's gentle motion. Williams stood beside Murphy and tried to think of something to say. The ship's captain was bellowing at the soldiers to go below and get out of the damned way. Hamish put his hand lightly on the Irish private's shoulder, unable to find any words. Dobson came up on Murphy's other side and passed him a bottle. The sergeants had inspected the Grenadier Company to check that none were sneaking alcohol on board, but somehow the veteran managed to produce brandy. Williams could not think how, and it made him realise how much he still did not understand about the lives of the soldiers. A volunteer was always an outsider. Still, much as he loathed drunkenness, he was for once glad that Dobson was providing the redcoat's most common comfort.

Seven companies of the battalion were crammed into emptied gun decks of HMS *Hasdrubal*, an old sixty-four long since past its best days. MacAndrews took the grenadiers and One and Two Companies on the *Corbridge*, a smaller merchantmen hired for the purpose. It was even more cramped and had evidently been much employed hauling coal, for the dust was everywhere. They were the only 'cargo' apart from a pair of engineer officers. The Light Dragoons and the Gunners were carried in other ships.

On the evening tide, the little flotilla set sail. Winds that held the main fleet in the bay off Cork were in their favour, and in less than a week they had joined the other ships, only to spend almost as long again at anchor. There was no opportunity to go on shore and officers and men alike suffered. Pringle had taken to his cot almost as soon as he had gone on board, and stirred little after that. Williams was almost as bad, but showed some signs of recovering while they were off Cork. Hanley more quickly found his sea legs, as did Redman, adding to his sense of superiority over Williams and creating an almost benevolent attitude in him. The ship's captain was a gruff Yorkshireman and ordered all ranks to remain off deck for all but an hour a day. Only once did he invite MacAndrews and the three captains to a meagre meal. They supplied the drink.

On 12th July the entire fleet, including the vessels containing the 106th, set sail for Spain and war.

PART TWO
Portugal, August 1808

18

Lieutenant General Sir Arthur Wellesley urged his weary horse over the rise and then pulled on the reins to halt the poor beast. He allowed himself a moment to take in the view over Mondego Bay and permit the three young staff officers trailing behind him to catch up. Their horses were only marginally weaker than the grey gelding he was riding, but as always he pressed his mount just a little harder than anyone else, whether in a hunt or on campaign. Tomorrow should be better. Two of his own horses had been landed that morning and the grooms had spent the rest of the day helping them to recover from the weeks at sea.

He patted the gelding's neck and could feel the animal breathing hard. It was a thin, half-starved creature, but the best the Portuguese commander could provide. Not that the man was any judge of horseflesh. Until a few weeks ago the worried, grey-faced man had been a professor of law at Coimbra University, until he and his students had taken up arms against the French and seized the fort overlooking the bay. After a few days, the Royal Navy had landed some companies of marines to provide a professional stiffening for this garrison. Wellesley was glad they were there, for it took a long time to raise and train an army and the Portuguese had only had weeks.

The students were a ragged-looking bunch. Only a minority had muskets, while a red rag tied around the arm was all that most of them had as a uniform. When he had ridden through the gates the enthusiastic salute offered by the young Portuguese volunteers had seemed almost a parody of the marines' smart presenting of arms. He had acknowledged it anyway, just as if it had been done by Guardsmen in London. In the same way he had saluted and offered his congratulations to the former professor.

The Portuguese were not yet organised, but they were welcoming and very keen and that in the end was what mattered. Things had been so different in Spain. Wellesley's original orders had been to take the army to Corunna and help the authorities in the province of Galicia. He had sailed ahead of the main convoy, but discovered no enthusiasm for the British expedition. The Galician junta welcomed English arms and money, but refused to accept any soldiers, let alone an entire army. With resources they could fight the French themselves, boasting of a major victory already won by a Spanish army farther south.

Disappointed, Wellesley had gone back on board the navy frigate and sailed to Portugal. At Oporto there was a bishop leading resistance to the French. The man was no soldier but seemed a talented organiser, and there was no doubting his zeal for expelling the French. It was the first taste of the greater willingness of the Portuguese to admit their weakness and co-operate, helped by the fact that there was already a British officer liaising with the bishop. The two countries were old allies, but Britain had done nothing to help the Portuguese the previous autumn when General Junot had led his columns into Lisbon. There had not been anything much they could have done, but that can have been little consolation to the Portuguese. Only the risings in Spain gave the chance of dividing the French forces in the Peninsula and making them vulnerable.

Oporto was too far from Lisbon and the main concentrations of French troops to be a good place to land the army. So Wellesley had gone back on board the fast-sailing HMS *Crocodile* and once again headed south. They could not land on the Tagus at Lisbon itself. The French would be bound to meet such a move on or near the beaches before the British Army was fully disembarked and ready. Added to that, there was the squadron of the Russian navy in the Tagus. The Tsar was an ally of Napoleon, and although his country was not actively at war with Britain, it was very hard to be sure of their neutrality. The Royal Navy were hungry for a fight, and hungrier still for the prize money it might bring, but Wellesley wanted to avoid any confrontation. It was enough having one enemy to fight.

Then the students had seized the fort at Figueiras-da-Foz at the mouth of the Mondego and resolved the problem.

'Fine sight, eh, Bathurst,' barked Wellesley to his Deputy Quartermaster General, who had just managed to persuade his exhausted screw of a horse up the last few yards of the slope. A young staff officer was beside him; the other had dismounted and was ruefully examining his mount's front left hoof. The shoe had lost two nails and looked ready to come free. The officer hoped it would last for the next hour. None of the three men had been quite prepared for the pace set by their thirty-nine-year-old commander. They were sore and weary themselves, but guessed that it would be a long time before they rested.

The scene before them was certainly impressive. Longboats shuttled back and forth to the shore loaded with tightly packed rows of seated redcoats or boxes, barrels and sacks of supplies. Behind were some of the sixty-eight ships which had sailed from Cork. The sea seemed to have calmed a little, and the big ships scarcely moved at anchor, but the rowing boats were still sometimes tossed by the waves. One looked to be in bad trouble and was being carried away by the current towards the rocky outcrops near a small headland. Bathurst pulled out his telescope and focused on the dark, almost black longboat. The soldiers sitting in the middle still looked rigid and impassive, but he could guess at their growing nervousness. There was no noise, but he could see a naval officer with his hand raised – probably a young midshipman not old enough to shave and yet still calmly giving orders in a high falsetto to men twice his age. For a moment the boat resisted the pull of the water, but then it was jerked suddenly towards the rocks. Oars reached out to push away from the boulders, but with another swell the boat struck hard against the rock and tipped.

Bathurst gasped. 'Poor devils,' he muttered as the little red figures and the white-shirted sailors were tossed into the grey water.

Again, through the glass it was eerily silent.

The general watched intently, but without resorting to his telescope. His eyesight was good, and there was nothing he could do to help the men from up here. Other boats were circling as close at they dared, and already one or two survivors were climbing on to the rocks themselves.

'Find out how many men we have lost today, as well as any supplies that have perished,' Wellesley instructed the young ADC.

'It could have been worse, sir,' ventured Bathurst. He had seen the little blue figure of the midshipman being pulled on to the rock by a redcoat and was pleased by that.

Wellesley grunted. There was an hour of good light left, and after that they would need to cease landing men until dawn tomorrow. Fane's brigade was already ashore. The Rifles had come first, little piquets of green-jacketed sharpshooters quickly forming all around the beach and linking up with the fort. The line battalions had strengthened the outposts. Now men from the other brigades were starting to join them. Some two thousand eight hundred men would be ashore by the end of the day, and that was a good start.

Judging that the others had now had enough of a rest – and that was the sole reason he had stopped for so long – Wellesley decided to move.

'On we go,' he said, and was already trotting down the sandy hillside. He needed to have a word with Brigadier General Fane and then ride back to the fort to receive the latest reports sent in by the Portuguese scouts. Bathurst and the two ADCs trailed behind, the one whose horse had a loose shoe going as gingerly as he could while still keeping up.

They passed a half-company of redcoats. Shoulder wings and white plumes on their shakos showed them to be grenadiers, and Bathurst then had to work out which regiment in the army had red facings to their jackets. As usual, the general was ahead of him as he nodded to the young lieutenant colonel who was standing talking to a group of officers beside the men.

'Evening, Moss, glad to see the 106th are with us,' called

Wellesley as he sped past, somehow persuading his grey into a canter.

'Thank you, sir,' called Moss eagerly at the departing figure. 'Always ready and always steady!' It was a new motto he had come up with for the regiment and hoped to make popular.

Wellesley's brief nod and gaze had scarcely been warm, but Moss knew that that was simply the general's way. Bathurst smiled cheerfully as he passed. The two men had met during Moss's service in Ireland.

'Nice to be on dry land again!' Bathurst called as he struggled to keep up with the departing figure of his chief. 'Must go.' He half turned in his saddle and waved back. 'Don't know where we can find a thousand mules, do you?' he called back, and then was gone, followed by the ADCs.

'Mules?' asked Hanley, as he and Pringle stood together at a decent distance from where Moss, Major Toye and the adjutant were talking.

'Bit like donkeys, only a lot more awkward,' said Pringle. 'Probably Welsh, I expect.'

'Then they must be noble animals indeed,' asserted Williams. 'No wonder the general wants them on our side. If such warriors join the French then we might be in trouble.'

'Curious thing to be worrying about on the day we have landed in an enemy-held country, though.' Pringle shrugged and Williams as usual exuded utter faith in the wisdom of his superiors, but Hanley remained puzzled. 'I would have expected the French to occupy his entire thoughts.'

Wellesley did think about the French, but it was not an immediate concern. The Bishop of Oporto had estimated General Junot's army at fifteen thousand men. Fresher intelligence suggested that this was a considerable underestimate. Some thirty thousand French soldiers had invaded Portugal the previous autumn. Wellesley was confident that these were now spread widely across the country. Portugal's people had risen in arms during the spring, just as the Spanish had done. The French had provoked them, for their soldiers looted freely, but there was a deeper rage at the invader who had so easily and quickly taken their land. Militias appeared all around the country. French patrols were ambushed and stragglers caught and killed, often after long hours of torture. The French response was savage, and Junot split his army up into smaller columns which marched through the valleys burning and killing.

The French spread fear, but the hatred was even stronger and more and more people chose to fight. Junot did not have enough men to garrison every town and village and so his soldiers kept moving, and as they did they plundered and raped. Reports made it clear that the enemy were dispersed in several groups and that none was anywhere near Mondego Bay. They had at least a week before Junot might even contemplate launching an attack, and in the meantime there was so much to do. How many men the French could concentrate by that time was harder to estimate. Wellesley was confident that his soldiers would defeat the same number of Frenchmen. Still, no general chose to fight on equal terms unless there was no alternative.

That was the wider problem, but at the moment – and indeed for the rest of the campaign – he must devote a good deal of his attention to mules, and to horses, oxen and carts. Animals took up far more space than men in transport ships, and needed better treatment if they were to survive the voyage and still be useful. His lone cavalry regiment had brought more troopers than horses in the hope of finding mounts after they arrived. The artillery were the same; indeed, an artillery battery was almost more demanding of horses than a cavalry regiment like the 20th Light Dragoons. More than half of his guns had no horses to pull them, or the extra ammunition and other supply carts they needed to function.

Then there was the ammunition and food required by the rest of the army. Already the arithmetic was running through his head. Armies consumed food at a staggering rate even before they used powder and shot for fighting. Whether they fought, marched hard or did nothing at all, the men and horses ate and drank. Men needed meat and bread or biscuit – or if they were given grain then they needed the opportunity to grind it into flour and then to bake the flour into bread, which in turn required copious amounts of firewood as fuel. Army regulations also entitled each soldier to an issue of alcohol every day. Horses needed food and fodder and good treatment if their health was not to decline.

The years in India had taught him that before anything else a general must keep his army fed and watered if it was to achieve anything. Having the supplies stowed safely in the holds of ships, or piled high on land in a depot, was in itself almost as useless as not having them at all. Everything needed to be moved to where the army wanted it and then to be immediately available. That meant transport, whether by pack animal or draught animals pulling wheeled carts. Without these, he could go nowhere. Yet in turn the baggage animals must have food and fodder, and so transport was needed for this and the animals involved would in turn want supplying. Oxen were strong – he had used thousands of them in India along with many elephants – but desperately slow. Mules were quicker, but needed more attendants.

He was unlikely to get a choice. Once the second fleet had arrived from Gibraltar in a few days and disembarked, he would have almost fifteen thousand men. From what he had seen it would be a struggle to find enough animals and wagons to move even half that number. The Portuguese were once again willing, but the country was poor, and even if every animal could be gathered they were unlikely to meet all his needs. There was no vast force of shire horses like those of England. So it was not a choice between oxen or mules, but a desperate search to find as many of each as he possibly could. To this end the general and his staff devoted their greatest efforts and would continue to do so as the days passed. They would ask, cajole, beg and, almost as importantly, pay their allies for every type of pack or draught beast that could be found.

Wellesley and his staff had much still to do that night and would ride quite a few more miles. The young gentlemen of the Grenadier Company were not concerned with such great matters and moved far less. Two hours after dusk, the piquet formed by one half of the company was relieved by the other half under Wickham and Redman. The men went back to cook their meals at the battalion bivouac just above the beach. No tents had been brought in the ships for the regiments, so all would sleep under the stars. A few of the officers owned tents, but none of these had yet been unloaded, and neither had the larger one destined to act as the mess. No one minded, and there was a jolly, festive atmosphere as they sat on convenient stones or the ground. Just under half of the regiment's officers were present as the rest were on duty. MacAndrews had rolled up in his blankets and was sleeping next to a large boulder. He would go on duty at 2.30 in the morning and be responsible for the battalion's piquets. Anyway, he had seen landings like this – and even larger ones – before and had found the day almost routine.

None of the more junior officers was able to copy him, even though some would share the duty. They were all far too excited. The French were nowhere to be seen, but still they were now just a few long marches away and the prospect of a swift encounter with the enemy thrilled them all.

Derryck had received a visit from his cousin Lieutenant Bunbury of the Rifles and was eagerly introducing him to everyone. He proved to be a personable young man with a fine singing voice. They sang 'Spanish Ladies' once again, and laughed uproariously when someone tried to fit Portuguese to the verse.

Williams knew that he would not be able to sleep and was happy to talk as long as anyone else was awake. It was almost a good thing to know that he would be back on duty at 2.30. He had hated the weeks at sea, but now it seemed strange to stand or sit on a surface that did not move and to be away from the constant creaking and moaning of a wooden ship. Today's landing had been impressive and spectacular. MacAndrews had told them to expect organised confusion and that had summed it up well. Their ship apparently came into shore earlier than it was supposed to, but the captain robustly refused calls to haul out to sea again and eventually the longboats arrived to ferry them off. The three companies of the 106th landed hours before the rest of the regiment, and this seemed to have irked the colonel, who had selected them for extra duties on the piquet line and given Major MacAndrews the hardest of the shifts as duty officer.

Williams had been in the first boat taken off their ship. Wickham sat in the prow with the major. Neither looked troubled as the boat rocked in the high breakers. The grenadiers' captain was as elegant as ever, although when he looked closely Williams noticed that his gloved hands were gripping the side of the boat tightly. Oddly, the volunteer found the more violent movements of the small longboat less disturbing than the rolling of the big ship, but perhaps this was just the prospect of getting on to dry land. The old merchant captain had leaned over the side as they left, calling down that he would be back to pick them up again in a month if they weren't dead by then. MacAndrews just raised his cocked hat in salute in reply at this reminder that so many expeditions to Europe had ended in failure.

It took twenty minutes to get ashore, and at one point the sailors at the oars seemed to be losing their battle with the current. They recovered, but as they managed to get back on course there was the grim sight of a corpse dressed in the red-faced green jacket of the 60th floating towards them. The man was face down, his long black hair still tied in its queue and his arms outstretched. For a while the body kept pace with them, bobbing just out of reach. Then came another wave and he vanished for a moment, only to reappear some way away. It looked unreal, and Williams found it hard to accept that the object in the water had so recently been a living, breathing man.

Only after they had landed did it wholly sink in that boats had been swamped and men drowned as the army was landing. Williams found the thought more than a little frightening and was disturbed by this reaction. He had always assumed that he would be brave, but now he was worried by the thought of drowning at the moment of landing, in spite of the fact that he had not. He felt horror – there was no other word for it – at the realisation that he could have died before battle had brought the chance of distinction and promotion. He was confident that he would succeed if the opportunity came, and that he would continue to rise in rank. Eventually he would be senior and wealthy enough to aid his family, and to ask Major MacAndrews for his daughter's hand. It all seemed clear and straightforward, even inevitable, and then came the sight of random and pointless death.

Hanley and Redman had come in the second boat carrying the grenadiers. Their trip was smoother and more steady, but they too were accompanied for some way by the dead rifleman. Redman tried to smile lightly, but was unable to think of a joke to demonstrate his calm. Hanley wondered who the man was, but felt that at least he looked more peaceful than the hacked and mutilated corpses in Madrid all those weeks ago. He regretted the fact that they were not in Spain, and yet was also eager to see Portugal, and especially Lisbon. He had read that there was a Roman theatre there which had been uncovered in an earthquake and was eager to see it. Yet he was not sure whether the French were between the army and the city, and suddenly he could not help laughing at the thought that he was planning to visit antiquities in the middle of a war. It seemed to make as much sense as the war itself.

Pringle came in the final boat with the engineer officers. Billy was glad to be off the ghastly prison of the never stable ship. He was sure that he must have lost weight, and yet in the mirror that morning his face had looked as round as ever. Given that he had eaten so little and spewed up so much, this seemed unfair. The third boat was also escorted by the rifleman, who always managed to stay out of reach. Pringle agreed when one engineer muttered that some poor fellows have such dreadful bad luck.

The company formed on shore and was almost immediately approached by Brigadier General Fane with orders. Fane commanded the Light Brigade, with the 2nd Battalion of the 95th Rifles and the 5th Battalion of the 60th – officially the Royal Americans, but now recruited more often than not from Germans and other foreigners. Both battalions carried the Baker rifle, which was far more accurate, although slower to load, than the line infantry's musket. For the moment the 106th was attached to Fane's brigade, as were two other battalions that had joined the expedition just before it left Cork. Everyone knew the arrangement was temporary, but for the moment it had got them ashore early on in the landings and that was a blessing. Fane's brigade major walked them – there were no horses ashore that early in the day – to the position reinforcing the outposts of the riflemen.

That had been many hours ago, and the rest of the day had been spent mainly in waiting. They moved position twice as the outpost line was expanded. Williams had never known a sun so powerful or felt so very hot. Hanley was used to it, although it did remind him of how delicious a siesta was on such a day. It seemed pointless standing in formation away from the shade. At one point they were put in an orange grove, but, this being the army, they were almost instantly moved one hundred yards and out of the shade back into the sun. Williams' face was almost as red as his jacket by the end of the day.

It was close to midnight when a single longboat ground ashore on another Portuguese beach. Two men had already sprung over the side and waded through the surf, holding their muskets high above their heads. They went forward, bare feet sinking into the gritty sand, until they reached a low mound of pebbles thrown up by the tide. Then they kneeled down and levelled their muskets, scanning the darkness for any threat. The moon had not yet risen, but the stars were bright, and over to the east was the dull glow of the lights of Lisbon itself.

The two men watched for more than a minute and then the one on the left raised his arm and gave a whispering call to those in the boat. One man jumped nimbly into the shallow water and strode ashore. Three more followed him, burdened down with backpacks, including those of the two scouts. They walked on to the beach and then piled the packs neatly and laid their muskets down on top of them. Then the three turned back and used their shoulders to push the boat out once more. The coxswain gave a few brief orders in a voice almost lost in the rolling of the surf. Expertly, the sailors brought the boat off a few yards and turned it, before rowing back to their ship, one of the Russian squadron anchored in the River Tagus.

The coxswain was glad to go. Normally, any time away from the hulking two-decked ship of the line, with its seventy-four guns and eight hundred crew, was a pleasant interval, but this had been different. There was something about the first lieutenant's orders that had been uncanny. Rumour said that the captain was ill, and no one had seen him for days, but he was still sure that no instructions had come from the flagship for this special mission. Twenty years in the service had taught him never to question an order and so he had done as he was told. Even those years had not quite cured him of thinking at all.

It was hard not to speculate about his passengers even if he tried to avoid it. Their leader was a dangerous man. His uniform was that of a major in the Tsar's own guard, one of the jaegers or huntsmen. That was enough to show that Count Denilov had grand connections even for an aristocrat. Yet the nobleman had the look of a killer.

The coxswain had fought in his share of battles, had hacked his way across decks crammed with sword-wielding Turks, and had battered many a man senseless in the fights in inns, alleys and on board ship that punctuated a sailor's life. He was not easily impressed, but even he had to admit the count made him nervous. What the hell was an army officer doing on board anyway, and with five of his soldiers instead of the marines serving with the ship? Well, for the moment, that was not his concern – at least until they had to return at the same hour in six nights' time and then on each of the next three nights. Three fires, spaced ten yards apart, would be the signal to come in and pick up the soldiers.

When one of the rowers missed a stroke, the coxswain decided they were far enough out from the shore to bellow a curse at the man. They were all nervous, he knew, but that was no excuse for poor seamanship. He tried to look on the bright side. There was supposed to be a war raging in Portugal, and maybe the count and his men would manage to get themselves killed. Sadly he doubted it. The soldiers looked more like killers than victims.

The sort of men you could not just knock down, but had to finish off permanently, or one day they would be back at your throat. Cut-throats led by an aristocrat who would as soon flog a man to death as look at him was the coxswain's judgement, and Portugal was welcome to them.

On shore the five soldiers put on their boots and then adjusted their packs, checking each other to make sure that their equipment rattled as little as possible. None of them spoke. The one-eyed sergeant tapped one man on the shoulder telling him to lead off. The sergeant followed, then the officer, and then the remaining three soldiers. All kept their muskets held loosely and ready to be brought up to the shoulder. The officer had thrust his double-barrelled pistol back into his belt and kept a grip on his sword to prevent the scabbard catching on anything. Almost silently, the six men slid into the night, intent on a theft that would restore the count's fortunes. No one who mattered would ever know how Denilov would achieve this miracle. Deaths were also necessary, but that was not something that had ever bothered him.

19

By the fourth day Hanley had become bored and sensed that the feeling was common throughout the 106th, and quite probably the army as a whole. Most of the ten thousand or so soldiers who had sailed from Cork had by now come ashore, but work continued with the much harder task of unloading the cannon and the horses of the artillery and Light Dragoons. It was nearly done, but the convoy from Gibraltar bringing the remaining four thousand men was expected to arrive the next day, and so the whole process must begin again.

The excitement of landing on an enemy-held shore had gradually faded as the days passed. There was no sign of the French and the army remained around the beach. The 106th performed piquet duty and provided work parties to help with the unloading and, on several occasions, to carry large quantities of stores half a mile or so for no obvious reason. The great adventure became bogged down in routine. Worse still, they spent hours drilling, just as they had done in Britain. They drilled as a battalion, as individual companies, and the adjutant also insisted on parading and training the more recent recruits and officers for extra drill. There was talk of brigade manoeuvres, but as yet these had not occurred.

There was no danger, no excitement, no fear even, and Hanley expressed his frustration. 'Aren't you sick of just sitting here doing nothing?'

'I am so sorry, is the war not to Sir's liking?' said Pringle. 'Shall I get the cook to bake a new one, with an extra helping of angry Frenchmen?'

With disappointment at the lack of adventure, a new sport began in the Light Company and soon spread to the rest of the 106th. Discovering that their French counterparts were known as voltiguers or 'leapers', the light bobs took to leaping any ditch or gap they could find. Even the officers joined in, pretending they were simply saving time by jumping rather than walking around an obstacle. Truscott was especially good at this. A day later someone began to walk along the top of a stone wall instead of beside it, and this became a new enthusiasm. Williams succumbed, producing hysterics in Pringle and Hanley when he slipped and fell down hard with one leg on either side of a wall. Experienced officers like MacAndrews saw no harm in these games; he remembered how in his first campaign he had seemed to have far more energy than he could possibly know what to do with. Moss felt it was undignified and issued an order banning the men from jumping. It was ignored unless there was one of the senior officers close by.

All in all Hanley and the other young officers felt as if they had never left England, but had still lost its comforts. The 106th now had its mess tent, where the officers could dine and drink, but the boat carrying the colonel's personal supplies had overturned on the way to shore and everything had been lost. Local wine had been procured, but as yet they had only a very poor port, and even the younger subalterns almost noticed the difference between this and Moss's finer vintages. The food was also now mainly reliant on the army's rations, for the few delicacies available locally had rapidly risen in price following the army's arrival.

Hanley did not mind more basic food and drink. Nor did he object to sleeping under the stars. Billy Pringle's tent had been stowed badly on the voyage and the attentions of rats and other vermin had left it in a pitifully holed state. Apart from that, there seemed no prospect of purchasing a donkey to carry it as soon as they moved inland. The nights were clement and there was a certain romance to sleeping on the sandy dunes rolled up in a blanket. Even some of those officers with tents were choosing to do this.

It was the waiting which he hated. Since they had landed – perhaps since he had watched that corpse floating lazily near the boat – William Hanley had felt the fear grow within him. Memories of the massacre at Madrid became more frequent. If he closed his eyes he could see the French sabres rising and falling, hear the grunts of effort from the troopers and the screams of their victims, and that appalling mewing from the Frenchman whose face was destroyed. It all seemed so real once again. England had seemed like another, quite separate world, distant in every way from such carnage, and even from the man he had been during the years in Spain.

Most of all he remembered his own terror, the scrambling panic as he had dodged the horsemen and then fled down the dark alleyways, running until he could run no more, his breath coming in gasps and his heart pounding within his chest. Would he run again? The thoughts of revenge, of somehow winning absolution for deserting Maria Pilar, had all gone.

Instead the worry that he would cave into fear and run tormented him more and more. He did not care about reputation, still less about the honour his fellow officers claimed shaped their lives. If he still had pride, then it was because he felt himself above such human vanity. An artist – and he was still one in his soul even if his ability fell short – should see the truth of things and not waste time with illusions. The only thing that truly mattered was the ability to create objects of wonder and beauty.

Hanley smiled at that, recognising his own pomposity, but still feeling that it contained some truth. He had been surprised to find himself reasonably content, at times even happy, with the regiment. Yet he did not care that much about the 106th, and in spite of the furious loyalty of his comrades, as far as he could see it was no different from all the other regiments in the army – probably in any army. He did care about his friends, about Pringle and Truscott, about Williams, who took life so very seriously, and some of the others. What he feared most was the thought that he might panic and abandon them. Compared to that, death seemed better.

That thought had grown and he found himself embracing it. A quick moment – the neat musket ball in the forehead and everything would be over. No more dreams, no more disappointments, no more search for purpose, just Catullus's 'never ending night of sleep'. It had the attraction of simplicity. Then he remembered the screams and the mutilation, and cold fear of agony and horror gripped him more tightly. The waiting gave too much time for thought and for fear to fester within him.

He started as someone patted him on the shoulder.

'Not drawing?' asked Pringle, sitting down beside him on the low bank overlooking the bay. Hanley shook his head. He had tried yesterday, but his pencil had frozen after only a few strokes. The image of the dead girl in Madrid haunted and fascinated him to the exclusion of everything else.

'Well, have something to eat.' Pringle held out a loaf of brown bread. 'Bills is bringing the salt beef, but we have this to wash it down with.' In his other hand was a green bottle. The cork was only lightly pushed back in and Pringle pulled it out with his teeth. 'I think you will remember this.'

Hanley took the proffered bottle and raised it to his lips. The other man watched him with a broad smile on his face. Hanley freely confessed to knowing little about wine, but the taste was certainly familiar. Recognition dawned.

'This is the colonel's favourite brandy.' Pringle nodded. 'This should cheer him up. Did you get this in the mess?'

'Not exactly. I bought it off an Irish lad from the ninety-fifth.'

'And how did he . . . ?'

'I understand that some of our riflemen are very good swimmers.'

'You mean this is the colonel's brandy.'

'No longer. Doesn't taste bad for its dunking either.' Hanley laughed, although he could not quite match his friend's delight. Williams joined them, carrying a bundle. They carved some of the salty beef and ate, the volunteer drinking from his wooden canteen. It was the regulation issue, painted light blue and with a stencil of the regiment's CVI numeral.

After a while Billy Pringle began patting his pockets. 'Oh yes, I have forgotten my solemn duty as your superior. Where is the damn thing? Never mind, it will not overtax even my mind to remember it. The general sent you both a personal message. Anyway, the big news is that we are to form line in two ranks.'

Hanley thought for a moment. 'But we always do.'

'Us and the rest of the army, but as you and Bills should know if you had studied the drill manual properly, that is not what the august Sir David Dundas tells us.'

'A line is supposed to be three deep, unless casualties have rendered a unit so weak that it cannot maintain its frontage,' said Williams.

'I am impressed. Is that a quote?' Pringle seemed even more ebullient than usual.

'My own invention.'

'Then I am very impressed, young Bills. One day you should write a very dull book on the most obscure subject imaginable. I suspect you have a natural talent.'

'I don't understand.' Hanley was genuinely puzzled. 'Why tell us to do what we are already doing?'

'You are not expecting the army to make sense, are you?' Pringle paused to take another swig from the bottle. 'That way lies the path to madness. Or possibly glory.'

'A three-deep line is more solid. The French and most other armies form that way.' Williams was extremely confident in his assertion. 'But the men in the third rank can't see much and have trouble firing effectively.' After a moment another thought occurred. 'It can be dangerous.'

'I thought war was supposed to be dangerous.' Hanley smiled.

'Really, no one told me. I may have to offer my resignation,' said Pringle with his mouth full of bread so that crumbs sprayed over the other two. Laughing at his own joke produced a fit of coughing. 'Sorry,' he added.

Williams ignored him, aflame with the urge to pass on hard-earned knowledge. 'I mean dangerous to the men in the second and front ranks. Sometimes the third rank shoots them.'

'What?' Hanley was incredulous. 'You are making this up, surely.'

'Certainly not.' Pringle came to Williams' support. 'You hear about it quite often. It was apparently common in the old days and still is for the French. Well, what's a couple more dead Frenchmen between friends. I fear once again you are expecting armies to act logically.'

'But to accept that you will regularly kill your own men? Why?'

'Pride, tradition, or because they have always done so in the past. It doesn't seem to stop the French from winning battles.'

'A deeper line is more solid,' repeated Williams.

'Anyway, the rest is about the formation to be adopted by the brigades of the army. We are on the far left, next to the Highland Brigade. On the march we will always be in the lead. Well, the two battalions of Rifles will be and we will support them. A couple of guns are attached to the brigade, so be prepared for some big bangs. Now have you got all that?' They nodded. 'Well, don't let it get too fixed as by the sound of things it will all be changed in a day or two once the new brigades have landed. That's the formation we would fight or march in at the moment, but since we aren't going anywhere and the French are nowhere near us it is largely academic.'

They were silent for a while, contemplating the mysteries of the army, until Williams spoke.

'I have a favour to ask you both.' His voice shook a little. He also went pale, something the others had noticed he was prone to do at moments of emotion. 'It is important.' Billy Pringle thought of a few flippant replies, but then judged that this was not the right time.

'At your service, as always,' he said. Hanley made a similar pledge.

'I have written these letters and would be most grateful if you could deliver them should I fall.'

'You are not going to die, Bills.' Pringle's voice was assured. 'None of us are. We are too handsome.'

Williams still looked earnest. 'Nevertheless, it happens. It would be a comfort to know that if either of you should survive [thank you very much, thought Pringle], then you would make sure that these notes reach their destinations. I cannot ask anyone else, but you two know more. I keep them in the bottom of my pack, wrapped in oilskin with my books.' He hesitated, and now flushed with embarrassment. 'One is for my mother. The other ... well, the other ... it is for Miss MacAndrews.' He scanned their faces intently, trying to see whether they were surprised or even amused. Both men were solemn and that reassured him.

'Of course, but it will not be necessary. You will see them both yourself one day. And you will be tall and proud as an officer.' Pringle tried not to sound too light in tone for he knew that Williams was as serious as only he could be.

'You have my word on it,' added Hanley, rather surprised at his use of the expression, but there was something oddly important about the scene and for once it felt natural.

'Mine too,' said Pringle. 'And that is the word of a man who was very nearly a parson.' He realised that was the wrong thing to say so added, 'More importantly, it is the word of a true friend.'

Williams took each man's hand in turn and shook it, staring fixedly into their eyes. After that he had to return to help a carrying party on the beach.

'Well, that was all solemn and more than a bit morbid,' said Pringle after the other man had gone. 'I hope you are not going to ask me to perform the same service for you.'

'I have no one worth sending a last letter.'

'Truly? No old enemy you would like to send a last batch of insults!' Pringle noticed that his friend was obviously moved. 'Not you too?'

Hanley looked at him. 'I confess thoughts of mortality have been prominent in my mind these last days.'

'You and I dare say just about everyone else in the army.' Hanley was surprised, although the exchange with Williams had begun to make him wonder whether his grim mood was more typical than he thought. 'The trick is not to let anyone notice. Anyway, you are not to die and that is an order. You can't leave me with only that ass Redman for company – oh, and Bills, of course, but it can all get a little too sober if you spent too much time solely with him.'

Hanley smiled dutifully. Oddly enough the thought that no one would care whether he lived or died had made him angry. A perverse part of him was determined to live just to spite the world that had cast him adrift. 'Well, if it is an order . . .' he said.

20

GENERAL ORDER, 7TH AUGUST 1808

Major General Spencer's corps having joined the army, the
regiments will be brigaded as follows, from the right

1st Brigade – 1/5th, 1/9th and 1/38th regiments
under Major General Hill

3rd Brigade – 1/82nd and 106th regiments
under Brigadier General Nightingall

5th Brigade – 1/45th, 1/50th and 1/91st regiments
under Brigadier General Crauford

4th Brigade – 1/6th and 1/32nd regiments
under Brigadier General Bowes

2nd Brigade – 36th, 1/40th and 1/71st regiments
under Major General Ferguson

6th or Light Brigade – 2/95th and 5/60th
under Brigadier General Fane.

The foregoing will be the general formation of the brigades in one
line, excepting that the light brigade will be ordered to take post in
front or in rear, or on either flank, according to circumstances. The
cavalry will be in reserve, and posted as may be necessary. A half-
brigade of artillery will be attached to each brigade of infantry.
Howitzers will be attached to the 1st, 2nd, 5th, and 6th brigades,
and the 9-pounder brigade will be in reserve.

'Spencer's now second-in-command to Wellesley,' said Moss, reading the rest of the general's order. A few weeks before it had been planned that the commander of the Gibraltar force would lead a brigade including the 106th. Evidently that plan had been discarded even before the force landed. 'Everyone clear about the new order of battle?' he asked Toye, MacAndrews and Thomas.

The senior major grinned. 'I notice they have split up the Highlanders. Very wise, or we could end up with another forty-five to deal with!'

Moss snorted with laughter. MacAndrews simply said mildly that there was an idea, and did anyone know where to buy the white cockades worn by Bonnie Prince Charlie's men.

'Well, we should be off at last.' Moss resumed his instructions. 'The advance will commence before dawn on the ninth. That will give us a few hours' marching before the sun gets too hot.'

'Where are we going, sir?' Toye's skin was heavily burned and already beginning to peel. It took great effort for him to resist picking at it.

'No details yet, but the talk was all of Lisbon last night at the general's table.' Moss had been invited to dine with Wellesley along with two of the other battalion commanders. He enjoyed giving the impression of special knowledge, although in truth the conversation had dwelt mainly on hunting and horses.

'Anyway,' he continued, 'by the end of tomorrow we will issue three days of rations to every man. I'd be grateful if you would have a word with Mr Kidwell about that.' Moss addressed the adjutant.

'Ammunition?' asked MacAndrews.

'Just sixty rounds per man at present. The rest will remain with the train, along with eighteen more days' worth of food.' Moss watched his two majors closely. His dissatisfaction with them had grown even stronger. It was not that they failed to perform their duties. Both men were efficient and reliable, but at the same time they seemed to lack any spark of enthusiasm. *Too old*, Moss thought, looking at MacAndrews' grey hair. Yet Toye was only a few years older than Moss himself, and always looked like a puppy nervous of being kicked. What was wrong with the man?

'Well, at least we are not too far from the front of the column,' said MacAndrews. 'Not so much dust.'

That was true, but seemed to Moss another symptom of worrying about the little things. 'Better yet, it puts us closer to the enemy if we should encounter the French unexpectedly. Shame we are no longer with the Lights, which ought to have ensured us of an early blooding. Anyway, it should not be long now. Remember, gentlemen, if in doubt, go straight at the enemy and show them British steel. I want the French to get to know the 106th – and fear us!'

Toye smiled politely. MacAndrews wondered at the colonel's growing tendency to make speeches at every opportunity. It was almost as if he were performing. 'The lads are ready,' he said simply. 'And the eighty-second look like a solid corps.'

'Yes, all in all, we are well placed. General Nightingall is a good man.' Moss's tone suggested generous condescension in this judgement. Before the others left his tent, the colonel's servant brought them a glass of indifferent wine and they toasted the regiment and the honours it would win. MacAndrews had an unsophisticated palate, but Toye was only just able to restrain himself from wincing at the sour taste. The loss of his personal stores was an additional annoyance, and perhaps added to Moss's disappointment with his senior officers. As yet there had been no opportunity to detach any of them from the battalion. Thomas would do, for an adjutant required a thoroughness and attention to detail which the man clearly possessed, however dull he was as company. The other two lacked animation, and the fire he wanted to impart to the entire regiment.

Moss grimaced as he took a sip of some truly foul port. It was the best his servant had been able to buy, and since there were only a few bottles, it was reserved for his own use and the mess would have to make do with even worse muck. Well, they would have to make the best of it and so would he. It fell to him to inspire the regiment, and by God he would do it. He would also have to make sure that his seniors understood the true situation. The years of waiting for another chance to distinguish himself were almost over, and the moment would not find him wanting.

'Mathematics has never been my strong point, but it seems an odd way to count,' said Hanley. A group of subalterns from the regiment were sitting around the table in the mess and studying a copy of the new general order. 'I mean, one, three, five, four, two, and six.'

'Well, it is the order in which we would stand when formed for battle,' offered Williams in explanation.

'Still seems odd. Why not just number us off from right to left? Or from left to right for that matter?'

There was stunned silence for a moment, so that Anstey's voice saying 'My trick, I believe' carried clearly from the game in progress among a group of officers sitting on stools outside. 'That's ten shillings you owe me, you rogues.'

'Seniority, William,' said Pringle in a tone that suggested this should be adequate explanation. Hanley still looked puzzled, prompting Truscott's strong pedagogic instinct.

'I'd never have believed it.' He shook his head. 'You are some-times quite the griffin. And you have been with us now for a couple of months? Truly amazing.

'Seniority is everything, and a grenadier most of all should know that. You do understand why your company is placed always on the right?'

Hanley said that he supposed everyone had to be somewhere, and that it was simpler if they were always in the same place.

Derryck broke out in a fit of giggles. Others were smiling rue-fully at such unbelievable ignorance.

'No,' Truscott continued patiently, as if speaking to an invalid or small child – or still worse a civilian – 'it is because you are senior to all the other companies in the regiment. Therefore you have the place of most honour, the right of the line. The Lights come next in seniority, so they are on the left, the second place of honour.'

Williams could see his friend framing the question and so answered before he had a chance. 'It goes back to the Greeks. A man carried his spear in his right hand and his shield in his left. It was the spear that attacked and the shield that defended, so the right was associated with attack and therefore became the place of most honour. The entire army was viewed as if it were one man, and so the right flank was the most prestigious place. If you remember your Thucydides . . .'

Truscott was grateful for the sanction of antiquity, knowing that Hanley would appreciate that, but was in no mood to listen to a long digression from Williams. 'With officers of the same rank,' he cut in, 'seniority is given to the man first appointed. We have two major generals, so naturally they are given the first and second brigades. Major General Hill has been longer in the rank, so equally naturally he and his First Brigade take the post of greatest honour on the right of our line.

'General Ferguson and his Second Brigade have the second post of honour on the left of the line. After that our brigadiers are stationed according to their seniority.'

He could see Hanley about to raise another question, but held up his hand to stop him as he felt it important to complete his explanation. 'The third place of honour is once again on the right of the line, just to the left of the First Brigade, and so that goes to the senior brigadier.' Truscott began to arrange cups on the table to mark the positions, ignoring a call of 'Hey, I have not finished' from Pringle. The explanation continued and Hanley struggled to follow.

'And so each brigade takes post according to seniority, working in towards the centre. The Sixth or Light Brigade is the only exception. It contains our riflemen and so is different to the others. Their duties require them to cover any advance or withdrawal and often to close with the enemy and skirmish. Therefore where they are actually stationed will vary, but nominally they are treated just as if they were the light company of a regiment and so stationed on the far left of the rest of us.' He looked at Hanley, expecting signs of enlightenment.

'It does seem very complicated,' he ventured. Truscott rolled his eyes.

'It is actually simple, William,' said Pringle. 'It becomes as natural as eating once you get used to it. May I have my cup back now, or will it break up the army?' He grabbed the pewter cup and quickly drained it. 'Alas for the Third Brigade. Morituri te salutant.'

'But surely the brigades could deploy in the logical sequence of their numbers,' Hanley suggested. 'Would not that be still simpler?'

'God save us from logical grenadiers!' Truscott decided to try again. 'That would ignore the places of honour and danger. The flanks of a line are vulnerable, so the best and steadiest officers and regiments should be there. Seniority ensures that this happens. It is the same for a battalion – though Heaven knows why we should grant precedence to grenadiers.'

'Because their minds work so slowly that they will stay in position even after they are dead,' offered Derryck.

Truscott ignored him as usual. 'It is the same within a brigade. Each regiment's seniority determines its position relative to the others. Surely you appreciate that.'

'I had simply assumed we went where we were told.' Hanley was struggling with the grammar of this new language.

'So tell us, fount of knowledge, where will we be in the Third Brigade?' asked Pringle mischievously.

'I understand that we are a new corps,' Hanley ventured.

'The newest, in fact.' Williams had decided to join in again. 'And so the most junior regiment of the line.'

'But the best!' asserted Derryck stoutly, and the more enthusiastic officers pounded the table in assent.

'Quiet in there. I can't hear myself losing money,' yelled a voice from outside the tent. They banged harder and cheered at that, and it took a while for the noise to subside.

'Oh, so does a lower number denote seniority?' Hanley felt he was making some headway, and was surprised by the expressions of universal dismay that he had only just realised something so obvious. 'Does that mean we shall be in the centre?' There was general and still incredulous amusement.

'In a larger brigade that would be true.' Truscott raised his voice to carry over the noise. 'But since we have only the Eighty-second with us, then our station is on the left. You see, it really is so very simple. Every company, every regiment and every brigade has its natural place. And then every one of us has his post within the company. We are threads within a much larger web.'

'Very poetic,' said Pringle. 'I have a suspicion you read books.'

'How about bricks in a wall, like the Spartans?' proposed Williams.

'Now you are confusing the man, he was much happier as a thread.'

'Bloody grenadiers,' swore Truscott wearily. 'At least he should know what is going on now.'

Hanley raised his head. 'So what precisely is a howitzer?' Groans came from all around the table.

'He's dead, sir,' said the one-eyed sergeant, massaging his knuckles.

Denilov had been paying little attention to the last few minutes of the interrogation, but a quick look confirmed that Varandas had died at last.

'Old bastard was tougher than he looked.' There was the faintest hint of respect in the sergeant's voice. Neither he nor any of his soldiers was as tall as their officer, but they were all broad shouldered and well used to hard toil. They had begun by simply beating the old man, and then the interpreter Roberto translated the count's questions, while the soldiers took turns to pound his face, ribs and stomach if the old man did not answer satisfactorily. For some time Varandas had stubbornly pleaded ignorance, until the pain finally grew too much and he began to moan the answers. Roberto licked his lips as he watched, first flinching at the blows, and later smiling as he enjoyed being on the side of men capable of unleashing such violence.

'It does not matter. I have learned all that is necessary.' That had happened a while ago, but it seemed reasonable to keep up the questioning, just in case there was something extra he might

206

learn. Denilov gave a dismissive gesture and the sergeant ordered two of his jaegers to carry the corpse outside. They took it into the garden of the cottage and tossed it into a large dung heap. Then they shovelled more of the waste to cover the body, complaining as each spadefull unleashed new waves of stench from the manure.

'You have done well, Roberto,' said Denilov in French.

'Thank you, sir.' The small man touched his forehead respectfully. As usual he was crouching, trying to be as inconspicuous as possible. His skin was sallow, his face pockmarked, and his eyes never stopped moving and never looked at anyone directly. The Russian officer made him nervous at the best of times and the brutal questioning of the steward had only added to his fear, but it had also increased his greed. He had been well paid so far, and there was the promise of more.

Denilov had hired him in an inn in Lisbon just a week ago. It had taken almost a month for the count to locate Varandas, for he had moved cautiously. Then a few more days had been needed before he was ready to go looking for him. The arrival of the British was a happy coincidence, for the confusion of a war would make it easier to go about his task. Who would notice a few more deaths, or quibble over lost treasure when rival armies were campaigning, looting as they went? The British Army's arrival would have pleased the old general, but Denilov had no doubt that it would fail. Not that it mattered, for he was so close now to finding the duke's hidden wealth. Varandas had finally revealed that he had arranged to conceal a chest full of the duke's property near Obidos. A local priest, trusted by the duke himself as well as his steward, had made the final arrangements. Now all they had to do was find the man and persuade him to talk.

'Do you know this place?' Denilov asked the interpreter.

'Obidos? Yes, sir, yes. I think, yes,' stammered Roberto. 'To the north, near the sea.' Once the servant of a French merchant, he had been caught stealing from his employer and dismissed. Since then he had become a petty thief in the back streets of Lisbon. He was useful because he spoke French, and few Portuguese spoke anything other than their own tongue. Denilov doubted he had travelled much outside the city, and suspected that his knowledge of the village he was seeking was vague at best. It did not matter. If he took them to the area, then they should find it without too much trouble.

'There was a woman here, I think. Yes, a woman, not long ago.' Roberto's expression was lascivious. 'The old man have some fun, eh? Not too old for that.'

Denilov had already noted that there were two sets of plates laid out on the table with the remains of a breakfast, while the bedclothes looked more disturbed than was likely if Varandas had slept alone. There were no women's clothes, and no signs of anyone else living in the cottage. Perhaps the steward summoned some whore from the nearest village, but Denilov doubted it and suspected Maria. So she had not given up. He had had little entertainment in the last weeks, and the idea of encountering her again was a pleasant one. Denilov smiled wickedly, making the nervous interpreter cringe, and the count could not resist laughing. Roberto looked confused, and then joined in the laughter, hoping to reassure his disturbing employer of his loyalty.

'Pity she not still here, sir,' he said with a leer. Denilov ignored him. If Maria had been here earlier today then she had taken a long time to find Varandas. Perhaps she had truly not known where he was, although obviously she had been able to track him down in the end. She was only just ahead of him, but he and his men should be able to move more quickly. Perhaps the girl had enlisted some men to help her, although it was unlikely she knew that he had also begun his own search. They would need to proceed carefully, but Denilov had planned to do that anyway, and could rely on his sergeant to keep the soldiers alert. Yet they could not afford to be too slow.

They left the cottage and headed north, always keeping one scout some distance in the lead and another keeping watch behind them. The countryside seemed unusually empty, and they saw almost no one. People were nervous of the two armies, and few travelled abroad unless they had no other choice. Once they saw half a dozen men in the distance and there was a glint from the sun striking metal, which suggested weapons. That night they camped in a small hollow, and did not light a fire in case it attracted attention. Several large bonfires were visible, and Denilov suspected that these had been lit by gatherings of militiamen and other enthusiastic volunteers, hovering around the countryside in the hope of ambushing isolated Frenchmen.

The next day their luck changed barely half an hour after they had begun to move. The night's cold had not yet burned off, and they were glad of the warmth of their drab greatcoats. The jaeger leading the file suddenly raised his hand to tell them to stop. They halted, each man scanning the scrubby bushes covering the sides of the little valley. The sergeant was just going forward to ask the soldier what he had seen when men erupted from the hillsides around them. There were at least forty. Many had pikes or pitchforks, but a few had traces of uniform and muskets or pistols. Instinctively the soldiers cocked their muskets and levelled them ready to fire, pointing the muzzles at the nearest peasants.

'Stop!' barked Denilov to his men. 'Lower your firelocks.' The jaegers obeyed, gently moving to point the muzzles at the ground, but none of them released his grip on the trigger. Roberto's eyes darted around, and the sergeant could see that he would break and run at the slightest opportunity. He whispered a threat, and although the sallow-faced man did not understand Russian he understood the intent and started nodding and smiling fervently in an effort to reassure him.

Then Denilov called out something in a language the sergeant did not understand. His tone was friendly, and the peasants looked doubtful. A man who seemed to be their leader took a few steps nearer and asked something in Portuguese. The count tried again, but neither man understood the other. Then Denilov spoke to Roberto in French.

'Tell him I am an English officer and we are English soldiers, their allies come to fight against the common enemy and liberate their country.'

There was a rapid exchange in Portuguese. 'He asks for proof,' whispered Roberto.

'Open your coats,' said the count calmly, speaking in their own language to his soldiers. He unbuttoned his own greatcoat and pulled it back to show them what he meant. Then Denilov switched back to French. 'Tell him he can see that we wear green jackets. We are elite English soldiers. Like your own *caçadores*. Hunters who hunt Frenchmen.' The uniform of the Guard Jaeger was different in cut and shade to that of the British riflemen, but the colour was all that really mattered. It was not French blue.

It took a while, but Denilov was confident and friendly, praising the Portuguese leader for the skill and obvious courage of his men. He offered the man a drink from his flask, and solemnly pronounced a toast to the two kingdoms of Portugal and England and their staunch alliance. One of the peasants guided them three miles to a dirt track which he assured them would lead to Obidos.

'Tomorrow, maybe next day,' translated Roberto. 'Or day after, he think.' Denilov wondered how widely many of these men ever travelled. He did not ask about the priest. That could wait until they were nearer.

21

On 9th August the British army marched inland. Patrols of the 20th Light Dragoons went first, although the cavalry-men had to nurse their horses carefully, for they were not yet fully recovered from the weeks penned in the makeshift stalls of trans-port ships. The army's staff had worked hard to obtain a supply of mounts, but had enjoyed very little success. The dismounted dragoons remained on foot, and so would stay back at the beach. So would a dozen guns, for there were sufficient horses only to pull eighteen of them across the poor tracks of the area.

After the cavalry came outposts provided by the 60th and 95th Rifles, then the brigades marching in their proper place. None of this was obvious to Hanley, struggling along carrying the cased King's Colour in the centre of the 106th's column. All he could see was the backs of the men from the company ahead of him through the thick dust which seemed to hang in the still air. Nobody sang, but in spite of the growing heat and the dust there was a sense of optimism and joy that they were at last moving. Everyone wanted to get on, and break the dull monotony of the war so far. Three times in the first hour the column stopped and waited before marching on again. There was never any indication of why this happened. Staff officers rode past periodically, but did not explain – not to him, anyway. He had that familiar sense of everyone else understanding what was going on and failing to let him in on the secret.

The Grenadier Company led the battalion as was proper. Wickham marched ahead of the centre of its formation as was equally proper, and spent most of the time regretting that he had not worn his old boots. This new pair looked smarter, but were still stiff and rubbed unmercifully. He glanced enviously to where Moss and the two majors rode to the right of his company. Once they were passed by Wellesley and his staff, and one of the officers stopped to exchange pleasantries with Moss. Wickham strained to hear, but was too far away and could not leave his position. Later, they would march less formally, but at the moment a rapid pace had been set and everyone had to remain at their posts. He noticed that the ADC had a well-cut pair of overall trousers, the insides reinforced with leather to take the wear of long rides and the outside seams decorated with brass buttons. The captain decided that he would have to get himself a pair as soon as he could. Presumably in time company officers would be permitted to buy and ride horses. Lydia would enjoy seeing him in such a rig.

The thought of his wife brought a momentary pang. The captain knew himself to be a physical, passionate man, and the enforced celibacy since the start of the voyage had been a great struggle. Lydia shared his enthusiasm, and even now, six years after they had eloped and he had first taken her, the desire was still there in both of them. In his case, there was also a desire for other women, but he had taken care to be discreet. Now that they were moving there was a chance that the army would leave this wilderness and so such pleasures might be found in a larger town. Lisbon surely should have many suitable establishments. It would be as well, for his enforced abstinence – the lack even of the company of ladies – had encouraged an even greater recklessness about his gambling. His debts had mounted alarmingly, far beyond his ability to pay without seeking more money from his brother-in-law. His luck needed to change and a few victories at the table would recover – or at least mitigate – his situation. Part of his mind wondered whether French bullets might solve the problem for him by removing Anstey or Brotherton, who between them held most of his promissory notes.

Wickham was jerked from his reverie by a call from Major Toye. He had to step quickly not to block the front rank of his company as he went to the side to join the mounted officers. After listening to the instructions he quickly gave the orders.

Ten minutes later Williams leaned all his weight against the iron-tyred wheel of a cannon and pushed forward. He heard Dobson mutter 'Move, you bitch' from the other side of the high wooden spokes. Twenty of the grenadiers had been instructed to help as many artillerymen shift the gun from the narrow ditch into which it had sunk. Together they heaved, as the drivers whipped the horses in their traces to urge them forward. Williams grunted as he strained to shift the heavy wheel. The gun carriage was painted grey like all the other guns, limbers and wagons of the Royal Artillery. The metal of the tyre was hot from the sun.

Finally the wheel began to turn, fractionally at first, and then with a surge it rose up the little slope, cleared the top and then flew forward. Williams was surprised everyone managed to keep their balance as the gun carriage shot forward. He grinned at Dobson.

'I thought they said this was a light six-pounder!'

'Aye, then we best be glad it weren't a heavy one,' replied the veteran. 'And be glad we ain't gunners. All those buggers are deaf.' He shouted the familiar joke to the blue-jacketed bombardier who stood next to him, rubbing his hands together. The man smiled and put a hand to his ear, pretending not to have heard. Then his face fell and he pointed ahead. Both limber and gun had bogged this time, sinking into a patch of soft sand no more than eighty yards farther on. This was supposed to be a road, but this section at least was badly rutted, broken by channels carved out when the heavy rains at the end of winter had caused a flood, or so dry that the soil was little more than dust. The three six-pounder guns attached to the 3rd Brigade were struggling to make progress, and so twenty men from the 106th's Grenadier Company had been sent to assist the gunners. It promised to be a morning of back-breaking work, but at least their packs, muskets and equipment were now being carried in an artillery wagon.

Williams walked beside Dobson as the group headed over

to extricate the gun once again. The volunteer was nervous, wondering whether or not he should say something to the old soldier. Two days before, he had been sent back from the out-post line with a message from Pringle to Wickham. He had cut through one of the olive groves clinging to the hillside, scrambling over the dry-stone walls. It was just chance, and at least he had been fortunate not to fall on top of them, but as he lifted himself on to one wall, he had found himself looking down on a couple making love. The man was on top and so intent that he did not notice the Welshman, but Williams could see that it was Redman. Jenny Dobson – well, Hanks now – stared him straight in the eye, and even winked as she kept moaning.

Williams had just turned and jumped down the way he had come, taking a longer route around the grove. He was still not sure whether he should have challenged Redman. The man was clearly no gentleman and could only have been insincere in his previous apology. Yet he did not want to fight a duel. It was not that he was frightened, simply that the advice of his friends had sunk in. He was so close now to his opportunity to win distinction that it was difficult to think of anything else. He must fight well and risk all to become an officer and then continue to excel until he was promoted to a high enough rank to support his mother and ask for the hand of Miss MacAndrews. Such aims could not be jeopardised by an affair of honour with a man who clearly had none himself. Williams thought himself selfish and hated the fact, but it still did not alter his resolution.

The question remained of whether or not he should tell the girl's father. It was hard enough to talk to the taciturn Hanks at the best of times, so he had already discarded the idea of speaking to the girl's husband. In truth it was none of his business. At the moment, there were too many others within earshot for him to think of broaching the subject. Even this made him feel a little craven. He wished that he simply had not chanced upon the scene of adultery. Better not to have known about it at all.

'Come on, Pug, here we go again.' Dobson patted him cheerfully on the shoulder as they took position around the bogged limber.

'Jackets off, lads,' ordered Sergeant Darrowfield with a nod at the bombardier whose own men similarly were stripping down to shirtsleeves. 'Think of good ale, and heave for England.' The men grimaced at any talk of liquid. Several had already more than half drained their canteens. Williams had drunk only a little – making use of yet another lesson he had learned from Dobson. He shook his head and leaned into the wheel.

The army made steady progress. The roads were not good, but Sir Arthur Wellesley had seen far worse in India. Throughout the day he was constantly on the move, riding ahead to inspect the terrain, going to meet Portuguese officers and civil officials, and always checking in person that everything that needed to be done was being done. He had long ago learnt to see the detail as well as the wider picture. He did not know all of his senior officers well, so he cast an eye over the appearance of their brigades. On the whole he was pleased.

Leaving the guns had been hard. In India guns mattered, and he did not want to experience another battle like Assaye five years before, where the enemy artillery had been far more numerous and larger-calibre than his own. As the day wore on he had been amazed that any of his men survived the deluge of heavy shot. Many did not, but the rest had kept on advancing and chased the enemy away.

Eighteen cannon was not many, especially since only one of the three batteries was equipped with the heavier nine-pounders. The French would doubtless have more guns and they would be well served. Portuguese allies were due to join his army the next day, but it seemed unlikely they would bring more than a handful of guns, if any at all. They lacked so much, although the thousands of muskets brought from England would help.

He would have to be content. There were no more horses, and so eighteen guns was all that he had. At least they were well served and fully crewed, even if the carriages were taking a hammering on the bad roads. He had already seen one gun's wheel shattered, but had been impressed by the speed with which his gunners had replaced it and continued. It would also have been better to have more cavalrymen. At Assaye he had personally led an entire brigade in a charge. Now he had only one weak regiment, and they were hard put to meet all his needs as scouts, patrols, escorts and couriers. Still, at least he now had his own horses ashore, and was able to change from one thoroughbred to another as they became worn out.

His infantry was good, and in the end that mattered more than anything else. The country he had seen so far was scarcely ideal for massed horsemen anyway. It was a drab landscape, lacking the intensity of colour and smell he remembered from India. He also missed the East India Company's own soldiers, the sepoys and sowars who looked so cheerful and fought so well. Yet his was a good little army, and he was keen to press on and confront the enemy.

It would not be his army for very long, and he freely admitted – at least to himself – that this added to his eagerness. He had studied the French carefully, had understood how the Emperor's men fought and how they had dazzled the world, smashing army after army. He also knew he could beat them and craved the opportunity to demonstrate this. It was ambition – victories in India could be dismissed, but success in Europe could not – for he was an ambitious man, but it was not merely that. Since he had decided to dedicate himself to a military life he had realised that his talents in this direction were prodigious. He had served under poor commanders in ill-judged and mismanaged campaigns and the experience had offended him. The waste and incompetence were repellent. He was not confident that similar failures would not occur if he ceased to hold command. Service to his country was central to his very being, the sense of duty as natural as breathing, and in his own mind anything done as part of state policy must be done well. Therefore it was better that he play the key role.

At most he had a matter of weeks, and perhaps less. Sir John Moore was on his way to reinforce the army in Portugal, returning from the fiasco of the expedition to Sweden. Muddled plans in London, and understandable suspicion of Britain's intentions on the part of the Swedes, had meant his army never disembarked. The whole thing had been a waste of time and effort, although Wellesley suspected little of this was Moore's fault. His reputation was high, but he was also disliked by powerful members of the government. Therefore, two even more senior lieutenant generals had been appointed as first- and second-in-command of the forces in Portugal. That was not all. More lieutenant generals were arriving and soon Wellesley would be the eighth-in-command of the army.

Sir Harry Burrard could arrive in less than a week; a letter had already come from him. Its content did not suggest any particular perception, let alone a clear sense of purpose. Fortunately another letter had arrived from Castlereagh, the Secretary of State and a friend. Wellesley's spirits had sunk as he read the details of the new appointments, but it had also instructed him to proceed with the campaign on his own initiative, and that was all that he needed. So now he would advance and seek out a rapid confrontation with the French. The previous night he had written to his old friend the Duke of Richmond, whose young son was serving as one of his ADCs. 'I hope that I shall have beat Junot before any of them arrive, then they may do as they please with me.'

So he had advanced. It was a risk, but a calculated one, and risk had never frightened him. He would find the French and beat them, opening the road to Lisbon. The job would be done properly before anyone else could make a mess of it. He would show them that he could beat disciplined Frenchmen as readily as the vast and colourful armies of Indian princes.

Wellesley and his staff rode back along the column. He was pleased to see that there were not too many stragglers. Some soldiers had fallen out from their battalions, struggling with the heat and the weight of their equipment. A soldier's pack was large and wooden framed and its straps cut into a man's chest, making it hard to breathe. It was said the French had a better design, and it would be worth taking a look at that when the opportunity was offered. Not that the British Army was likely to change its equipment simply because it was badly designed.

'George, see that anyone who can't walk is taken forward by cart. No one is to leave the column.' The ADC sped away to arrange things. Wellesley did not want to lose any men unnecessarily. Some would genuinely not have recovered from the inactivity of the voyage. More importantly men away from their units for any reason were liable to misbehave. They would wander off and molest the population, stealing food and valuables, even raping and murdering. An army whose recruitment was aided by magistrates contained many dangerous and bad characters. Some of his meagre force of cavalry were patrolling the flanks of the column to prevent any redcoat from straying. He had some provosts – the army's policemen – but not enough.

In the last weeks the French army had marauded through Portugal, committing every sort of atrocity. Napoleon's men routinely foraged and plundered, but now they were massacring men, women and children alike. They hoped to terrify the Portuguese, but had spread as much hatred as fear, and now the hand of every peasant was against them. Lone Frenchmen were apt to have their throats cut. Wellesley was determined that his own men would not provoke similar hatred and reprisals.

Wellesley waved a greeting to General Bowes as he passed. The red-faced Bowes was yelling as he supervised a group of men trying to free an ammunition wagon sunk into the mud. A string of Irish oaths almost drowned out the brigadier's encouragement. It had taken massive and persistent effort to persuade the authorities to give him two companies of the Irish Wagon Train to carry the expedition's supplies, but the men and their vehicles were already proving to be worth their weight in gold.

The general and his staff continued their ride, and soon a harsh cacophony of metallic screeches announced the approach of the main baggage train. For some reason the drivers of the local ox carts never greased the axles. The contrast with the regimented efficiency and uniform vehicles of the wagon train was stark, but these hundreds of carts made the campaign possible. Behind them came thousands of mules, driven by some of the most villainous men he had ever seen in his life. They could have gone faster, but it was necessary to keep together, and so they kept to the steady two-mile-an-hour plod of the oxen.

Slowly, the long column snaked forward to find General Junot and to smash him.

22

The Portuguese officer stared blankly after Hanley finished talking to him. He tried again, speaking slowly and clearly in Spanish.

'These ragamuffins can't even understand their own damned language,' said Lieutenant Colonel Moss rather too loudly from behind him. Hanley could see the allied officer understood the tone if not the content of this scornful comment. He bristled, yet was clearly still polite when he spoke. Hanley could understand only a few words. The accent was so strong and so very different to Castilian. He knew that he could gain at least a general understanding of written Portuguese, but had not been prepared for the difference in sound.

The 106th's Light Company were providing outposts on the second evening of the march and Moss had been visiting them when a group of armed Portuguese had arrived. They were motley in appearance. Two had faded and patched blue jackets, but most were in simple white smocks. Each wore a broad-brimmed civilian hat, but no two were alike. A few had large feathers of various colours tucked into them. Most of the men had simple hide sandals, leaving their toes bare. They were part of the Portuguese General Friere's forces who had come to join the British, but no one was able to understand what they wanted. Then Moss remembered Hanley and immediately sent for him.

The ensign had tried to explain that he had lived in Spain and not Portugal, and that the languages were different, but Moss had brushed such trivialities aside.

'We don't need to conduct a debate. Just find out what it is these fellows want.'

Hanley had tried, and only felt more foolish as each effort failed, and more aware of the colonel's frustration and anger. It was one more disappointment for Moss, reinforcing the realisation that if the battalion was to succeed then he must do everything himself.

Finally, Hanley felt that he might just as well try French. The response was immediate. The Portuguese officer smiled and replied in French that was barely accented and in many ways better than Hanley's own. The man announced himself as Lieutenant Mata of the 4th Artillery Regiment. A wheel had broken on one of their few guns and they needed the help and tools to replace it.

Hanley explained the situation to the colonel, who had already lost interest. Moss told him to lead the Portuguese to the half-battery with the 3rd Brigade and let the gunners sort it out. Hanley did so, and asked Mata to tell him about the French invasion and what Junot's men had done. It was a grim story, and if he had not seen the massacre in Madrid he would have been inclined to dismiss it all as tall tales and lies born from hatred. Yet it depressed him. His admiration of the Revolution and its promotion of reason, of the new Emperor and his imposition of order, was still a warm memory. In a way it made it worse that these high ideals had been corrupted into such savagery. Mata loathed the French with a ferocious bitterness, and Hanley could not think less of him for this. He had also come to hate them, and yet there was still something terrible about seeing the well-educated young lieutenant – he was yet another product of Coimbra – consumed by such rage.

They met Pringle on the way, and after the introductions Billy's cheerfulness lightened the tone of the conversation. It helped that there was something essentially ridiculous about French being their only means of communication. Even so Hanley was glad to leave the Portuguese with the gunners.

★

Williams stood as one of the sentries guarding the regiment's baggage. Dobson should have been there, but the man was too drunk even to stand, and so Williams had managed to persuade Sergeant Darrowfield to turn a blind eye and permit him to cover for the veteran. Earlier in the day the volunteer had noticed that Jenny Hanks had a bruised cheek. A few hours later Private Hanks had appeared on parade with an eye blacked and the signs of a recently staunched nosebleed. Neither he nor Dobson said anything, but it was well known that they had gone off on their own and that the veteran had come back first.

Dobson had started drinking as soon as the parade was dismissed. It had been many months since he had taken more than his 'daily tipple', and it was clear that there was more to the incident than a father demonstrating to his son-in-law that it was not safe to lose his temper with his wife. Dobson clearly knew or guessed something, although Williams himself had remained silent. Yet the regiment was always a hotbed of gossip and Jenny was a fool if she thought that everything would remain secret.

Williams watched her now as she carried a pail of water towards the main camp of the regiment. He watched her flirt and joke with the men she passed, but the girl had always done that and in the main it was harmless. Soldiers' families lived their lives very publicly within the larger family of the regiment, and inevitably most grew up with a thick skin and a robust sense of humour. Then Jenny spotted him, smiled, and came over.

'Ma says thanks, Mr Williams. Dad will sleep it off by tomorrow. Old bugger ought to know better.'

'You don't have to be old to be a fool, Mrs Hanks.'

The girl made a face and lowered the bucket to the ground. As she straightened up she raised a hand to brush back her brown hair. The immediate glance to see his reaction revealed that this was not purely a natural gesture.

'I don't want to follow the drum all my life. There's a world out there of cities and fine things and I mean to live like that one day. It's mine to take.'

'Redman won't give you that,' said Williams, surprising himself with his directness.

'Him – he's just practice.' The sixteen-year-old's tone was surprisingly scornful. 'And the others. They give me nice things, but it's only a start.' She eyed him for a moment. 'I'd do you for free if you like. To say thanks.'

She enjoyed his obvious shock. Williams was dumbfounded and simply shook his head. Jenny chuckled, her laugh that of a child without traces of her recent cynicism. 'Well then, perhaps you could lift my pail for me? It's fine once it's off the ground.'

Manners immediately took over, and since Williams was not at attention, he bent forward and reached for the handle. As he came low Jenny darted forward and kissed him lightly on the cheek. 'That's from Ma,' she said, then dropped her tone to a whisper, 'and this is from me.' Her lips moved on to his, and before he realised it his mouth was open to her tongue. His eyes widened and he dropped the pail the few inches to the ground. It stayed upright, but splashed on to the hem of her brown skirt.

'Clumsy bastard,' she scolded him lightly, adding a wink, which instantly gave Williams the picture of stumbling across the girl and Redman. He was too flustered to apologise. 'Don't worry, I'll do it.' Jenny retrieved the pail herself. 'Where you men would be without women . . . I don't know.'

'Well, thanks, Mr Williams, from me and Ma both.' The girl walked away, seeming to sway in her stride more than was usual and more than the one-sided weight of the bucket would require.

Williams gulped, and renewed his vigil, trying not to think about the last few minutes. The strangest thing was that in spite of everything he liked the girl.

The next day they saw the first signs of the French. They entered a town and saw houses broken into and looted. Others had chalk marks on the doors where French billeting officers had allocated each one to soldiers from different regiments. They had left only a day before and had not stayed long so the damage was limited. In the evening light Hanley went with Truscott, Pringle and

Williams to look at the medieval abbey. They had rarely seen him so animated as he enthused about the grand old building. Even Pringle admitted that he had never before had so much pleasure looking at a lot of tombs.

When the army marched onwards they were given a clearer illustration of the enemy's rapaciousness, when they passed a convent whose ceilings and walls had been roughly stripped of every piece of their gilt decoration. Hanley came close to tears when he saw the wreckage, the floors covered in plaster. Then he worried that the attacks on buildings seemed to affect him more than the mistreatment of people and felt guilty about this. Most of the other officers were disappointed to find the convent empty of nuns. They had nearly all read romances in which nubile young noblewomen were incarcerated in convents by their stern parents, and sat in their cells waiting for a heroic rescuer to arrive. Even Pringle had been surprised at the degree of lust even the mention of nuns provoked in normally staunchly Anglican officers.

He wondered for a moment how many nuns had lived here before the war. With each step he took his boots crunched the pieces of fallen plaster underfoot. He was in a small room – probably really a cell, he thought – and tried to imagine what it would be like to live in such seclusion. His family had meant him to be a parson, once his father had grudgingly accepted that the child's absurd seasickness was not going to be cured. He had gone along with the idea because it was easier than challenging it. Even then Pringle had liked an easy life and Oxford had provided many pleasures. He had never really worried about what would happen afterwards, but always knew that the Church was not for him. His beliefs were vague and, although observation of the clergy in general suggested this was not a fatal flaw, he had known that he would not follow that path, which seemed so safe and dull.

He had first suggested going into the army as a joke and had been surprised at how readily his father had warmed to the idea. After a while so had he. He liked having so many of his decisions made for him, and found much of the company congenial. Pringle smiled as he overheard Hanley remonstrating with

Williams after the volunteer had made some scathing remark about the trappings of popery. Truscott's deep laughter echoed along the wide empty hall.

Pringle let them go. There was something oddly secure about the little room. He sat down on the straw mattress. For some reason the French had not taken or ripped this apart as they had done in the other cells. His hand felt something tucked down next to the timber frame and drew out a battered little black book. Idly he flicked through the pages. The print was tiny, and he took off his glasses and brought the book close up to his face. Much to his surprise it was neither Latin, nor religious. As far as he could tell from guessing the Portuguese words, it was a romance, telling of knights and damsels in the Middle Ages. There was something written by hand on the inside of the cover. As he continued to flick through the pages, and as was so often the case, his mind turned to thoughts of women. Perhaps a young and pretty inmate of the convent had kept this book as a secret pleasure. He smiled at the thought.

'Señor, señor!' The voice startled him, as did the feel of hands clasping his knees imploringly. He had not heard the woman rush into the room and throw herself down before him. 'Señor, are you English? I beg you to help me, please!'

Pringle dropped the book on to his lap and fumbled for his glasses. The woman was swathed in a black robe which covered her bowed head. He caught one glimpse of a face before she leaned forward to press her forehead against his knees. Voice and movements suggested youth, but until he had hooked his spectacles over his ears he could not see clearly. When he did – after nearly poking himself in the eye in the process – he could not help laughing. It was a nun in distress.

'Do not mock me, señor, but pity me!' The woman's accent was strong, making a soft voice even more charming. 'I believe the English to be gentlemen and I have nowhere else to turn for help!' She looked up imploringly. Only her face was uncovered, but it was a remarkable face with a frail beauty which even under normal circumstances would have made any man feel protective. Her complexion was dark, and her eyes paler grey than any Pringle had ever seen before. Now they were glazed with tears. 'Oh, please help me, señor.'

'Do not cry, Sister.' Pringle reached out and lightly grasped the young woman's shoulders. 'My name is Lieutenant Pringle. I am an English officer and I am at your service.' The words sounded pompous even as he said them. He felt that he was either dreaming or inside a romantic novel. It would have been hard to answer any other way. For a moment he wondered where his friends had got to, and why the noise had not brought them back. He tried not to laugh again at the absurdity of the situation, but could not stop himself.

There were more tears and Pringle murmured reassurances and even went so far as to pat her head. It was a little hard to know quite how to treat a nun. As she was kneeling so close to him and kept grabbing his legs he was very aware that she was also a woman and no rough and ill-fitting habit could conceal the fact that she was also an attractive one. Gently he raised her chin and smiled as encouragingly as he could. His other hand took one of hers and pressed softly.

'Now, what help do you need?' His thumb began stroking the palm of her hand.

The story came out slowly, with several fresh outbursts of tears. She told him that her name was Sister Maria, and she had a very long surname which Pringle knew he could not pronounce and was struggling even to remember. She was an orphan, but her uncle was rich and had given a generous endowment to the convent, where she was raised until now she was nineteen. Pringle would have guessed her age at a few more years than that, but was not about to quibble. She had not pulled her hand away and he continued to rub his thumb over the palm. His other hand had left her chin and was pressing the rough material of her sleeve.

When the war started her uncle had taken ship to England. He was a merchant in the wine trade and had many connections in that country. Once again the story smacked of fiction, but at that moment it was very hard not to believe. Well, actually it was hard to care with an attractive young woman so desperate for his company – and so close. Pity that she was a nun, but at least his life had become more interesting for the moment, however brief it proved.

'That is why he assured me that I could always trust an Englishman,' said Maria, staring up into his eyes. 'They are a good race even if they are heretics.'

'Generous of him. Sound chap, your uncle,' was the best Pringle could manage. Maria had shifted her arm and his own hand slid round till it was above her ribs. Instinct was taking over and she did not seem to mind as he traced the outline of her body. The material of her habit was surprisingly thin.

'Before my uncle left, he sent a large sum of money to me to provide for the nuns during the crisis and to permit us to continue our charitable works. He guessed that the French would be cruel, but alas, even he did not truly appreciate their viciousness. He gave the money to a priest who brought it to a little church five miles west of Obidos and hid it near there. Then he came to me here at the convent, but on his way a party of French soldiers arrested him as a spy. They hanged him by the crossroads.'

'Goddamned rogues,' murmured Pringle. Maria did not seem to register the blasphemy. Billy was struggling to listen. Both his hands had moved to hold the girl's body. She did not seem to register that either, although he found it rather hard to believe. Her tale had the ring of fiction about it. At the moment that did not seem to matter.

'Only his servant escaped and he brought the news to me.'

'Brave fellow, I'm sure.'

'Then he ran away with his own and his master's horses.'

'Swine.'

'I must go to Obidos and speak to the priest of that church. He will know where the money is hidden. Then I can bring it to my abbess and she will be able to use it to help the needy.

'Please help me to do this thing. It is not safe to travel alone. There are French soldiers everywhere and they spare no one. Even nuns have fallen prey to their lusts.' Maria paused and looked down as if only now noticing that Pringle had his arms around her. The Englishman coughed and then withdrew his hands, muttering an apology. Even then he wondered whether she was truly so naive. Surely a real nun would have been more outraged or even oblivious?

'Oh, you are so sympathetic, so kind and honourable,' she continued. 'Will you escort me there and protect me? It is much to ask, but I beg you as an English gentleman to aid me now in my distress. Please, señor, please, I am begging you on your honour.' Once again her head pressed against his knees imploringly.

'Well, of course, if it's a question of honour . . .' said Pringle, tentatively patting her head, but taking care to suggest nothing beyond mere sympathy.

He remained sitting for a good five minutes after Maria left. Already the whole thing seemed unreal. Yet he had agreed to meet the nun at a crossroads shrine outside the town at three o'clock. Unless the orders had changed, the army would not be moving again today. He would bring horses and a few friends for added safety and they would take Maria to find the church and its priest, and then escort her back in safety with her money. It seemed simple enough, apart from borrowing horses, finding the man and evading any prowling French patrols. Simple, he thought to himself, and wondered why he had agreed so readily, even though he knew that he could never resist a pretty face. For all his bluff, at heart he was a romantic – or perhaps a damned fool, and maybe there was no real difference. Now he needed to find some more damned fools to help him.

Hanley, Truscott and Williams appeared in the doorway. Pringle smiled.

'You will never guess what has just happened,' he said.

23

'Perhaps she isn't coming?' asked Hanley. They had been waiting for a good half-hour. A few travellers had passed, but there had been no sign of Maria. All three of Pringle's friends had readily agreed to come. Indeed, he suspected that he could have recruited most of the officers in the regiment – probably in the army – with the prospect of helping a nun in distress. The idea was romantic, but far more than that everyone was still restlessly energetic, frustrated by a so far disappointing war and an enemy who had failed to turn up and fight.

Together the four men had called in favours, and spent almost the last of their money to borrow four horses. None was too impressive, but even so solemn oaths had been sworn to return them to their owners before dawn. All four men had felt the excitement of questing knights. It was now beginning to wear off in the baking afternoon heat.

'Perhaps you imagined the whole thing?' suggested Truscott. 'Could all be a touch of the sun. After all, to call her Maria.'

'All the women in this country are called Maria,' said Pringle stoutly. His doubts had grown, however. The whole episode now seemed unreal, the 'nun', her story and her behaviour like something from the stage.

'Well, a lot of them anyway,' acknowledged Hanley.

'She felt real enough.'

'Please remember that she is a nun,' put in Williams.

'Yes, don't get any ideas.' Truscott shaded his eyes to look up into the sky. The sun was still beating down and part of him wanted to lie in a shady spot and do nothing for a very long time.

'Unless she is a figment of your imagination, in which case you are free to indulge in any sort of depravity.'

'That almost makes me regret to have to say that she is coming.' Pringle was pointing to a black-robed figure riding a donkey out of the town. The four Englishmen assumed respectful poses. Maria greeted them demurely and instantly won their devotion. She was humble and grateful, and even Williams' suspicions of the Roman Church in all its forms were quickly turned into admiration for a godly young person willing to take risks to help the unfortunate. At the same time he could not help noticing that for all her simple and concealing clothes she was a remarkably attractive woman. He tried to suppress that thought and failed utterly. When she gave him the slightest of smiles he beamed back enthusiastically.

It took them more than an hour to ride to the little church. They passed a few whitewashed farms, but saw no villages. Even Obidos itself was out of sight, hidden by some low hills. There was no sign of the French, and barely any indication of people of any sort. The few travellers they passed tried to avoid their gaze and hurried away.

'It used to be more important,' explained Sister Maria. 'Almost three hundred years ago a little girl was carrying water to her mother when she saw the Virgin herself standing tall on a boulder. She was very beautiful, and the sight of her face gave wisdom to the child to know instantly who it was.' Williams only just managed to restrain a sceptical sniff.

'Later the child became an abbess in my order. In the meantime a local nobleman paid for this church to be built.' They had arrived and could see that it had a grand tower with a small but very high hall. 'For over a century people came to light a candle at the shrine and pray for healing. There were some miracles.' Maria's tone was matter-of-fact. 'These days, people rarely visit.' Signs of decay were obvious in the crumbing stonework and loose tiles.

'Why did they stop coming?' asked Hanley.

'There are other shrines and new miracles.' Maria shrugged,

and the gesture struck Truscott as somewhat incongruous in a nun, but then since he knew little about how such ladies were meant to behave he thought no more of it.

They fell silent as they stopped by the arched gateway to the churchyard and cemetery. Dismounting, they tethered the horses and the donkey to a hitching post that did not seem too rotten. Maria was about to go through the gate when Pringle stopped her. He drew his pistol and went first. All three of the officers had loaded pistols as well as their swords, and Williams had his musket. There was no sign of life in the church, and perhaps for that reason Billy Pringle felt the need for caution. The four men searched about for any threat, and kept Sister Maria in the middle of them.

Pringle lowered his pistol when he came to the small doorway set in the main double doors of the church itself. It seemed a necessary mark of respect, but he was still wary. He turned the handle and tried to use no more force than was necessary to open the door. Its hinges creaked alarmingly. He looked in, but it took a moment for his eyes to adjust to the dim interior after the bright sunlight. There was nothing – no movement and no sign of life. He went in, pistol ready down at his side.

Nothing happened. He looked up at a high vaulted ceiling and towards the ornate plaster altar. No, not plaster, he thought, but gilt decoration whitewashed in the hope of fooling French plunderers. Pringle's footsteps echoed in the empty church. There was no other sound. He beckoned to them, and Maria and his three friends came in.

'The place seems deserted. Might the father be away?' he asked Maria. 'After all, he did not know when you would come.'

She ignored him and walked across to a side door. Pringle followed. 'Stay here,' he said to the others. 'Oh, and somebody keep an eye on those horses. I fear we have had a wasted journey. Don't want to make it worse by having to walk back!'

Maria had already vanished. Pringle followed her, just in time to see the nun go through another door leading off the passage. When he reached it he could see her standing still in the centre of what looked like a kitchen. Her head turned back to stare at him, her expression blank. Pringle heard a noise from the corridor behind him, but before he could turn something hit him hard on the back of the head. There was an instant of searing pain and then nothing. He fell heavily, twisting his glasses off so that the edge of the wire frame left a cut on his nose.

The one-eyed sergeant nodded with satisfaction. Then he gestured to his men. Two left the building and made their way round to the front of the church. Another followed him down the corridor. All had fixed bayonets. Denilov followed, holding Maria tightly by the arm and with a cocked pistol pressed against her head. The remaining soldier left the priest, bound to a chair and already badly bruised, and covered the unconscious Pringle.

The two soldiers grabbed Williams by the arms before he knew they were there. He had propped his musket against the wall as he took a long drink from his canteen. He nearly choked as the water went down the wrong way.

Truscott and Hanley heard the main door kicked savagely open and then saw Williams flung through to land hard on the floor. Two soldiers in dark green jackets and trousers followed him, their muskets levelled directly at the officers. With another loud bang the side door slammed back against the wall and two more soldiers rushed into the room. There was no time to raise or cock their pistols. Then a taller man came in, holding the nun and aiming a double-barrelled pistol at her head. There were epaulettes on his shoulders and a gorget at his throat.

'Welcome, gentlemen,' he said in English. 'I would take it as a personal favour if you would both drop your weapons. So would Maria, as otherwise I shall be forced to blow her head off.'

The pistols clattered to the ground.

'And your swords.'

Hanley and Truscott each took a light hold of their swords and drew them slowly. Clutching the hilts with just thumb and index finger, they let the blades drop.

'Excellent, I can see we shall be such good friends,' said the count. The other soldier dragged Pringle into the hall and rolled him up against the wall. Hanley and Truscott both rushed to see how badly he was hurt. Prodded by bayonets, Williams scrambled across the floor to join them.

'Who the hell are you?' demanded Truscott, relieved to see that Billy Pringle was only unconscious and did not seem to be seriously hurt.

'Merely a visitor to these shores. You are in no position to demand any more information than that. Indeed, you are in no position to demand anything at all.' Denilov barked an order in a language none of them recognised and three of the soldiers took a step closer and stood watching the Englishmen. Their bayonets looked sharp, and the men themselves well practised in their use.

'It is good to see Maria, again. Sister Maria now, of course. That would seem such a waste for a woman of your undoubted talents, my dear.' The girl glared at him, but said nothing. The tall officer pushed her a pace away from him, then yanked off her headscarf, shaking loose her long curling black hair.

Williams stood up and took a step forward, but then the soldiers levelled their bayonets and he halted.

'She doesn't look much like a nun,' whispered Hanley.

'She is still a woman, and he is a brute.'

The officer laughed. 'Where did you find these fools, Maria?' She spat some insult at him in rapid Portuguese. Hanley recognised just a few of the words.

'Definitely not a nun,' he said.

'What the hell is going on?' asked Truscott, his annoyance fighting with sheer confusion.

Denilov did not look at him, but simply watched Maria. 'Shall I continue? It wouldn't be the first time, would it, my dear.' She was crouching now, hands crossed over her chest and clutching her shoulders. 'Your modesty seems new. But then, perhaps you have always needed it for some of your clients.'

'I have tried to forget what I needed for you, Denilov.' Maria spat the words at him, using English this time.

The officer smiled. 'Ah, that is the old Maria. Come, my dear, we have things to discuss. Forgive us, gentlemen.' He gave a languid wave and ushered the girl out through the side door. The sergeant and one of the soldiers followed, carrying the Englishmen's weapons.

'Just what the hell is going on?' said Truscott once again, this time whispering to his friends. He and Hanley sat with their backs against the cold stone of the wall. Williams was standing, and in some vague way felt this was a small act of defiance.

'We are prisoners of the French,' replied the volunteer.

'Do the French wear green?' asked Hanley, happy to be talking rather than simply waiting in silence surrounded by murderous-looking armed men.

'Some of the German regiments do,' said Truscott. 'And the cavalry, but these fellows aren't cavalry.'

'They might be if they steal our horses.' Williams grinned at his own joke. It was better than thinking, for try as he might he could see no way of surprising and overpowering the guards.

'They are not Germans. I don't know what language that was, but it was not German. Maybe Polish?' Hanley ventured. 'Or Russian. Denilov sounds a bit Russian to me.'

'What the devil would Russians be doing here in Portugal?' asked Truscott.

'What the devil are we doing here?' replied Hanley.

'Helping a nun who looks rather like she is really a fallen woman,' said the lieutenant.

'She is still a woman and needed our help.' Williams' voice had all its usual certainty when he spoke of anything connected with honour. He took a slight step to one side. The soldiers raised their muskets. One brought his up to his shoulder and aimed directly at the volunteer's head. Williams went back and held his hands up by his sides. After a moment the guards lowered their muskets. 'How's Billy?'

Truscott leaned over. 'Sleeping peacefully. Far too peacefully for the man who got us into this.'

'The French treat prisoners well, don't they? That's assuming they are renegades fighting with the French.' Hanley was trying not to remember the sabres cutting down the panicking crowd in

Madrid and wanted some reassurance. There was a menace about Denilov which made him deeply uneasy.

'Not renegades. Russia is allied to France. They are supposed to be civilised, though.'

A scream cut through their nervous conversation. It was bitter and filled with agony. Williams once again made a move forward and did not halt until a bayonet was almost touching his chest. 'Now look here,' he said rather weakly.

'That did not sound like a woman,' said Hanley.

'The priest.' Truscott winced as another cry of pain shattered the stillness of the church. 'It would be too much to hope it's Denilov.' Another scream followed. 'Poor devil.'

'I think I may have to kill these men,' said Williams quietly.

'An admirable sentiment, but not a practical one at the moment.' Truscott gave Pringle a shake. 'No, still out cold.'

There were no more screams, but in some ways the silence was almost worse. A few minutes later Denilov came back into the room. There was no sign of Maria. He ignored their questions and simply levelled his pistol to point directly at Truscott's head. Then he waited for silence.

'Thank you, gentlemen. I now have what I came for. I suggest you forget Maria. There are plenty more whores in Lisbon, if none quite so special. Still, such things will no longer be your concern. I regret that we never had time for formal introductions.' He pulled back the hammers to cock both barrels of his pistol. The three soldiers did the same with their muskets and Williams wondered whether any sound had ever been so loud. He tried to prepare himself for one last spring, knowing that he would die before he could reach even the nearest of the soldiers. Fear fed his anger.

Then the sergeant came in through the door set into the main entrance. He raised a finger to his lips. Voices came from outside. The sergeant whispered something to Denilov and the count smiled.

'Even better,' he said. He kept his pistol firmly aimed at them as he walked backwards. The soldiers did the same. Only at the last minute did they turn and run through the side door. Williams dashed after them, but the door was slammed and bolted before he reached it and he simply hurt his shoulder when he barged into it. Truscott had gone to the main door. He looked out and saw green-coated cavalrymen in the gateway to the churchyard. One saw him and shouted.

He jerked his head back in and flung his weight against the door, feeling for the bolt.

'French cavalry!' he called.

Hanley came to help him. 'So are we really going to be prisoners of the French this time?'

'I'm damned if I am,' shouted Williams, and the other two did not even notice that he had sworn. The volunteer was looking for something he could use as a weapon.

A flurry of gunshots came from outside. There were shouts, and then more shots. Hanley was about to suggest lifting Truscott up so that he could peer out of one of the high windows when a musket ball shattered the glass.

The shouting died down and then there was silence. Pringle moaned and woke up.

'Did I miss anything?' he said weakly. They ignored the question. Someone tried to force the main door and then a voice shouted.

'They're Portuguese,' Hanley said with relief. 'English, English,' he shouted as loudly as he could and then unbolted the door and opened it. Two muskets were immediately levelled at them. The Englishmen stepped back to let their allies in. Hanley tried his Spanish, but with the same lack of result as before.

'Ah, Monsieur Hanley, is it not,' said a familiar voice. Lieutenant Mata smiled from behind his two soldiers. It was a fortunate chance which made explanations easier. That was just as well, as in a few moments the Portuguese troops had searched the church and discovered the body of the tortured priest. They were used to such sights by now but that did nothing to diminish their anger. Hanley had intended to tell only of the French cavalry, but he had liked Mata when they met and found himself recounting the whole story.

'You take risks, my friend,' was the only comment the lieutenant made at the end of the tale. Hanley was not sure that the Portuguese officer was convinced that a group of Russian soldiers were responsible for the murder. The French had done as much and worse so often that his instinct was to blame them.

One of their borrowed horses had been wounded in the skirmish. The Portuguese had finished the animal off and, short of fresh meat, were already butchering the carcass. They had taken two horses from the French patrol, however, and Mata loaned the British officers one of these mounts. The Portuguese had also found the redcoats' weapons, dropped just outside the church, and returned them.

It seemed a long ride back to camp. Billy Pringle began by asking a lot of questions, but lapsed into silence when no one answered him. Failure and defeat gnawed at all of them. They were young, and even Hanley was now willing to think of himself as a soldier. This was their first war, and they expected to win. Exuberance, restlessness and boredom had made each relish the adventure of aiding a damsel in distress. Maria had proved herself no innocent, had lied to them and manipulated them. There was still a vague sense that they had let a woman down, and that hurt their sense of honour. Far, far worse was the wider sense of defeat. Soldiers were supposed to fight and to win. They had done neither, and the humiliation ran deep.

Finally, when they were nearly back at camp, Truscott relented and told him what had happened. He had wanted to blame his friend for entangling them in this futile misadventure, but could not. It did not matter how they had become involved. They had been tested and found wanting. It was very hard to bear.

The British and a small force of Portuguese continued to advance, pursuing the French as they retreated back towards Lisbon. Most of Junot's army was still scattered and distant, and only a single strong brigade faced the allies. On 15th August Pringle was able to include in his diary that the first shots had been fired. At least the first shots of the official war involving the British army. He had begun religiously writing up a journal each day since the landing, something he had never managed in his life before. He did not write about Maria or their adventure at the church, but that did not stop him thinking about her. Failure tasted bitter.

Neither Pringle nor any of the 106th saw anything of the fighting. There were shots from ahead of the column for a good half-hour. In spite of their continuing advance the firing seemed to get more distant. Later, as darkness was falling, there was a new burst of firing, and the heavier sound of ordered volleys as well.

There had been activity ahead, but while General Hill's brigade was hurried forward, the 3rd Brigade and the 106th were not required. Moss was obviously frustrated, and eventually managed to get some information from one of General Spencer's aides as the young man passed. The Rifles had driven the French back. Later it became clear that the green-jackets had become excited and chased too eagerly after the withdrawing enemy. They had outstripped the supporting companies and then run into a formed French battalion. Recoiling, the riflemen had formed a loose rally square on a hilltop and spent a nervous night waiting for a major attack which never came.

The French had withdrawn again and the next morning the British Army followed them. Williams was surprised to find Dobson becoming more cheerful with every day that passed. The closeness of the enemy seemed to excite him. The colonel was also in an ebullient mood, joking with officers and men alike.

'Pitiful,' was his comment when they saw a rifleman with a bandage on his bare head leading three French prisoners back down the column. The men had been stripped of their cross-belts and packs so that their long loose dustcoats flapped in the breeze. Their wide-topped shakos were covered in drab cloth and they wore baggy brown trousers made locally. Only the headgear marked them out as soldiers. All three were young and looked sheepish. 'Absolutely pitiful,' said Moss again. 'Just scruffy children from the slums. How the hell these creatures have terrified Europe is beyond me.'

'Just conscripts,' suggested Toye. 'Boney has sent lots of his youngest troops to Spain and Portugal. And I suppose the least willing soldiers are always the most likely to surrender.'

MacAndrews was riding just behind them and wondered whether this was a slur aimed at him, but decided that Toye was simply being thoughtless. He remembered the confusion and fear of capture. 'Junot does have a lot of third battalions in his army. Quite newly formed most of them.' The French Emperor had recently expanded his army and most of the new units contained few experienced men.

Moss grunted, slightly resenting his elderly major's detailed knowledge. 'Still, it does help to explain the news from Spain. If the French army there was composed of children like that then no wonder the Dons beat them.' Reports had arrived of a French army forced to surrender by the Spanish. There had been many tales of Spanish triumphs in the past – the Galicians had boasted to Wellesley about them while turning down his direct assistance – but all had turned out to be inventions. This one seemed to be true, and was encouraging. A defeat in Spain would make it far less likely that the French could reinforce Junot in Portugal.

'Battle in a day or two,' said the colonel. 'I can smell it. And if the dagoes can beat the Frogs then we should go through them like a hot knife through butter.'

Neither of the majors chose to mention Buenos Aires, where the 'dagoes' had beaten a British expedition and forced its capitulation. Still, Wellesley was no Whitelocke.

All three officers raised their cocked hats respectfully as they passed a more melancholy scene. A group of riflemen were piling up earth on a new grave. That night Pringle could record in his journal the death of Derryck's cheerful cousin, poor Bunbury of the 95th. The news had very briefly cast a gloom over the 106th's mess, but soon the talk became louder as the wine was passed around and songs were sung. Orders had arrived for the army to advance the following day. The baggage would be left behind and the brigades would go straight into an attack on the French, who seemed at last to have halted. Hanley thought the laughter and talk of that evening to be a little strained, sometimes almost hysterical, but then wondered whether that was his own nervousness. Williams withdrew fairly early and read his Bible by candlelight under the stars. Pringle stayed in the mess and tried to ignore the noise as he made a short entry in his journal.

'I earnestly hope that this will not be the final entry in the diary of William Pringle, Lieut. 106th Foot,' he wrote at the end. Please God, let that be true, he thought. The war already seemed a lot more dangerous and confusing than he had expected.

24

The young ADC had made a mistake, but there was no time to do anything about it now. An hour before dawn, when he had passed on the orders to the brigade major, he had told him to form left in front. The formation should have been by the right as normal. By the left meant that all dispositions were reversed. The 106th formed ahead of the 82nd and both battalions had the Light Company at the front of their column and the grenadiers at the rear. For Hanley and Trent with the colour party it made little difference. They were still in the centre of the battalion, but were now looking at the backs of a different company. Pringle and Redman were in place behind the flanks of the Grenadier Company and so were at the very rear of the 106th. Pringle raised a quizzical eyebrow at the adjutant riding beside him.

'These are the orders,' said Thomas in response. 'Something must have changed.' He had seen the general's orders issued the night before, which specified that the brigades would march right in front. That allowed a rapid deployment into the normal fighting line either to the front or to face the right flank. Marching left in front made it easier to turn instead to the left. 'I had better check, though.' Thomas could dimly see a cluster of horsemen and hear raised voices. He spurred his horse over to join them, but before he could reach them the group broke up. Moss came towards him, surging ahead of the two majors.

'We go as we are,' he called to the adjutant. 'It's wrong, but puts us closer to the enemy, so I shan't complain.' He did not stop, but rode quickly back to the head of the column. Toye looked nervous as he passed. MacAndrews just shrugged. Before Thomas had reached his station he heard Sergeant Major Fletcher's voice booming across the open plain.

''Talion will advance.' A pause and then 'Forward march!' The drums started and the band began to play 'The British Grenadiers' as the 106th moved off.

'They're not bothered about surprise, then,' whispered Williams to Dobson, who marched in front of him.

'They'll know we are coming. Make them nervous to listen to us for a while. No one wants to think on a day like this. Chin up, Pug. We'll show 'em.'

'Silence in the ranks,' yelled Sergeant Darrowfield, who chose to ignore Murphy's loud whisper of 'Miserable sod'.

Sir Arthur Wellesley wanted the French General Delaborde to notice his army's main central column. Altogether he had some nine thousand men, with the bulk of the cavalry and a dozen of his precious guns. They marched straight at the French position on the hills in front of the little village of Roliça. He could just see the whitewashed houses clustered around the church through his telescope. The sun was not yet fully up, and he would need another look when they got closer. He spotted a hillock in the plain which ought to offer a good viewing point. At the moment he could see darker smears on the hillside, which might be French troops. He glanced to the left, but could not yet see very much. Delaborde had a single brigade – no more than four or five thousand men including a regiment of cavalry. Yet another French brigade under General Loison was only a dozen miles away, and if he came to reinforce Delaborde he would come from those hills.

The French wanted to delay the British until Junot could concentrate enough troops to smash them. Wellesley guessed that Delaborde was also keen to inflict a bloody nose on the advancing British. There was a desire both to add to his high reputation and to encourage his soldiers by showing them they were better than the enemy. Sir Arthur counted on this to keep the French brigade in place long enough to trap it. So he wanted Delaborde to be mesmerised by his central column, to see them and only them. In the meantime Major General Ferguson would take two brigades on a march round to the left. A smaller Portuguese column led by Colonel Trant – an English soldier of fortune who seemed reliable in spite of the fact that he was rarely sober – went to the right. If the French commander was stupid or sufficiently overconfident, then it might work.

'Very pretty,' said Henri-François Delaborde as he rubbed his hands together. It was an hour and half later, and he and his staff had watched the British columns process across the rolling plain towards them. There was an air of a field day about it, especially now, as the enemy brigades deployed immaculately from their columns into line. One of his younger ADCs applauded. The general silenced the man with a look. His spirits were rising – if only it were not for this damned rheumatism in his joints.

'At least we are fighting a proper army again,' commented his chief of staff. Junot had disbanded Portugal's regiments soon after his arrival. When the Portuguese rose against the French, they consisted of hastily organised forces, often little more than mobs. It had been brutal, inglorious work suppressing them. The French had done it, resolving always to be far more brutal than the enemy, but such tasks would win no man promotion or praise from the Emperor. It did not help that the Emperor was still in France, for he was never as lavish with decorations in campaigns where he did not lead in person.

'They march and form well,' grunted Delaborde in agreement. 'And they look handsome,' he muttered as he clicked his glass open. Through the telescope the nearest battalions became more than a red strip. He could see black shakos and white cross-belts. 'At least eight battalions. Maybe a few more. Call it two or three brigades.'

'We are outnumbered, then.' His chief of staff's comment was neutral.

'We are French,' Delaborde said automatically. There were a few companies of Swiss infantry with his brigade, the remainder of a battalion left behind in garrison, but they were almost as reliable as his countrymen. 'How many did the Chasseurs spot over on the right, Jean?'

A fresh-faced staff officer consulted a note. 'At least a brigade, General. Rosbifs again. A couple of guns and a handful of cavalry.'

'How close?' The British flanking column was covered by the olive groves and the rolling hills. Delaborde had spotted a little dust and the occasional glint of metal, but had not been able to make out anything more definite from his position. A patrol of his green-uniformed cavalry had already located the enemy, however, and soon sent him a detailed report. They did not spot Trant's smaller column, made up of Portuguese, and coming by a longer route.

'An hour, maybe an hour and a half.'

Delaborde guessed that it would be nearer an hour and a half. The British manoeuvred well, but their marching did seem slow. Still, it would take careful judgement. He wanted the British centre to stay deployed. In lines the enemy infantry would move even more slowly, for the ground was broken and rolling, and every dry-stone wall, grove and rocky outcrop would force them to halt and re-dress their ranks. Time was what mattered. Delay and tire the enemy. He had no intention of fighting from this position, but wanted the English general to believe that he was locked into place.

'Jean, ride to the battalions and tell them to send forward their voltigeurs.' One out of the nine companies in each French battalion was trained to skirmish. They were the equivalent of a British light company, with yellow and green plumes, yellow collars and epaulettes to mark their elite status. French skirmishers were considered the best in the world. 'Tell them to move fast when they hear the order to pull back. Just tease the British for a while.'

Delaborde watched the four voltigeur companies come up from behind the ridge and walk over the crest and down the other side. After a while they disappeared from his view. He wondered about riding forward to check that they did not go too far, but stopped himself. He could trust his captains. Then the sparkle of a tiny reflection caught his eye. There was a group of enemy officers on top of the highest hillock below him. He smiled. That was where he would have gone himself. He guessed that the British officers were scanning his light infantry with their glasses.

Delaborde walked his horse over to an eight-pounder cannon set up on the crest, one of the six guns with his brigade. There should have been two more, but there were not enough horses to pull them so they had been left in garrison. An artillery lieutenant saluted and his men stiffened to attention.

Delaborde nodded to the man. 'Worth a shot?'

The lieutenant was only twenty-one and was flattered that the general sought his opinion. He was nervous for a moment, then the pride of being a gunner took over. There were mysteries of military science which he understood better than any general save the Emperor himself. He shook his head. 'Be a waste, General. Might give them a headache, but no more.'

It was the answer Delaborde had expected. 'Fine, we shall wait. You'll have plenty of good targets before the day is out.' He glanced back and saw the limber and horse team waiting, an ammunition caisson and its horses behind that. The artillery were ready to pull back on his order. There was no need to say any more. He rode farther down the line, his half-dozen staff officers following.

MacAndrews noticed, or perhaps just sensed movement on the ridge ahead of them. He shaded his eyes as he strained to see. He blinked and then noticed little figures coming down the slope.

'Sir.' He pointed. Along with Moss and Toye, he reached for his telescope. MacAndrews' glass was old and had a small crack on the top left, but he soon found some of the figures and could see they were French.

'Their light bobs by the look of it,' said Moss. 'Good, the ball is about to start.' They were still almost half a mile away from the French position, so it was too far to rush. Moss wondered whether to ask the brigadier for permission to go back into column from line. That would speed up the advance, but then it would require careful judgement to switch back into line before they bumped into the enemy. A marching column was vulnerable. He decided against it.

The 106th marched steadily forward. The colours were now in the centre of the line, and every now and again the big silk flags flapped lazily in the light wind. Hanley was finding the weight of the flag a heavy burden, and poor little Trent beside him was bright red in the face and clearly struggling. Neither of them had noticed any movement in the enemy position, and no one had mentioned anything to them. They assumed the French were out there, but had to take this on trust.

Pringle, Williams and the other grenadiers were glad to be in line rather than column. Marching at the rear had meant swallowing the dust of those ahead of them. Yet it was odd to be on the left of the battalion – the 106th was still in reverse order. They marched on under the hot sun. Williams could feel his back soaking with sweat and his mouth felt dry and tasted of salt. For some reason he could not understand he never sweated much on his face. He tried not to think too much, just concentrate on the steady plod forward. The band was following them and had gone through its entire repertoire so was playing 'The British Grenadiers' for the third time. The 82nd's band seemed still to be beating out the jauntier 'Downfall of Paris' and the two tunes fought for mastery.

Ten minutes later one of General Nightingall's aides rode up to Moss. 'General's compliments, and the battalions are to deploy the light companies to their front.' He rode on to pass the order to the 82nd.

'If you will oblige me, Mr Toye,' Moss said to his senior major, who rode over to the end of the line. The colonel turned and looked for a moment at the colour party in the centre of the line – his line – and the thrill of leading his own regiment into battle flooded over him. Then he noticed that young Trent with the Regimental Colour looked fit to drop. Better relieve the boy as it was set to be a long day. 'Mr Thomas,' he called to the adjutant behind the two-deep line of men.

Up on the ridge, Delaborde called an enquiry over to the gunner lieutenant.

'Worth a try,' he replied. The British infantry lines were now closer, and before too long the slope would actually make them harder to hit. If they fired now then they might well manage half a dozen shots before the British reached the cover of the slope.

'The one straight ahead,' the officer said to the sergeant in charge of the gun crew. 'Just a degree to the left.' He peered along the bronze barrel, resting his head near the large wreathed N cast into the metal. The sergeant put the steel trail spike into its slot. With the help of two gunners he lifted the green-painted carriage and turned the gun the merest fraction to the left. The lieutenant looked along the sights again. The notch at the end of the barrel was almost perfectly in line with the two flags at the centre of one of the distant red lines. He ordered an adjustment to the screw that controlled elevation. This was as much guesswork as science, but in this case the young officer judged well.

MacAndrews and Moss both saw the puff of dirty smoke up on the ridge. A moment later Moss thought he saw the dark blur of the cannonball and drew in his breath because he was sure it was heading straight for him. It seemed to hang in the air, the shape now clearly a sphere, and then a massive force hammered against the air as the ball whipped past faster and louder than anything he had ever known.

The eight-pound shot struck the adjutant beneath the right shoulder as he turned in the saddle back towards the colour party. It ripped off his arm in a gout of blood and bone fragments, sending the arm still in its sleeve cartwheeling through the air. Hanley saw every detail, even though it all happened so fast. There was no sound. Thomas's mouth was open in a silent scream as he fell backwards in the saddle. The ball was dropping in its flight and moving too fast for Hanley to spot it flying ahead of the whirling limb. He saw Trent flicked aside like a rag doll as the shot took away the right side of his neck and shoulder, leaving his head almost hanging off. A moment later Thomas's arm hit him and the sharp tip of broken bone buried itself in the already dead ensign's chest. Still falling, the ball struck the sergeant behind Trent in the stomach and cut him in two, but Hanley did not see this and only heard the sickening thud and felt warm liquid sprayed over his own back.

MacAndrews managed to catch Thomas before he fell from his horse, and hold him there. The adjutant's blood soaked into his own jacket and overalls as he held the man in place and yelled out for the bandsmen. One of the sergeants ran forward to help support the dreadfully wounded adjutant. Trent's corpse sunk to its knees, still clutching the colour, and after what seemed like an age it dropped to the ground. The flag covered him.

Hanley vomited. He bent double, using the pole of the standard as a prop and spewed the contents of his stomach on to the floor. The sergeant behind him patted him on the back. 'Better out than in, sir,' he said.

Derryck was summoned from his company. As the next most junior ensign, it was his task to take over from his dead friend. Hanley thought he looked pale as he raised the Regimental Colour, whose red cross on a white field was drenched with Trent's blood. Yet Hanley guessed he must have looked pale himself. Another sergeant was summoned to take the place of the dead man, for the colours must always be protected. Four drummers carried Thomas away in a blanket. He had lost consciousness and that was probably a mercy.

Up on the ridge, Delaborde had been focused on the 106th when the eight-pounder shot struck them. He saw the flags dip and smiled.

The advance continued. The cannon fired again, but the next ball bounced high and harmless over the battalion. The next was closer, but also missed. A fourth ball flicked the high plume on Wickham's cocked hat, plucking the hat from his head. He laughed hysterically for a moment, picked up the unscathed hat and waved it at his men. The grenadiers smiled or cheered him. Then their captain took another long draught from the bottle he carried in a wicker case clipped to the belt with his haversack. He had been drinking hard since before dawn, and the brandy was now more than three-quarters gone.

The British Army kept up its steady pace. The lines wavered

at times because of obstacles in their path, or on a handful of occasions when the French cannonballs found a mark. Still they came on. To the left of Nighingall's brigade General Fane sent his riflemen on ahead. Soon there were sporadic shots. The 106th's Light Company were also engaged. A private with red facings came limping back towards the battalion; another man with the light companies' shoulder wings and a green plume to his shako was supporting him.

Moss sent Toye to reprimand the unwounded soldier and send him back to the firing line. He had issued strict orders that no one was to assist an injured man. They were to be left until the bandsmen found them and brought aid. Otherwise it offered an easy escape to the timid.

MacAndrews was riding behind the battalion's line now that poor Thomas was gone. This was the normal position for the second major, but Moss liked to have both of his senior subordinates with him. It was important, however, to have a mounted field officer to check the alignment and steady the ranks from behind. MacAndrews was glad to be away from the restlessness of the colonel. It was no safer as a position, but did give him just a little more freedom.

The firing from in front and to the left grew heavier for a while, and then slackened. As they continued forward it stopped altogether. Word came back that the French had gone, withdrawing behind the village to a higher ridge.

It was not long to noon, but the battle had not yet started in earnest. After a brief rest, the British Army went forward again. With only a handful of casualties, most of the 106th's bandsmen had not yet been detached to carry the wounded. The band played 'The British Grenadiers' once again. 'We're popular today,' muttered Murphy to Dobson. Williams grinned, but his legs felt heavy as he marched forward, and he knew it was not with fatigue.

25

Wellesley watched the French battalions withdraw over the plain towards the higher ridge and was impressed by their discipline. If he had had more cavalry he might have been able to make things difficult for them, but the French had as many or more green-jacketed Chasseurs as he had dragoons from the 20th. Switching his gaze, the British general could see Ferguson's flanking column approaching. He turned to the right and saw the head of the Portuguese force doing the same thing. Evidently General Delaborde had seen this and timed his retreat nicely, withdrawing past the little cluster of whitewashed houses that made up the village of Roliça. His horse shifted beneath him, but the movement to calm the beast was wholly unconscious. Unsurprised by the failure of his subterfuge, he resolved to try again.

It took some time to reorganise the British Army for a new attack. The plan would be the same. An advance by the main force to pin the enemy in place, and then the flanking columns would envelop the enemy. Wellesley rode to each of the brigade commanders in the centre, warning them not to commit to a full attack until Ferguson and Trant had got behind the French on the ridge.

The plain became much more broken as the 106th neared the high ground. The line became ragged, in spite of the best efforts of the sergeants to keep the men in place. Moss kept advancing. The French were no longer visible, having pulled back behind the crest. As the battalion came closer to the slope even the enemy skirmishers dotted along the top of the ridge disappeared from view. The ground was rocky and the mounted officers had to ride with great care. Moss decided to dismount, realising that the going would only get worse and that there was little chance of getting a horse up the steep slope. Anyway, it was better to lead the charge on foot – just like in Egypt. As soon as the colonel dismounted so did both majors.

It had taken the French artillery some time to take up new firing positions on the ridge. This had spared the advancing redcoats a good deal of fire. By the time the enemy gunners opened up, the 106th and other battalions in the first line of the British formation were largely obscured by the slope. Regiments in the rear were less fortunate and came under a steady fire. Pringle happened to turn his head at the very moment a round-shot struck the line a few hundred yards behind the 106th. There was a plume of dust just in front of the redcoats, then a smear of red blood as shattered pieces of musket, equipment and flesh were flung into the air. He could dimly hear the sergeants bellowing at the men to close ranks. The regiment had yellow facings and a yellow colour. That would make them the 9th Foot from Hill's brigade.

Moss stumbled on the loose boulders and nearly fell, but just managed to steady himself. The main slope was very steep, but a gully opened ahead of the 106th and seemed to offer a better path to the top. Heavy firing broke out somewhere to the left. It was not volley fire, but the individual shots of skirmishers. Moss could not see where it came from. Even the 82nd had disappeared from view, hidden by the folds in the ground. Moss jumped up on to a boulder. Behind him he could see the 9th still advancing. To his right were a few pairs of skirmishers from the light companies of Hill's brigade – the green plumes were clear. Otherwise it was very hard to see anything.

The skirmish fire grew even heavier. The attack was clearly going ahead, and it was time to play their part.

'Mr Toye, Mr MacAndrews, would you be so good as to join me.' Moss decided to be especially casual in his instructions, fighting back the excitement within him. Toye was only a few yards away. MacAndrews had to come through the line next to the colour party and join them.

'We're going straight up the ravine,' said Moss. 'I will take the left wing with Major Toye. You bring the right wing up to support us. We'll form column at quarter-distance. It will not be neat, but if we feed one company in at a time it will give us some control.' He turned to look back at the gully. 'I doubt it gets wider. The main thing is to press on, get up there as fast as we can and then form when we reach the crest and find some space. Major MacAndrews, I'd be grateful if you would tell the colonel of the Ninth what we are doing and ask for their support.' Moss had an impish grin. 'No time to lose, let's move.'

Orders were issued. The manoeuvre was untidy, but it brought the Light Company to the mouth of the gully and the others ranked behind them. MacAndrews kept the right wing off to the side before putting them into column to give the other companies a little more space. In the meantime he remounted and rode back the three hundred yards to talk to the commander of the 9th.

Moss licked his lips, and then gave the order to fix bayonets. Men slid the long steel spikes from their scabbards, slipped the rings over the muzzles of their muskets and clicked them into place. Moss and the other officers drew their swords. With the two wings operating separately, the colour party was put between the second and third companies in the column. Hanley and Derryck could not see the colonel over the heads of the men in front, but they could hear him.

'Boys, we are going to take this hill from the Frogs. I am going first. If any man beats me to the top I'll give him a guinea. Now, 106th, follow me!'

Moss set off at a jog. The gully's slope was gentler than the craggy ridge, but it was still steep. Ranks and order quickly disappeared. The ground was soft, with patches of loose scree. Men stumbled, fell and cursed as they struggled upwards. Soon, the muscles at the backs of their legs were aching, and most were breathing hard. The gully had been shaped by a stream fed by rainwater and over the years the stream had moved. Channels opened off the main gully and some men followed these. Moss was still at the front, and Major Toye was using his sword as a stick as he tried desperately to keep pace. Men from the Light Company were around him, and a sergeant helped him up when he slipped and slammed into the ground.

There were bushes and briars growing out of the sides of the sunken path. Some could be trampled and others had to be avoided. French cannon were firing from up on the ridge and more than once round-shot bounced low across the banks of the gully. Then a shell fired from a stubby-barrelled howitzer arced slow and high to drop into the little ravine. It spun crazily as the fuse burned, then the powder inside exploded with a fierce crack and sent jagged fragments of the iron case scything through the air. One piece sliced the top off a sergeant's skull as neatly as a boiled egg. Another slammed into a private's pack, knocking him down and shredding his blanket, but leaving the man unharmed.

The colonel kept going as straight as he could, following the path that looked most direct even if it was not the widest. The men behind tended to follow the more obvious routes. Companies split and mingled. The younger and fitter men, and the more aggressive, pressed onwards, while others slowed and fell back. The colour party stuck together and followed the colonel. The slope was usually steep enough for Hanley to see Moss now. He was thirty yards ahead, but along with Derryck and the sergeants guarding them both, the group managed to keep in sight of their commander.

One group of soldiers took a side path and quickly emerged on the slope itself. A crackle of shots from French voltigeurs dropped one of them immediately. The men raised their muskets to fire in reply. Then another of them was hit, this time in the knee. The man screamed and was dragged back into the gully by his comrades. The other wounded man lay on his back, his stomach a mass of blood. He moaned pitifully and called out for his mother. From the shelter of the gully's banks the redcoats fired back at the French skirmishers.

At the mouth of the ravine MacAndrews could not see any of the advancing men. It had taken some time to form his right wing into column. There had been no sound of volleys from above, so that at least was encouraging. The artillery fire was slackening and there were periodic shots from skirmishers. Anyway, there was nothing to do now but follow orders.

'Come on, boys,' he called, and led the five companies up the ravine.

Even Moss was beginning to struggle as the slope took its toll. Yet he knew they were now a long way up and that the top could not be too much farther. He had slowed to little more than a brisk walking pace. He did not look behind him. A good officer must trust that his men will follow him, and anyway he had no doubt that they would. The gully was now wide enough only for three men to pass. A man from the Light Company was almost abreast of him. A sergeant from a centre company was on the other side, jabbing his half-pike's butt into the ground and using it to drag himself upwards. Moss grinned at them and somehow found the energy to run again, bounding up the next few yards of the gully. Its banks were growing lower and suddenly he ran out on to a wide grassy field. They were not at the top, but the slope up to the crest was gentler and not long. They were in a horseshoe-shaped depression, with spurs of higher ground on either side and stretching behind them. No enemy were visible.

The colonel allowed himself a moment to breathe deeply. The sergeant beside him looked bright red in the face. The light company man dropped to his knees and was panting. There was the sound of boots on the soft ground from behind them as more men arrived.

'Don't worry, boys, you'll each have your guinea anyway.' Moss now allowed himself time to turn back and look down the slope. A few dozen men were fairly close behind. He could just see the colours turning round a bend in the gully. It was harder to see anyone else. Captain Headley of the Light Company jogged up beside him and seemed both cheerful and unruffled by the rapid scramble up.

'Warm day, sir,' he said.

'Ideal for walking,' replied Moss. Major Toye looked close to collapse, but straightened up as he arrived. The blade of his sword was dirty for several inches along its length from where he had stuck it into the ground. Even worse, it had bent slightly out of shape from carrying his weight. Toye held it up and could not help grinning.

'You should join the Lights,' joked Headley. Like all Light Company officers he carried a sabre with a curved blade instead of a straight sword.

Moss cut them off. 'Sergeant Keene!' A flash of memory had supplied the man's name just before he spoke.

'Sir!' responded the sergeant, who had reached the top just behind Moss and was delighted to be recognised.

'Form a line, right marker over there!' Moss pointed to the spot. There were already some thirty men with them from all the different companies of the left wing. The sergeant chose a corporal for the right marker and formed them up next to him. As more soldiers arrived, they were added to the left of the line. In a few minutes there were sixty men in two ranks facing up the slope. Three sergeants stood behind the line along with a single drummer and two young ensigns. Moss and Toye stood just to the right of the formation and Headley to the left. The colour party arrived and took post in the centre behind the little line.

Before they could advance some red-coated soldiers appeared on the crest among a patch of bushes. The men had deep blue facings and fronts to their jackets. More appeared, and they began to walk down the slope towards the men of the 106th.

'Who the hell are they?' Toye said aloud.

'Must be Fane's men,' replied Moss with assurance. The French wore blue, or those loose greatcoats they had already seen. Only the British Army wore red.

A formation of redcoats marched in step directly in front of the 106th. They were in company strength, an officer with his sword held high marching on their right.

'Bloody fools must be lost,' said Moss. 'They're going the wrong way.'

The scattered group of redcoats now raised their muskets upside down in the air and began to shout.

'*Suisse! Suisse!*' They were nearest to Headley, who began to walk towards them. He looked baffled. The formed company kept moving towards the 106th and then halted on command.

'Where are you going?' yelled Moss. 'Who is in charge?'

The red-coated soldiers raised their muskets to their shoulders, the men looking as if they turned to the right. There was a series of clicks as musket locks were pulled back.

'What the devil . . .' Moss was stunned. 'We're English, you damned fools.'

The officer's sword swept down. '*Tirez!*' The red-coated soldiers from one of Napoleon's Swiss regiments pulled the triggers of their muskets. Flints sparked and set off the powder in the pans which flared and ignited the main charge. The noise and the flame and the bursts of smoke were almost simultaneous as the volley thundered out at the 106th.

It was difficult to fire down a slope. Men instinctively aimed too high and most of the bullets sailed above the heads of the 106th. Hanley felt the King's Colour being plucked at by the musket balls. One shot was true, and struck George Moss squarely in the forehead, flinging his head back as the lead ball drove deep into his brain. He was dead before he hit the ground, an expression of intense surprise on his face.

26

Toye noted the colonel's death without any great emotion. It was simply too sudden.

'106th, present!' he yelled. The men brought their muskets up to their shoulders.

'Make ready!' Flints were pulled back till they clicked into place. The men had fixed bayonets, which would not help their aim or reloading, but Toye wanted only one quick volley from them. The Swiss company paused as they reloaded. It was almost as if everyone took a deep breath. The scattered group who had inverted their muskets in an effort to surrender milled about, and then started to run back into cover.

'Fire!' The 106th's own volley was a little ragged, but much better aimed. Firing up a slope tended to be more accurate. Dense smoke blotted the enemy from view, but Toye was beside the main formation and could see men dropping all along the front rank of the Swiss line.

'Charge!' he yelled. 'Let them hear you coming, boys!' Toye was already running, his weariness forgotten and his bent sword held out in front of him. The 106th cheered and charged after their major, rushing through the smoke towards the Swiss. The latter had still not loaded. One man raised his musket anyway, clicked back the hammer and let it fall on an empty pan. Others tried to keep loading, but most started to edge backwards. One of the wounded men from the front rank was screaming in pain. When the 106th were ten yards away the Swiss wavered and then fled. Their officer grabbed a man and tried to hold him back, but when the soldier shook him free the officer joined in the flight as well.

Four Swiss were left on the ground, one of them dead. Toye halted on their position, his men too weary to chase the enemy any farther.

'Well done, lads,' he said. He turned to look back down the slope. A dozen or so more men from the 106th were making their way out of the gully. Then he spotted Moss's body, his limbs splayed out in an unnatural position.

'Sergeant Keene, detail four men to carry the colonel back down the hill.'

More movement made Toye look to the spur on the left behind them. A line of men in dun-covered shakos and long buff coats was coming over it towards them. The French infantry were three deep and a short distance behind them was another company. They were scarcely a hundred yards away.

'Company, about turn!' Toye shouted as loudly as he could. The response was hesitant, the order a surprise, but after a moment the men turned around. 'Reload!'

The sergeants and ensigns as well as the entire colour party were now in front of the formation. There was some added confusion as they tried to push their way through. Hanley and Derryck turned and stood with the colours in what was now the front rank. The sergeants stood in the second rank to cover them. The wind had picked up as they had gone higher and the two flags streamed out behind them. Around them the men scrabbled to reload, some taking the skin off their knuckles as they plied ramrods too close to a fixed bayonet. It was a race, and the French were bound to win.

When they were fifty yards away the first French company halted. The second had wheeled to its left and was moving to extend the line. The new arrivals from the 106th ran up the slope to join Toye's men.

The leading French company fired with a sound like heavy cloth ripping. There were dull thumps as balls struck home. Hanley's cocked hat was jerked off his head. Beside him a redcoat was hit on the cheek and knocked backwards. Another man screamed as he was struck in the stomach. Two men were dead and six wounded. The sergeants dragged the wounded back and pitched the bodies of the dead forward. Normally a line would close formation to the centre, but this one was too small so the men from the rear rank were simply urged forward to fill the places of the casualties.

Toye wondered about charging. The French company that had fired now fixed bayonets and began to walk forward. The second company halted and made ready. Toye could see some of his men loaded and hoped for the best.

'Present!' he yelled. 'Aim low, boys, aim low!' Perhaps two-thirds of the 106th were loaded. Some of the other men pulled back the hammers of their muskets anyway.

'Fire!' Hanley flinched as a musket went off just inches from his left ear. For a moment he was stunned, unable to hear. Smoke billowed around them, and then the wind took it and blew it back in their faces. Hanley coughed, the stink of burnt powder in his throat. Although ill prepared, it was a good volley. Four men dropped in the leading French company and their officer reeled backwards, dropping his sword as he was struck in the shoulder.

Then the second French company fired. Hanley felt a hammer blow to the very top of his chest and was knocked backwards. Then he saw nothing. The King's Colour dropped from his hands, the dust staining the big Union flag. Captain Headley's left arm was broken and hung lifelessly, but for the moment he was in shock and felt no pain. A sergeant from his light company was hit in the thigh and lay on the ground, trying to tie his sash into a tourniquet. As he worked he cheered the men on. Other wounded just moaned.

The French charged with a great cry of '*Vive l'empereur!*' Behind the 106th the Swiss reappeared and fired a ragged volley into their rear. Toye was struck in the side. A sergeant was hit in the back of the skull and dropped on to Hanley. Half a dozen more men were down. The British soldiers turned in confusion. Men spread out and were facing in every direction as the yelling French infantrymen came towards them, the tales of their coats flapping, the points of their long bayonets reaching forward hungrily.

A Frenchman who looked no more than a fresh-faced boy drove his bayonet deep into the stomach of a redcoat who was trying to load his musket. The man gasped as the wind was knocked out of him, then began to scream as the young French conscript struggled to free his blade. Beside him a long-moustached veteran neatly dispatched another redcoat with an economical thrust, giving his musket a slight twist to free the blade. A corporal of the 106th had only just finished loading his musket and shot the veteran at point-blank range, blowing off the back of the man's head in a spray of blood and brains. He jabbed at the conscript, who ducked, but was then himself stabbed through the thigh by another Frenchman. He tried to spin round and thrust at his opponent in spite of the hot agony of his wound, but another French bayonet took him in the throat. Most of the redcoats did little to defend themselves, stunned by the ferocity of the attack and knowing that it was hopeless. They dropped muskets and raised their arms or held them butt upwards in the air, just as the Swiss had done.

At first it did not stop the French. Bayonets lunged forward. Men screamed as the points slid into their flesh. Toye was shouting, wishing that he knew some French and trying to attract the attention of an officer. Faced with death anyway, some of the redcoats grabbed muskets again or struggled with the French soldiers.

A group of Frenchmen led by an officer had gone straight at the colour party. A sergeant had picked up the King's Colour and lowered it to point the heavy and ornate spearhead at the approaching enemy. It was a clumsy weapon with a blunt blade, but he snarled as he slashed the air with it. The French officer stopped, took careful aim with his pistol and shot the sergeant in the chest. A moment later he thrust his sword left-handed at Derryck, who was struggling to hold the standard in one hand and draw his own sword with the other. The youngster hissed with pain, but did not cry out. As he fumbled with his sword, a sergeant stabbed his half pike over his shoulder at the officer's face. The Frenchman went backwards, flailing for balance, but avoiding the wickedly sharp point. A French soldier tried to stab

Derryck, but managed only to graze his arm. The ensign freed his blade and cut clumsily at the man, wincing with the pain from his arm. The Frenchman parried the blow, raising his musket high. He clubbed the butt down on the young officer's face, smashing his nose and knocking Derryck down. The sergeant's half-pike took the Frenchman in the eye. He screamed and clutched at the blade, but before the sergeant could free it the French officer dropped into a lunge and opened his throat. Blood jetted in a fountain over the falling colour and the dying sergeant himself.

He was the last redcoat to resist. The others were dead or wounded or trying to surrender. The Frenchmen herded them into a group. Several more of the 106th were stabbed in the process. Toye grabbed a man who had just bayoneted an already wounded soldier and was promptly stabbed himself, the blade going deep into his leg. Still he shouted protests. Only the arrival of a mounted officer – his long blue coat covered in lace and his cocked hat plumed, so evidently a man of rank and probably a general – rode up and yelled at the soldiers to stop. They obeyed, a little sullenly in some cases. Two French officers held up the 106th's colours to the general for his inspection. Toye found the sight utterly humiliating.

Other Frenchmen walked among the dead and wounded, stripping both of any valuables. Derryck coughed when a man began to rifle his pockets. The ensign sat up. Had the general not been there, the French soldier would have been tempted to finish the boy off. Instead he helped him up. Derryck staggered over to the other prisoners. A sergeant, his head roughly bandaged, went out to help him. One of the French soldiers barred his way until an officer barked an order.

'Bad business,' said Headley, who had come to sit beside Toye.

'Damned bad,' was all the major could think of saying in reply. 'They must have been on the spurs behind us. You couldn't see a thing down in that ravine.' There was a fresh burst of heavy firing from somewhere down the slope. 'The rest of the battalion?'

'Probably,' agreed Headley. 'They're taking their damned time, though.'

The firing was coming nearer, and this prompted a flurry of

activity among the French. The prisoners were urged to their feet and ushered back. Altogether there were five officers and more than twenty men, of whom all but six were wounded, some several times and mostly with bayonets. They helped each other to limp up the slope. The French gave them a dozen guards as escort, as well as the two officers proudly carrying the captured colours. Derryck was sobbing, far more from his sense of failure than the pain of his injuries, although that was bad enough.

Williams and Dobson peered over the ledge of the ravine, having taken care to remove their shakos. They were careful, and a gorse bush gave them some cover. None of the French appeared to notice them. The right wing had also broken up as it climbed the gully, men defiling off into the various channels. The Grenadier Company had led, and as Dobson glanced behind him he could see quite a few more men scrambling up the slope to join them at the lip. He gestured at Sergeant Darrowfield for them to come on as quietly as they could. They had climbed up on the left spur above the hollow, where the leading men of the 106th had been overwhelmed. There were bodies clustered on the slope and most were in red jackets.

Reaching back, Williams carried out the difficult operation of pulling his telescope out of the long case he strapped to the side of his pack. Dobson helped him.

'You ought to change this for something smaller, Pug,' whispered the veteran. Dobson looked back at the French formations and the activity behind them. 'Bastards,' he said bitterly, 'they've got our colours.'

Williams had focused on the French line, the strong magnification bringing their faces very close. They were no more than a hundred and fifty yards away and through the glass he could see every detail. Now he shifted the heavy telescope to the slope behind them. He moved past a group of Frenchmen and then back on to them. The two French officers laughed as they marched triumphantly up towards the crest carrying the flags of the 106th. A pair of infantrymen marched behind them with muskets formally on their shoulders.

The colours symbolised the regiment. They were its pride and its honour. Losing them to the enemy, especially while anyone in the battalion still lived and was able to fight, meant utter humiliation and disgrace. Williams felt shame and despair overwhelming him. Then came anger.

'We'll get them back,' he said firmly.

Dobson patted him on the shoulder and gave a grim smile which the volunteer did not see. Williams had moved to look at the little column of prisoners. He spotted Toye and Headley and some ensigns he knew only by sight. Then he noticed Derryck leaning heavily on a sergeant. There was no sign of Hanley. Williams felt a pang at the loss of his friend, but then the emotion fed his cold rage. He turned his glass to look up the slope. There was a patch of woodland behind the French and nearer the crest. Around it were scattered boulders. If they could reach there with only a few dozen men then perhaps they could pin the French until help arrived. Most of it was open slope, but there were a few hollows which would provide some concealment.

Shouts from the French interrupted him. For a moment he guessed that they had been spotted, perhaps because he had not been careful enough and had let the sun shine off his glass.

'It's the major,' said Dobson excitedly. 'Good old MacAndrews.'

Williams did not bother with the telescope; instead he looked over to the right and saw a formed body of the 106th marching over the far spur. There were at least a hundred and fifty, moving in two slightly ragged ranks. An officer – Major MacAndrews – marched ahead and to their right, his white hair blowing wildly as he waved his cocked hat in the air.

French officers shouted orders and began to re-form to face this new threat. Then there were more cries as another group of redcoats appeared from the same part of the gully Moss had followed. These men had yellow facings instead of the 106th's red and must be from the 9th. Some sixty men formed up so that now the French were threatened from the front and the flank.

Sergeant Darrowfield crouched down beside Williams. The volunteer pointed up the slope.

'It is only a suggestion, but if we could reach the trees we can come in behind them. Even a handful of skirmishers will help the battalion. More than that, if we move quickly we can take the colours back. Maybe free the prisoners as well. We just need to get as far forward as we can without being spotted.'

Darrowfield nodded. It made sense.

'Dob and I will go first. We've had longest to look at the ground.'

'No you will not,' snapped a familiar and hated voice. Ensign Redman was panting for breath, but his tone still dripped with contempt. 'There is no time for your glory hunting, sir. I am in charge and will decide what is best.'

Darrowfield reported quickly to Redman and explained the plan, having the sense to make it a suggestion, just as Williams had done with him. Redman peered over the bank and saw that the small force from the 9th and MacAndrews' men were almost ready to attack. The French had formed in an L-shape with half a company facing the 9th and the rest towards the larger force of the 106th.

Williams had to acknowledge that Redman was a good enough soldier to see the opportunity, much as he despised the man.

'Yes, that is our duty,' he said firmly. Then, with a mocking smile, he turned to the volunteer. 'Mr Williams, I'd be obliged if you would lead us up to the trees. One man will be less conspicuous. If you get there then Dobson and I will follow.' He looked at Darrowfield. 'If we make it then you, Sergeant, will bring the other men. No one is to fire unless they start shooting at us. Ready?' There were nods from the men around. As Williams took off his pack to move more quickly, Redman leaned down and whispered in his ear.

'If you haven't got the guts for this I can send someone else.'

Williams said nothing, hiding his rage at this insult. Instead he scrambled up the bank. There were three cheers – three British cheers – and he glanced to his right to see that MacAndrews and the 106th were moving forward. He took a deep breath, pushed up and sprinted forward, making for the first of the little hollows, but when this provoked no shouts or shots, he swerved around the cover. His haversack, pouch, bayonet scabbard and canteen were banging against him as he ran, and he felt his musket's sling slipping from his shoulder, so he grabbed it and held it across his body. He was breathing hard, his legs aching as he ran up the slope, dodging boulders.

Still no one seemed to notice the lone figure as he zig-zagged up the hill. There was the sound of a heavy volley, followed almost immediately by another. The French were clearly pre-occupied with the main attack. Williams ran on. He came to a boulder at the edge of a little depression and pushed down hard on the stone to leap over the hollow. He was amazed to see two red-coated soldiers look up at him. They seemed even more sur-prised. One jerked upwards and Williams' trailing foot caught the man a glancing blow on the forehead. The volunteer's shako fell from his head, but he could not worry about that.

Williams landed awkwardly, but kept running. He reached the shelter of the clump of thin trees a few moments later and only then turned to look back. The two soldiers had vanished. Their uniform had not looked British to him, but obviously they were now crouching down in the hollow. He decided they were not a threat and waved his hand to signal back at the grenadiers. Darrowfield waved his half-pike in response and two figures – Dobson and Redman, came over the lip. Williams decided to push on through the wood. Brambles plucked at his white breeches, and a button snapped off his gaiters, but the undergrowth was not thick enough to slow him down very much. There were more volleys, markedly more ragged this time.

He ran between two larger trees and found himself in a patch of open ground in the middle of the wood. A path cut through it, and on this stood four Frenchmen, who stared at him in surprise. They were the two officers with the colours and their escorts. Before consciously reacting, Williams turned his musket to point at the nearest officer and pulled the trigger. The detonation seemed enormous. The officer was flung backwards, taking the colour with him. A great red stain was spreading on the bright white front of his dark blue tunic.

Williams charged. There was a weird, guttural yelling filling the air, and it took him a moment to realise that it was coming from him. There had been no time to fix his bayonet. The French were better prepared and the two soldiers stepped forward to protect the remaining officer. The first man had a corporal's gold stripe on the sleeve of his loose greatcoat. His face was sallow, his bared teeth yellow and stained as he thrust forward at Williams. The volunteer parried the blow, knocking the Frenchman's musket aside with his own. Then he used the motion to swing round and slam the brass butt of his musket into the Frenchman's chin. The second enemy soldier jabbed at Williams, but the blow missed as he turned and the bayonet stuck in his haversack. The corporal was down, his jaw hanging loose and obviously broken. As the private struggled to free his weapon, Williams swung back the other way and slammed the butt into the man's forehead.

The officer had struggled to draw his sword while holding the heavy and unwieldy flag. It was the Regimental Colour, and the large red cross flowed around him for a moment, obscuring his vision. Williams dropped his musket and stooped to pick up the French corporal's weapon. As the officer cleared the silk of the flag from in front of his eyes and held his sword out ready, Williams pulled back the hammer with a click that seemed almost as loud as the gunshot a few moments ago. The corporal was moaning horribly.

Williams did not know whether the strange-feeling musket was loaded. Neither did the officer. Slowly he pointed it at the Frenchman.

'Prisoner?' he said.

The officer was small and thin. He thought for a moment and then shrugged. '*Oui, monsieur.*' He dropped his sword. Williams gestured at him to lower the colour to the ground and to sit. Hesitantly, the Frenchman did so.

'Fortunes of war,' said Williams slowly. The man gave a half-smile.

At that moment Dobson came through the undergrowth and on to the path. He looked around him at the two colours and the three prostrate Frenchmen.

'Bloody hell, Pug,' he said admiringly.

Williams smiled. 'Where is Mr Redman?'

Dobson's face became wooden. 'He didn't make it.'

27

It was hard for Wellesley to read the battle. His centre brigades had attacked early, before the flanking forces could make their presence felt. Men had made their way as best they could up the four main gullies in the steep slope. He could see little of their progress no matter where he went. The sound of firing had massively increased, and had for some time contained full volleys as well as individual shots. There were very few French visible and only occasionally could he spot groups of redcoats. It was difficult to resist the urge to head up one of the gullies and take personal charge of the fighting. He could sense the same instinctive reaction in his brigade commanders as he rode from one to the next. They could go up soon. He needed to give the attack more time, and follow only when he could usefully direct the fighting.

MacAndrews took his line to within twenty paces of the French before he halted the men. It was a gamble and meant they took three enemy volleys. The first dropped a dozen redcoats, the second half that, and the final ragged flurry of shots sailed harmlessly over the heads of the 106th.

'Present!' he ordered. 'Make ready!' The Frenchmen could see what was about to come. Even at twenty paces the muzzles of the English muskets looked huge and ominous.

'Fire!' MacAndrews' command was followed by an almost perfectly timed volley, filling the air between the two lines with thick smoke. '106th will fix bayonets!' yelled the major before any of the men could begin to reload. 'Fix!' Men reached back to grab the hilt of the spike bayonets. 'Bayonets!' They drew the blades and put them on to the warm muzzles of their muskets.

'Charge!' MacAndrews rushed forward. In his hand was not his regulation sword, but the basket-hilted broadsword he had grown accustomed to during his service with the Highlanders. It was a heavier blade and well sharpened. A handsome thing, and a fine tool for killing.

In this case there was no need. The French line had been wavering before the volley had scythed through its ranks. Men had dropped – some silent and some screaming. The sergeants behind the three ranks struggled to keep the men in place, but when the British cheered and came through the smoke, the French infantry broke. The 9th charged a moment later from another direction and completed the rout. When MacAndrews reached the French position there were only some thirty dead or wounded men sprawled in the grass. Their comrades were already disappearing over the crest of the ridge. The prisoners and their escort had already gone. The 106th followed. MacAndrews did not want to let them get too far, but hoped to reach the crest itself.

'There were two Frenchies in among the boulders. Wearing red, the cheeky buggers. They got Mr Redman with a bayonet. I settled them.' Dobson spoke flatly, but there was a defiance in his eyes suggesting that he was in no mood to answer more questions. Blood on his long bayonet backed the story. Yet Williams found it hard to believe. The two men had looked docile to him. Somehow he simply knew that Dobson had found out about the ensign and his daughter. Williams wondered whether murder had been done. It was a shocking thought, but then so many things had already shocked him today. He wondered whether he could do anything about it and then surprised himself by contemplating even whether he should.

'Who's this?' asked Dobson, jerking his thumb at the French officer.

'I am Sous-lieutenant Jean Galbert of the Emperor's 70th Regiment,' the man replied in confident English, much to Williams' amazement. 'And I am your prisoner. Or at least the prisoner of your officers, when they arrive.'

'All alike, aren't they,' said Dobson. 'Bloody gentlemen. Oh, sorry, Pug.' He gestured at the volunteer. 'Now see, monsewer, Mr Williams here is an officer. Well, will be after this.'

That surprised Williams. He had not thought that anything he had done might be enough to gain him his commission. The battalion had lost the colours and he had retrieved them. Even thinking that made him wonder whether Dobson was right. Then the nagging thought returned that he might be a party to murder.

There was the sound of shouting and of men forcing their way through the undergrowth. The grenadiers burst through the trees. Captain Wickham was with them, and Sergeant Darrowfield behind him. The captain looked wild and so different from his normal suave and controlled manner. He was shouting at the top of his voice and waving a sword in one hand and a pistol in the other.

Galbert rose to greet him. Wickham did not break stride, but ran towards the Frenchman. He pressed the pistol to Galbert's chest and pulled the trigger. A gaping wound erupted in the French officer's back as he was flung backwards. Wickham ran on, still yelling and cheering wildly.

'He's drunk,' said Dobson mildly. Darrowfield shrugged as he passed, but carried on after his officer. Most of the grenadiers followed.

Williams looked down at the dead Galbert. 'Murderer,' he said in a hoarse whisper. 'You damned murderer!' he screamed at Wickham as the captain charged on. Dobson grabbed him round the shoulders and stopped him from giving chase.

'He's drunk. No sense in him. It's just bad luck.' Williams was shaking with fury.

Half an hour later Major MacAndrews had gathered more than six hundred and fifty men from the 106th. Several companies were badly depleted, but with some improvisation the battalion was formed in line in something approximating its normal order. The right wing companies were stronger, close to their full complement, reduced only by a few casualties and stragglers. On the far left of the line, the Light Company had only forty men under the command of Lieutenant Black, the former militia officer. Companies Eight and Seven were so weak that they had been merged into one, as had Companies Six and Five. There was also some shifting of men between the other companies to make them viable as manoeuvre units. Altogether the Left Wing mustered barely two hundred men. The colour party – the flags held by the next most senior and junior ensigns and guarded by other sergeants – was placed between Companies Four and Three in what was now the rough centre of the battalion. Stragglers kept coming in, and for the moment Lieutenant Anstey was tasked with forming them into a squad that would act as reserve. To the right of the 106th, the 9th Foot formed their own line and waited. On the crest, they were overlooked by a higher fold in the ridge which hid the French from them. MacAndrews conferred with the colonel of the 9th and an ADC of General Hill's, who had climbed up to find out what was happening. They agreed to hold the position for the moment.

At first the French probed the British position tentatively. Two companies of voltigeurs came over the higher crest and began to snipe at the British battalions. In response the light companies went forward and spread out across the slope, working in pairs and trying to drive the enemy back. More serious was the arrival of two French field guns, manhandled into position on the ridge. At such a close range, the gunners had to push the cannon forward until they were actually pointing downwards at the British.

The first balls went high, so the artillerymen reduced the charge of powder. This time, when the guns were fired and leapt back up the slope on their carriages the balls struck the far left of the 106th's line, each eight pound shot smashing two men to pulp. Yet the angle was difficult and this success was never equalled by later salvoes. There was anyway little time for the gunners to practise. Almost immediately two French battalions marched over the crest. They came in column, two companies abreast and the other six companies in pairs at quarter-distance behind them. To Williams it was as if a succession of smaller lines came over the ridge. The French cheered and beat their drums in the rhythm of the charge. Officers ran out ahead, wildly gesticulating with their swords. One man was almost dancing in his urge to show contempt for the enemy. The voltigeurs parted to let them through. A few shots were fired by the British skirmishers before the whistles of their officers called them back and they withdrew to take up their positions on the left of the battalions.

Both British battalions let the French come close. At thirty paces they came to the present and fired. Men were felled all along the front rank of each column. Miraculously the dancing officer emerged unscathed. The French stopped, muskets came up to their shoulders, and their leading companies fired a ragged volley. The colonel of the 9th was struck in the chest, but refused to be moved until the attack had been repulsed. Next to Williams, Private Murphy was hit by a ball that ripped off the top of his right ear. He cursed long and hard in Gaelic, but did not pause as he reloaded his musket. Other men fell and were dragged out of the ranks. Sergeants yelled at the men to close up towards the centre.

The British fired a second volley and then charged. Both columns recoiled, the men in the rear companies turning and running, those in the very front going back more gradually, and a few pausing to fire the odd defiant shot. Just behind the crest their officers managed to stop them and began to re-form. The two British battalions halted and re-dressed their ranks. They were now closer to the enemy. One of the French guns loaded a canister, a metal case filled with musket balls. When the gun fired the case disintegrated as it left the barrel and the balls sprayed out like the blast of a giant shotgun. Seven men from the Grenadier Company of the 9th were flung backwards as if by the slice of a great scythe.

The adjutant of the other battalion ran over to tell MacAndrews that their colonel was dead, and that the senior major advised driving forward to the crest. MacAndrews agreed. The light companies were sent forward again to snipe at the French gunners and to keep the voltigeurs in check. Then the two lines went forward at a steady pace. The guns got off two rounds of canister and cut more swathes through the redcoats before the gunners lifted the trails and wheeled the cannon back over the crest to limber up. The voltigeurs could not resist both the light companies and the full battalions and followed a few moments later. The redcoats cheered as they reached the top of the hill. Then they were struck by the volleys from the two French battalions, now re-formed into line and waiting on the far slope. Captain Mosley took a ball in the shoulder, which spun him round. He staggered, but remained with the company, trying to ignore the pain. The 9th replied first with a volley. MacAndrews ordered platoon volleys from the 106th, sections of a company firing in sequence so that the fire rippled up and down the line and never stopped.

Private Scammell turned over the sergeant's body and searched his uniform with practised hands. His mate, Private Jenkins, kept watch. There were lumps along the seam of the dead sergeant's tunic and so Scammell slit it with a knife and revealed the coins hidden there. He smiled to himself and held the silver up to show Jenkins. There was an officer underneath the sergeant. The man lay on his back and both his face and chest were covered with dark blood. Scammell recognised him as the new one from the Grenadier Company, but neither knew nor cared about his name. Well, he thought, let's see if he's rich.

The officer stirred and his eyes came open. He gasped for breath. Hanley gasped again when he saw the predatory expression on the face that loomed over him. Then the man smiled a gap-toothed grin.

'You all right, sir?' asked Scammell, disappointed, but as ever willing to make the best of things. 'Can you stand?' Hanley nodded. He tried to speak, but his voice was no more than a croak. His chest and throat ached as he sat up.

'You're a lucky bugger, sir, begging your pardon.' The private was cheerful and held up a twisted piece of metal. It was Hanley's gorget, the horseshoe-shaped ornament worn by all officers on their neck. A ball was buried deep in the brass. 'If it had missed that you'd be dead.'

They helped Hanley up. Breathing was hard and painful, but a quick inspection showed that he was not actually wounded. 'Where is everyone?' He managed to get the words out with difficulty.

'The battalion, sir? Somewhere up there. Me and Jenkins here have been trying to find them. Still, we'd better take you back to the surgeon,' said Scammell hopefully.

'No. No. The battalion.' Hanley was firm. He did not know why, but simply wanted to be with friends. He wondered what had happened to the colours.

Scammell shrugged and the two privates walked with the officer up the slope. They did not hurry. The firing was heavy from beyond the crest, so that suggested that the battle was there, and so probably was the battalion.

Williams had lost all track of time. His mouth was dry from biting off cartridge after cartridge and tasting the salty gunpowder. His cheeks were stained black and his shoulder ached from the recoil of the heavy musket each time he fired. Dobson loaded and fired in front of him and there was no time to think of what the man may have done. Simply go mechanically through the motions of loading, just like during the long hours of training, and then fire forward into the smoke. He could not see the French, but they were there, and now and again balls plucked through the dense cloud. With a dull thump like a man slapping a ham, one shot hit Private Tout, standing beside him.

He looked puzzled and turned towards Williams. 'Oh, sir, they have killed me,' he said in a flat voice, and then toppled backwards.

Williams had just raised another cartridge to his lips. He paused for a moment. Then he bit off the ball, put a pinch of powder into the pan, dropped the musket's butt to the ground, poured the main charge down the muzzle, and spat in the ball. The ramrod slid easily from its holder. He reversed it, thrust down once and then twirled it again before sliding it back into the rings. Musket back to fold into his bruised shoulder, pull back the hammer. He aimed at where he had last seen the French. Let his breath half out and squeezed the trigger. The noise was indistinct over the general clamour of battle, but the butt slammed into his shoulder and he began again.

Billy Pringle stood on the right of the Grenadier Company and so on the very right of the battalion's line. Properly that was the captain's place, but Wickham had succumbed to the excitement and the brandy and was now sleeping both peacefully and soundly in the shelter of a copse guarded by a lightly wounded private. He was the only officer remaining with the company, although fortunately the sergeants had been spared. There was anyway little enough for him to do. The neat platoon volleys had degenerated into every man firing as quickly as he could load. There were no more orders to give for the moment, so he simply stood and tried to look brave and confident in the hope that it might encourage the few men able to see him. He could dimly see the French line through the curls of smoke. Worse, he could see them moving a cannon into place on the flank of the infantry.

Someone appeared at his side. It was Hanley, looking pale and bloodstained.

'I thought you were dead!' Hanley looked blank, and so Pringle yelled even louder to be heard over the rolling gunfire.

'You mean I'm not!' Hanley had cupped his hands around his mouth to shout. As he lowered them, he felt a sudden pain above the elbow of his left arm. He looked to see his sleeve torn and blood spreading darkly.

'Damn,' he said. Pringle produced a handkerchief and began to bind the wound. Beside them a group of blue-jacketed men from the Royal Artillery struggled to roll a light six-pounder gun up the slope. Most of the men of the half-battery were there, all combining to drag just one of their guns up to the top of the ridge. Pringle was amazed they had managed it. He watched the gunners go through the well-practised routine of loading and took great satisfaction when the crew stepped back and the match was applied to the priming tube. The gun leapt backwards as it roared. For once the smoke seemed to clear and Pringle saw three of the French gunners plucked away from their own cannon as the canister threw up dust around it.

Lieutenant Brotherton appeared, once again acting as adjutant. 'Tell the men to cease fire, Billy.' He leaned forward to shout the instructions. 'We're going forward again.'

As the British infantry had gone higher up the ridge, Sir Arthur Wellesley had found it easier to follow their progress. The fighting was heavy, but it was clear that they were making headway. It was time for him to move up, and for a while he lost all general perspective of the battle as he rode his horse up the easiest route he could find. Soon he and his staff were passing the debris of battle. An ADC was sent to bring up the 20th Light Dragoons from the reserve, telling them to follow this path and then to form in a single rank at the top of the ridge. It might just convince the French that he had more cavalry.

The enemy was already giving way. He doubted that more than a third of his own army had yet been engaged and those troops would not have outnumbered the French. Even so they were forcing the enemy from one position to the next and that at least was encouraging. Less satisfying was his inability once again to molest the French as they withdrew. The enemy's retreat was disciplined, and well covered by their Chasseurs. His cavalry were too weak to do much to interfere, although their mere appearance may have hastened Delaborde on his way. The French commander was forced to abandon three of his cannon when there was not time to get them through a narrow defile. They did take the horse teams, and without those the guns were of little use to Wellesley at the moment. Still, they were a mark of success, and an encouragement to his – his only for a short time, but still his – new and young army.

Delaborde was almost as content as he rode back alongside one of his infantry battalions. They had delayed the enemy, and inflicted at least as many losses as they had suffered. The redcoats had shown courage, but did not seem to be the equals of the Emperor's men in skill. His opinion of General Junot was low –

the man was a hussar at heart and they never had any brains – but even he should be able to smash the British once he had mustered a large enough army. Delaborde had done a good deal to give him the time for this and would have to make sure that the Emperor was aware of his achievements. The rest was up to Junot.

Williams raised his canteen in the vain hope that there might be just a drop of water left. He had never been so thirsty. His tongue felt huge and swollen, his mouth like sandpaper. Most of the battalion was sitting in a rough line across the ridge where they had fought. The French had gone, and he assumed other regiments were following them. There was still the occasional musket shot, but he had heard no heavy firing for some time.

He stood beside Pringle, but neither was in any mood to talk. They were simply weary, and in both cases their ears were still ringing from the noise of volleys. Hanley had gone back with the other wounded to have his injury dressed and all the canteens found on the dead had been sent back with them. Captain Wickham had also gone with the party, and Williams was glad that he did not have to look at the man, for his anger was still raw. Dobson had gone with the carrying party and for the moment the volunteer was also glad that there was no need to talk to the old veteran. It was easier not to think and not to care. He knew that if he lay down, even sat, he would be asleep within moments. Pringle no doubt felt the same, and to set an example to the men forced himself to stand. The lieutenant suddenly turned and grinned at Williams.

The volunteer tried to speak, coughed, and then managed to croak, 'It isn't quite how I expected.' He meant the way the battle had simply stopped, at least for the 106th. There had been little drama. The enemy pulled back and they were too exhausted to chase them any more. There did not seem much pattern to anything, and already his memories of the day were becoming jumbled.

Pringle just shrugged. Then he brightened as he saw a staff officer ride up to MacAndrews. Hopefully this meant orders, and in due course rest.

28

The mood was strange in the mess of the 106th that night. It was not until late in the evening that the tent was set up and the wooden tables and stools laid out. Everyone was tired, yet MacAndrews sent Brotherton around to make sure that all officers who were capable of attending and not supervising the outposts came to the evening meal. It was simple enough fare, all of it cold and accompanied by a modest supply of cheap wine. Moss's luxuries were a thing of the past, as was the colonel himself. So much else had changed, and a visual reminder of this was the bullet-riddled and bloodstained colours crossed over each other and propped up against a stand of sergeants' half-pikes at the end of the tent.

At first the talk had consisted of greetings and enquiries about others. Hatch went pale when told that Redman had fallen, but managed a feeble joke about anything to avoid paying him ten shillings. Some officers were known to be dead. Others were with the surgeons and had a more or less good chance of recovering. Thomas still clung to life, although when MacAndrews had visited him his face had looked grey and it was hard to believe that the adjutant could possibly survive. Even if he did, his soldiering days were over and the best he could hope for was half pay or a good profit from selling his commission, which might stave off the worst ravages of poverty. Several officers were missing, Toye and Headley among them. At first it was not known whether they had simply not been found, and lay dead or wounded in some bleak hollow on the ridge, or whether they had been taken. Williams was able to say that he had seen them led off as prisoners. When the armies came back into contact no doubt messages would pass across the lines and include lists of captives taken. In time prisoners of equal rank might actually be exchanged for each other and return to their own side. Throughout the long wars with France the behaviour between British and French armies had been correct to the highest standards of the civilised world. The savagery of the French campaign against the Portuguese was no obvious reason for ending this.

That made him think of Wickham shooting Galbert out of hand. Anger was fading to a dull contempt, but there was also a real fear that such random murder could just as easily be committed by a Frenchman. He was too tired to be really afraid for the captured officers of the 106th, even poor Derryck. Weariness combined with resignation, for there was nothing that he could do. Dobson had anyway once told him that the dangerous moment was just after surrender. If a man was not murdered in the first hour then he would probably be treated well.

Since Major Toye was missing, that left MacAndrews the senior officer in the battalion. Captain Howard held a brevet majority and had done so for several years, but that meant only that he was a major when on detached service. In the regiment he was simply a captain and not even the most senior, for there were two others above him. Pringle and Truscott tried to explain this three times to Hanley without any success. To him it was baffling that the army should have two parallel systems of rank for its officers, so that a man might be called major or colonel, but was only a captain in his own regiment. Hanley's wound had been cleaned up, stitched together and bound. He had been fortunate because the ball had not struck the bone.

MacAndrews was for the moment in charge of the 106th. He accepted this in a matter-of-fact way, unwilling to get too excited, for it might prove very brief. Toye might return, and it was quite likely that even if he did not someone would purchase the post left vacant by Moss. A few months ago, as an ageing captain without prospects, he would not even have dared to dream that he might lead a battalion into battle. Now he had that chance, and he would do his duty. He quickly dismissed thoughts of seizing the opportunity to make a name for himself. Moss had tried to do that, and it had led to something close to a disaster as well as to his own death. The 106th had fought hard and – most important of all – had recovered its colours. They had come out without disgrace, but still had much to prove. That was more important than any ambition of his own.

At the end of the meal MacAndrews stood. He did not have Moss's flair for making speeches. He also knew this was not the time for a lecture. They were good men, most of them around the table, and they did not need to be advised. It was never pleasant to lose comrades, but the growing chatter had suggested they were coping. It was simply part of the soldier's life. There was also no need to announce that he was now in command. He was senior and so naturally assumed the role. Nothing needed to be said.

'Gentlemen,' MacAndrews began once the hubbub had subsided, 'I am pleased to pass on the compliments of Lieutenant General Sir Arthur Wellesley, who was gratified to commend the attack of the 106th and the Ninth Foot. We are to be mentioned in his dispatch.' They pounded the tables at that, at least as enthusiastically as they used to do for Moss's speeches. Sacrifice was always better when it was recognised. Being mentioned in a dispatch was an honour to the regiment and something of which they could all be proud. MacAndrews raised a hand for silence.

'We have lost some good fellows today. They have gone, but the 106th lives on. Gentlemen,' he raised his glass, 'I give you the King and the Regiment.'

'The King and the Regiment,' echoed the men almost in perfect unison.

'So what precisely happened?' MacAndrews looked straight into Williams' face as he asked the question. It was close to midnight, and the major had been working solidly since the evening meal. There was so much to be done – updating the regiment's muster role, balancing the companies and making sure that all officers required to replace their seniors were aware of their new duties.

It had generally all gone smoothly, but it had taken time and the major could have done without this additional problem.

'We became cut off from the rest of the company as we climbed up the ravine,' said Williams. 'Dobson and I got to the top first, a short while before you and the main body arrived over to our right. Sergeant Darrowfield joined us with some of the men and we prepared to turn the enemy flank, and if possible recapture the colours and the prisoners. Mr Redman arrived and took charge. We went forward in small groups and after some fighting managed to recover the colours. Mr Redman was our only casualty when he and Dobson ran into two Frenchmen in red uniforms who were hiding. Both of the French were also killed. Soon afterwards Mr Wickham arrived.'

MacAndrews watched him for a moment, wondering whether any more detail would be offered. He had already spoken to Darrowfield and Dobson, and had tried without much success to get some sense out of Wickham. He had also seen Redman's body and those of the two Swiss – their identity had been confirmed by some deserters from the same regiment – soldiers around him. The corpses had been stripped. It was always amazing how quickly this occurred. Soldiers looted and so did their families. The local villagers seemed even quicker off the mark, and more inclined to take anything just in case it might be of use or value. Redman still had his white shirt and drawers on. All three men had been killed with bayonets. One of the Swiss had been stabbed through the throat, and the other had several wounds to the stomach. Redman had been killed by a single neat thrust to the heart. There was a look of surprise on his pale face and vast bloodstains on his shirt, which might explain why it had been left, although the looters had stripped the Swiss, whose wounds must also have bled. MacAndrews guessed that Williams had also visited the spot. Darrowfield had been evasive, while Dobson had simply told his story briefly and baldly. He and the ensign had dived for cover into the hollow. The two enemy soldiers had killed Redman and he in turn had killed them.

'Were there many Swiss there – the men in red?' the major asked.

'I only saw two. Nearly fell on top of them when I went up.' Williams had learnt from the other soldiers – most of all from old Dobson himself – to avoid the gaze of officers and remain at attention staring blankly ahead. MacAndrews stood and walked from behind the little camp table, coming so close that that old trick would not work.

'Did they seem notably aggressive? Quite a few men from the Fourth Swiss Regiment have deserted to us.'

'Not at the time. They let me pass. However, they were probably too surprised to act. I know I was.' Williams smiled with this confession and then immediately realised it was a mistake. MacAndrews' gaze was hard.

'Yet moments later these cowering soldiers – probably men trying to give themselves up – furiously attacked and killed one of our officers?' MacAndrews let the question hang.

'So it seems.'

'Do not toy with me, sir.' The major was shouting, and Williams barely managed to stop himself from jumping back. MacAndrews calmed himself. 'It is not unknown for disgruntled privates to kill unpopular officers in the confusion of battle.' His tone was quiet now. 'God knows I have known it happen often enough. Sometimes the officers may be considered to have deserved being killed. Sometimes not.'

He paused again. Williams said nothing. It was obvious that MacAndrews shared his belief that Dobson had killed Redman. Maybe he too knew of the probable cause, for MacAndrews had an ear for everything that went on in the battalion and no doubt was aware of the gossip about Jenny.

MacAndrews' face was now just a few inches from Williams. 'Such things happen, but can never be condoned. If a man so much as raises his hand to an officer he is flogged. If the attack is serious he is hanged or shot. There can be no exceptions. Not even for men of good record and proven courage.' The Scotsman let that sink in. 'Therefore, I must ask you on your word as a gentleman, whether you know that Ensign Redman's death was not at the hands of the enemy.'

Williams' throat was dry. He licked his lips and coughed before he was able to speak. 'I do not know otherwise, sir, and saw nothing.'

MacAndrews noted the precision of the reply. For a good minute he stared at the volunteer.

'There remains the matter of the French officer who was captured.'

'I saw Captain Wickham kill him,' replied Williams firmly.

'He was leading a charge, was he not?'

'That is true, but Sous-Lieutenant Galbert had surrendered to me and been disarmed.'

'It may interest you to know that Captain Wickham has formally commended you for your bravery, and recommended that you immediately be commissioned into this regiment as ensign.' In fact Wickham had remembered little of the day, but had readily responded to MacAndrews' suggestion.

'That does not change the truth of what I saw. I do not believe I can accept this reward at the recommendation of such a man.'

MacAndrews returned to the table and sat down on the canvas chair behind it. He studied the volunteer for a while.

'Does it matter from whom the recommendation comes?' he asked after a while. 'You have the makings of a good officer.'

'Not from such a man who would murder the helpless.'

'That is a strong word. The blood of any man can run very hot in battle.' MacAndrews held a low opinion of Wickham and felt nothing but contempt for his behaviour, but could do nothing about that.

'He was drunk, sir.' Williams made no effort to conceal his own scorn. Until today he would never have dared so openly to criticise his company commander. Yet he felt oddly different. Nothing had prepared him for the reality of battle. For the sights, at times ghastly and at other times strange, or even oddly beautiful. The smells had sometimes been even more shocking. He could never have guessed that human bodies could be so mutilated and that they would stink so much when it happened.

MacAndrews paused again. 'Many men drink in battle.' That

was true, but Wickham had gone far beyond mere Dutch courage. He had not been able to do his duty by the end of the engagement. Still, some otherwise brave men struggled the first time they went into battle. MacAndrews could pardon that, as long as it did not happen a second time.

Williams felt the silence pressing in on him. He could only half believe that he was refusing to take the commission which he had longed for. Yet he knew he could not face himself if he owed his rise to such circumstances. 'I regret, sir, that I cannot accept Captain Wickham's recommendation. I do wish to continue serving as a volunteer with the 106th Regiment if I am granted that honour.'

'Think carefully about this. You behaved with considerable gallantry and recovered colours whose loss would have been an appalling stain on the honour of this regiment. That deed is greater than those usually performed by gentlemen seeking a commission.' MacAndrews was unsure whether to be impressed or vaguely annoyed by the Welshman's stubbornness. He wondered how he would behave in the same circumstances, knowing that his own pride and sense of what was right might have made him just as big a damned fool. 'Would it change matters if I made it an order?'

'I still could not in honour obey,' said Williams mulishly. Realising what he had said, he added, 'With the utmost respect, sir.' A thought he been playing with for some time voiced itself. 'Perhaps it would be a kind thing to tell Mr Redman's parents that he fell leading a gallant charge to recapture the colours.'

MacAndrews permitted himself a tiny smile. A damned fool in love with honour and still seeing the romance in soldiering. That did remind him of himself, but he was not about to admit that.

'Redman came nowhere near the colours,' he said. 'You went first anyway.'

'Nevertheless, he was in command, sir, and led the main body.'

'As you say,' MacAndrews relented. There were so many letters to write and at least this would make one of them easier. It would be harder to phrase the words to the colonel's father – and his affianced. Damn, he had forgotten her. He looked again at Williams. 'Very well. You are dismissed, Mr Williams. Good night to you.'

29

The 106th mustered seven hundred and eighty-four men and twenty-seven officers when it marched out with the rest of the army on the day after the battle. In spite of its losses it was still stronger than several other battalions. Hanley marched with the Grenadier Company. His left arm was bandaged and held for the moment in a sling, and so it would have been impractical for him to carry the colour. He was more than a little surprised to find that this disappointed him and that he felt a vague sense of failure, but he said nothing about this to his friends.

Williams felt strangely free. There was a curious, even perverse satisfaction in turning down the commission. Somehow it made him feel in control of his own destiny. During the fighting he had felt fear and horror, and yet also something of that same clarity and control. It had all seemed so simple and he found himself able to think clearly and do what needed to be done. Nothing had been quite as he had expected, and yet his initial revulsion at the deaths of Redman and Galbert had diminished. There would be another battle soon, for it was widely known that the French were gathering their forces. It would be a much larger battle, and he could only assume that that would make it more ferocious. That prospect made it hard to think over much of the past. He had merely shrugged when Dobson had greeted him with a gruff 'You still with us, Pug?' He was not yet sure how he felt about the veteran, although he had no doubt that he could rely on him when the fighting resumed. It was simply harder to decide what mattered.

Billy Pringle was happy to live only in the moment. They had won a victory, if a small one, and he shared the near-universal confidence that they would beat the French main army as soon as they confronted it. Wickham was following on with the regiment's baggage. He had emerged from the battle with a bad cut to the head – Pringle suspected the result of a fall rather than enemy action. Today he complained of aches and a fever and so excused himself from duty, telling Pringle to look after the lads for him and that he hoped to be well again tomorrow. Billy did not mind. Most of the day would be spent in marching south. The army was heading back towards the coast, for new convoys of reinforcements had arrived and Wellesley was moving to cover their landing. The French had gone back inland and so it was unlikely anything would happen for a few days. There seemed nothing in particular to worry about and he was content to let the future take care of itself. There was something reassuring about having the army make all his decisions for him.

The British followed the coast road south. It passed through rolling hills and at times they could see the sea to their right. Williams had never seen water look so blue until he had come to Portugal. In the sunlight it sparkled. Even from this distance it helped to make the day seem cooler, although the sun bore down and the dust covered everyone and everything with fine powder. Pringle paused for a moment to let the company pass him, checking as they did that everyone was coping and that none of the men needed help carrying their equipment. As Hanley passed, the man mouthed a word and made Pringle smile. Yes, he had been thinking of Xenophon – the great cry of the Ten Thousand was 'The Sea! The Sea!' For those ancient Greek mercenaries it had marked the end of the journey and of their toil. That wasn't true for the 106th, but still it was a pleasant sight and a diverting thought.

That evening the army camped on the high ground around the village of Vimeiro, which lay on the main road. Some way to the east were the heights of Torres Vedras and then Lisbon itself. To the west the road wound down to the coast at the tiny hamlet of Porto Novo, overlooking the bay where the reinforcements would land.

MacAndrews was still very busy, and once again had to work late into the night. Brotherton helped as much as he could, but for all his enthusiasm he could not yet match Thomas, who knew the battalion so well. They had left a small party at Roliça with the wounded who could not be moved, the adjutant among them. Somehow he still clung on to life. Other regiments had also left men and a small hospital had been set up in the church. MacAndrews had spoken to the surgeon to discover which of the wounded still with the battalion were ready for duty. The list of names with the details of injuries and current condition was in front of him now.

It was one more list in a life that now seemed to consist entirely of lists. He was generally content with the mood of the battalion. They had taken a blow, but had recovered and felt that they had proved themselves more than a match for the enemy. Personally, he was not yet sure of that. By all accounts the French had been heavily outnumbered and so were bound to be forced from the position in the end. Even so the 106th had performed well, and so it seemed had the rest of the army. The general appeared to know his business, but then since he was soon to be superseded much might change. Well, there was nothing he could do about that. The arrival of the convoy meant that ships would be return- ing home afterwards and post could be sent. There were letters to write expressing regret to the families of the fallen officers. He had determined in his own mind that all would be of the same length, but the habits of seniority also meant that he decided to begin with the one to Moss's father. Then he must also write to General Lepper. Perhaps at the end he would still have energy enough to pen a few words to his dearest Esther. Perhaps. Duty as always would come first.

The convoys of ships had come from Harwich and Ramsgate and between them brought another four thousand men. There were six battalions of infantry and a couple more companies of riflemen from the 95th. There were also artillerymen, but the familiar problems of finding horses to pull the limbers made these less immediately valuable. The surf was high and the bay offered only limited shelter. Some boats were overturned and men drowned, but after two days almost everyone had been landed and had marched the few miles to join the main force around Vimeiro. The new regiments had all dispensed with hair powder and queues, and brought the formal order from Horse Guards ending the hated practice. Some of the 106th were a little disappointed that this made them less unique in the army, but the general mood of joy quickly spread to them.

This was increased by a lively expectation of battle. On the evening of 20th August word had spread that the main French army had left Lisbon and was coming towards them. Now that the reinforcements had landed, preparations were under way for the army to move out once more. With the sea behind them the only way to go was forward to meet the French. The new arrivals, and the regiments that had seen little service at Roliça were especially eager to prove themselves. The 106th and the other units that had done the bulk of the fighting were equally keen to demonstrate how it was done.

Sir Arthur Wellesley's mood was less optimistic as he was rowed ashore in one of the last boats to make the landing that day. Lieutenant General Sir Harry Burrard had arrived, and this signified the end of his period of independent command. Nothing could alter that, and he had gone out to greet the general on board the frigate that carried him. Carefully and respectfully he had explained the situation. Junot had at last concentrated some fourteen thousand men and was advancing. It was good that he was not waiting longer to gather more of his army. Perhaps he felt that some garrisons needed to be held to keep some control over the Portuguese. More probably he was simply confident that this was enough to crush any British force. Yet, with the two newly arrived brigades, the British could muster more than sixteen thousand men, not counting the Portuguese contingent, whose effectiveness was not yet proven.

Wellesley had grown animated as he explained his plan, using a map spread out on the table in the frigate captain's cabin. There was a chance for bold action. Junot was overconfident and was also unlikely to know about their reinforcements. If the British Army marched to the south they could loop behind the French. At best Junot would be cut off from Lisbon and the loss of the capital should encourage even more Portuguese to rise against the French. At the very least they should catch the enemy strung out on the march and be able to choose when and where to defeat the French general. Everything was ready. Two days' food had been issued to the men, more would be carried in the wagons, while the ammunition train and other essential baggage would be ready to march before dawn.

Burrard had listened politely, but when he finally spoke the man seemed far older than his sixty or so years. He commended the zeal and gallantry of his junior, but had to reprimand his recklessness. If there was a chance, there were risks too, and those were unnecessary. Sir John Moore was said to be nearing the coast. With his forces they would be more than twice the strength of the French and whatever he did Junot would not be able to match those numbers in the foreseeable future. Time was on their side, not that of the French. A battle might even be unnecessary altogether once the odds became overwhelmingly in their favour. The army would stay at Vimeiro and wait.

As the little boat rocked in the swell, Wellesley felt the spray on his face and thought longingly of the years in India when he had been given freedom to do the right thing and to act. Burrard had preferred one last night on board ship rather than spending it under canvas, which meant that in all practical respects he remained in command until Sir Harry came ashore the next day. He could not disobey a direct order. The army would stay in camp, but he would make sure that they were ready to move in the unlikely event that Burrard came to his senses. The old man had been more concerned with minor details of administration, with orders for two men from the regiments to be seconded to his staff as additional ADCs. Influence at work, no doubt, but there was nothing wrong with that in itself.

The longboat ground ashore. Wellesley took the proffered hand of one of the sailors and leapt out into the knee-deep surf. No, he could not disobey a direct order, but until the moment Burrard took formal charge he would continue to act as he saw fit. Junot was close, and with luck the light dragoons would locate the French during the night. If Junot attacked, or left himself vulnerable, then Wellesley would fight unless specifically ordered not to do so. There was still a chance to do things properly.

Billy Pringle thought that Wickham looked in good spirits. He sat outside his tent, playing cards with Anstey, Howard and several of the usual gamers. Mosley was missing, left in the makeshift hospital at Roliça, recovering from having a surgeon cut out the ball embedded in his shoulder. The cards were favouring the grenadier captain tonight and he laughed and joked happily with the others. At first he had reached up to his head periodically, and then given the slightest of winces, suggesting serious pain which he controlled with effort. Pringle still liked Wickham. Few men were as pleasant company. Yet he had come to wonder about the man. It was hard to know him, to see past the consummate actor and the elegant charm. Pringle had seen little of Wickham during the battle. He had certainly been drinking heavily in the hours before, but so had many others. Pringle himself had taken a good few gulps from his own flask, although once they had begun moving he had changed to water. They had become separated while going up the gully, but the forced and awkward silence of others made him wonder about the captain's conduct. He had tried to get more out of Williams, but the volunteer had looked especially stiff and on his honour and said that he was unable to speak. It had been the same when he asked about Redman.

During a break between games Pringle had asked Wickham how he felt.

'Bearing up,' came the cheerful reply. 'Have felt a bit of a fraud leaving all the work to you today.' As ever the smile was charming. Pringle immediately found himself making noises about how he should not consider such things, was sure he was making light of it and that he must wait until he had fully recovered.

'It's a ghastly nuisance. Lucky too, I suppose. An inch or two's difference in the Frenchman's aim and, well, who knows . . . A shallow grave and the end of old Wickham, who tried his best and was never any good at cards.'

'Would have saved me some gilt anyway,' said Howard, who was one of the heaviest losers. 'If I see that Frenchman I'll have to give him a thrashing on account.'

'I'd steer clear of him, if I were you,' put in Anstey. 'Some people's heads offer bigger targets!'

'Some of us do have a majestic profile, it is true,' responded the captain. 'Others can afford a small cranium since it is not required to contain anything.'

'Seriously, though.' Wickham steered the conversation back to himself. 'It is not all that bad. If the Frogs do come up to scratch tomorrow I'll manage. Am sure I will. So wake me early if Johnny Frenchman comes a-calling. Can't have you fellows fighting without me – you might get lost and attack the wrong side!' He let the scornful laughter subside. Then he looked Pringle in the eye, betraying just the faintest hint of moisture in his own. 'If not I may have to impose on you to run the company for another day. I am sure I can trust them in your hands.'

It was just what would be expected. Brave self-doubt conquered by a determination to do his duty if there was serious work to be done – concern for others and bluff confidence. That was the proper behaviour for a gentleman, so why did Pringle not quite believe it? No, that was wrong. He was simply not sure whether or not to believe the captain's sincerity. In the end did that matter? Weren't they all actors to a greater or lesser extent, following the rules and doing what was expected? What was important was what he actually did and they would not see that until, or if, the battle came. So Pringle stayed with the group and enjoyed the talk.

Williams read his Bible by the guttering light of an almost exhausted candle. He would have to see whether he could acquire a new one. It was a strain to make out the tiny printed words, but he read from the Psalms and memory tended to take over. A polite cough betrayed the presence of Hatch, Redman's friend.

'Seeking comfort?' asked the ensign.

'And finding it, as always.' Williams wondered what the man wanted and was ready to respond to any mockery. Then he wondered whether Hatch was suspicious about the death of his friend.

'Never helped me much. Had to recite so much at school. Deuteronomy mostly. Our headmaster was a miserable old sod. Lots of stuff about children being stoned for disobeying their parents. Not encouraging.'

'There is a lot more beyond that, and anyway every passage has its purpose.'

'Scaring schoolboys mostly. Quite liked the Song of Solomon when I grew older. There's riper stuff around, though.' Hatch looked extremely awkward. He also seemed to be fully sober and that was rare by this hour. 'Look, Williams, I wanted a word with you.'

Again there was an immediate flash of suspicion. Did he know something? It seemed unlikely. As far as he could tell Hatch had been with the main part of the battalion throughout the battle. 'Please speak freely,' said Williams.

'You know Forde is dead?'

Williams nodded.

'I was next to him when it happened . . . A cannon shot . . . Odd thing was that it did not touch him. It whipped just past his head and didn't give him so much as a scratch. He just gave a sigh and died. Some of the older fellows say they have seen it before. It's the wind or the shock or something.' Williams had never seen Hatch treat anything so seriously. 'Anyway, he died. So have so many. I do miss Redman.'

'I was sorry about that,' said Williams to his own surprise. 'You know we had our differences, but I would never have wished for this.'

'That is good of you, very good.' Hatch seemed deeply moved. 'He was an ass, but he was a good fellow. And brave too. None braver.' Williams nodded since it seemed to be helping the man. 'Well, that is my point. We may all be dead soon. You and I both. I know that we too have had our differences over these last months. Well, that's not important now. I just wanted to say . . . that is to ask . . . well, to take your hand and say that there were no hard feelings.'

Williams still could not quite convince himself that no game was involved and that the mockery would not resume. Yet Hatch seemed utterly sincere, indeed deeply emotional, and clearly needed this gesture. Williams stood and held out his hand. Hatch took it and shook it fervently.

'Thank you, Williams. Now we are square whatever happens. Thank you.' Hatch stepped back. 'There should be no arguments unresolved. This does not mean we need become friends.'

'Well, perhaps,' said Williams vaguely.

'No, I really do not care for you, but that does not matter.' The tone was matter-of-fact, not scornful or hostile. Hatch turned and walked away. Williams shook his head and returned to the Psalms. They were so much easier to understand than people.

MacAndrews sent Brotherton to tell Wickham. The order had come through late, but Captain Wickham of the 106th was to report to General Wellesley's staff immediately, as a preliminary to being attached to that of General Burrard. Wickham's friends had obviously been working on his behalf. Staff postings offered hard work, but brought far greater comforts and rewards than the more anonymous service with a regiment. MacAndrews had no doubt that the captain would be healed enough to take up his new duties, for this was a great opportunity. Well, ambition was natural enough, although MacAndrews had a deep-seated suspicion of the staff, perhaps because he had never been given an opportunity to serve in such exalted circles himself.

That was the last order he needed to give today. He had written five letters of condolence, and decided that now he might at last turn to his own correspondence. He had dismissed his clerk, the round-faced and bespectacled Corporal Atkinson, to get some sleep. This he would do on his own. He pulled out the locket that he always wore around his neck and flipped open the catch.

The miniature of Esther had been painted fifteen years ago and yet still captured her better than any other image. The smile was full of mischief. The portrait of Jane was less good, made when she was thirteen and awkward sitting for the artist. The girl had grown so much and he would need to have a new likeness made.

It was odd, but although he thought of them always he found it hard to picture their faces whenever he was away from them. He knew what they looked like, but struggled to see it. The pictures were a comfort and a reminder, and he stared at them for a long time, before he dipped his pen and began.

My dearest wife and sweetest daughter
Are you well? I think always of you, even as I go about my
duties. You are both with me, are part of me. I miss you and long
to be with you again.

He heard the sentry challenge someone outside, but tried for a moment to ignore the noises of the camp. Then the flaps of his tent were pulled open.

'Hello, Mr MacAndrews,' said his wife. 'Do you have a welcome for two weary travellers?'

30

The girl's smile was lavish, and her slim beauty made even stronger by the harsh shadows of the firelight. On the day of the battle Pringle had managed to forget about Maria. The battle itself already had a strangely dreamlike quality in his memory, and everything before it seemed both hazy and unimportant. The fact that he had been unconscious for much of the time doubtless added to this. Now Maria was back, but she was no longer a nun. Her long hair framed her face. She wore a tight-fitting orange-brown jacket and a flared skirt. This was short, like those worn by many of the Portuguese women, and revealed her ankles sheathed in white stockings and light black shoes tied up with straps around them.

Maria knew she was being inspected and leaned back in the camp chair she had been ushered to. The motion let her hemline rise another fraction, and helped to display her figure to full force. She reached up apparently absent-mindedly to smooth her long hair back over her right ear.

Pringle revelled in looking at the young Portuguese woman, and he could sense that Truscott, who sat on a boulder beside him, was almost equally appreciative. Hanley and Williams were on piquet duty, but he could sense that many of the officers of the 106th were finding reasons to drift nearer to the fire made by the officers of the Grenadier Company.

Lieutenant Miguel Mata coughed. 'We need your help,' he said slowly in French. Pringle had a basic knowledge of the language and Truscott spoke it well. 'I think you owe me a favour.' The former student turned gunner – though in an artillery regiment with scarcely a cannon to call their own and no horses to move the few they had – had arrived with the girl. He was clearly bursting with pride to be in the company of such a beautiful woman, flattered that she chose him out of a literal army of men. Truscott silently suspected that the young officer did not know how far out of his depth he was. Pringle just thought ruefully that he had got the nun, while Mata had damn well got the courtesan.

'Shall we take a walk and speak more privately?' said Maria in her excellent but accented English. Truscott wondered whether she exaggerated this to sound more exotic and fascinating. If so, then he had to admit that it worked.

She slipped her arm into Mata's, who beamed happily as they walked out from the regiment's lines. He no longer cared that the conversation was in English. Maria let Pringle take her other arm.

'Denilov is an evil man, and a desperate one,' she explained. 'He has gambled away his family's wealth and cannot honour his debts.'

'How do you know all this?' asked Truscott.

'Men tell me things.'

'I am sure they do,' said Pringle before he could help himself. For a moment her expression was once again that of the nun. Both Englishmen felt sheepish. Mata had understood none of the exchange and smiled with contentment.

'I met Count Denilov at a reception more than a month ago. There were usually a few Russians at these affairs ever since their fleet arrived off Lisbon. But he is a soldier, not a sailor, an officer in the Tsar's guards, and seemed a fine gentleman. He can be very charming.'

Truscott grunted. 'I'll take your word for it.'

'My uncle – at least that is what he is in public – had already fled and I had no secure protector. I might have found one among the French, but there are some things I will not bring myself to do. Not ever.' The bitterness in Maria's voice was surprising and seemed genuine, although Truscott was no longer sure what to believe about her. She had decided that a good deal of the truth had to be revealed, even though she still found it hard to trust anyone after Denilov's betrayal. 'It was already dangerous to travel outside the city and I needed help. Everything I told you about my uncle and the money left to help the convent is true, I assure you. The duke is a generous man. With the money are some things he promised to me. I want only what is my due. I have come with Mata to show that I am honest. He is a good man and will make sure the money goes to the sisters. I want no more than my due.'

'Which is?' Pringle had spoken, surprising Truscott, who had thought he was the only one listening with any scepticism to Maria's story. His friend had voiced the question he had himself been on the verge of asking.

'Jewellery. Especially pearls. The duke used to like me to dress as Cleopatra and she was famous for her pearls.'

'Among other things,' muttered Truscott. 'And Denilov promised to get them for you?' he said aloud.

Maria nodded. 'But I realised too late he would take everything and leave me nothing. He is a beast.' She shuddered, and for the first time Mata looked concerned. She smiled at him reassuringly, and pressed her hand to his cheek. The former student, who was still little more than a boy, beamed.

'He fooled me and I told him everything I knew, even the name of the man the duke had put in charge of the business. I did not know where he was, and by the time I had found him, Denilov and his soldiers were also looking. Varandas the steward was an old man who did not approve of me, but I managed to persuade him to tell me what he knew.

'Denilov must have followed. I doubt the old man is still alive, for he must have told the Russians everything.'

'They may have persuaded him, just as you did,' suggested Truscott.

'Not as I did.'

'I see.'

'Do you? Do you really know?' The flash of temper vanished in an instant. Maria shrugged, startling Mata with her sudden movement. 'Does any man really know?

'Denilov knows only how to kill. You saw what they did to the poor priest. He would do that to anyone if it suited his purpose or merely to amuse himself. Anyway, it had become a race, but it was hard for me to be faster than them. I needed help and I found you.'

'Not that it did you much good,' said Truscott. The bitterness of failure had faded during the battle, but now returned to savage his pride.

'Or us for that matter.' Pringle rubbed the bruise on the back of his head, which had throbbed unpleasantly on today's march.

'How did you get away from Denilov?' Truscott had not meant to sound so blunt, but the question had to be asked.

'How do you think?' Maria's expression was both hard and bitter. Then she sagged. 'I was lucky. Before too long we ran into a French cavalry patrol. They fired before asking who we were. The vile man they had with them as interpreter was killed beside me. Denilov tried to tell the French that they were allies, but before they stopped shooting I managed to run. The Russians couldn't chase me and persuade the French that they were innocent allies at the same time. Both the French and the Russians came after me later, but it was getting dark and they were nervous of running into any militiamen out for their blood. I hid and they did not find me. As I said, I was lucky.' She thought for a moment. 'Very lucky.'

'You understand that I had to ask.' Truscott was almost apologetic.

'I would have done so if you had not,' said Pringle, surprising his friend. 'Anyway, this rather brings us to the point. What are you asking us to do?'

'Not here.' They were still near the camp of another battalion, and Maria had already attracted plenty of interested glances. 'Could we walk somewhere a little more private?' she asked.

'Armies aren't exactly designed for privacy,' muttered Truscott. They walked towards the beach, heading away from the brigade's lines. They passed occasional sentries, pausing in conversation until they were again out of earshot. For a while they let Maria explain, not interrupting her assurances of honesty.

'There is a farm on the little road east from here. Perhaps two miles away, maybe less. It is owned by the duke. The money is hidden in a panel set into the fireplace. What looks like solid stone slides back to reveal a niche. That was all the priest knew and so all that Denilov knows. I know how to open the panel.'

'How do you know Denilov has not been there already and opened it up through brute force?' Truscott sounded interested, although far from committing himself.

'Perhaps he has, but that does not mean we should not try. It does mean we should hurry. Still, he would not find it easy to reach the farm. The priest was vague and it is marked on no map. It is different for me.'

'Why?'

'Because I was born there.'

Pringle thought again how little he knew about the woman. She had deceived them before and now she came asking them to risk their lives again. He had survived one battle, and another was expected. Pringle could not quite make up his mind whether that meant there were so many dangers to life and limb that another did not matter. The shame of being bested by Denilov's men was still raw, but it was very hard to trust Maria, particularly because he was so aware of her beauty and how that sapped his resolve. The intimacy of walking beside her was intoxicating, and there was a promise when she gently squeezed his arm.

'We cannot simply wander around at will, you know. We are officers and have duties.' Truscott saved him from having to say something.

'Miguel will help me.' Maria repeated the statement in Portuguese and the young officer fervently assured her of his willingness. In spite of her reluctance, she resorted to French to include him. 'Yet it may be difficult for him to move through your army and its patrols. Apart from that, he has only a few men he can trust.

'At the very least, will you take him to your officers and ask permission for him to take a patrol through your . . . I do not know the word?'

'Outposts,' said Truscott. He thought for a moment, and then nodded. 'That at least is something I am happy to do. Shall we go?'

'Take the lieutenant.' Maria smiled. 'I may look a little unofficial.' She spoke quickly to Mata, and again touched his cheek with one hand. 'Mr Pringle can escort me back to your camp in a moment. I am sure a nun is still safe with him.'

Truscott's eyes flicked suspiciously from Maria's innocent expression to his friend, but Mata was all eagerness to go about their task and he quickly led the man away.

Maria let them go, their shapes soon lost in the dark shadows. 'I do love the scent of salt in the air,' she said and stretched, arching her back.

'Shall we walk back?' Pringle asked after a moment, but there was no enthusiasm in his voice.

'That way,' the girl said, pointing towards a small copse. Her head leaned to one side as she looked up at him. 'I still need to persuade you.'

'Perhaps you cannot.'

Maria shook her head. 'I am very persuasive.' She took his hand and led him among the trees. Pringle decided to stop thinking.

'I'm going with them,' said Billy Pringle, ensuring that he did not look any of his friends in the eye. It took all his willpower not to keep breaking out into a grin.

Truscott sniffed. 'I am not surprised.' Hanley looked puzzled, but Williams did not seem to notice. The other two had gone out to meet them as they returned from piquet duty and explained Mata's request.

'We owe the lieutenant, I suppose,' said Truscott, weighing his words. 'After all, he and his men pulled us out of the soup. We have to be grateful for that.'

'Enough to take another foolish risk?' Hanley could not quite believe what they were saying. No one replied. 'I mean, aren't there rules about this sort of thing?' Again there was no response. 'What would MacAndrews say?'

Truscott shrugged. Their earlier exploit had been no secret and they could not simply wander off without permission. Yet he doubted anyone would try to stop them. It was a humbling judgement on their significance. Not that it mattered any more. Pringle was his closest friend in the regiment and, if he was going, then Truscott would go with him. He knew the others felt the same, and would go in spite of every misgiving.

Williams was checking the lock on his musket. He nodded. 'They need to be stopped,' he said simply.

'So that's settled,' said Hanley wearily, still not quite sure how and why this was happening, but unwilling to be parted from his friends. He did not have much else in the world left to him.

'We are to meet Maria and Mata in twenty minutes, just behind the piquet line on the east road,' said Billy Pringle.

As they walked off, Truscott let Hanley and Williams go a short way ahead and then whispered to Pringle, 'I hope it was worth this.' Billy Pringle's only reply was a beaming smile.

The moon was bright and silvered the landscape as they marched towards the farm in search of treasure. Williams always found such nights a little unreal in their beauty, but in this case that seemed appropriate. Pringle had gone to MacAndrews and got permission to take a patrol out in company with Portuguese soldiers during the night. As far as he could see the major had just wanted to get rid of him quickly, although he wondered whether MacAndrews knew far more than he was revealing, because his expression suggested that he thought Pringle and his fellows were damned fools. Co-operation with the Portuguese was one of the standing orders, however, and perhaps that was why he gave them permission. On the other hand Pringle had heard that the major's family had arrived and guessed there could be other reasons for such a curt dismissal.

Pringle had gone to confirm the matter with the brigade major, who had to be woken and promptly told him to take his patrol to the devil and stop disturbing honest men at their rest. As he departed, there was a shout telling him to make sure to tell the officers on the outposts unless he wanted his damned fool head blown off by his own side.

Mata had brought half a dozen of his men. They were all young, but each had a musket, a bayonet and a pouch full of ammunition. He also had a mule to carry the box with the money and another donkey for Maria to ride. Everyone else walked. Hanley had insisted on coming in spite of his arm. So had Dobson.

'I'm your front-rank man, Pug,' he had said. 'I go where you go, because it's our job to keep each other alive. We can look after Mr Hanley too while we're at it.'

A little reluctantly, Williams had agreed. Part of him was glad the old soldier was there, because he reckoned that he was at least as tough as Denilov's killers.

It took longer than he expected to walk the mile and a half to the farm. They went stealthily. The army had lost contact with the French, but that did not mean there were no stray patrols about. Then there were the Russians. None of the Englishmen wanted to be surprised a second time.

They did not lose their way, and only once did Maria have to think for any time to decide on their path. It seemed she really did know this area well. They did not speak save when they had to, for Dobson had from the beginning told them to hold their tongues, because the noise would carry much farther than they thought.

There were no lights in the farm when they arrived. They crouched down behind a dry-stone wall to have a closer look. It lay at the end of a lane leading off from the main track. Two smaller buildings sat on either side of the main house, which alone had two storeys. All three buildings cast long shadows in the light of the rising moon. Maria whispered that the smaller ones were a barn and a cattle shed. A large family worked the place as tenants of the duke, but there was no way of knowing in these times whether or not they were actually there.

'No dogs,' whispered Dobson to Williams. 'If there's no dogs at a farm then there's no people either. Leastaways not those with a right to be there.'

Maria either did not hear or ignored him as she continued her description. 'There are two doors to the house. The main one is at the front, and a small side door to the kitchen at the right end of the rear wall. In the old days they would not be bolted, but today . . . ' There was more than a hint of bitterness as she added, 'My family kept the place better.'

Two of Mata's men returned from a wide circle of the buildings. They had seen nothing. Williams was close enough to sense Dobson's contempt. 'They're just young 'uns. Don't know they're born, let alone how to fight,' he whispered. 'Best way in is from the top down. Daft buggers never guard the top floor properly. Look.' He pointed. 'See the far wall. There's just a single window at the top. Force the shutters and in that way.'

Williams was tempted to ask him how he knew so much about housebreaking, but realised this was not the time and was not sure he would like the answer. He crouched as he went along the wall to join Pringle and Truscott and explained Dobson's suggestion.

Truscott was unimpressed. 'How the hell do we get up there?' They were soon joined by Mata and Hanley, and there was a long whispered conference. In the end they formed a plan. Two of Mata's men went to watch the entrance to the lane. They were to fire if either Denilov or any French approached and then run back to the house, which by then the others should have secured. Mata and four men would go in through the front door, while the British officers used the kitchen door. Williams and Dobson were allowed to try to force their way in through the upper window if they could. When the plan was explained to Maria, she baulked and refused to be left behind and this led to more discussion. Finally she agreed to follow at a distance behind the three British officers and wait for the signal to join them.

When the two main groups moved off, Dobson grabbed Williams' shoulder and held him back.

'Wait,' he whispered. 'After that parish meeting the whole bloody world must know we're coming.'

'If anyone is there.'

'You're a soldier, Pug. Always expect the worst. Now wait.'

Williams could see the five Portuguese walk slowly up the path to the farm's main entrance. His friends swung wide to the side of the house, Maria just a few paces behind them. All of them cast long shadows and looked conspicuous in the moonlight. He tensed, waiting for the sudden flames and noise of shots.

Nothing happened. Mata reached the main door. He crouched and two of his men presented their muskets and aimed at the big shuttered windows on either side of the door. The other two closed up on the officer.

Pringle and the others had vanished around the side of the house. Mata waited to give them time to reach the kitchen door. Sword held in his right hand, with his left he grasped the large iron ring of the door and tried to turn it. To his surprise it moved and he felt the catch lift. As gently as he could, he pushed the door inwards, wincing when the hinges creaked so loudly that he thought the whole world must hear.

The kitchen door was also open. Pringle turned the handle and then slammed his shoulder against the door, flinging it open and half falling into the room. Truscott and Hanley both pointed their pistols through the open doorway. There was no one in the kitchen. Pringle had fallen against a high-backed wooden chair, one of three placed around a heavy wooden table. There were plates and pots on it, and more hanging from the walls and around the fireplace. The room smelt faintly of rotting meat.

Mata heard the bang as Pringle forced his way into the house, and pushed the main door harder. It was very dark inside and for a moment he could see nothing. He took a pace in, his sword held out before him. There was another door a yard or so in front of him and a second one to his right.

'Bugger,' hissed Dobson as he saw movement in an upper window just above the main door. Williams saw a tiny red spark fall through the air. One of the Portuguese soldiers felt something heavy strike his shoulder and thud into the dirt beside him. He looked down and saw a small sphere no bigger than a child's ball. A fuse burned in it.

The explosion was thunderous, the red flame sudden and

blinding. The two Portuguese soldiers covering the lower windows died instantly as the sharp fragments of metal smashed into their bodies. More jagged pieces scythed through the air to strike the men next to Mata, knocking them down. The lieutenant himself was unscathed, but left stunned by the noise. The doors opened and, before he could parry the blows, bayonets reached out and stabbed him. Hissing with pain, he dropped his sword and slumped down.

'Grenade,' said Dobson. Nominally they were grenadiers, but Williams had never seen one of the old-fashioned weapons for they were erratic and almost as much a danger to the man throwing them as to his target. The British Army had stopped using them regularly more than fifty years earlier.

The sound was muffled in the kitchen. Truscott and Hanley were at the inner door, which was locked. Maria had already followed them into the room and helped Pringle to his feet.

'Sounds like a war,' muttered Pringle. Truscott pulled back a pace or two to charge the door. Maria screamed when a figure appeared at the outer door and slammed it shut. Glass in the nearby window shattered as it was hit with a club. Then a round object was thrown into the room. A burning fuse flared as the iron grenade clattered on to the floor and began to spin wildly.

'The table,' yelled Pringle. He began to lift the nearest leg. Truscott joined him while Hanley flung himself at Maria and used his good arm to drag the girl down behind them. Grunting, the two lieutenants managed to tip the heavy timbered table on to its side and ducked behind it.

There was a pause that seemed to last forever and then an explosion louder and more appalling than anything they had heard in the battle. They felt the solid table shake with the impact of wickedly sharp shards of the grenade's casing. Some pattered into the plaster wall behind them. Both doors were flung open and soldiers came through them with levelled bayonets. Truscott was swaying from the shock of the blast, but managed to fire, and the man coming through the outer door grunted and slumped to the ground. Pringle and Hanley turned to face the inner door and pulled the triggers on their pistols at almost the same instant, so that the reports merged into one. Both shots missed.

Behind the soldier came Denilov, the twin barrels of his pistol aimed squarely at Maria. He glanced at the others.

'The same fools,' the Russian officer said with contempt.

31

Williams pulled himself up on to the wall when he heard the second muffled explosion. Dobson grabbed his legs and dragged the volunteer back with all his strength. The two men fell, locked together, but the older man's strength was greater. They rolled and Dobson was left on top. One hand clamped tight across Williams' mouth.

'Quiet, you stupid bastard,' he hissed. Williams struggled and suddenly he felt the cold touch of a blade on his throat. Somehow Dobson had drawn a knife without letting go of his grip. For a moment the image of Redman's corpse flashed through the volunteer's mind.

'Quiet and let the buggers think they've won.' Dobson spoke softly as if reassuring a child. 'We can't help them at the moment. If we rush in we'll just die as well.' Williams stopped struggling. The veteran waited for a moment and then took the knife and then the hand away.

'What if they are being killed now?' Hamish managed to keep his voice low.

'Then there ain't a goddamned thing we can do about it. It's not about dying, Pug. It's about winning. So now we wait and keep quiet and let them think the danger has gone.'

'What about the two Portuguese?'

'Forget 'em. We can't talk to the devils anyway. They're just children. If they run then they don't matter and if they come back and fight on their own then they get killed.' The veteran spoke brutally. 'Now we wait.'

★

The three British officers kneeled on the floor with their hands tied behind their back. Hanley was in agony as their captors had torn off his sling and bent his wounded arm back in spite of his hisses of pain. Mata was in a worse state; stabbed in the right arm, stomach and thigh, he lay on the stone floor of the farm's main room. When they had been brought into the room, Maria had dragged herself free of the Russian soldier who held her, and run to help him. She tore her scarf into strips and bound up the young officer's leg and arm. The Russians let her, and watched as the girl searched for something to bandage the much bigger wound to his belly. Denilov had gone to post two of his men as sentries. His sergeant was dead, killed by Truscott's lucky shot, but the latter had not yet had time to take in the thought that he had actually killed for the first time. The Russian soldiers were puzzled by the death, for the one-eyed NCO had seemed indestructible. They were not disconcerted. Death was part of a soldier's lot, and they were all still breathing, which was the main thing.

The room contained little. There was a small round table, two stools and an elderly rocking chair. Candles and an oil lamp on the table gave some illumination, but there was no fire in the grand fireplace.

Maria looked around, but there was no cloth or other material to act as bandage. The girl shrugged and reached back to lift up the tail of her tight jacket. Very deliberately, but without looking at anyone, she unhooked her skirt and eased it slowly downwards. The two Russian soldiers watched appreciatively. One even permitted himself a wicked smile. The Englishmen also watched.

As the girl lowered her skirt she leaned forward, her long black hair hanging down around her face. Her petticoat was white and seemed very bright in the flickering light. It was also short, falling only a little past her knees, and as Maria bent over, its laced edge rose up at the back and showed her stockinged legs and some of the bare skin above them.

Pringle was about to comment when he decided that it was better not to break the silence. Then he noticed something glinting next to Mata's foot. It was a fragment from one of the grenades, presumably caught on the wounded man's clothing or kicked in here accidentally.

Maria stepped out of her skirt and dropped it in front of Mata. It covered the jagged shard of the grenade. The Russians watched every motion as she knelt down and took the skirt and with a fierce effort ripped it along the seam, and then tore the pieces again. Mata winced as she raised him to bind the cloth around his stomach, but then managed to apologise and thank her.

Pringle noticed that the piece of metal had vanished when the girl stood up and walked over to the three kneeling Englishmen. One of the Russians barked an order, but Maria gestured at Hanley and touched her own arm to show that she wanted only to look at the wound. Then she turned her back on the guard and crouched down to tie another strip of her ruined skirt as a fresh dressing on the wound.

'Come a bit forward,' she said, and Hanley obeyed, shuffling towards her on his knees. Then Maria stepped back, and walked around behind him to see better. As she passed behind Pringle she dropped the piece of grenade casing into the palm of his hand. He felt the sharp metal cut his skin as he tried to shift it and twist with his fingers so that the edge was against the rope binding his wrists.

The door opened and the two Russian soldiers instantly took on more alert postures as Denilov came in. He glanced around the room.

'A little obvious, even for you, Maria,' he said suavely. Then he spat a fierce rebuke at his men. Guessing that something was going on, he paced behind the kneeling British officers. It was chance, for he had not seen anything, but when he was next to Pringle, Denilov suddenly slammed his fist into the side of the Englishman's neck just above his jacket collar.

The pain was searing as Pringle was knocked over on his side, gasping for breath. The little shard of metal dropped on the ground. Denilov noticed it, shook his head, and kicked the fragment off into the corner of the room.

'How very tiresome,' he said as he walked towards the fireplace, and then he slapped Maria hard across the cheek. A trickle of blood came from the corner of her mouth, but the Russian count caught her as she fell and flung her forward against the carved stone fireplace. Truscott and Hanley shouted in protest, until one of the guards clubbed each of them in turn with the butt of his musket. All three Englishmen lay on their sides, struggling to get up.

'Come Maria, you know that you will have to tell me sooner or later. Open the hiding place.' Denilov slapped her again, this time on the other cheek, knocking her down as she tried to get up. 'I am losing patience. You will show me in the end. How much do I have to hurt you and these others before that happens?'

The tall Russian aristocrat looked around the room. 'As you wish.' He nodded to one of his men, who promptly kicked Mata in the belly. The former student hissed in agony, but somehow managed to stop himself from yelling out.

'Very brave.' Denilov's tone was mocking. He nodded again to his man. This time the soldier jabbed down with the butt of his musket against the wounded man's thigh and then ground the weapon over the wound.

Mata screamed in agony.

Williams staggered from the weight of Dobson standing on his shoulders. Both men were tall, but they were trying to open a window some ten feet above the ground. Lacking a watch, the volunteer did not know how much time had passed since the grenades had gone off. It seemed like an hour, but was maybe only half that. They had seen no sign of Mata's remaining two men.

Dobson had led him in a wide circuit to come at the farmhouse from the lee of the barn. That meant they had only a short stretch of open ground to cover, and the veteran reckoned that the enemy would anyway be watching only the approaches to the doorway. Now the old soldier's boots pressed down hard as Dobson used all his considerable strength to prise open the shutters. Williams felt him sway backwards, as he fought for balance when the left-hand one finally snapped its catch and swung outwards and back.

The burden slackened and Williams looked up to see that Dobson had grabbed the window ledge with one hand and was pulling himself up. Both men had left their packs, shakos, canteens and haversacks back behind the wall. They kept only their ammunition pouches. Dobson disappeared into the room and then a moment later emerged again and reached downwards. Williams passed up the old soldier's musket and then his own. Both had their bayonets already fixed. Dobson quickly took off the two musket slings and tied them together. That gave them a cord a good six feet in length. The veteran looped one arm around a beam and held the sling in his other hand, letting it hang from the window.

Williams took a few paces back and then ran at the wall, leaping upwards and grabbing at the dangling musket sling. He caught it with his right hand, but nearly lost hold when he slammed against the wall, and only just clung on. A moment later his left hand also found the sling and he began to pull himself up. Hamish had never been much good at climbing, had always watched baffled as others seemed to shoot up the cables like monkeys, but somehow it seemed easier on this night. He managed to push out with his feet and then almost walk up the wall.

Then the shots came. First there was one, and then two in reply from the front of the house. There were shouts, and after a flare of panic Williams realised that it had nothing to do with their own efforts at breaking in. Whoever it was – and he hoped it was Mata's men and not a French patrol – then they would keep the Russians busy.

When he neared the window, Williams' boots slipped on the stone and he slid hard against the wall. Dobson cursed as the sudden weight yanked at the slings, but then saw that the volunteer had his elbows on the window ledge. The veteran let go of the sling and instead grabbed Williams' hand. Gasping with effort, Hamish pulled himself into the room. It was long, running the length of the entire floor, and was probably in normal times a storeroom and sleeping quarters for the labourers on the farm. Even in the moonlight, Williams could see that it was now empty save for a few rags.

'You're getting fat, Pug,' whispered Dobson with a grin.

There was another shot from outside, answered by one that seemed to come from the floor below. They took their muskets and walked as stealthily as they could to the far end of the room, where a staircase led downwards. Williams led the way, and no matter how lightly he trod each step produced what seemed like thunderous moans from the wood.

When the shooting started, Denilov sent one of his men to the front of the house to see what was happening. Then he went back to his task. Maria had ignored him at first. Then she had cursed him as they repeatedly hit the wounded Mata, whose screams grew fainter with each blow. Then she had sobbed and begged him for mercy.

Denilov continued to ask the same question over and over again. In the end Mata passed out and could not be revived. Maria continued to weep and to plead.

The Russian officer drew his double-barrelled pistol and pointed it at the girl. Then, as if on a whim, he turned and walked towards the three British officers. Truscott had somehow managed to get back up on his knees, so Denilov pointed the pistol at his forehead.

'It is up to you, my dear,' he said to the girl.

The first Russian ran on to Williams' bayonet. The volunteer was advancing down into the corridor when the man rushed around a corner, his own firelock held across his body. The bayonet slid easily between the man's ribs and there was only a short intake of breath before he was dead. Dobson pushed past as Williams struggled to free the blade. In the end he let the body drop and then put his foot on the man and finally dragged it out.

Dobson was by an open door when there was a shot from inside the room. For a moment a soldier was illuminated by the flame as he fired out of the window. Then Dobson saw little apart from the bright red glow seared into his vision. He squinted and stalked the man, as the Russian mechanically loaded his musket.

A musket ball fired from outside whipped past the soldier's head and instinctively he flinched. As his head moved he caught sight of the veteran. The Russian turned, his ramrod still in the muzzle of his musket, just as Dobson stamped his foot forward and lunged. The man flung his firelock up in a wild defensive sweep which succeeded only in knocking the redcoat's bayonet higher than he had aimed it. The point drove into the Russian's throat. He choked, blood jetting out on to his chest. His musket was now on the floor and both hands went up to clutch at the blade. Dobson ripped the blade free and then stabbed again, driving deep into the man's belly. The Russian writhed for a moment, gurgling horribly, before he finally went still.

Williams was behind him in the doorway, and Dobson came back to join him. They went out into the corridor and could see light coming from under a door. Then there was a woman's scream. Dobson barged Williams out of the way and flung himself at the door, which splintered and collapsed. The light inside was very bright after the dark corridors and Dobson blinked as he stumbled and fell into the room. A Russian soldier lunged at him with his bayonet, and the veteran rolled to avoid the attack, losing his own musket in the process.

As Williams came through the door, Denilov aimed his pistol at him. Maria flung herself at him, jogging his arm so that the first shot smacked into the wall next to the door. Dobson dodged another lunge from the Russian, and then Pringle kicked at the man's shins. The soldier staggered and Dobson sprang at him, grabbing his knees and knocking him down. The two men wrestled on the floor.

Denilov struggled free of the girl and then managed to slam his pistol against the side of her head. The second barrel discharged in the process, and Maria felt the ball flick her hair as it passed and flattened itself against the stone of the fireplace.

Williams came towards him, bayonet at the ready, but took care to avoid treading on Mata. Denilov dropped his useless pistol and had enough time to draw his sword. He raised the blade in a salute and a challenge.

'Just a common soldier,' he sneered.

'I am a gentleman, sir,' said Williams. Then he raised his musket to his shoulder. Denilov was no more than two yards away and there was just time for surprise and fear to register on his face before Williams shot him through the body. Powder smoke filled the room as the noise of the shot echoed off the stone walls.

Denilov gasped something in his own language and dropped to his knees. Then he slumped forward. Blood pooled darkly around his body.

Dobson swore as the Russian soldier bit his shoulder, then head-butted the man and pummelled him as he reeled from the blow. Using his greater weight, he held the man down with only one hand and with the other unscrewed the Russian's bayonet from the musket that lay near by. It was awkward, but eventually he freed it and stabbed the man repeatedly until he lay still.

'There's one more,' warned Truscott, and at the same moment the door to the kitchen was forced open. The last Russian soldier saw Dobson stabbing his comrade and aimed his musket. Williams ran towards him, and without thinking threw his musket and bayonet at the man as if it was a spear. It flew awkwardly, but made the Russian swing back his own weapon to parry the clumsy missile.

Williams was still too far away to reach him as the man pointed the muzzle of his musket at him. He shut his eyes. The shot was deafening, but to his astonishment Williams felt no blow. When he looked the Russian was stretched out on the kitchen floor, moaning. Mata's two men had come into the house when the Russian at the window had stopped firing. The first one in was no more than fifteen, and had never thought of anything beyond his studies until a few months earlier. Yet he did not hesitate as he entered the room and saw the dark-uniformed man poised to fire. He shot first and much to his astonishment hit the target.

Mata was badly hurt. He could not walk or ride, but the thin-faced student must have been tougher than he looked because he had not died. His men were not so fortunate. When they found

315

the bodies of the two who had only been wounded by the grenade, they found that their throats had been cut. The fifteen-year-old promptly did the same to the wounded Russian and no one acted quickly enough to stop him. Nor did any of them truly blame him.

All the dead were dragged out. Maria cleaned Hanley's wound and did an even better job of bandaging it with the last remnants of her skirt. They lifted Mata as gently as they could into a bedroom and laid him on a bed. Before he let them do this he had watched as the girl ran her hands over the carved animals decorating the fireplace. She reached behind the head of a bull and with some effort pushed at a metal catch, which sprang open a panel. Inside was a small chest, the key still in the lock. She got Williams to lift it out and lay it on the table before she turned the key and opened it. The gold glistened red in the candlelight. There were hundreds of coins – not a fortune perhaps, but still more money than Williams had ever seen in his life. There was also a bag, which the girl took. She untied the top and slipped her hand inside to check the contents, but did not show them to anyone else.

It was nearly half past two in the morning by Pringle's watch and Truscott's piece made it even later than that. They all needed to return to the battalion and their proper duties, promising to come back with a surgeon as soon as they could. Mata's men would stay with him, as would Maria and the money.

'He will be cared for by Cleopatra,' she had announced. A bruise was spreading across her cheek, but Maria looked both assured and determined. Billy Pringle also thought she looked damned attractive, especially as she still lacked a skirt.

Maria noticed where his glance had strayed and smiled, catching his eye when he looked up.

'I suppose we could not wait half an hour?' he asked Truscott hopefully.

'My old schoolmaster used to say that you could only eat cakes if you had brought enough for everyone,' replied the lieutenant.

'I knew there was a good reason why I always hated teachers.

However, Bills isn't keen on cakes and poor Hanley is wounded and must be careful.'

'Still leaves me. Save your strength.' He led his friend away to join Hanley and Williams by the pile of their packs and other equipment. 'All ready?' he asked.

'Just waiting for Dob,' said Williams. 'Said he had to go back for something.' The veteran appeared a moment later. He was carrying a long bundle wrapped in rags and strapped to his slung musket, and had his hands clasped together.

'Beg pardon, sirs, but I reckon we've earned this.' Dobson's tone was assured. 'Hold out your hands, Mr Truscott, sir.' The lieutenant did as he was told, and a moment later there was a jingle of coins falling on to his palms. 'Better take Mr Hanley's share as well, sir,' said Dobson as he turned next to Pringle. 'Him still being a bit Nelson.'

'Where did you get this?' Truscott could feel the coins in his hands. There must have been at least a dozen.

'From that Russian bugger, sir. There was a bag of it in his pouch. Arrogant bastard hadn't even hidden it.' The veteran's tone was contemptuous. 'He don't need 'em any more.' Dobson reached Williams. 'Come on, Pug. Reckon you'll be needing this soon. They're gold. Officers need a proper uniform. Makes it easier for the enemy to shoot at them.'

'I'm not an officer yet, Dob.' It was odd to be handling a dead man's money, but Dobson's manner did not permit a refusal. None of them was a rich man, and taking spoils from the enemy was as old as war itself. The only one who ventured any concern was Pringle. His gratitude to Maria had grown abundantly when she had slipped a note to him just before they left, whispering to him that the man named would be able to find her if Pringle came to Lisbon in a month's time. Billy Pringle relished the thought of that reward. To take money in addition seemed excessive.

'I'm not sure we should take this.'

'Easy for you to say,' said Truscott sharply. 'You've got more out of this than the rest of us.'

'Do you mean . . . ?' began Hanley wonderingly, before Truscott cut in.

'I mean nothing,' he said. 'Thank you, Dobson. It is generous of you to share.'

The old soldier simply nodded.

Hanley looked at Pringle and let out a short laugh. Williams looked on uncomprehendingly.

'We must get back. I think there will be a battle soon,' said Truscott.

'You know,' said Pringle, 'I had almost forgotten about the French in the midst of our private little war.'

No one bothered to reply. Truscott was rubbing his wrists as they slowly came back to life. Hanley's arm was paining him, and Pringle's neck began throbbing from Denilov's blow to it. Williams was puzzled again by how quickly the intensity of violence faded and the memories began to seem unreal. Dobson, for whom none of this was new, quickly cleared his mind as he always did on a march, walking in that steady rhythm that eats up the miles.

They walked in silence. Fatigue was catching up with them, but they knew that they would get little or no sleep that night. There was a dull satisfaction that this time they had won, but that only went a small way to easing the aching muscles in their tired legs. Hopefully it would be another quiet day of routine. On the way back they ran into a patrol of the 20th Light Dragoons led by a sergeant whose accent proclaimed him to be German.

'More bloody foreigners,' muttered Dobson under his breath. It took a while to convince the suspicious NCO of their identity, but fortunately the officer they were taken to remembered Truscott from the dinner in England. They were escorted back, reaching the 106th's camp just after four.

32

The sun rose over the hills to the east, from where the French would come, if they came at all. Williams pulled the peak of his shako down as far as he could to shield his eyes from the glow. Soon he would no doubt be cursing the heat, but for the moment the first hint of warmth was very welcome. Along with the rest of the army, the 106th had stood to an hour ago and since then had been standing in line, just behind the long ridge to the west of the village of Vimeiro. The night had been cold and uncomfortable, for they had been ordered to sleep in their uniforms, with packs and muskets ready to hand. Old hands had stuck their legs into the arms of their greatcoats and buttoned them on upside down. Then, with their blanket wrapped over the top, they had slept soundly. Williams had tried this once and found it far too restrictive.

So instead he wore the coat normally, used his pack as a pillow, and pulled his blanket over the top. He felt a mixture of elation and weariness after their strange adventure, but even if he had calmed enough to get an hour's sleep then the cold would have kept him awake. He would never have believed that a place could be so hot in the day and yet so savagely cold at night. Not wanting anyone to think him nervous, he had pretended to sleep, listening to Pringle snore away for a good half-hour. Truscott had gone back to his own company, and Hanley had been silent, but Williams wondered whether he too had lain awake during the short time for rest they had. He was sure that Dobson went to sleep as soon as he lay down, for the old soldier had a remarkable knack for napping at any opportunity.

It had been a relief when the bugles had blown to rouse them. It was still dark, and Williams felt numb, his limbs lifeless as he stamped and rubbed his hands, trying to get warm. Activity had helped, as had the cup of piping-hot tea brought by Pringle's soldier servant. Billy Pringle actually disliked tea, but had so far failed to convince Private Jenkins of this. He took a few sips, thanked the ever cheerful soldier, and then passed the cup round.

The army had been ordered to be ready. Rations were issued, ammunition pouches filled, and packs worn as the battalions roused themselves in the darkness. There was a smattering of shots from the piquet lines, as sentries discharged their pieces, checking to see whether the powder had grown damp. In a few cases it had, and then the redcoat added a fresh pinch to the pan and tried again. Those muskets which failed to go off after this had to be painfully unloaded.

Williams had flinched at the first shot, but was relieved that no one seemed to notice in the dark. He still felt drowsy and cold, and tried to convince himself that it had only been the shock of the sudden noise. Yet suddenly he knew that he was going to die today. When he closed his eyes he saw the Russian soldier levelling his musket and the fear flooded back. He had been lucky – they all had. It was hard to believe that his luck would hold.

It was all for nothing. The pride he had felt in refusing to be commissioned ebbed away and he called himself a fool for missing the chance. At least then his mother could have been proud of a dead officer son. It was not death itself he feared, for even in the cold pre-dawn he had stubborn confidence in his religion. He just knew that he wanted to live. There was so much left undone – so much he did not understand or had never known. Once again Williams was glad of the darkness for he knew his eyes were glassy. A vision of Jane MacAndrews sprang immediately to mind. How could he have been such a fool not to speak more clearly? Did she know how he felt? He had assumed his admiration must be obvious, but as he thought about it he knew with dread certainty that the girl was most likely completely unaware of the strength, and most of all the sincerity, of his devotion.

The rumour had gone around the battalion that the major's wife and daughter were here, although how this was possible he could not imagine. He had not seen them, but now he prayed that they were and longed for just one sight of the girl before he died.

Williams started when a hand touched his shoulder.

'Sorry,' said Hanley. 'But could you give me some help with these belts?' Although his left arm remained in a sling, he insisted upon performing his duty. Williams took the sword belt and sash and eased the belt over Hanley's right shoulder. It was easier to be looking after someone else than thinking.

'Damn, but it's cold,' Hanley continued. 'Maybe it's because we are so near the sea. That wind just goes through you.'

'There, that should do. How is the arm?' asked Williams.

'Oh, fine. I'm just wearing this to get some sympathy!' Hanley joked, but in truth the pain in his arm was much stronger than it had been, and the slightest movement made him wince. Fear was growing that the Russians had done serious damage, and his mind raced as he pictured himself under the surgeon's knife. What sort of artist would he be with one arm? For all that he tried to sound casual.

'I knew it,' said Pringle, looming out of the shadows. 'I am in command of a company of idlers.'

'That seems appropriate.' Hanley reached down to lift his sword slightly from his scabbard. 'You know, I didn't even draw this last time. It's probably blunt anyway.'

'Well, club 'em with it,' suggested Pringle.

'If there's time I can have a go with my whetstone,' offered Williams.

'How do you carry so much, Hamish? I reckon if I said I needed a pianoforte, dining table and ten chairs, you'd offer to whip them out of your pack.' Pringle's laugh was a little louder and higher pitched than usual. He stopped abruptly and lowered his voice. 'Now, William, you are behind the company today with the sergeants. Make sure everyone stays in their place and keeps up. Hamish, you are on the left next to Darrowfield and his rear rank man. If anything happens you take over and become left marker. I know I can count on both of you.'

'Do you know anything?' asked Williams tentatively.

'Yes, she's here, but no, I haven't seen her.' His laughter this time was less forced. 'Or did you mean about the less important question of what the army is doing? Waiting, as far as I know. No advance has been ordered, but we are to be ready for one. Or to meet an attack. The French are out there somewhere.'

General Delaborde cursed the rising sun and the slow progress of the French columns. Under his breath he exercised particular inventiveness in cursing his commander, but as Junot and his staff were riding just a few yards ahead he had to be discreet. At least the damned man was acting. The British were expecting reinforcements to arrive soon and it made sense to attack now. Some thirteen thousand men – somewhat fewer than the British believed – had been concentrated from the garrisons and columns scattered around Portugal. That should give them an advantage of a few thousand over the British. The French had fifteen battalions of infantry, more than had been mustered in one place since the previous autumn. Twenty-four guns rumbled along as fast as their pitiful teams could pull them over these bad roads. That was more than the English had had when he met them at Roliça. They certainly had more cavalry than the enemy, although as they toiled through these hills any fool could see that this was scarcely ideal cavalry country – but then Junot was an old hussar, so whether he thought at all remained to be proved. Still, there might be an opportunity for their use, and at the very least it should help to locate the enemy.

At that moment a dragoon cantered up to give a report to Junot's staff. The rising sun made the man's copper helmet glow red. Cavalry had their uses even in this country. Delaborde could not make out the large white numerals on the soldier's saddlecloth which would identify his regiment. Not that it mattered. The three Dragoon regiments with the army were all provisional formations, formed from detachments taken from the depots of

322

all the different line regiments and grouped together to form a temporary unit. It was not an ideal arrangement. Officers and men did not know each other well, and all were aware that their careers would not be made in such an ad hoc formation. Still, they were French cavalry and would be more than a match for the small number of English horsemen. The Portuguese cavalry were not even worth considering.

Delaborde urged his horse towards the group of staff officers around Junot, ignoring the ADC, who had turned towards him at the general's beckoning.

'Henri, we have good news,' said General Thiebault, the chief of staff, moving his horse in front of Delaborde. Junot pressed on, ignoring the approach of his subordinate. 'The English are not moving and are camped at some squalid little place called Vimeiro.'

'It's night, why should they move?' Delaborde was in no mood to be cheerful. He knew Thiebault to be a good soldier, and knew what his brigade had done on the Pratzen Heights at Austerlitz. He also knew that the chief of staff was clever, and well read for a former private soldier, and that for all his talent there was no one he trusted less. Thiebault never shared credit, but was generous with blame and acid in his readily expressed views of others.

'Nevertheless, the duke's plan appears to be leading us to a great victory.' As always with Thiebault, his words were carefully chosen.

'We're not going to get there by nine.' Delaborde was deliberately gruff. 'Worse than that, he's split up my division. More than half of my lads are off poncing about with Brenier somewhere over there.' He waved his arm back to the north-east. The brigade he had led at Roliça had been detached and marched by a different road.

'They will swing round the enemy's left flank and pin them just as we attack them from the front. It is a neat plan.'

'If they arrive on time and if the British sit around with their eyes closed.'

'As I say, our patrols report that they are not moving. Why should they expect an attack?'

Delaborde snorted at that. 'We've spread out too far. Half of my division is with Brenier, and the other brigade coming up behind us. How the hell am I supposed to control them?'

'As you know, the divisions were only formed a few days ago. Our brigades are used to operating independently.' Thiebault remained suave. 'I am sure the duke will make excellent use of both you and the brigades.'

'Better than if we fought together as a division?' Thiebault shrugged, but Delaborde did not want to leave the matter. 'I tell you, he is scattering the army when we should be concentrated. These aren't just peasants or militia. It's an army.'

'A small part of a very small and minor army. The English are famous for their sailors, not their soldiers. It is not as if we are facing Russians or Austrians.' The reminder of Austerlitz was blatant.

'True, but it is an army none-the-less. I have fought them. They can manoeuvre and are stubborn when they fight. Oh, we can beat them, but only if we treat them with respect. We're not chasing rebels any more. This will be tough, and I for one would be happier if the army was still concentrated.'

'Much must be risked in war,' Thiebault declared airily. 'We have surprise on our side.'

'The sun is almost up. I'll wager you a thousand francs that they see us coming.' Delaborde gave a knowing grin. 'You can afford it, after all.' Stories of Thiebault's looting were legendary even in the army that had stripped Portugal of everything it could find.

The chief of staff refused to be drawn. 'I must rejoin the Duke. Perhaps you should check on your second brigade.' Delaborde resumed his cursing of the army's high command as he rode back down the column.

The 106th stood down with the rest of the army when it was fully light and the enemy were nowhere to be seen. The men breakfasted and set about the many tasks that had been too difficult in the dark. Hanley borrowed a small mirror from Truscott and after he had shaved Pringle and Williams took their turn. After he had finished Pringle rubbed his smooth chin and smiled.

'It does make it easier to think, doesn't it,' said Hanley.

Williams then set about cleaning his musket, checking the flint and spring. He honed the already sharp point of his bayonet and did his best to put an edge on Hanley's sword.

'Probably be better off finding an armourer with the Light Dragoons,' suggested Truscott, who had come to retrieve his mirror.

'Where are they?'

'Somewhere down in the valley, I think. This side of the village,' ventured Truscott.

'Is there time for me to go down, Billy?' asked Williams.

'Better not risk it. We might be sitting about for hours or moving in five minutes. *Mirabile dictu*, Sir Arthur has failed to confide in me.'

'Oh, the benefits of an Oxford education. "Wonderful to relate" even sounds pompous in English. Anyway, I had better return to the less erudite conversation of Four Company. Private Knowles has secured a ham for us, so I have no doubt that the three of you will arrive when it is time to dine. That being so, I might just as well invite you. You can provide the wine.' Truscott waved lazily as he headed off.

Williams wanted to read his Bible and soon walked off to the edge of the brigade area. It was Sunday and a Highland regiment from the next brigade was holding a church service. They had posted sentries facing outwards around the semicircle of seated men as a reminder of the days when the Presbyterian kirk had been illegal. The minister had a quiet voice and Williams could catch only a few of the words. He sat on a rock, laying down his pack and resting his firelock against it, and tried to read. His eyes scanned the pages, but the words did not seem to register. It was not fear now. His mind just seemed empty.

'Am I interrupting?' The voice was the one that filled his dreams. Williams sprang to his feet, turning as he did so, brushing against Jane MacAndrews, who had been leaning to look over his shoulder. She stepped back in surprise, steadied herself, and then smiled.

Williams was overwhelmed by her beauty. Her face seemed so fresh, her eyes so bright, and that striking red hair mutinously strayed from under the broad-brimmed straw hat she wore. A ribbon bound the brim close to her face to guard her white skin against the power of the sun's rays. He recognised the russet riding habit she had worn in England and that time by the river. The apology decayed to murmurs and then collapsed into silence. Williams just looked at her, struggling to find the courage to speak. His resolution of the early morning, that he would tell her how he felt or at least how highly he esteemed her, battled with his shyness and lost.

Jane was a little puzzled and eventually decided that this conversation would require considerably more effort. 'Well, I must say I am surprised. I had expected to find you at least a captain by now!' She laughed and Williams laughed easily with her. There was no malice in the joke, and he thrilled because her tone conveyed genuine affection. Jane MacAndrews smiled again. In spite of his freckles and peeling skin she thought him not ill favoured in appearance and bearing.

'Still just a humble volunteer.' He was tempted to tell her of his refusal of a commission, something which he had not even spoken to his friends about. Instead he let his curiosity triumph. 'Has your father said anything?'

Jane made a face. 'Father has said nothing to me at all save for a brief hello and an even briefer kiss. Mother has not had much more luck with him. Did you know he gave up his tent to us and slept outside rolled in a blanket?'

Williams shook his head. 'I would guess that he felt obliged to share the fortunes of the men. I am sure he must be pleased to see you both.'

'Hmm, perhaps. He is probably a little angry as well. I don't believe he thought Mama and I would be able to make our own way out to Portugal.'

'He commands the battalion. He has to appear strict, but I am sure deep down he is glad that you have come.' Williams took a deep breath. 'I know that I am.'

'Mama will be pleased,' said Jane mischievously. 'She likes to be welcomed.'

'I . . . that is, I did not . . . of course, a fine lady.' The girl struggled to keep her face impassive as Williams babbled nervously. Even at nineteen she felt so much older and wiser than these young boys. 'That was not my meaning. Miss MacAndrews, I . . .' He coughed and struggled on so that Jane almost felt a little cruel. Almost. 'Miss MacAndrews, forgive my bluntness, but you are . . .' Williams floundered.

'Ah, here is Mr Hanley, with my fine steed.' Jane was rather relieved at the distraction. She had hoped that their earlier moments of intimacy and friendship would by now have allowed Williams to overcome his shyness. Yet once again he was nervously inarticulate in her presence, and she was beginning to find this slightly annoying. 'I have not ridden a donkey since I was a child. Mama insists on calling hers an ass, and then pretends not to understand.

'It is good to see you, Mr Williams. Now, would you favour me with a lift, for that is quite beyond poor Hanley at the moment.'

It took a moment for Williams to understand her meaning, and then he leaned forward and cupped his hand. The girl's brown leather boot seemed light and delicate in his hand. In truth she needed only the slightest of lifts, and no doubt could have managed without assistance.

'Good day to you both,' she said, and with a flick of her crop headed away. 'I wish you good fortune and pray for your safety.' The two men watched the girl go. She looked so out of place surrounded by an army and yet exuded utter confidence.

'So did you tell her?' asked Hanley.

'Tell her what?'

Hanley looked at his friend. 'Well, you know best.'

Williams thought for a moment. 'Are my feelings that obvious?'

'Oh no, a blind and deaf man might not notice.'

Williams sighed. 'I managed to tell her that she is.'

'Is what?'

'I did not get that far.'

'Well, she is, and there's no doubt of that.'

Hanley had not spoken much of his past life, but Williams had guessed a lot. 'You are more experienced in these things. I do not really know and haven't felt . . . Well, I have never felt like this. Do you understand ladies?'

'Understand women!' Hanley could not help laughing. 'I doubt there is a man alive who really does that. There is only one consolation. They don't understand us either.'

There was a ripple of noise along the ridge. Men pointed away to the south-east, shading their eyes with their hands to look into the sunlight. Excited conversations broke out. Williams and Hanley followed their gaze. There was a thick cloud of dust above the horizon, the sort thrown up by thousands of marching feet and the iron-rimmed wheels of heavy guns and wagons. The French were coming.

33

The second dust cloud was quite distinct through the magnification of the glass. It was low and thick, which meant infantry and guns. Horsemen threw up a higher, thinner cloud. A force of cavalry alone would be little more than a diversion, but the second column suggested real power and had to be taken more seriously. Sir Arthur Wellesley snapped his glass shut. The nearest French column was doing precisely what he had expected and would most likely strike at or near the village of Vimeiro. Most of his army was positioned to meet just such an attack, or on the ridge to the west of the village which protected the bay. The second French column – with perhaps half of Junot's army – was swinging round to threaten the British left. Only a single brigade was posted to meet such a threat. That would not be enough, but there was no threat at all to his right wing and the troops already in the centre should be adequate to hold it. That meant he could shift brigades from his right over to the left.

Beckoning to his staff, the British general began to issue orders. Only one brigade would remain to hold the western ridge and the other three were ordered to march behind the village and follow the valley to the north-east, strengthening his left. With so many orders going out at once, Captain Wickham was given the task of taking instructions to Brigadier General Nightingall's brigade. They were not far away, for Wellesley and his staff had been observing the progress of the enemy from the highest point of the ridge. Still, it was pleasant to be given something to do, and even more satisfying that the duty would take him back to his own brigade.

Wickham's surprise at his transfer to General Burrard's staff had been brief. After all, such distinction was only his due. The meeting with Colonel Fitzwilliam had been awkward, but similarly short. The colonel – he was really only a captain like Wickham himself, but Guards officers possessed army rank much higher than their regimental responsibilities – had always been grudging in his duties towards him. Still, today he had been polite enough and had complimented Wickham on his service in the previous action and asked solicitously about his wound. He had even handed over a letter from his wife, on whom the colonel had called before embarking. That gave pause for thought. Lydia was warm-natured, and might all too easily be taken advantage of by a smooth hypocrite like Fitzwilliam. Probably the man had behaved like the pompous prig he was. Probably. He would have to read the letter carefully.

The order was soon delivered, and Nightingall's ADCs carried instructions to the 82nd and 106th as well as the other detachments with the brigade. Wickham rode his horse back at a gentle pace, justifying this because he had only the one bay mare and did not want to tire the beast out at the start of what might be a long day. Had he known of this appointment he would have bought a second horse from among those whose owners had fallen. Still, perhaps today would offer more opportunities in that respect. He could not resist passing his own battalion on the way.

'Morning, Billy,' he called out to Pringle. 'Morning, boys.' Wickham's smile was warm as he gave a leisurely wave to the Grenadier Company.

'What is it like living in such exalted circles?' asked Pringle.

'Oh, endless work.' In fact Wickham had so far done little, other than engage in light conversation with several of the other aides. He was good at being pleasant. Indeed, he could not help feeling that his elevation was not only deserved, but overdue. After all, he was an experienced officer, with years of service in the militia before he had transferred to the 106th. Had those who should have promoted his interests done so with proper zeal, he would long since have been well on the path to distinction and higher rank. As ever, jealousy and spite had held him back.

Pringle looked up at his company commander and wondered. His speech was sharp and there was no sign that he had been drinking. In fact, he already had the assurance and arrogance of so many young staff officers. 'What is going on?' he asked.

'The Frogs are coming. Two big columns, so I imagine there will be some hot work before the day is out.' Wickham was speaking loudly, and almost shouted as he added, 'Still, nothing my boys can't handle. Give them hell, lads!' He dug his heels into his little mare and urged her off. 'Back to work!' he called cheerfully over his shoulder as he rode away. There were some smiles among the grenadiers, but no wild enthusiasm. The captain had left them, and for the moment was out of the small world of the company. Wickham raised his crop to Williams as he passed. The volunteer nodded curtly in return. Miserable little bugger, thought Wickham, who had no clear memory of the battle a few days before.

The 106th formed into column behind the 82nd. Other brigades had to move off before them and it was a good half-hour before they began the march down off the ridge. A group of women were waiting for them as they came towards the bottom of the slope. Most were soldiers' wives with their children. Mrs and Miss MacAndrews were also there, and had indeed arranged for the other women to stand as a group and see off their men. Jane was holding a baby in her arms, leaving its mother free to deal with her three other offspring.

The group cheered the battalion as it passed, Major MacAndrews riding at its head. A touch of one finger to his cocked hat was the only acknowledgement of his wife's vigorous waving. Seeing this, Esther ostentatiously blew him a kiss and the men of the Grenadier Company who led the column sent up a great cheer of their own. Williams was on the far side of the rank, but just glimpsed Jane making the baby's hand give little waves. Pringle bowed to her. When Four Company passed, Truscott did even better and left the formation to give a small bunch of wild flowers to the girl. Jane stopped working the baby's little arm and took them with her free hand. She smiled and curtsied and the passing soldiers raised another happy shout. When Truscott had gone back, Jane leaned over and gave the flowers to a small girl in a ragged dress. The child looked utterly thrilled at the gift.

It was a strange way to march to battle. MacAndrews forced himself not to look as they passed, still more not to look back. He had spoken to Esther for a short while the previous night, and had even fewer words with Jane. It was a thrill to see them again, even if he had not wanted them to come and still feared for them. At the very least they would see things which no lady should have to see. He had to hope that nothing worse would happen. His wife had solemnly promised to keep far away from the fighting and not allow curiosity to get the better of them. She would probably keep her word, but that was not to say that something unexpected might happen. There were a handful of other officers' wives with the army, although he doubted that there was another single, respectable young lady here.

Esther had explained how they had gone to Harwich soon after the 106th had embarked, having already written to Brigadier General Acland. MacAndrews had forgotten, or perhaps had never known, but Esther had helped nurse back to life a cousin of the general while they were in the West Indies, and called in a favour.

'And of course, I worked my charm,' she had added complacently. 'So did Jane. How could they possibly have refused to help two poor ladies? They are supposed to be gentlemen, after all.'

MacAndrews had tried to be discreet, but the battalion was a small place and as close as a family and he knew that word would soon spread. Only briefly had he wondered whether he would be thought a fool for giving up the tent to his wife and daughter and sleeping outside himself. It had been the right thing to do, and he had never bothered too much about the opinions of others. He could not be seen as acting commander to enjoy privileges and comforts denied to so many. None of the ordinary soldiers' wives had been able to call in a favour from a general if they had lost in the ballot for permission to come. There was also a superstitious part of him that warned against being too happy the night before a battle, lest fate decide to exact a payment. He was no more or less afraid than before any other battle, but this minor self-sacrifice oddly made him feel better.

The battalion marched on. From their position still several miles away Junot, Thiebault and Delaborde saw the dust thrown up by marching feet and knew that the British were altering their deployment to meet Brenier's men marching around the flank. A messenger went to the rearmost brigade of Loison's division and sent them to reinforce Brenier's attack. They were ordered to press on as fast as they could to catch up. The attack could then be made by two brigades – equivalent to a division, but not a real division, thought Delaborde ruefully. Even so, it should be able to punch through anything the English could offer.

Wickham found the pace set by General Wellesley gruelling and knew that his poor mare was getting tired. He was now annoyed that Fitzwilliam had not taken him back to the beach when he went. Instead he was to stay and so be ready to report more fully to Sir Harry when he landed. After ordering the brigades to march to the left, Wellesley had gone gingerly down the forward slope of the ridge to check on the positions around the village. Once off the hard going, he set off at a canter, and was soon through the cluster of whitewashed houses around the village church and among the olive groves and dry-stone enclosures of the hill beyond it. Everything had seemed in order with the two brigades posted there. A third formation provided support behind the village. Then Wellesley had sped off along the track behind the eastern ridges. He had personally taken the brigade commanders and shown them where he wished them to form to protect the left. That done, and the first battalions already moving into place, the staff had hastened back to Vimeiro itself.

It was now mid-morning, and sporadic gunfire announced that the French were in contact with the army's outlying pickets. Wickham lagged behind as the general and his staff rode back down the valley. His mare was struggling, its sides flecked with a foam of sweat. No one seemed concerned. As yet there had been no more sign of Fitzwilliam, let alone of General Burrard. Damn Fitzwilliam. He knew what a staff officer's duties meant and could at least have loaned him another horse. Wellesley and his senior staff had already changed mounts once today, while the junior aides were all mounted on expensive and well-cared-for thoroughbreds. As a mere captain of a line regiment, who was starved of funds by the jealousy of others, he had not been able to afford anything better, and anyway the only horses for sale were those whose owners had died in the first battle.

Wickham lost sight of the main group when they went through the narrow streets of the village. He must have made a wrong turn, for he came out along a dirt track between two low houses with sloping, red-tiled roofs. The church, surrounded by a high-walled graveyard, was to his right. He kept going, thinking that he could cut over in that direction and catch up. His mare could now manage not much more than a brisk walk and he did not want to tire her even more by going back. It was the longest he had spent in the saddle for many weeks, and although he had enjoyed it, he could also feel aches beginning to develop.

The track swung round towards the churchyard and Wickham followed it. The firing had become heavier. He tried to spot the general and his staff, but it was hard to see much as the hillside rising up in front of the village was covered in vineyards. There were soldiers from the 43rd Foot in the churchyard, knocking loopholes in the walls. They were a light infantry regiment, and reckoned – not least by themselves – as one of the finest battalions in the army. They had white facings and every man wore shoulder wings and had a green plume on his shako, while their badges were shaped liked hunting horns. The men looked fit and confident, their officers brimming with swagger. Wickham had wanted to join one of the light infantry regiments, but had been thwarted by the refusal of his 'friends' to aid him in purchasing such an expensive commission. He hailed a captain supervising the work.

'Mornin'. Getting warm, I fancy.'

'Deuced warm. Though not as warm as the reception we'll give Johnny Crapaud if he comes this way.' The captain had a long, horse-like face, his thin lips drawn back to reveal teeth stained heavily from smoking. 'Any orders for us?'

'No, I am looking for Sir Arthur's staff.' Wickham enjoyed the implication that he was on first-name terms with the general. 'Have you seen them?'

The captain shook his head. 'I'd try up the hill. The firing is getting heavier and I suspect he's the sort of man to stay close. Good luck to you!'

'And good hunting to you too,' said Wickham, walking his weary horse onwards. There was a strange noise now over the firing. An odd sort of rumbling, followed by rhythmic shouting. He could not catch the words, but it was unlike anything he had ever heard before. He threaded his way slowly through the gardens and rows of vines on the slope. It was still hard to see anything, although now and again he glimpsed lines of redcoats. A green-jacketed rifleman from the 60th Rifles limped past him, his left leg clumsily bandaged. Wickham asked the man what was happening, but the man just shook his head. Most of the 60th were Germans – belying their official name of the Royal American Regiment – and many of these spoke little or no English. In truth Wickham sometimes struggled with the accents of some of his own soldiers in the 106th.

The rumbling noise and the chanting were coming closer. Then cannon boomed out their deep-throated challenge. A few moments later there was a sound like rolling thunder as a battalion volley echoed down the slope. Then there were three cheers – three distinct and very British cheers, which turned into wild cries. Wickham could see nothing, but the chanting had stopped. He came through the gate of a vineyard and could at last see clear up the slope. A line of redcoats was surging up towards the crest of the hill. Their formation was ragged as they rushed forward through a thinning cloud of smoke. In the centre their colours fluttered with the motion. A Union flag, and another with a red cross on a black field. That meant black facings so it must be the 'dirty

335

half-hundred', or the 50th Foot to give them their formal title. The dye from the black cuffs on their jackets tended to run in the rain, making the men's hands, and anything they touched, black.

Staring more closely, Wickham noticed huddled lumps looking like bags of old clothes dotted across the slope. Most were in a drab light brown, but there were a few in red. A group of horsemen rode after the redcoats as they vanished over the crest. From over to the right came more volleys and another great surge of cheering. It took some time for Wickham to get even halfway up the slope. By then the redcoats of the 50th were coming back over the hill, chivvied back into place by their sergeants. The line started to re-form. Wounded men limped back or were carried by bandsmen to where the surgeons waited with their saws sharpened and ready. The group of staff officers also reappeared. Wickham recognised General Fane from the time when the 106th had formed part of his command. Lawson, the brigade major, gave him a warm welcome.

'Wickham, old man, what are you doing here? Thought your lot were miles away dozing in the sunshine.'

'Oh no, I do my loafing on the staff these days,' replied Wickham with a grin. 'Looking for Sir Arthur at the moment, in fact.'

'Saw him ten minutes ago before the attack. Prettiest thing you ever saw, by the way. Two big battalions of them came up the slope and ran into us. Hollering like furies they were, but we gave them a shot and then the cold steel and they didn't fancy that at all. Imagine they'll be back, though. If you want General Wellesley I would head over that way, towards Anstruther's brigade. By the sound of things they have been welcoming our friends as well. Quickest way is straight along the top of the hill. Might be a bit lively, though!'

Wickham now felt obliged to ride along the hilltop. Had Lawson not added that final comment he would have headed down the slope, but now he was committed and his reputation would suffer if he appeared even slightly cautious. Damn the man, he thought.

*

'Form here. Sergeant, you're right marker. First Company that way!' Delaborde pointed to where another sergeant stood holding the company's pennant. 'Well done, the Eighty-Sixth. We nearly had 'em. One more push and we'll drive them back to the sea. Make 'em swim back to England!' He rode among the survivors of the beaten attack and tried to re-form the two battalions of the regiment. Junot had flung them forward against the high ground in front of the village without anything more than a cursory reconnaissance. A couple of battalions from Loison's division had gone in at almost the same time, but there had been no real co-ordination. Even the guns that had advanced with them had been an afterthought. They had driven off the English skirmishers, but then come over the crest to meet formed lines of redcoats waiting in ambush. It had been a bloody shambles and they had been chased back the way they came, losing a couple of hundred men for nothing.

Junot was a fool, but at least now he seemed to be learning some sense. A battery had deployed and was firing steadily at the hill. It might not kill many English, but it would keep the heads of their light infantry down and, better than that, would encourage his own lads. He and Loison would re-form their four battalions, but this time fresh troops would lead the attack. These were their best, the grenadier companies taken from every battalion in the Army of Portugal and formed into elite units. The men were big and confident. Yet even now the fool was taking half-measures. He had two grenadier regiments in the reserve, but was letting only one attack. The other would wait to exploit the advantage. Delaborde returned to silently cursing his cretin of a commander, but now there was work to do.

'That's it. Three ranks here. Come on, boys, that was just to warm us up. We'll show those English vermin how real soldiers fight. Hey, Lucien, is that you? Glad you're still with us.' He waved an arm in greeting to a veteran whose long moustache was streaked with grey. 'Just like Marengo. Looked bad early on, but we hammered those Austrian bastards by the end of the day. Remember the wagons crammed with food we captured. And

337

those women we caught. Ha, you remember, you old rogue. You too, Jacques! How can they resist men like us! The Emperor may not be here, but you know how he rewards the brave. The Cross of the Legion of Honour to the first man to break their lines!'

34

The 106th sat in line and waited. They were on the long gentle slope where the valley curved round to the north. The
Light Company had gone forward along with the 82nd's Light
Company and the detachment from the 60th Rifles which had
been added to the brigade two days before. The men were still
a little uncertain about the soldiers in green jackets and red facings, most of whom were foreign and looked grim. MacAndrews
thought they were excellent soldiers, although in his case he
remembered the fine Hessian riflemen from America. For the last
few days it had been bothering him that he could not remember
the name of the captain with the glass eye whom he had come to
know well. The man used to take out the eye and wear a patch in
battle in case he lost it. Damn it, he wished he could think of the
name. Must be in his sixties by now at the very least.

Waiting was always one of the hardest parts. However dreadful
the situation was once the fighting began, you had little time to
think, and anyway bigger problems to occupy you. Waiting meant
that the mind wandered, or still worse became empty and made
a man sluggish. MacAndrews needed to set an example. He took
a gentle stroll along the front of the battalion, exchanging a few
words with each of the company officers. Brotherton went with
him, but the two men said little. It was important to exude confidence and look relaxed. What was said hardly mattered, and he
lacked Moss's talent for dramatic speeches. What was that slogan
of his – always ready and always steady. The words weren't bad,
but it seemed so false.

MacAndrews liked walking. When the action began he would

mount, for the small difference in height for a man on horseback allowed him to see a good deal more. For the moment he was happier on foot. He nodded to Pringle when he reached the far right of the line. Brotherton chattered away to the lieutenant with some nonsense about cricket.

'Hello, lads, good luck. I know I can count on you.' MacAndrews' voice was gruff when he spoke to the men of his old company. All sorts of thoughts came into his head of other things he could say – advice about aiming low and keeping in formation. They did not need it. They were well trained and if they were not ready now then nothing would change that. To say more risked babbling away and making everyone nervous. Better to appear unruffled, even cold. He was not there to make people like him.

MacAndrews wandered back along the line towards the colours in the centre. He looked up the slope at the rear of the 82nd. They were in the front line with the 106th three hundred yards behind them in reserve. To the left was Major General Ferguson's brigade, with the 71st Highlanders next to the 82nd and beyond them the 36th with pale green facings and the 40th with buff. These were supported by Brigadier General Bowes' brigade in reserve level with the 106th. The 6th Foot with yellow facings were closest to them and the 32nd Foot, nominally from Cornwall and with white facings, were on their left. All seven battalions were sitting on the parched grass. Three guns were deployed on each flank of the first line and the gunners busied themselves with the tasks that gunners always seemed to have to perform. As usual there was much shouting, and the noise drifted across the otherwise silent air.

'Feeling homesick, sir?' asked Brotherton, for by chance the major was looking at the Highlanders. In truth MacAndrews was pleased to be next to the Scottish regiment. They were not quite his old 71st, for that regiment had been disbanded after the American War when as usual Britain had rushed to cut the expenses of its army. This was a new corps, but they had already made a name for themselves, and there was something familiar about the faces he saw underneath the dark-feathered bonnets.

340

The regiment had been involved in the South American debacle and their uniforms had suffered as a result. Only the pipers still wore kilts, for material had been short, and the rest were clad in tartan trousers. The men looked fit and ready, and everyone spoke highly of Lieutenant Colonel Pack, who commanded them. Yet he did not know the regiment and nothing could bring back the one he remembered, or indeed his own youth.

'It will be good to hear the pipes again,' he said after a moment.

'Just like Savannah?' said Brotherton happily.

'Have I told you about that one?'

'I may just have heard it! Anyway, today we don't want them to know we are waiting.' The pipers were silent. So were the parties of bandsmen that had followed their regiments, but were today without their instruments and ready to carry the wounded.

General Solignac was surprised to see the English soldiers. There must have been close to one thousand of them in a thick swarm of skirmishers near the top of the ridge ahead of him. He stared intently through his telescope. There were some men in green and he guessed these were light infantrymen of some sort – perhaps armed with rifles.

'Do the English use rifles, Pierre?' he asked one of his ADCs, who was always studying books about the armies of the world. It was strange how easy it was to buy copies of the drill manuals of other nations. Not that the tedious detail contained in them was much use.

'Yes, General. They have formed a special corps.' Pierre was not actually sure about this, but had a vague memory and had long since learned that it was always better to sound positive.

Solignac grunted. 'Not to worry. They are slow to load and a man who likes to do his killing at a distance tends to be shy when anyone gets close. Push to the bayonet and they'll run.'

The sight of the enemy soldiers was such a big surprise because Solignac's brigade was supposed to be in reserve, sent to support General Brenier's brigade in its attack on the English left flank. Yet there was no sign of Brenier and they had heard no shooting so he could not have already come into contact with the enemy.

'Should we wait, sir?' asked the *chef de battalion* of the 12th Light Infantry. Solignac had already marked him down as a cautious man.

'The Emperor does not reward hesitation.'

'But General Brenier?'

'Is nowhere to be seen.' Daft sod was probably lost, thought Solignac. 'The enemy are in sight and we have three excellent battalions of the finest soldiers in the world.' Actually he knew they were all third battalions, who until recently would have remained at their depots, but Solignac wanted his commanders to feel confident.

'There may be supports.' The cautious light infantryman voiced another doubt. How had the damned man ever got promoted this far!

'Then they are badly deployed, which means these English don't know what they are about.' Solignac was dismissive, but resisted the temptation to show his scorn for the man. 'We will drive up that hill and then get down into the valley the other side. After that the way is open to come in behind their entire army. Gentlemen,' he looked at each of the three battalion commanders in turn, 'back to your regiments. I want you in column of attack. The Twelfth on the right, the Fifteenth in the centre and the Fifty-Eighth on the left and back about a hundred yards. Keep deployment intervals.' That meant there would be enough space between the columns for each one to form into line if necessary. The columns had a two-company front, with each company in three ranks. The Voltigeur Company – the battalion's specialist skirmishers – would deploy forward, so there would be three rows each of a pair of companies and a seventh company in reserve behind that. Attack columns moved fast and sent a succession of waves against the enemy. The disadvantage was that only a minority of the men could fire, hence the need to be able to deploy into line if they came up against strong opposition. 'Come, gentlemen, let's show these English that they should have stayed in their ships. I want to attack in fifteen minutes.' Actually

342

he expected the preparations to take nearer twenty-five minutes, but there was never any harm in giving them a sense of urgency. 'Move!'

General Brenier was still more than a mile and half away. He had been ahead of Solignac until they reached a steep gully near a cluster of farm buildings. There was no bridge, and the track simply went down one steep bank and up the far side. The ADC who first reported it was gloomy and Brenier could see why. The men and horses could get across, but they would need to dig at the bank and make a path for his four cannon. That would take too long, so instead he looped around, following another branch of the trackway which went farther north.

Solignac had reached the same spot an hour later. It took his men half an hour of sweat to drag their three eight-pounder guns across. He pressed on, the reserve having become the spearhead of General Junot's flanking attack.

The drums began to beat and Solignac's three battalions marched forward. Two were from light infantry regiments, who felt themselves to be the cream of the French army. Some of their officers wore Hessian-style boots like the glamorous hussar regiments. All had jackets much shorter than the long-tailed coats of the line infantry, but today these were rolled up on top of their packs. Instead they wore their blue-sleeved waistcoats. Some men still had their regulation blue breeches and black gaiters, but many had lost these to wear and instead sported a range of replacements. A good number had loose trousers made from the red-brown cloth most used by the Portuguese peasants. The 58^{ieme} were a line regiment and they sported the long loose coats worn by so many of Junot's soldiers. In the centre of each column a gilded eagle was proudly carried. The line regiment's standard had its flag attached, bearing its name and battle honours, along with a general call to valour and discipline in gold letters. The light infantry battalions had each left the banner in store and carried the eagle without any decoration on its blue staff.

343

Three companies of French voltigeurs ran ahead of the attack. In the final years of the last century – the first century in the new calendar of the Revolution which Napoleon had only recently abandoned – French light infantry had shattered the armies of royal Europe. Fighting as individuals, using cover and keeping to no rigid formation, they had sniped at the enemy lines, eating away at them slowly until they collapsed under the weight of a formal attack by the French supports. It was simple and it worked and the French were very good at it.

Yet today there were only about four hundred and fifty volt-igeurs against almost twice as many British skirmishers. Three companies of these were from the 60th and their rifles began to pick off the more conspicuous Frenchmen long before they could hope to give an accurate reply with their muskets. Officers and sergeants were singled out, along with any man who came on too boldly. The range was long, and only a few shots struck home, but it was enough to stop the French skirmishers. Only when the formed columns came up did the British light infantry give ground. They did so grudgingly, stopping to fire intermittently. Men dropped from the columns as well as among the voltigeurs, but it was not enough to slow them down. Solignac saw the thick line of redcoats retreat behind the ridge and scented victory.

The British lines had got to their feet as soon the firing began. Ranks had quickly been dressed, encouraged by barks of command from the sergeants. The waiting continued, but the anticipation was now more immediate. Pringle glanced along the front rank of his company. The faces looked a little pale, even though most had been heavily burnt by the sun since they had arrived in Portugal. Expressions were blank or a little pinched. He turned back to face up the hill. A few figures came across the crest, some obviously limping or helped by comrades. The firing was coming nearer.

A few minutes later the light companies and riflemen appeared. They came down the slope quickly, running back to rejoin or shelter behind the first line. Pringle could not catch the order, but he saw a ripple of movement as the 82nd fixed bayonets.

It seemed eerily quiet now that the shooting had stopped and he could hear great shouts coming from the direction of the enemy. There was an even louder cheer when the first French column breasted the rise. A second appeared almost immediately afterwards some distance to its right. The French infantry were dressed in blue and marched proudly on in ranks that were still remarkably well formed given the rough terrain.

One column was in front of the 71st, the other approached the 36th. Pringle wondered for a moment why his own brigade was not being attacked, but then a third column, this time dressed in drab coats, appeared and headed towards the 82nd. Each French formation was some eighty men wide. Successive three-deep lines followed the first.

The three cannon to the right of the 82nd boomed out, the heavy carriages leaping backwards in recoil. They were firing canister and ripped great holes in the front of the drab column. Men were flung back or pitched forward like rag dolls. The column did not check. The French soldiers stepped around the dead and dying, and as the sergeants hustled them back into place the ranks closed up and once again the formation appeared immaculate. As company followed company, men stepped over the mangled bodies, but no one stopped. Over on the far left the other British cannon fired, but Pringle could not see the damage they did. The French columns came on. In the next burst of shouting Pringle could just make out the words '*Vive l'empereur!*'

Smoke plumed out all along the front of the 36th and the Highlanders as a great roll of musketry echoed down the valley. The 82nd fired a moment later. The range seemed long to Pringle – maybe eighty yards or even more – but he watched as the front companies of the French column quivered. Drab-coated men fell all along the line.

The French stopped. A few men tried to flee, but were forced back into their places by the sergeants standing behind the third rank. Officers ran out ahead, trying to urge their men to follow. Most instead raised muskets to their shoulders and fired a ragged volley.

The British were advancing. The 82nd gave three cheers and advanced at a steady pace. To their left the other regiments matched them. They moved forward, bayonets lowered to present a row of sharp points, but the men marching at normal pace and keeping in step. Pringle watched as the front ranks of the nearest column seemed to sway like a flag in the wind. He wished he could borrow Williams' glass to watch more closely, for it was fascinating being a spectator. He looked down the line to where MacAndrews sat on his horse but there was no indication that they were about to move.

Some Frenchmen reloaded and fired again when the British were no more than twenty-five yards away. A few men fell among the 82nd and were left behind as the line kept on. Then there was a louder cheer and the redcoats were let off the leash. Led by an officer on a grey horse, they surged forward and screamed out a challenge as they charged the enemy. Pringle noticed that the highlanders somehow seemed to speed up faster than the two English battalions on either side of them.

The French held on until almost the last moment, and Pringle expected to see the lines meet and fight a bitter battle with bayonets and the clubbed ends of muskets, but then the enemy were running. The men higher up the slope and farther from the charging redcoats went first, turning in flight. Soon the enemy were streaming back over the ridge, with the redcoats running on in pursuit. For the moment order had gone. The red lines disappeared over the ridge.

A staff officer rode to the centre of the 106th. Shortly afterwards MacAndrews gave the order for the battalion to form up four deep. It was an unusual order, with each company halving its frontage and doubling its depth. It made the battalion more manoeuvrable and allowed it to form square more quickly, but it was something they had rarely practised. There was a muttering until the sergeants bellowed out for silence. The change was made smoothly enough. Then they began to advance in support of the 82nd.

Wounded men were hobbling or being helped or carried

by bandsmen down past them. Other redcoats lay dead, or still moaning softly in the dry grass. One raised an imploring arm at Williams as they marched past. He shook his head and hated himself, but kept in formation, having to check his stride and then hurry to catch up as he and the men behind him passed over the man. Nearer the top of the hill the bodies were thicker, and most were French. There were also lots of the rough white cow-hide packs the French used scattered about the slope. Dobson scooped one up, and to Williams' amazement managed somehow to rifle through it one-handed, still holding his musket to his shoulder with the other. He produced a bag which seemed to contain some sort of meat and contentedly reached back to push it into his haversack. Then he dropped the French pack. He had never once broken stride.

When they reached the top, they looked out to see the red lines some way ahead. They were now scattered and broken into groups, but still surging forward. They were also splitting into two bigger clumps as the Highlanders and the 82nd went more to the right. The French were fleeing, the teams pulling their guns frantically trying to keep pace across the uneven plain. MacAndrews nodded with approval when he saw the 82nd and the Highlanders halt to re-form. It gave him more time to catch them up. They were soon going forward again, however, and he could see that their lines were more than a little ragged. The French guns became trapped at the foot of a slope which for a short distance was too steep for them to climb, and a great cheer went up as the Scottish infantry fired a volley and then surged forward to capture them.

Sudden movement caught MacAndrews' eye. To the right of the two lead battalions of redcoats, new columns were spilling over the high ground. They were dressed in the long drab coats of French infantry and beside them was a squadron of cavalry with green jackets and brass helmets. The French were coming and were heading straight at the flank of the ragged British lines. General Brenier had finally arrived.

35

Wickham wanted a drink, and even more than that wanted to sit or lie down and rest for a while. Most of all he was sick of sitting on his mare presenting a target to every French gunner out there. After leaving Lawson he had ridden along the ridge-line. That had not been too bad. There were riflemen ahead of him and the nearest French were some two hundred yards away. Once only had he heard the whirring of a spent musket ball pass his head. Still, it was a considerable relief when he reached a cluster of olive trees and knew that these would shield him from the sight of Lawson or anyone else. It was also good that no one was close for his hand was shaking as it held the reins and he could not control it. Once past the trees he swung down more on to the slope. It might have worked if Sir Arthur's staff had not been peacefully sitting their horses on the crest about fifty yards farther along. There was no choice but to join them.

A solid shot punched the air just feet away from him as he arrived. He could not help flinching.

'Was it something you said to them?' commented Colonel Fitzwilliam cheerfully.

Wickham gulped, but managed to answer. 'No, the French just recognise talent and so that is bound to make me a target.'

'Well said, old boy.' Fitzwilliam had a low opinion of Wickham – indeed knew too much of the man to have anything else – but that might well change if he showed true courage. After all, what was more fundamental in revealing a man's quality? 'Sir Harry has come ashore this morning. However, he has most generously declined to replace Sir Arthur in command now that the battle has commenced. Sensible too, really, since Wellesley knows our dispositions far better. He is waiting back behind the village at an appropriate distance. Doesn't want to be in the way, of course, or confuse matters.'

'Should I report to General Burrard?' Wickham asked, trying to conceal his hope of spending the remainder of the battle in more comfortable and safer surroundings.

'No need. He has let me come forward and said that you could remain as well. Didn't begrudge us having some fun. You'll like him. He's a grand fellow.'

'Yes, he sounds it.' Wickham tried to conceal his disappointment. 'And I must thank you for helping to secure me this assignment.' There, that would help. A gentleman could readily be expected to show a little discomfort in anything so emotional as admitting gratitude.

That had been nearly an hour ago. He had been forced to be still and appear insouciant as the French round-shot bounced among them. One had taken the rear legs off an ADC's horse, so that the poor beast sank down, screaming in agony. The rider had sprung off easily enough, but there were tears in his eyes when he shot the animal between the eyes to end its suffering. That was the only hit, but many of the others seemed close enough. It was also the only emotion any of them showed – apart from almost schoolboy enthusiasm when the second French attack came in and the British artillery opened up against the oncoming columns. They were using a new invention, the spherical case-shot invented by Colonel Shrapnel. The shells had a long range, but, if the fuse was cut to the right length, exploded over the head of the enemy. They were packed with dozens of pistol balls and these and the shattered casing itself showered down on the target much like a round of canister.

'Damned fine!' called Bathurst, the Deputy Quartermaster General, as one shot exploded directly over a French gun and massacred its entire crew. There was much agreement and even a smattering of applause.

They had moved little during the second French attack. The

two columns of grenadiers had been stopped just as abruptly as the earlier assaults. There had been less skirmishing this time, but even so some enemy skirmishers had come close enough to fire at the cluster of mounted officers. A ball had gone through Fitzwilliam's hat, much to the Guardsman's amusement. Afterwards he kept sticking his finger through the hole it had made and grinning.

· They did not move until there was a heavy burst of firing and loud cheering from the village behind them. The second regiment of French grenadiers, Junot's final reserve, were led by Kellerman, a cavalryman by trade and a cunning officer. He took them behind a low hill which kept them out of view of the British on the ridge and hooked round down the road into the village. The 43rd in the churchyard and nearby buildings stopped them. It was a vicious fight, fought at point-blank range and often enough hand to hand. Men had stabbed and shot each other in the narrow alleys of the village and among the tombstones in the graveyard. By the time Wellesley and his staff arrived – Wickham's mare had recovered enough not to trail too much and he managed to stay with them – his nearest brigade commanders had already brought up reserves to complete the rout of the French grenadiers.

The area around the church was a charnel house. Bodies lay in the street, in the graveyard and surrounding buildings. All the walls were pocked with musket shots. A French grenadier lay propped against the wall of the yard, his stomach slashed open and with his entrails poured out beside him. Near by was a redcoat from the 43rd with his skull almost cut completely in two. Wickham looked around at the carnage. The smell was dreadful, but he found the sights more distasteful than horrific.

Seeing that the attack had been thoroughly repulsed, Wellesley rode back through the village. Behind it the two hundred and forty men of the 20th Light Dragoons waited, supported by as many more Portuguese cavalry and a troop of officers from the Lisbon constabulary. The French attacks had all been broken, their reserves were spent and now there was an opportunity to put them fully to rout.

'Now, Twentieth, now is the time,' Sir Arthur himself called out to Colonel Taylor. Wickham thought back to the dinner the 106th had enjoyed with the dragoons just a month or so earlier. Somehow it seemed more like an age.

The Light Dragoons were ready. Taylor had formed them in the centre, his two squadrons side by side and each in two ranks. He would have preferred a reserve, but did not have the men. The Portuguese horsemen extended his line on either flank. He would also have preferred to have the troopers of his own regiment, who had been unable to find mounts, but that could not be helped. The country was open enough to the south-east of the village and he led his men across the plain at a walk. There was a thrilling scraping of blade on the metal mouths of scabbards as he ordered his men to draw their heavy, curved sabres.

A line of French cavalry in green appeared and tried to form ahead of him. Taylor gave the order and the Light Dragoons went into a trot, the men rising in their saddles. The Portuguese hesitated and then copied them, so that they began to hang back a little on either side. At two hundred yards he accelerated into a canter. The French were not moving and that seemed odd. There was a danger now that he had started the charge too soon, expecting them to come forward to meet his men, but that could not be helped. Anyway it should not matter. If the fools met him at the halt then they would be broken in an instant.

Taylor glanced to the left. The Portuguese had gone. His head flicked to the right. The Lisbon police were still there, but the regular Portuguese cavalry had gone, turning their nags around and streaming to the rear. Oh well, too late now, he thought as he raised his sabre high and bellowed out the order to charge, rising in his stirrups. His trumpeter, young Morrison, resplendent in his yellow jacket and mounted on a grey, was just behind him as he should be, and Taylor winked at the boy encouragingly. Then he turned and concentrated all his attentions on the enemy as the last few yards flew by.

The French Dragoons had their long straight swords thrust out in the charge position, wrists turned so that the blades pointed forward and slightly down. Yet they were not moving and the herd instinct of their horses took over as the line of British cavalry rushed at them. The animals shifted in the ranks, then some turned and started to run away. Wide gaps opened in the line and the British horsemen flooded into them. Sabres rose and fell. Taylor cut hard at the man in front and to his right. His sabre grated for a moment on the peak of the man's helmet and then bit deep into his face. The Dragoon screamed and clutched at the dreadful wound, which formed a gash from eyebrow to chin. Taylor was already past and slashed across his body at a man to the left, but was parried, his arm jarring with the shock. The chest of his horse barged into the Frenchman's horse, and the Dragoon was tumbled from his saddle.

Just two of the British cavalry fell in the brief melee. Several more received wounds, but none was stopped and the French Dragoons were cut or knocked from their saddles or fled as the 20th rolled through them and kept going. The line was broken now, but a concentrated mass of blue-jacketed horsemen galloped onwards across the plain. In a moment they were among the disordered French infantry, the remnants of the grenadier battalions driven back from the village. They had been attempting to reform, but were still scattered, and almost all turned to run for safety as the British horsemen bore down on them. A few – the experienced ones – clustered together into closely packed knots and tried to present a row of bayonet points to any cavalryman who came at them.

It was natural for the Light Dragoons to pick on the easiest targets. The men who ran were helpless, and it was exhilarating to ride among them, picking a target and then cutting down. A British corporal took care to wait until he was just passing one of the running grenadiers. Then he would slash backwards, slicing deep into the man's face. The second time he did this the top of the grenadier's head sheared off neatly. The corporal did not smile or exult, but simply pressed on to the next victim. Other men were wilder. Some of the rawer troopers hacked at the backs of the fugitives. More than one man found himself knocked off his feet, but would then stagger up to discover that the only damage was a great hole in his backpack. Another trooper laughed as he rode alongside a Frenchman, watching the man nervously glancing up at him. Then he hit him hard with the flat of the sabre, and laughed all the more as the man staggered, losing his shako, and then blinked, looking confused. Another man from the 20th passed and cut down deep into the man's skull.

Taylor was enjoying the moment. He was an urbane, sensitive and educated man, a product of Christ Church College and he had already killed or wounded five enemy soldiers. The French were at their mercy and his boys were doing well, and Taylor wanted more. There was a thrill to this slaughter, a sense of power and invulnerability, and he spurred onwards. Morrison was still with him and Taylor knew that he must soon tell the lad to sound the recall. Yet they were doing so much damage that his senses told him a few minutes more would harm the French fatally. He saw a close-packed knot of Frenchmen moving slowly back across the plain. There must have been fifteen of them and more fugitives headed towards them. He saw their leader, a lieutenant whose single epaulette was tarnished and whose hair was white, grab a fugitive with a musket and turn him round so that he joined the front rank. Unarmed men were thrust away from the formation as useless.

'To me, Twentieth, to me!' Taylor called. If he could break this little formed body then the French morale must be shattered. Morrison was with him and four troopers headed over to join the group. There was also a corporal, King of C Troop, his helmet gone and his cheek flapping from the cut of a blade, but still looking determined. That was good. 'Come on, boys, let's finish them! Follow me!'

The seven horsemen formed a rough line, with Taylor ahead and in the centre. They yelled as they pushed their horses forward, using their last energy in a gallop to carry them over the short distance to the little cluster of Frenchmen. The elderly lieutenant halted his men, and got his front rank kneeling with the butts of their muskets pressed into the ground and the points held up to spear into the horses' chests if they should dare to come close. There were just four men in the front rank and only three with loaded muskets standing behind them, but the lieutenant waited until the British were no more than ten yards away when he bellowed at them to fire.

It was a small volley and Taylor could see they had left it too late, and then a ball punched into his chest and struck the heart and his eyes faded and then he knew nothing. Involuntarily his arm pulled on the reins and his horse swung to the left, colliding with Morrison's grey. The horse of one of the troopers was hit and collapsed, throwing him high and far over its neck to strike the ground with a sickening thump. The charge was stopped in its tracks, as horses barged into each other or swung away. Taylor was dead and the French lieutenant leaned out to shoot the cavalryman on the ground with his pistol. Corporal King sheathed his sabre and pulled out his carbine. He looked grim, but since his cheek was slashed his expression was not clear. One Frenchman fired a musket at him and the ball passed close to his shoulder, but he did not flinch. He checked that there was powder in the carbine's pan, and raised it to his shoulder. Firing from horseback was always chancy, but he took deliberate aim.

The ball nicked the French lieutenant high on his left arm, spinning him round. The man staggered, but then straightened up and raised a defiant fist at the British cavalryman. King was disappointed not to have killed the man, but had at least shown him that you did not shoot helpless men. Then he heard the trumpets sounding and saw a line of French Dragoons coming across the plain, the sun glittering off their brass helmets and the blades of their swords. They were formed and fresh, and the British were scattered and weary. It was time to go. King looked for the other troopers, but could see only Morrison. 'Come on, lad,' he said, his voice distorted by his wound, and the pair headed back the way they had come, moving as fast as their blown horses could carry them. Behind them, the French horsemen hunted down anyone who fled too slowly.

Wickham and the other staff watched the 20th return from

their charge. More escaped than he had expected, for they had watched the French reserve cavalry approach. Wickham thought he heard Wellesley mutter under his breath, 'Gallant, but unwise.'

It was a different regiment of French Dragoons which charged down against the flank of the 82nd and 71st as the redcoats milled around the captured French guns. They began the charge a little too soon, for their colonel scented an opportunity. Unformed infantry were helpless against cavalry and he did not want to give the English a chance to rally and re-form. Yet the slope was rocky and uneven and this slowed his men as they came down it. The French infantry columns were farther back and not so quick off the mark.

Officers shouted warnings, and one captain of the 82nd tried to organise his company and any other men he could find into a line facing the oncoming cavalry. He and his sergeants tugged at men and forced them into line. Some men from both regiments were going back. Colonel Pack of the 71st knew that the difference between steadiness and panic was as narrow as the blade of a knife. It would not take much for both regiments to collapse into rout. He also knew that there was no point fighting from a hopeless position and that sometimes it was right to retreat. One of the French columns halted and the leading two companies brought their muskets up to their shoulders. It was long range, but half a dozen of his own men fell, their feather bonnets rolling in the dust. The French Dragoons were getting closer.

Pack turned and saw salvation. A battalion was marching towards them and was now only some five hundred yards away. They were in four ranks and looked solid enough, with a red cross on a white field as their Regimental colour. The 106th, then, but he did not much care who they were, only that they had come upon a wish. He smiled and then raised his voice over the chaos. 'Back! Back! Rally back!' He rode among the milling Highlanders, shouting and pointing them back. His officers copied and so did those of the 82nd. The bulk of the men were soon running back towards the 106th. The captured French guns were abandoned.

The captain of the 82nd gave his ragged line the order to fire when the French Dragoons were still more than a hundred paces away. A single horse fell, but it slowed the charge just a little and might give them a bit more time.

'Back!' he yelled. 'Get back!' and set off at a run towards the supporting battalion. The men ran, packs and pouches banging with the motion. The little valley was filled with some eighteen hundred redcoats running back towards the formed battalion. Both colonels sent their adjutants and other officers riding on ahead to form the men when they came level with the 106th. The French Voltigeurs ran forward in pursuit, stopping sometimes to fire at the retreating British. A few redcoats fell. The dragoons spread out into a loose mass as they chased, but the ground was difficult and their horses ill fed after six months in this benighted country. Some managed to catch up with the slower fugitives. The long swords stabbed or slashed down. Redcoats screamed as the steel took them.

Looking over Dobson's shoulders, Williams could see the little figures falling as the horsemen swept among them. The 106th marched on, but the pace seemed so slow and there was nothing they could do to save those men. The volunteer tried not to think about it, and then suddenly an image of Truscott instructing him in manoeuvres using the wooden blocks leaped into his mind. Looking back, it now all seemed so childishly simple in practice, and devilishly difficult in reality. Williams was glad he was not making such decisions today. He glanced to his left and could just glimpse MacAndrews, riding in front of the colour party. The major looked impassive, staring straight forward as if he did not have a care in the world. Reassured, the volunteer smiled, and looked back to his front. The enemy now seemed very close.

36

MacAndrews was in fact very happy, even if he did not show it. His battalion was in the right place at the right time. Had they been farther forward their own flank would have been turned by the French and they would have been in no position to resist. Had they come more slowly then they would have been too far behind to help the 71st and the 82nd. Coming in four-deep line had made the difference, for they had marched a little faster, and he had to admit that the brigadier's instincts had been right on that.

He ordered the 106th to halt. The Highlanders were rallying and re-forming on their left and the 82nd on their right. The artillery were still far behind, but they now had three strong battalions to face the French assault. The enemy seemed to have realised that their victory would not now be so easy. They had halted and their dragoons were pulling back to reorganise, ready to support the infantry attack. General Brenier put three of his four battalions in his first line. The fourth was behind the centre battalion as a reserve. All were in attack column on a two-company frontage. Officers and NCOs shouted and chivvied the men into position on both sides. After ten minutes the French were ready.

'*En avant!*' called General Brenier. '*Marche!*' The drums began to beat and the French infantry marched forward, the tails of their long coats flapping. They went at one hundred and twenty paces a minute, the drummers marking the time. One, two-three, one, two-three, on and on in the quick rhythm that would carry the attack on to and through the enemy. The soldiers began to shout as they came, bawling out '*Vive l'empereur*' whenever the drummers paused between each sequence. Over four thousand voices echoed down the valley. '*Vive l'empereur!*'

The rhythm of the beating drums hammered at the waiting British. Williams found himself counting silently along with the beats. He even mouthed the French chant. Private Murphy began muttering aloud in time with the rhythm.

'Old trows-ers! Old trows-ers!'

Dobson joined in, and then more men on either side as the nonsensical phrase spread throughout the battalion.

'Old trows-ers! Old trows-ers!'

Williams laughed and joined in.

'Old trows-ers! Old trows-ers!' The chant was loud now, the men of the 106th bellowing out the words as if to challenge the French.

MacAndrews grinned as he listened to them. He looked to either side and saw that the other battalions had now re-formed and were ready. General Nightingall and his staff were on a low knoll just behind the 106th, and as MacAndrews watched the general waved his cocked hat forwards.

'Mr Fletcher, prepare to advance.'

The RSM cleared his throat. 'Silence in the ranks!' The chanting stopped. ''Talion will advance. Forward march!'

The three lines of redcoats stepped out towards the oncoming enemy. The French were close now, less than two hundred yards away, so close that the skirmishers on both sides ran back to the flanks. Still the drums beat and the men shouted '*Vive l'empereur!*' Officers ran ahead of the column, willing their men onwards to crush the thin British line. The British advanced more quietly, and then the pipers of the 71st struck up and the wild, savage music carried over all the other noise.

MacAndrews was ahead of the colour party, and walked his horse forward without looking behind him. He did not really need it, but the call of the pipes made him draw his basket-hilted sword. For a moment he laughed at the thought that he was still ready to kick off his shoes and run headlong at the enemy like the wildest clansman. Company officers marched at the right of their men.

'Steady, lads, steady,' said Pringle quietly. Other officers repeated the simple phrase or stayed grimly silent.

The French were closer now. Pringle could see the faces of the men in the front ranks, watched the mouths open wide as they chanted '*Vive l'empereur!*' Most of them had moustaches and looked like old veterans. It was hard to believe that anything could stop them. The clean-shaven British looked like mere children by comparison.

At one hundred yards the French columns stopped for a moment and fired. MacAndrews felt the balls fly past him. There was a low sigh from behind him and out of the corner of his eye he saw a flicker as the King's Colour fell for a moment. The ensign carrying it was dead, but one of the sergeants picked up the flag and carried it until the next most senior ensign could be summoned from his company. Other men fell. The captain of the 82nd who had organised the line against the cavalry was hit on the kneecap and had to grit his teeth as he tried not to scream. A piper of the 71st was down, shot through both thighs, but he propped himself up against a stone and a moment later was playing again, the music urging the men on as the Highlanders advanced past him.

The British did not check. Sergeants forced men to close up the gaps and the red bundles of rags were left behind the lines as they moved on. There were two cannon beside the central French battalion and these deployed now. MacAndrews tried not to watch the gunners as they hefted the gun barrels from the travelling to the firing position and flipped the covers over to hold the trunnions in place. They rammed down charges and then balls fixed to their wooden sabots.

The French columns were moving again now and the drumming and chanting had resumed. '*Vive l'empereur!*' '*Vive l'empereur!*' First one gun fired and then the second a moment later. A ball struck the Grenadier Company of the 106th and decapitated each of the four men in one file. One moment they were whole, and then the heads seemed to disintegrate, spraying blood and brains over the men around them. The bodies stayed upright for an instant, blood gouting from the necks, and then folded down. Sergeant Darrowfield yelled at the men to close up.

''Talion halt! Present!' Fletcher's voice commanded instant obedience, but MacAndrews let his enthusiasm get the better of him and called out the final order himself. 'Fire!'

Only the first two ranks fired, for it would have been dangerous for the men behind them. Some three hundred and fifty muskets flamed out and blanketed the front of the 106th in dense smoke. A dozen muskets misfired, although most of the men did not notice. They could not see, but the volley slammed into the front of the central French column and flung men bodily backwards. There were screams and dull thuds as the heavy metal balls struck home. British muskets were larger-calibre than the French and the soft lead balls easily lost shape and smashed bone as they drove deep into flesh. More than twenty men were dead, and twice that number wounded. Some of them would not survive the night. The chanting and drumming had stopped and been replaced by cries and sobs of pain.

MacAndrews was about to give the order to fix bayonets when he glanced back and noticed that the blades were already screwed on to the tops of the men's muskets. For the life of him he could not remember giving that order.

''Talion will advance! Forward march!'

The 106th went through the smoke of their own volley at a steady pace. On either side of them the Highlanders and 82nd were doing the same. The pipes were still playing, the whining notes making themselves heard over everything else. The British volleys had devastated the fronts of the French columns. The enemy had stopped. Officers yelled and tried to restore order. The left and the central columns started to deploy their rear companies in an effort to form line and return the British fire. It was too late.

'Charge!' screamed MacAndrews, and kicked his heels into the sides of his horse. The 106th cheered and ran forward after him.

The other regiments were charging too, the pipes now sounding more ragged as the pipers struggled to keep up. The French cannon fired again, and two canisters burst among the 106th, scything down clumps of redcoats. Private Murphy was nicked on the arm, but hissed a few blasphemies through his teeth and kept going. Shots were fired from the fronts of the French columns, and one of the companies trying to deploy was panicked into firing and sent musket balls into the British and their own comrades alike.

The columns broke. Men turned to flee, and although the sergeants behind the companies stopped the first ones there were too many and suddenly there was just a flood of fugitives surging to the rear. MacAndrews glimpsed a gilded eagle flying over the disintegrating column and headed towards it, thinking what a fine thing it would be to take such a trophy. He was ahead of his men, and cut down clumsily at a French soldier who looked confused, but still thrust his bayonet up at the Scotsman. MacAndrews' blow sliced into the soldier's shako, which stuck absurdly on his blade, and was still heavy enough to knock the man down, even though it did not break the skin. Then there were men around him all trying to surrender and the major realised that the fighting was over.

Williams sprinted ahead of the other grenadiers towards the French guns. He was not thinking, simply acting, desperate to reach the artillerymen before they could reload and fire or escape. He had barged his way through the formation. Dobson was close behind him, and perhaps others, and he glimpsed Darrowfield coming almost level with him, his half-pike reaching towards the enemy. Then the sergeant stumbled and there was a horrible scream as the head of his pike stuck in the ground and the blunt butt rammed itself through his belly. Williams did not see this, but kept running. Dobson stopped and cradled the dying Darrowfield in his arms. They had known each other a long time, and if not friends were old comrades. Darrowfield sobbed in agony, and blood trickled from his mouth. Bloody daft way to die, thought Dobson.

Williams ran on. The gunners were frantically swabbing out the gun barrel to extinguish all the burning embers and stop them setting off the next charge prematurely. Men had both the charge and a metal canister ready in their hands. Williams wished now that his musket was loaded, but it was too late to think about that, and so he yelled a challenge at them and forced his legs to go faster. A gunner in dark blue jacket and matching trousers came at him, swinging a heavy rammer. Williams ducked the blow, and slammed the butt of his musket into the man's groin. The Frenchman doubled up, and Williams hit him on the head for good measure as he rushed past. The next man had a short sabre, but the volunteer parried the cut with his bayonet, flicked the weapon aside and then jabbed the point into the man's throat. There was a look of horrified surprise as the gunner dropped his sword and clutched at the gaping wound. He hissed and blood jetted out over his tunic and on to Williams' hand as the volunteer pulled back the blade.

A voice was yelling obscenities and Williams dimly realised that it was his own. He was at the gun itself now, and two more Frenchmen came at him. One was an officer, his sword long and expertly held as the man bared his teeth wildly. He lunged at Williams, who only just managed to duck so that the blade sliced through the grenadier's wing on his right shoulder, cutting through the wool decoration. The sword stuck, and Williams felt his jacket tear as he in turn jabbed at the officer's face with the butt of his musket. The Frenchman jerked back and received only a glancing blow. At the same moment the gunner swung a heavy trailspike and hit Williams in the body, knocking him sideways. His musket fell from his hands as he landed and rolled on the grass.

The man was coming for him, the iron club raised once again, as Williams got up to his knees. Most of his right sleeve and a lot of his jacket had been ripped away, and he glimpsed the French officer trying to disentangle the remains from his sword. Half up, Williams sprang towards the gunner, hitting him in the stomach and knocking the man down beneath him. One hand grabbed the Frenchman's throat and his right fist pummelled the man's face bloody. The officer had freed his blade and now came towards them.

'Monsieur!' Hanley interrupted, his left arm bandaged and in a sling, but with a cocked pistol in his right hand held straight at the Frenchman's chest. Several grenadiers were behind him, muskets levelled.

The artillery officer stared at them for a moment, then shrugged and lowered his sword. He threw it on the ground in front of Hanley.

'Take it, Bills,' he said. 'You did the hard work.'

The French attack had been shattered. The three leading battalion columns broke when the British lines charged, and the supporting column joined in the rout as the 82nd closed on it. The Highlanders recaptured the French guns they had taken earlier. One of their corporals also took Brenier himself, finding the French officer wounded and pinned underneath his dead horse. Some British guns arrived and helped to speed the rout. They fired at the dragoons, which were the last formed body of troops, and when the riflemen of the 60th also began to snipe at the green-coated horsemen, the French cavalry withdrew.

Just before Sergeant Darrowfield died, the pain seemed to fade and he became lucid. He smiled at Dobson. 'I didn't tell anyone, Dob. I swear I didn't. I like Mr Williams, and good riddance,' he gasped. 'Never liked that bastard Redman. I am glad Pug killed him, but I never said anything. Not me.'

Dobson said nothing, for he could see that the light in the man's eyes had faded. His own were glassy and he did not notice Ensign Hatch standing just a few feet away, unscrewing the cap from his flask.

Sir Arthur Wellesley knew that all of Junot's infantry had been broken and more than half of his guns captured. The battle had spread over a wide area, almost two miles separating the fighting around the village and the defeat of the French flank columns. Junot had flung his brigades in individually and they had been thoroughly torn apart as a result. Now Major General Ferguson

363

had sent a report that he had the remnants of one of the French brigades trapped in a valley and asked for permission to attack and complete their destruction. The French were shattered and now all it needed was for the British – and their Portuguese allies – to advance and complete the victory. The Light Dragoons were in no shape to do much, but nearly half the infantry had not yet fired a shot. They were fresh and eager and the enemy would not be able to stop them. It was only noon.

Wellesley sensed the moment, but the army was no longer his to command. At long last General Burrard had arrived, and so the younger man had ridden over to his senior to report and to urge him to give the obvious order. It did not matter that Burrard would take some of the glory, for there should be plenty to spare.

'Sir Harry, now is your time to advance. The enemy is completely beaten, and we shall be in Lisbon in three days!' Wellesley's voice rose in pitch in his enthusiasm.

'Congratulations, Sir Arthur, on a nobly fought action. But you and the men have done enough for one day.' For all the generosity of his words, there was a grudging tone to Sir Harry's reply.

Wickham agreed. He for one could do with eating and then sleeping for the rest of the day. Wellesley's face betrayed the faintest trace of his anger and frustration, but the decision was no longer his and he obeyed. He was *nimmukwallah*, and would obey whatever fool his government appointed over him.

The farm where they had left Mata and the others had lain in the path of the French flanking column. Pringle, Hanley and Williams borrowed horses and rode out to the place when the fighting was over. The surgeons were all too busy after the battle to come with them, and Truscott was waiting for his turn, shot in the arm in the last moments of the battle. None of the other three had seen it happen, or known about it until afterwards.

When they reached the farm the dead of the night before lay in a row in the barn just as they had left them. Their pockets had been turned out, but otherwise the French had not disturbed them as they passed through. There was no sign of Mata or his men, no sign of the chest of money, and no sign of Maria.

'It did happen, didn't it?' asked Hanley. Neither of the others could think of a good reply, but Pringle's hand went down to pat the pocket holding Maria's note. The name was that of a priest, the address that of his church. Pringle smiled.

'Oh yes,' he said. Billy Pringle thought back to the nun desperate for help and anticipated his reunion with the courtesan, now that the French seemed well and truly beaten. Poor Truscott was wounded, but apart from that it was proving to be a very good war. Far better than the dull life of a parson!

EPILOGUE

Williams sat on a stone and looked out into the night. There was a large fire on the hill across the valley and little black figures capered around it like the warriors of some savage tribe from Africa or America. They were Portuguese peasants, but had shown themselves barbaric enough as they emerged when the fighting was over to strip the French dead and wounded. More than a few injured men were knifed as they lay, and the redcoats had been sickened by the display, but unable to protect the enemy casualties as they were ordered back to the ridge they had occupied before the battle. Hanley said that it was all the French could expect after the way they had behaved in Portugal and Spain, but even he had blanched at some of the sights.

'I don't understand it,' said Williams finally. 'The French were at our mercy and yet we sit here and do nothing.'

'Not up to Caesar, I'll agree,' said Pringle with a grin. 'But generals are generals. The story is that Wellesley was all for it, but Burrard suspected there might be more French out there.' It was said that Sir Hew Dalrymple had now arrived from Gibraltar to take over from Sir Harry, so that the army had its third commander in as many days. 'Who knows, he could be right.'

'You do not actually believe that, do you?' asked Hanley.

'Well, no, of course not, but I am just trying to show you how a responsible lieutenant should behave. No croaking.'

'It has not quite sunk in yet. I'll be glad of the extra pay, though.' Hanley had been made lieutenant. He was the senior ensign and so due for promotion, and all the casualties had created many vacancies.

366

'Ah yes, we lieutenants live as kings.'

'You may be a captain soon,' said Williams.

'Maybe.' Pringle was determined not to take anything for granted. He had the years of experience and seniority, but someone might still purchase over his head, and in any event he was not keen on leaving the Grenadier Company. 'Anyway, now that you have been an officer for a grand total of five hours, we should be asking you how it feels, Ensign Williams.'

'Not that different really.'

'Can't you manage a little more exuberance?'

'Hurrah!' said Williams flatly.

'Why did MacAndrews say he'd shoot you himself if you did not take it this time?' asked Hanley.

'Does it matter?'

'Not really, but the story might have passed the time.'

Williams reached down to touch the sword that lay beside him. His promotion had not yet truly sunk in, but the officer's weapon reassured him that he had not imagined the whole thing. He was now an ensign, and even if he had spent enough time in the ranks to know how scornfully most soldiers thought of these most junior officers, he could sense the excitement within him. It was a pity that he had not been able to keep the sword he had taken from the French artillery officer. When the man offered his parole, there was no choice but to return to him this symbol of his honour.

Dobson had presented him with this blade just over an hour ago. The veteran had taken it from Denilov – it was the bundle he had so mysteriously carried back to camp.

'Told you you'd be an officer, Pug,' he had said, his face split into one of the widest grins Williams had ever seen. The old soldier seemed truly delighted. Then he had snapped to attention and delivered a salute which would not have disgraced a sergeant major of the Guards. 'Congratulations, Mr Williams, sir,' he said with the greatest formality.

Williams smiled at the memory and gently eased the sword from its scabbard. The hilt was ornate, with a crest which he guessed was from the Russian's family. The blade was curved, and grenadier officers were supposed to carry a straight sword, but it was so perfectly balanced that even his inexperienced eyed could tell that it was an excellent weapon.

The gift meant one less expense in the next few days as he purchased the uniform and equipment of an officer. Hopefully his share of the money Dobson had taken from the Russian officer would allow him to buy the rest. Soon there would be macabre auctions, as the property of fallen officers was sold so that the profits could be sent to their next of kin, and Williams knew that he would have to take part in these ghoulish affairs. Dobson had helped him in so many ways, and it simply no longer seemed to matter that he had probably killed Redman. Williams worried that his sense of morality was being eroded, but was too tired, and still too happy, to give it much thought.

There was the sound of violent retching and they all looked up as Hatch stumbled past. He was obviously quite drunk. He glared for a moment at Williams, sitting there in the remnants of his torn jacket. Hatch was trying desperately to remember something, but his senses were gone for the moment. It was important, he knew that much, and yet it stubbornly eluded him. Perhaps it would return in time.

'You look like a beggar,' he said, and lurched off into the darkness.

'He's got a point,' said Pringle. There was a polite cough and they all sprang to their feet. Jane MacAndrews stood on the edge of the light from their small fire. A soldier waited behind her, and they recognised Truscott's servant, Private Knowles.

'How is Mr Truscott?' asked Williams, for once clear and confident in his speech to the girl.

'He is asleep. They have taken his arm, unfortunately, but the surgeon says he has an even chance.' The girl had seen Truscott being carried to the makeshift hospital after the battle and had held his other hand throughout the operation, managing somehow to ignore the ghastly grating of saw on bone. Then she had sat with him alongside Knowles until he drifted into sleep. Her face looked drawn and her eyes were dull.

'Thank you from all of us,' said Pringle. 'I know how much help you will have been.'

'I did nothing.' She sighed. 'The poor, poor boy.'

'It will have been a huge comfort.' Hanley tried to lighten the mood. 'I wouldn't be surprised if half the regiment shoots themselves just to hold your hand.'

Jane smiled dutifully, but then her happiness became genuine. 'I hear congratulations are in order. I am proud of you all. Especially you, Mr Williams.'

Williams beamed, and then dropped down on one knee and grasped the girl's hand. Pringle and Hanley stepped back a few paces to give him room.

'Miss MacAndrews, praise from you is sweeter than any reward.' The words came out fluently, confident at last. 'I must tell you that I hold you in the very highest esteem. Indeed, that I . . .' For the first time he hesitated, amazed at his own boldness. 'I love you.' He kissed her gloved hand lightly. There were traces of blood on the glove.

Jane's expression was fond, but overwhelmed by weariness. 'That is truly kind of you, Mr Williams. I am genuinely touched.' He remained with his head bowed over her hand which he clasped tightly.

'I am not in a position to ask for anything,' he continued. 'Not yet, but perhaps one day?' Then he relapsed into silence and once again pressed his lips to her hand.

'Well, at the very least we shall be friends, as I have said before, and I suspect the firmest of friends,' said the girl after some time had passed. 'Now I am tired. May I perhaps have my hand back?' Williams looked up worshipfully and she dazzled him with a smile.

'Is that it?' whispered Pringle into Hanley's ear.

'Don't mock. That was probably the same as a night of passion for us. Bills is an odd cove.'

'Well, I suppose it is a day for things to end unexpectedly.'

HISTORICAL NOTE

True Soldier Gentlemen is a work of fiction, but it is fiction grounded in fact.

In August 1808 an army under the command of Sir Arthur Wellesley landed in Portugal and began Britain's direct involvement in what would become known as the Peninsular War. Six years later, the British Army had chased the French from Spain and Portugal, had invaded southern France and made a major contribution to the collapse of Napoleon's empire. In 1815, Wellington faced and defeated the Emperor himself at Waterloo. It was one of the great achievements of the British Army, and it sparked a flood of personal accounts and histories. The memoirs written by veterans, including a substantial number of men from the ranks as well as officers, provide a wealth of material regarding the lives and experiences of Wellington's men, and I have drawn heavily upon these. Very many of the episodes of the story are based on real incidents.

Regency attitudes differed greatly from those of the present day. Scarcely anyone questioned a system that allowed the purchase of commissions, but purchase was in fact relatively rare except in fashionable regiments. Officers were expected to be gentlemen, but many were not especially wealthy and relied on seniority for promotion. This was often slow, especially if their regiment did not see active service and suffer heavy casualties. Many men grew old as subalterns or captains. There were probably very few veterans of the American War still with the battalions in 1808, but it is certainly not impossible that a man like MacAndrews could have existed.

Gentleman Volunteers were far more common. By the height of the Peninsular War almost one in twenty officers earned his commission in this way. It was a peculiar institution, with a man serving in the ranks, but living with the officers. The path was followed by men who lacked not only the money to purchase rank, but the influence to secure direct appointment to a commission without purchase. There was no guarantee that a volunteer would be made an officer, and it could take a considerable time before they proved themselves and a vacancy occurred.

The vast majority of army officers had modest funds and little influence. Promotion was slow. Conspicuous valour might win them a step in promotion, but in most cases they had to wait their turn and rely on seniority. For this, as well as other reasons, most welcomed the prospect of active service and heavy casualties. Uniforms, equipment and other necessities were expensive, and officers' pay at best barely sufficient. They were gentlemen, but for many their claim to that status rested on fragile grounds.

Regency England is probably now most familiar to us from the genteel world of Jane Austen. In many ways the situation for her heroines mirrored the lives of junior officers in the army and navy. Belonging to the gentry by birth and education, but not truly wealthy, such young women had to hope for a good marriage. The alternatives were posts as companions or governesses, honourable penury, or in extreme cases even prostitution. Such fears underlay the gentility and the rituals of courtship and flirtation and give the stories some of their edge, even though they are only occasionally mentioned. The safe world of Austen concealed real risks.

For officers the dangers were different, but no less real. They had little control over postings. A man's career might stagnate in Britain, or be ended abruptly by disease if the battalion was sent to the West Indies, which consumed units at quite staggering rates. War service brought more opportunities for advancement at the risk of death and dreadful injury – and indeed increased the chance of succumbing to disease. All the time a man's conduct was regulated by strict rules. No gentleman could strike another, unless in a formal duel. As in wider Regency society, most army officers drank heavily and many gambled freely. There were plenty of opportunities to disgrace themselves and be forced to resign. There were also constant frustrations as better-connected or wealthier men advanced their careers far faster than was possible for most. Officers who chose to marry, or who had to assist their parents and siblings, struggled even harder to cope, but many somehow managed to do this.

Jane Austen created a witty and incisive portrait of the real world for young women of her own class. Many army officers lived in the same world. The even bleaker conditions of the poor register only slightly. The gentility of Austen's stories also has little hint of the wider war with France going on in the background. In particular, the contrast with the savagery of the Peninsular War could not be more marked. Yet many army officers experienced both, and it is something of this contrast that I have tried to convey in this story. Hence the inclusion of Wickham, made possible by Austen's final comments about him, under the convenient assumption that the 'restoration of peace' she refers to was the Peace of Amiens in 1803, rather than the end of the Napoleonic Wars in 1815.

I have probably allowed my characters greater knowledge about the reasons for the Peninsular War than is actually likely, although I have tried to give a little sense of the vague perspective of junior officers. Soldiers throughout the ages have rarely been party to the wider reasons of why they are sent to fight. The roots of the conflict lay in Napoleon's 'continental system', through which he hoped to close all European ports to British ships and trade. Since he was unable to defeat the Royal Navy and invade Britain, his aim was to ruin its economy and force the acceptance of peace on his terms. Portugal refused to comply and so in November 1807 French forces under General Junot invaded the country. They had moved through Spain with the co-operation of the Spanish, who were allied to France – Trafalgar had been fought only two years before. Portugal was quickly overrun and this success encouraged Napoleon to turn against his ally. Spain's government was corrupt and unpopular, and it seemed an easy matter to remove the Bourbon monarchs and appoint his own brother Joseph as King of Spain.

It proved to be one of Napoleon's biggest mistakes, but it is unlikely that anyone would have guessed this at the time. Uprisings against the French forces occurred all over Spain. The French responded with great brutality, and the massacre in Madrid on 2nd May with which the novel begins was just the most famous of many incidents. It is now probably best known from Goya's painting *El Dos de Mayo* and its companion piece depicting a French firing squad. The savagery of the conflict quickly escalated as each side outdid the other in reprisals. Today the Spanish know the conflict as the 'War of Independence', and it was fought as much by armed bands of guerrillas as by formal armies. Goya's *Horrors of War* present haunting images of its brutality.

The risings in Spain provided Britain with an opportunity that was quickly seized. Wellesley's army had originally been organised to mount another expedition against Spain's South American colonies. The attempt on Buenos Aires in 1806 had been a humiliating disaster for the British, but the lure of lucrative colonies was always a strong one. Instead, the government responded to an appeal for aid from a Spanish embassy. The state of war between Britain and Spain was not formally renounced until some time afterwards. In the event, however, the Galician junta that ran the war effort in north-western Spain did not want the assistance of British soldiers. So Wellesley sailed on, to receive a better welcome in Portugal.

The campaign there occurred very much as described in the story. Lieutenant Bunbury of the 95th was the first British battlefield fatality of the war. Hindsight tells us that these early encounters were the first of the succession of battles won by Wellesley's army. None of this later success was inevitable. The record of British expeditions – especially to continental Europe – was extremely poor. So was the reputation of the British Army. Alexandria in 1801 and Maida in 1806 (which gave its name to Maida Vale in West London) were rare victories amid a long series of failures. They hinted that the reforms of the army under the aegis of the Duke of York and carried on by imaginative generals such as Abercromby and Moore were beginning to bear fruit. Yet the redcoats had yet to prove themselves. Numerically, Britain's army was dwarfed by that of Napoleon and powers like Austria, Russia or Prussia. It was simply not large enough to confront the main strength of the Emperor's army on its own. The Peninsular War offered a chance for it to face French forces spread very thinly as they struggled to control Spain and Portugal.

It was understandable that at first French generals like Junot underestimated their British opponents. At Roliça the forces actually engaged were similar in numbers, although overall the British outnumbered the French by more than two to one. It was therefore inevitable that the latter would be forced from their position, and it was merely a question of how long this took. At Vimeiro the French attacked a somewhat larger British Army, although again the numbers actually engaged were more equal. Junot attacked recklessly and met far tougher resistance than he had expected. It was easy afterwards for the French to blame his mistakes and the relative inexperience of much of his army. It would take several years and more British victories before French commanders learned more respect for their opponents.

I have described these actions as accurately as I could. The 106th Foot did not exist in the form described here. (A unit with that number was briefly included in the Army List, but was probably never organised in reality and certainly did not see active service.) The regimental number was far more important than any name or regional affiliation until the end of the nineteenth century. Therefore, in the story the battalion is usually referred to as the 106th rather that the Glamorganshire Regiment. I chose that county simply because it happens to be my home and because there was no such regiment in reality. Wales was generally under-represented in the Army List, with only the 23rd Royal Welch Fusiliers being formally affiliated to the region. The battalions of that regiment recruited widely and actual Welshmen were never more than a significant minority. I have given the 106th red facings to their jackets in honour of the 41st Foot, one of the ancestors of the Royal Regiment of Wales (and now combined with the Royal Welch Fusiliers in the Royal Welsh). The 41st did not serve in the Peninsula, but saw considerable action in Canada during the 1812 War.

The routine of the battalion, its organisation and drill are as accurate as I can make them. It is all too easily forgotten that long periods of training underlay the success of Wellington's army. For both officers and men the bulk of this training occurred at the battalion level. Gentlemen were expected to behave with courage and set an example to their soldiers, but as officers they also had to learn how to manoeuvre and control their men, as well as the less tangible skills of leadership. Much of this occurred in Britain and is all too easily ignored. Examples of the wooden blocks used to explain the manoeuvring of a battalion can be seen today in the National Army Museum in London.

The conditions of the men in the ranks are only glimpsed in the story to reflect the perspective of junior officers. Discipline was harsh, and could be arbitrary but then civilian justice for the poor was sometimes even worse. In some ways the lot of the redcoats' families was even more bleak. The scene where the wives draw lots to see who will accompany the regiment is based firmly on reality – indeed, such things would be hard to invent. The prospects for those left behind were often bleak, and such ballots were carried out at the last minute to prevent desertions. Some officers' wives did follow their husbands to the Peninsula, although there were probably very few there as early as August 1808. It is far less likely that an unmarried daughter would have gone with her mother, but I have permitted this because I wanted Jane to be there for this and future plots. I will keep looking to see whether I can find a real precedent for this, but have so far failed.

I have based the exploits of the 106th at Roliça and Vimeiro closely on those of the 29th Foot (formerly the Worcestershire and Sherwood Foresters and now part of the Mercian Regiment). This is largely because the exploits of the real redcoats were in reality more impressive than almost anything a novelist could plausibly invent. I have not stuck rigidly to this in every respect, however, and this remains a novel. In the real battle Lieutenant Colonel Lake led the 29th in a premature attack and was killed when he and part of the battalion found themselves attacked by French infantry who had been bypassed as the redcoats advanced up one of the gullies. Lake had won a high reputation for himself in India and the attack appears to have been a genuine mistake. For a while the colours of the 29th were lost to the enemy. These were soon recaptured, however, and the regiment re-formed and repulsed a series of French counter-attacks. Wellesley singled them out for praise in his dispatch. The 29th would later fight with considerable distinction at Talavera and other engagements. Moss is not supposed to be a reflection of Lieutenant Colonel Lake, nor is the fictional 106th, and the tensions within its ranks are not intended in any way to be representative of the real 29th Foot. In later stories the 106th will no doubt mirror the fortunes of different regiments.

Bizarrely enough, there was a Russian fleet in the Tagus in 1808 and no one was entirely sure whether the Russians would side with their French allies. In the event they maintained an uneasy neutrality. Many Russians felt humiliated by the 1807 Treaty of Tilsit and the new friendship between Tsar Alexander and Napoleon, but it must have been very hard to guess whether or not the French Emperor would ever lose his dominance. There was also little love for Britain, however. Count Denilov is an invention, exploiting this strange situation. I needed a more personal enemy for my heroes and having a Russian seemed a greater novelty than a Frenchman.

True Soldier Gentlemen is the first in a series of novels, intended to follow the characters through the years of war with France. Much lies ahead of them. There will be more battles in Portugal and Spain, some in Canada, and in the long run they will end up on the ridge at Waterloo. Ahead of our characters lie adventure, romance, plenty of battles and powder smoke and – this being Wellington's army – no doubt a fair amount of amateur dramatics.